He was handed a single photo, showing Shea following a slightly heavy, middle-aged woman in a parking lot. "That's Cynthia Miller. Shea followed her inside the mall. When Mrs. Miller came out, Shea was behind her. Then two men and Shea grabbed her and forced her into a van."

Ethan's stomach clenched. Just what did Shea think she was doing? Going after Cole's murderer was one thing, but terrorizing and abducting women? How had she gotten so deep that she was actually doing the exact thing she'd fought so hard to shut down? What the hell had happened?

"Ethan, you with me?" Gibson asked.

"Yeah, sorry. What?"

The sympathetic smile the older man flashed told Ethan that Gibson knew something of his and Shea's history. "I was just saying that this vehicle is for your use. We don't anticipate Shea returning to the compound at least until tomorrow afternoon, so you have time to go over the maps and reports, scope out the location, and cement the details of your rescue plan."

Nodding, Ethan turned his gaze back to the approaching darkness. He'd come here to save Shea or die trying. This was a possible one-way trip for him, and Ethan accepted that as his due. He'd taken so much from her. The least he could do was give her his life if necessary.

Also by Christy Reece

Rescue Me
Return to Me

Books published by The Random House Publishing Group
are available at quantity discounts on bulk purchases for
premium, educational, fund-raising, and special sales use.
For details, please call 1-800-733-3000.

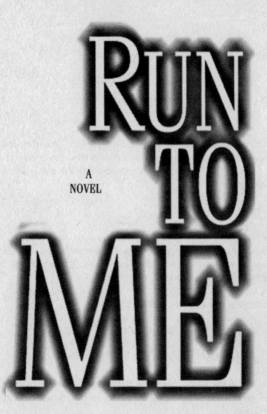

RUN TO ME

A NOVEL

CHRISTY REECE

BALLANTINE BOOKS • NEW YORK

Run to Me is a work of fiction. Names, characters, places, and incidents are the products of the author's imagination or are used fictitiously. Any resemblance to actual events, locales, or persons, living or dead, is entirely coincidental.

A Ballantine Books Mass Market Original

Published in the United States by Ballantine Books, an imprint of The Random House Publishing Group, a division of Random House, Inc., New York.

BALLANTINE and colophon are registered trademarks of Random House, Inc.

ISBN 978-0-345-50544-6

Cover design and illustration: Tony Greco

Printed in the United States of America

www.ballantinebooks.com

9 8 7 6 5 4 3 2

To my sweet and beautiful sisters,
Debra and Denise,
who love the mountains of Tennessee
as much as Shea does.
Thanks for always being there for me.
I love you.

prologue

Ixtapa, Mexico

Naked and exposed, she lay on the bed. Angry tears flooded her eyes, blurring the white ceiling fan that whirred above her. With her arms wrenched over her head and tied to the bedposts, the rope around her wrists abraded and tore at the sensitive skin as she twisted and tugged. The binding around her ankles was so tight, she had lost feeling in her feet.

If only they had left her legs free, she'd be able to take out a few of the sons of bitches. But they knew that. Knew how dangerous she was. Knew she'd come here to kill them. She had failed. Waves of helpless fury rolled through her. Twice in a lifetime she'd failed Cole. She hadn't loved him as she should have, and now her plan of vengeance against the people who'd killed him had been destroyed by her own stupid carelessness.

She lifted her head, straining her neck, and searched for an out, some kind of hope. She saw none. The room was large and white . . . a white so intense it hurt her eyes. No color, no warmth. The furniture, carpet, walls, even the drapery, all a shocking white. Her neck aching, she dropped her head back onto the pillow. A pristine, colorless prison. For some reason, the lack of color increased the terror building inside her.

Going deep cover had been a stupid idea. Even as she'd cooked up the plan, she'd doubted her ability to

carry it off. She had many skills—going undercover
wasn't one of them. A part of her hadn't cared . . . had
only wanted to make Rosemount pay for killing Cole. If
she'd been able to take the bastard out, even losing her
life would have been worth it. Now that hope was gone.

Rosemount would kill her. How? When? It no longer
mattered. The one thing she wanted, had worked for . . .
lost to her forever.

An insistent little voice inside her whispered. It reminded her that there was someone else who wanted revenge just as much as she did. Someone who felt
responsible for Cole's death. Someone she'd once loved.
Would he take over for her? Once he learned of her
death, would he come here and wreak havoc for what
they'd done to Cole? What they would soon do to her?

Sobs built, threatened to explode. Her heart screamed,
"No!" She didn't want that to happen. He was out of
this life, out of this business. He needed to stay out of it.
She could die easier, knowing that Ethan Bishop was
safe.

Across the room, a door swung open, then closed.
Footsteps approached. She froze, not wanting him to see
her struggle. Refused to let him see her fear. He would
want to see her weak and afraid. Damned if she'd give
him anything he wanted.

Her eyes narrowed, glaring at the man who'd caused
so much pain and destruction. Below average height,
slender, almost thin physique. Curly, mousy-brown hair
framed a thin, freckled face. Thick, round glasses made
his mud-brown eyes appear abnormally large. Her astonishment the first time she'd seen him had been hard
to hide. This was the man who'd been kidnapping innocent people for profit? The man responsible for Cole's
death? He looked like he would run from a puppy.

Donald Rosemount was below average in every way.
There was nothing at all remarkable or attractive about

him. Thousands could pass him on the street and never see him—one of the reasons he'd been able to maintain his anonymity. He looked ordinary, common. Unfortunately, he possessed an uncommon evilness.

"Well, my dear, don't you look nice and juicy." The slimy smile curling his thin lips made her want to gag. She refused to give him that satisfaction.

Trailing a skinny, death-cold finger up her neck, he caressed her cheek. His smile grew wider. "I'm going to enjoy taming you."

She hid her quiver of revulsion with words: "Over my dead body, you freaking pervert."

"Dead? Oh no, my beauty. Admittedly, my tastes are a bit, shall we say, unorthodox, but having you dead doesn't interest me. There are so many other ways I can enjoy you."

"Going deaf, asshole? I said. Over. My. Dead. Body."

Excitement flashed across his face. "You're going to be difficult, aren't you?" He pulled a small leather case from his pants pocket. "I've got just the thing to ensure your full cooperation." Withdrawing a hypodermic needle and a small bottle of clear liquid, he prepared an injection.

Her muscles locked. Drugs? Suddenly death was much more preferable. Why couldn't he just kill her and be done with it? Or did he think he could get her to talk first? She almost laughed out loud. She didn't have anything to tell. Hadn't been in touch with the home office in months. This was an unauthorized op. She hadn't been approved to come in and kill him. LCR didn't kill if they could help it.

This wasn't LCR business. It was hers alone.

A flush of hot pink brightened his cheeks as his eyes glittered with sick anticipation. "Sad to say, this won't hurt near as much as I would like. I've asked time and again that additional pain additives be mixed in, but my scientists swear it dilutes the effectiveness. So I had to ask myself, What would I rather have? See you go through agonizing, hideous pain . . . but only for a short period? Or do I opt for just a slight physical pain and settle for the satisfying knowledge that an LCR operative is doing my bidding, without any remembrance of who she is or what she used to be?"

Confusion flickered on his face. "I have to tell you, it was a difficult decision. Seeing you writhing in pain would be so damned satisfying. Noah McCall and his people have caused me endless hours of aggravation. But alas, the pain would be short-lived and, after a while, could become somewhat boring." He lifted a bony shoulder. "I do detest boredom."

Her mouth was desert dry, making it hard for her to speak. "Rosie, before we met, I thought you were a halfway-interesting creep. Now I know you're nothing but a wormy slug pretending to be a man."

The tightening of his mouth was the only indication that her words bothered him.

Without permission, her body stiffened as the needle came closer. "Whatever you do, you will pay for it. I promise you that." A useless threat, but it was the best she could do under the extreme terror pounding through her. Dear God, anything but drugs!

"Doubtful, my little wildcat. But even if I do, it won't be from you." He twisted her arm and pressed the needle into a vein.

She screamed. Not in pain—it hadn't hurt. No, it was the pure anguish of being bound, helpless. Sweet God, she'd promised herself she'd never be helpless again.

Her eyes closed against the smug visage above her, images of her life danced behind her lids. The stepfather who'd raped her, the mother who'd allowed it, the hope and hopelessness of one foster home after another. And then Ethan . . . strong, confident, the love of her life, but in the end, just as damaged as she. Then later Cole, her husband, her salvation and her biggest failure.

Images blurred together, a colorful mishmash of sweet memories and gut-wrenching sadness: Cole's beautiful eyes, Ethan's strong arms, Cole's disillusionment, and Ethan's scarred, grief-stricken face . . .

A warm flush of heat and then agony ripped through her. She screamed again.

And then there was nothing. No past. No present. No future. Her life was without form, her memories dissolved, her soul stolen.

Darkness fell.

one

Three Months Later
Last Chance Rescue Headquarters
Paris, France

"You're sure it's her?"

"Yeah. She doesn't even bother to disguise her appearance."

Noah McCall shot from his chair and faced the window behind his desk. "I can't believe she'd betray LCR. Nothing in her profile indicated this thread of evil inside her."

Gabriel Maddox stayed seated as he watched the head of LCR flounder for an answer. Seeing Noah show emotion no longer surprised him, but the changes in his boss were still fascinating. Before McCall met and married his wife, Samara, Gabe would have sworn nothing other than God himself could have forced an honest emotion from the man. But in the months since he'd been married, Noah had done a complete about-face. Oh, he could still be a coldhearted bastard and no one dared cross him, but Gabe had heard him laugh on more than one occasion, and last month, when he announced that Samara was pregnant, damned if the man hadn't blushed.

"How many abductions has she been involved in?"

"We're sure of two," Gabe said.

"I could have sworn she was about the straightest arrow LCR ever hired."

Not a patient man by nature, Gabe knew better than to rush his boss in making a decision. Especially as hard as this one would likely be. Didn't take a genius to know that the former LCR operative known as Shea Monroe would have to be dealt with, possibly taken out.

This decision wouldn't be easy for McCall. He'd hired and trained every LCR operative since its beginning. Some of the younger ones called him Pop behind his back, though it was always said with an enormous amount of respect and even affection. Noah McCall had saved every one of their worthless hides and turned them into something. They might sometimes resent the tough restrictions he placed on them, but not one of them would speak against him.

Still, when an LCR operative went rogue, it affected everyone. Taking Shea down wouldn't be enjoyable but might well be necessary.

McCall dropped back into his chair. "Anyone talked to Ethan lately?"

It sounded like a casual question. Gabe knew different. Noah McCall didn't ask casual questions. Ethan Bishop had left LCR under a dark cloud. Few people knew the full reason for his dismissal, but speculation that he'd become a loose cannon was the number one theory. Gabe knew this speculation was correct.

"I talked to him a few months back," Gabe said.

"So he doesn't know about Shea?"

Gabe felt a slight nudge of guilt. "Didn't see the need to tell him. When she went missing, we assumed she disappeared on purpose. Since Cole's death, Shea's not been at her best. Telling Ethan wouldn't have accomplished anything other than making him feel more like shit than he already does."

Noah turned his dark eyes on him and Gabe suddenly felt like an insect about to be skewered.

"And now that we know she's working for the organization that killed her husband, you don't think that's something he'd be interested in learning?"

The answer Gabe gave was so lame, he inwardly winced as he said it. "Ethan doesn't work for LCR any longer."

McCall continued that black-eyed stare. "You want me to tell him?" His voice had softened, which meant only one thing—he was about to lose his temper.

Drawing a deep breath, Gabe gave the answer he didn't want to give. "No, I'll tell him." He shot his boss a narrow-eyed glare. "You know he'll go after her, don't you?"

"Of course."

"Then why?"

"Because despite the evidence, I think Shea's worth saving. There's no one in the world better able to see Shea for what she is. If she's turned, Ethan'll know what he has to do. If she's in trouble, he'll bring her home."

"And if she's turned, she might just end up killing him."

An odd light flickered in McCall's eyes. "Or she might end up saving them both."

Gabe stood, knowing his boss wouldn't change his mind, no matter what objections he gave. Noah McCall was of the opinion that almost everyone had something good in them. Since he'd turned around a lot of lives, Gabe wasn't going to argue with him. But he'd seen what Shea had done to his friend. Loving a woman that much was damned dangerous. Shea had taken advantage of that love, and Ethan would never be the same man again.

Gabe stalked out the door. Bypassing the elevator, he stomped down ten floors. Ethan didn't even own a phone. The only way to reach him was to fly there. His gut plummeted. Few people knew about his problem with enclosed places . . . the fewer, the better. By the time he made it to the podunk town in the Tennessee hills where Ethan had buried himself, Gabe would be in a lousy mood. Ethan wouldn't be happy to see him and would most likely try to throw him off his property.

On the other hand, a good fight never hurt anyone. His mood lightened. Damned if he wasn't suddenly looking forward to the trip after all.

East Tennessee

The sun blasted a welcome searing heat. Sweat poured off Ethan, splattering and dimpling the dirt like slow, fat raindrops. Wiping his hand across his brow, eyes squinted against the brightness, he gazed around at the progress he'd made. After months of doing nothing but chopping down dead trees and clearing brush, he was beginning to see a small amount of progress. Yes, it would have been simpler to hire people to do this but not nearly as satisfying. This was his land. No one would care about this property as much as he did. It was his blood and sweat that would create something out of nothing. Besides, what the hell else did he have to do?

After throwing another tree limb onto the already full truck bed, Ethan jumped into the cab and started it up. One last load—then he'd shower and head to town for supplies. Once a month, he forced himself into town. He'd already put it off three days longer than he should have. Out of coffee for the last day and a half, he felt like a rabid dog, on top of having a hell of a headache. The fast-food place a few miles from town would be his first stop. A giant cup of their strong brew would ease the pain. Hopefully, by the time he made it to the store he wouldn't want to kill anyone.

Under the rumble of timber slamming to the ground, he heard the quiet purr of an expensive car headed up his hill. Mercedes, maybe? Not a Jag. Whoever it was, they were lost. He was the only one who lived on this road.

He clenched his jaw, hating that he'd have to see another person on his property, even for the short amount of time it would take to get them off. His fingers combed through a week's worth of growth on his face, pushed through his shoulder-length hair, soaked with sweat. Nice thing about looking like a serial killer—most people who saw him turned around and ran the other way. Whoever was headed this way would soon do the same.

A sleek silver Mercedes rounded a corner and hit the top of the hill. The sun's glare against the windshield couldn't disguise the identity of the dark-haired man behind the wheel.

"Shit." The dull pounding in Ethan's head blasted toward jackhammer status. *Gabe Maddox.* Last time he'd talked to Gabe, he'd told him to go to hell. Looked as though he hadn't taken the advice. Figured . . . bastard was stubborn like that.

Ethan glowered at the other man, letting him know up front that he still didn't want him around. "Don't believe you were invited."

Unfolding his long body from the leather seat, Gabe flashed an arrogant grin that was so popular with the ladies and pissed most men off because of it. "If I waited for an invitation, I'd never see you again."

"That's the idea."

"Sorry . . . I'm on orders."

"Noah sent you?" Now, that was a surprise. Last time he saw Noah McCall, the man had damned near choked him to death. Not that he hadn't deserved it, but he figured McCall would just as soon pretend that Ethan had never existed.

"Yeah." Gabe jerked his head toward the house. "Mind if we talk inside?"

"Why?"

His eyes searching the hills warily, Gabe shrugged and headed toward the log house without Ethan's consent. "Don't like being out in the open like this."

"Damned stupid, coming from a claustrophobic."

Gabe turned to glare at him but kept walking.

Ethan threw his gloves down and stalked past Gabe, into the house. His home was only a few months old, but his furniture was almost as ancient as the surrounding hills. His things served their purpose, and that was all he cared about.

He tugged open the refrigerator and pulled out two beers. Tossing a bottle to Gabe, Ethan leaned against the counter, unscrewed the cap, and took a long swallow.

Easing down into a rickety chair at the scarred, aged table, Gabe swallowed a mouthful of beer and gazed around. "Nice place you got here, man."

"Thanks. I'll tell the decorator you said so. Now, what the hell do you want?"

Gabe took another swig of beer, set the bottle on the table, and blew out a long sigh.

A strange tension zipped up Ethan's spine. "Must be something major for you to take so long in answering."

"It's Shea."

The words were quietly spoken, but the impact to his heart and mind were like bombs exploding. He turned toward the kitchen window, unwilling to allow his former friend to see the naked pain. "She dead?"

"No. If only it were that simple."

Ethan turned sharply and growled, "What the hell does that mean?"

"She's gone sour."

Ethan snorted his disbelief. "Shea wouldn't turn south. I'd believe you turned before her."

"Gee, thanks for the vote of confidence." Gabe waited

a beat, allowing Ethan to absorb his statement. "We've got positive intel."

"I don't give a flying fuck what you've got. Shea Monroe would never betray LCR. Not for money . . ." He shrugged. "Not for anything."

"Noah feels the same way."

"But you don't."

Gabe didn't flinch from Ethan's direct gaze. "You know Shea was never my favorite person after she and Cole married."

"Shea did the right thing by marrying Cole. But that's beside the point. Give me what you know."

"First I have to have your agreement on something."

"What?"

"Noah wants you to find her. If she's turned, you're to bring her in. If she's in trouble, he wants her rescued."

"Why me?"

"Says you're the only one who'd be able to determine if Shea has truly turned."

Crossing the room, Ethan slumped into a chair across from Gabe. Noah McCall had fired his ass for very valid reasons; Ethan didn't blame him. Besides, he owed Noah his sanity and his life. The man knew he'd do almost anything for him. But this was Shea. And Noah knew Ethan would slay dragons and fight an army for the woman he'd once loved and lost. Yeah, McCall was right on the money to ask him to go in. No one had more to lose than Ethan if something happened to Shea.

He owed Shea Monroe a whole lot . . . more than he could ever repay. After all, not only had he broken her heart, he'd also gotten her husband killed.

"Begin!"

The young man rushed toward her, fast and hard. His mouth was crimped, tight with determination; his eyes reflected the fear and nervousness of a new recruit. She waited. At the last second, she pivoted and swooped out of his way. He stumbled across the mat, teetering, unable to recover his balance. She twisted and delivered a swift, controlled kick to his head with the side of her foot. Blankness crossed his face an instant before he thudded to the mat.

She whirled, confronted another opponent, and put him down just as easily. Eventually, they came at her in twos. With no emotion and little thought, she dispatched them one by one onto the mat.

Panting lightly, she turned to her teacher and bowed. His eyes gleamed with appreciation and lust. She had the ability to recognize emotions without feeling them herself. Sometimes she wondered what they felt like . . . emotions. Most times, she didn't think about it. She served a purpose. It gave her no satisfaction, no sense of completion. Their expectation and her fulfillment of that expectation filled her day and that was it . . . nothing more.

Today was a demonstration, not training. Her superiors required her to show the new soldiers what was expected of them. If these had been highly trained fighters, she would have had more trouble. These young men were nothing more than inexperienced, unformed amoebas. They would be shaped, molded, and taught how to kill. Until then, she, among others, would show them how inept and ineffectual they were.

One of the younger men lay before her, unmoving. She blinked down at him. Why didn't he get up? Two others came, grabbed him by his shoulders and feet, and hauled him away. She blinked again, her knees weakening, she stumbled. Noise like a thousand tiny bees roared in her ears. What was wrong with the man? Why were his eyes still closed?

"That's enough for today."

She turned to her teacher, confusion flooding her mind with questions. "Why doesn't he move?"

When his eyes narrowed into slits, she knew she had angered him. Speaking was allowed only to answer a direct question. It was not her right to question anyone at the compound. Punishment would follow if the teacher chose to report her.

"Your duties are over." His hand wrapped around a hank of her hair and gave it a vicious tug as he pulled her to the door. Since this was the only place anyone other than the master was allowed to discipline her, she was accustomed to the sharp sting. "Go to your room. You don't want to be late."

Alarm exploded. No, she couldn't be late for her vitamin shot. She received an injection each evening to make her stronger . . . more focused and capable. She always looked forward to it because it did make her feel better. By the time she was given the shot, she was always weak, her mind blurring and asking questions for which she had no answers. The vitamins would race through her system, and within minutes, she would once more be strong and renewed, no longer confused or disoriented.

Dashing down the hallway, she ran into her bedroom. Hands shaking, breath coming in near-panicked spurts, she halted when she saw him, knowing he would instruct her further.

"You are almost late. I almost had to wait for you."

She forced herself to ignore the wild hammering inside as her eyes lowered in supplication and obedience. "My apologies."

"You know I don't like to wait. If it happens again, I'll withhold your vitamins for a few days. Once again you'll see how important obedience is. Do you understand?"

"Yes sir." She had been punished this way in the past. Throughout the long nights and interminable days, agony filled her. Visions and nightmares of demons screamed into her mind while pain rippled through her body as though glass shredded her insides into millions of pieces.

Through each punishment, she had been taught a proper lesson, correcting her behavior for one infraction or the other. The lessons had been well learned and well deserved. Only after apologizing and begging for forgiveness was she once again favored with an injection. She worked hard never to disappoint her master again and force him to punish her.

"Take your clothes off."

Relieved that she had been forgiven, she clawed and tore at her clothes, dropping them on the floor. Once nude, she stood before him, waiting for more instructions.

"On the bed. Now."

Crawling onto the bed, she lay facedown and lifted her bottom, allowing him to inject the vitamins into her buttocks. She paid no attention to the tall, silent man standing in the corner of the room. His emotionless blue-eyed stare meant nothing. He was here at the master's command, as he often was. His presence wasn't hers to question.

As the vitamins swept through her, she closed her eyes in anticipation of relief. Peace and serenity would soon permeate her entire being, and she would be renewed with energy and stamina. Then, when allowed, she would go forward with whatever pleased her master.

His will was hers, and she was his to command.

two

The drone of the private jet beneath his feet barely penetrated Ethan's consciousness. Photographs spread out before him held his total concentration. The surveillance cameras were exceptionally good, especially when picking up someone with exquisite bone structure.

Gabe was right. Shea didn't bother to hide or disguise her face. It wasn't as if she stared into the cameras—she just acted as though they didn't exist. She had to know she was being photographed. That every movement of that gorgeous body and every expression on her face would be picked up. Why would—

Breath seized in his lungs. Shea was still beautiful, her full mouth just as bewitching as before, but something was missing, and that was the part that ripped at him. The face he'd seen a million and one times in both his dreams and reality was the most animated, expression-filled face imaginable. But this woman, who looked identical to Shea, down to the velvet-black beauty mark just below her left eye, revealed no expression or emotion. It was a mask of sheer beauty and nothing more . . . like a mannequin.

For a brief, wild moment, he wondered if Donald Rosemount had somehow achieved the creation of a lifelike robot. Crazy idea, but no more so than the thought that Shea Monroe had turned bad. Shea didn't have it in her to be bad.

Ethan's first glimpse of Shea was a vivid, poignant

memory. He had walked into an LCR training room and jerked to a stop at the sound of the most joyous laugh he'd ever heard. Whirling around, he'd spotted three attractive women. While his eyes appreciated each of them, it was the one in the middle he couldn't stop staring at. Never had he seen a more lively, animated, or precocious expression. For a young man who'd left joy and happiness behind years before, the sound of her laughter, seeping into his soul, immediately began to heal something inside him. Sparkling green eyes had stared at him with unashamed curiosity. A wide smile curved her full lips, inviting and encouraging him to smile back. At that moment, Ethan had known his life would be changed forever.

Most LCR operatives had come from a bad circumstance, some worse than others. Shea's innate openness gave her the ability to share her experience with Ethan. None of the circumstances she'd endured had been her fault. Ethan had felt enormous pride in her for not only escaping but also wanting to help others escape. Her courage astounded him; her heart humbled him.

The obnoxious buzz of his new cellphone interrupted thoughts he'd rather not dwell on anyway. Didn't do a damn bit of good other than to remind him how freaking stupid he'd been.

Ethan flipped the phone open. "Yeah?"

"Nice to know your phone etiquette hasn't changed."

As Ethan settled back into his seat, his mouth kicked up into a grin. "Heard you got married, old man."

Noah McCall snorted. "Old man, hell. You're a year older."

"Yeah, but at least I'm not tied to a ball and chain."

Extreme satisfaction tinged McCall's voice. "You've met my wife. No ball and chain could ever be so beautiful."

Remembering the petite, dark-haired beauty Noah

had once ordered him to protect, Ethan had to agree. "You're right about that. I understand you're going to be a dad, too. Having over a hundred adopted kids not enough for you?"

"You guys all grew up and left me. At least with a baby, I can have a few extra years."

"Congratulations. I'm happy for you." Ethan meant that sincerely. No one deserved happiness more than the man who'd saved so many.

"Thanks. Now, tell me how you're doing."

"Fine . . . till Gabe showed up."

"I knew you'd want the opportunity."

"Hell, you knew I couldn't turn it down." Ethan picked up a photo again. The expressionless face still bothered him. "You got any more intel?"

"Another abduction last night. Wealthy American's wife. Taken outside a shopping mall in San Diego. No ransom demand yet, but the abduction's similar to all the others. Meaning it'll take another day before we find out how much they want."

"Shea involved in this one, too?"

"Looks like it . . . from what we can see from the security cameras in the parking lot."

A thought came to him, something he hadn't asked before. "And they've all been returned, after the ransom's delivered?"

"Of the ones we believe Rosemount's responsible for, all but one was returned."

"What happened?"

"Not sure. Her body washed up on a beach in Florida. Throat sliced open."

Ethan rubbed the persistent throb between his eyes. "Was Shea involved in that one?"

"Don't know. The victim was nabbed outside a friend's home. No cameras available. There was a request for money . . . it wasn't paid in time."

"Hell," Ethan said quietly, "he was making a point."

"Yeah, not one we want to see repeated."

"The ones returned . . . they couldn't help?"

"No. Drugged and blindfolded the entire time."

"How many have been taken so far?"

"With this particular pattern, seven that we know of."

"All American?"

"Only two from the U.S. . . . including the one last night. One from Italy . . . the rest from Mexico."

"And you're sure it's Rosemount's group?"

"Oh yeah, we've seen several of his henchmen. Took us some time, but we were finally able to track one of them. Lost him for a while, then our people picked up his trail in Ixtapa."

"And Shea's been involved in two . . . make that three . . . after last night?"

"We've got positive intel on those three, not sure about any others." McCall blew out a long sigh. "You know her better than anyone. You think it's possible she's turned?"

"Not just no. Hell no. She's gone deep cover . . . that's the only explanation. Cole's death messed her up." Ethan was grateful that Noah didn't say the obvious. Cole's death had affected someone other than Shea. "Shea always acted first and thought later. And you know deep cover was never her strong point. She's probably in so deep, she can't get out. But no way in hell would she turn."

"I trust your judgment. You got everything you need?"

"Got an exact location yet?"

"Not yet. Last time our people checked in, Ixtapa was still as close as they'd gotten. They'll be waiting on the ground for you and should have more by now."

"Good."

"Sure you don't want Gabe with you?"

"No, it's best I go in alone."

"I don't want you sacrificing yourself. You can't get her out, make damn sure you get out alive."

Ethan didn't bother to respond. If Shea was no longer on this earth, he didn't see much point in being on it either. He'd just make sure he took Rosemount with him.

"I'll be in touch when I can."

McCall ended the call with a gruff "See that you are."

Picking up another photograph, Ethan tried to read something in her expression. There had to be something . . . anything that would give him an idea of what was going on in that beautiful head. The photograph was black and white, so her vibrant colors didn't show. Shea had startling green eyes and deep, rich auburn hair. But still, there should be something . . . some kind of emotion or expression. There was nothing. She looked like a beautiful doll.

What had happened to the vivacious, emotional woman who could laugh or cry with such ease? He remembered being completely stunned the first time he saw her cry. Ignoring his grumblings, she'd dragged him to a chick flick with a happy ending. The theater had been dark, so it wasn't until they were walking to the car that he saw her frantically wipe at her eyes, as if she didn't want him to notice.

Seeing Shea cry had done something to his heart that day. Melted it? Who the hell knows. He remembered grabbing her shoulders and pulling her to his chest. She'd broken down then, soaking his shirt. He'd held her, kissed the top of her head from time to time, and relished every tear she shed. A part of him envied the ability she had of so freely expressing her emotions. Wondered how that would feel.

He always thought that might have been the day he'd

tumbled off the precipice and fallen completely in love
with her. Only to crash and burn a few years later.

"Mr. Bishop, we're landing."

He nodded at the flight attendant, gathered the reports and photographs, and slid them back into the
large envelope. Tonight, when he was alone, he'd take
them out and try to make sense out of the unexplain-
able.

The plane made a soft bounce against the tarmac, and
within minutes, Ethan was saying good-bye to the small
crew and heading down the stairway toward the man
and woman waiting for him.

The man, medium height with a handlebar mustache
and a wide smile, greeted him, "Ethan, good to see you.
I'm Gibson." He gestured to a tall, slender woman.
"This is Maria."

Ethan shook their hands, accustomed by now to hearing only first names. LCR often used fake names, so he
doubted either had used their real ones.

"Good flight?" Gibson asked.

Ethan jerked his head in a nod. "I understand there
was another incident last night?"

Gibson waved his arm toward a dark green SUV
gleaming in the late-afternoon sun. "Let's get out of this
heat. We just got some new information I think you'll be
pleased to see."

Ethan hadn't even noticed the warmth of the day, but
poor Gibson's mustache drooped with sweat. He headed
for the vehicle and jumped into the front passenger seat,
not for the first time appreciating the powerful influence
of LCR. Bypassing customs was one of the many perks
operatives were allowed.

While Maria drove, Gibson handed him a packet and
updated him on what they'd learned. "We believe she's
in a compound about thirty miles outside Ixtapa. Of
course, the land belongs to a corporation buried within

other corporations, but we're almost certain Rosemount owns the property."

"And Shea's been seen at the compound? We got anybody on the inside?"

Maria shot Ethan a regretful look. "Our people have seen someone who strongly resembles Shea walking around the perimeter, but we've been unable to infiltrate the compound. We've seen Rosemount's men go back and forth, so we're fairly sure he's been there. Since the man is almost a complete recluse and none of us knows what he really looks like, we, of course, can't verify that."

Ethan nodded, aware that this was how Donald Rosemount had avoided capture for so long. Only those people who worked for him knew what he looked like. The ones who no longer worked for him no longer lived. An added danger for Shea. Getting her out was one thing, but if she'd seen Rosemount, and Ethan assumed she had, the bastard wouldn't rest until Shea was dead.

"The woman abducted last night . . . the one from San Diego. We have anything on her yet?"

Maria shook her head. "No ransom demand yet. We're still a few hours from that."

Ethan glanced up from the photographs of Rosemount's compound. "He doesn't bring them to his compound?"

"No. We believe he keeps them close to where he had them taken. That way, he can return them without too much difficulty. It works very well for him," Gibson said.

"And Shea was definitely involved in the one last night?"

He was handed a single photo, showing Shea following a slightly heavy, middle-aged woman in a parking lot. "That's Cynthia Miller. Shea followed her inside the mall. When Mrs. Miller came out, Shea was behind her.

Then two men and Shea grabbed her and forced her into a van."

Ethan's stomach clenched. Just what did Shea think she was doing? Going after Cole's murderer was one thing, but terrorizing and abducting women? How had she gotten so deep that she was actually doing the exact thing she'd fought so hard to shut down? What the hell had happened?

"Ethan, you with me?" Gibson asked.

"Yeah, sorry. What?"

The sympathetic smile the older man flashed told Ethan that Gibson knew something of his and Shea's history. "I was just saying that this vehicle is for your use. We don't anticipate Shea returning to the compound at least until tomorrow afternoon, so you have time to go over the maps and reports, scope out the location, and cement the details of your rescue plan."

Nodding, Ethan turned his gaze back to the approaching darkness. He'd come here to save Shea or die trying. This was a possible one-way trip for him, and Ethan accepted that as his due. He'd taken so much from her. The least he could do was give her his life if necessary.

Sleep always came fast and deep, like dropping off the edge of a cliff and free-falling into black velvet nothingness. No dreams or memories encroached on her unconscious mind. When something covered her face, seconds passed before she comprehended the meaning. Then adrenaline surged, racing through her. Forearms braced against the bed, she tried to shoot straight up, ready to dispatch whoever had been sent to test her, possibly kill her. The hand over her mouth was strong. The big body lying on her powerful. Did he plan to use her before he killed her? That was different from the others, but not surprising. Another test . . . one she would win . . . ensuring another victory for her master.

She bucked up against the hard body. The hand on her mouth didn't allow speech, but she had nothing to say to this man. He had come here to teach her a lesson; she would do her best to make sure he learned his own.

Warm breath caressed her ear. "Shea . . . it's me. I'm taking you out of here. Understand?"

Since he lay still, she assumed he was waiting for an answer. She nodded.

As if her acquiescence was all he wanted, he lifted his body and sat beside her. She rolled away and grabbed her gun from under the pillow in one motion. Standing on the other side of the bed, she pointed it at the dark figure.

"What are you doing?" The voice a harsh whisper. "It's me, Shea. Ethan."

That deep, gravelly voice . . . did it sound familiar? Did she know an Ethan? As her hand held the gun steady and pointed toward the shadowed image, her bare feet padded cautiously around the bed. She wanted to get closer, to see if she somehow recognized him.

"Put the gun down. Now." The tone held a cold fury.

She ignored the order, took another step closer.

"I'm not going to tell you again. Put. The. Gun. Down."

Whether she recognized that voice or not, it was filled with anger and meant her harm. She pulled the trigger.

With lightning speed, he knocked the weapon away. The gun landed with a soft thud against the plush carpet. She dove for it. The man slammed into her, covering her with his body.

"What the hell's the matter with you?" he growled.

The rage in his voice told her she would not get away from him as easily as she had from the others. She lay beneath him, quietly panting, waiting until he gave her some leeway. Then she would strike again.

He muttered, "Fuck this."

Blinding pain struck her temple, and blackness surrounded her once more.

Rat-a-tat-tat. Rat-a-tat-tat. Donald Rosemount jerked from a sound sleep, horror filling his gut. *Gunfire!* He sprang from the bed. Every molecule in his body filled with terror. Someone had found him. He had to get out . . . had to leave. He could do it. No one would see him. He could sneak out of the house, jump into his Hummer, and be gone before anyone could find his room.

Halfway across the midnight-dark room, he pulled to a stop. What was he thinking? There was no need to panic. His people would protect him . . . that's why he surrounded himself with the strongest and most skilled. Their number one priority was his protection. No one could get to him, much less harm him.

Heart still pounding, he dropped to his hands and knees and scurried back to the bed. *Just in case.* Wiggling under the bed, he pulled out his Colt .357 Python. His entire body attacked by violent tremors, he struggled to get his hands wrapped securely around the weapon. Still on his knees, he peeked over the surface of rumpled covers. The gunfire sounded more distant now, as if the fight had been taken outside. Arms braced on the bed, he pointed the gun at the door. Anyone who came in would get their head blown off.

Minutes seemed like hours. Finally the gunshots ceased. Only silence remained. Were they gone? Who had it been? Had his people killed the bastards who'd dared invade his home? The big gun in his hand a reassuring reminder of his power, Donald stood and slunk across the floor, his bare feet soundless on the thick carpet. At the door, he stopped. Ear plastered against the wood, he listened. Nothing.

Cold sweat trickled down his spine. Gnawing his bottom lip nervously, he eased the door open, winced at the slight creak. He peeked out. The hallway was empty, a distant pain-filled groan the only sound to penetrate the deathlike silence. Sweaty hands wrapped around the gun, Donald ventured out. He looked left and right— still no sign of life. On tiptoes, he crept across the width of the hallway and looked down from the third-floor railing to the giant entryway. Two bodies lay on the marble floor. His men. Were they dead? Though they were replaceable, it would be inconvenient to find new ones.

Fury replaced fear as Donald stomped down the stairway. Somebody better have a good explanation of how his home had been invaded. Heads were going to roll!

At the second-floor landing, he stopped and took stock. A man hung halfway over the railing. Again, one of his. Not bothering to check to see if he was alive, Donald continued down the stairs.

On the main floor, Donald treaded softly. Whoever had broken in was most likely either dead or gone, but he was too smart to take chances. Groans from one of the men on the floor added to his ire as he tiptoed toward his study. He inched his head in, saw no one. Nothing disturbed.

There was only one other reason for someone to break in. Rage bubbled and boiled. They'd come for the woman.

He ran out of the room, then jerked to a stop at another groan from the man in the foyer. Edwards, who'd been with him for over three years, lay faceup. Blood oozed from a wound in his thigh. Donald stooped down, nudged the man's shoulder with his gun. "Who was it, Edwards?"

"Don't . . . know." He grimaced, took a breath. "Big man with long blond hair . . . scar on his face . . . took the woman."

Donald straightened, weighed his options. Edwards wasn't bleeding that much, but burying him would be less trouble than healing him. Besides, he'd allowed the bastard to take his woman. Hands no longer shaking, he pointed the gun at the wounded man's head. Horror widened Edwards's eyes barely a second before Donald pulled the trigger.

He ignored the groans from the man lying beside Edwards. Shooting his brains out would be gratifying but wouldn't accomplish his objective. His people needed to see what happened when orders weren't obeyed. His home had been invaded; valuable property had been stolen. There was only one creature he depended on to carry out their punishment. Everyone else would watch. Lessons must be taught.

But first he had a rescue mission to set up. His woman had been taken from him. His people would bring her home . . . or die.

three

"Be still." Ethan smacked the shapely bottom of the squirming woman draped over his shoulder. Long strides ate up the distance as he ran down the road outside the compound and plunged into the overgrowth where he'd stashed the Jeep. Blood seeped from his side, the pain secondary to the shocked fury zooming through him. She'd tried to kill him. He couldn't believe it, and if someone had told him this would happen, he would've called them crazy. But he'd seen her. Moonlight from the bedroom window had shone directly on her face. A lovely, ethereal countenance with a deadly, blank expression. She'd shot him and hadn't blinked an eye.

If that sixth sense, telling him what was about to happen, hadn't reared its head, warning him to move, he'd be lying on that bedroom floor in a pool of blood. Would that have fazed her? Would she have stood over his lifeless body and felt remorse, or would she have just shrugged and walked away?

Ethan opened the back of the vehicle and tossed the bound and gagged Shea inside. Yeah, she'd have some bruises, but damned if that didn't give him a certain sense of satisfaction. Her bruises were a hell of a lot better than having a bullet in his gut.

Hand against his side to stanch the bleeding, he jumped into the driver's seat and started the engine. Blasting out of the bushes, he roared onto the rut-filled dirt road, toward the small airstrip. Once they were on the plane, he'd rip the gag off and demand an explanation. Not that there was one he'd accept. *Holy hell, the woman had tried to kill him.*

Things had gone so smoothly, he should have known there'd be a hitch. After spending hours studying the layout of the compound, he sat on his ass, at the top of a hill shadowing the compound, and observed. For two freaking days he'd watched people walk around the perimeter. One of those people had been Shea, and not once had she looked as though she was under coercion or threat.

The mansion, Spanish in design, was a Peeping Tom's wet dream. Balconies, giant windows, and wide, arched doors gave him plenty of opportunity to view the inside. Only five guards were on duty, eight-hour shifts. He saw no reason he couldn't practically march into the mansion and nab Shea with little resistance.

He waited till three in the morning, figuring the guard he'd seen nodding off the other two nights would be doing the same. And he had. Ethan found a sturdy tree limb hanging over a wall. Within seconds, he'd swung from the branch and been on the other side. On the way to the mansion, he'd slashed the tires of several vehicles and taken out three guards. Not killing if he could help it. No point in killing if it could be avoided. That was an LCR rule and one of the few he almost always followed.

Even her bedroom, on the second floor, had been damned easy to find. He should've known there'd be a wrench somewhere. He'd just never expected it from Shea. Good thing he'd brought clothes with him. If not, he would've had to search her closet. Something he'd definitely not had time to do. Putting shirt, pants, socks, and boots on a woman was a bit of a reversal, but he'd managed it in less than three minutes. Would've taken less time if he hadn't been bleeding like a stuck pig.

As he turned onto a paved highway, he spared a look at the brightening sky. Would be dawn soon. They'd be long gone before—

Glass shattered. The backseat window exploded. Bullets slammed into the door. Damn! A white van was closing on them fast. The three men hanging from its side gripping high-powered rifles meant business.

Head lowered, Ethan floored the gas and zigzagged back and forth across the road in an effort to avoid as many bullets as possible. Another blast . . . passenger window shattered. Bullets hammered holes into the seat beside him. If Shea had been sitting there, she'd be dead.

His bloody hands gripped the steering wheel as he took a left on two wheels, tires squealing. "Dammit, Shea, when we're out of this shit, I'm going to spank you till you can't sit down. What the hell were you thinking?"

No response. Not that he expected one, since she was gagged. Besides, she was probably plotting back there, waiting for another chance to kill him. Damned if he'd let that happen.

His eyes flicked up at the rearview mirror. The road was empty. Good . . . lost them. Now he just needed to get to the airstrip, get Shea out and . . . The Jeep sputtered, slowed to a roll. Ethan glanced at the gas gauge. Empty. The tank had been hit. A miracle the vehicle hadn't exploded.

With no other option, Ethan turned off the road. The Jeep nose-dived into a small ravine and shuddered to a stop. He shoved the door open and jumped out. In seconds he determined how far they were from the airstrip. Dense woods and jungle surrounded them. He'd made the run from the compound to the airstrip two nights ago . . . knew the area well. Shit, ten miles at least. No way would they make it in time. The pilot had instructions. If they weren't there by five o'clock, he was to assume something had happened and leave. It was already four-fifty.

A distant sound . . . the roar of an engine . . . headed his way. Ethan snagged his backpack, tucked his SIG Sauer P229 into his waistband, and stalked to the back. Yanking open the door, he grabbed a violently wiggling Shea.

"Be still, or I'm going to knock you out again. You hear me?"

Booted feet rammed toward his balls. Ethan jerked away but not in time. His eyes crossed as blinding bursts of agony slammed into him. He dropped his pack, let go of Shea, and bent double. As darkness edged his vision, he had the grimly humorous thought that at least she'd taken his mind off his throbbing side. Pulling in deep gasping breaths, he staved off unconsciousness, then began to work on the extreme nausea clawing at his gut.

Hands on his knees, he observed with dispassionate interest as Shea squirmed until she fell, with a hard thud, from the back of the vehicle. She rolled on the ground and then made it to her feet. Hands still tied behind her back, legs tied at her ankles, she hobbled away. The gag in her mouth muffled what he could only assume were threats against him and insults to his ancestry. Not that he cared. At this point, he was as close as he'd ever been to saying to hell with her.

One last deep breath. Feeling slightly less ill, he straightened. Backpack in hand, Ethan took off after her. Dawn made a slow spread of light across the sky, easily allowing him to see the short progress she made before falling. He reached the top of a small rise and found her lying faceup, in a ditch, panting. Her green eyes showed no emotion. Had he ever seen those vibrant eyes with such a cold, blank expression? Did she hate him that much?

As much as he'd have liked to sit down in the ditch

with her and have it out, he couldn't. The growl of a vehicle grew closer and closer. If it was something he could hijack, he would. Most likely, Rosemount's goons had caught up with him.

He dropped into the ditch and waited. The white van that had chased and almost killed him sped by. No telling when they'd return and find Ethan's abandoned Jeep. He and Shea needed to be long gone by then. He hauled Shea to her feet, slung her over his shoulder, and loped into the jungle.

As he stomped through the underbrush, tiny grunts and groans came from her gagged mouth, but she'd stopped squirming. Only by cold determination did he fight back his fury. When they were a safe distance away, he'd drop her on her ass, take off the gag, and get an answer. Until then, she could grunt and groan as much as she wanted.

Though blood trickled down his side with every step, Ethan knew the gash was little more than a flesh wound. He'd stop soon and bandage it . . . not yet, though. They needed to get as deep into the jungle as they could. Rosemount's men might give up after a few hours. Till then, he had no choice but to continue. Jaw clenched with resolve, Ethan forged onward.

She ignored the bruises and exhaustion as she planned her attack. Neither the identity of the assassin nor who'd sent him mattered. It wasn't the first time she'd been tested in this way. Her training included periodic surprise attacks. She'd easily dispatched the previous ones, but this man was stronger, highly skilled. Not part of a training mission. So why hadn't he killed her when he could? Was he an enemy of the master? Did he plan to ransom her as a hostage? That was unfortunate because the master would not pay for her. He had told her that repeatedly; had insisted that she repeat it herself.

She was his pet, trained to do his bidding, but held no value.

She would escape, of course. Her training ensured her survival. What this man intended to do with her was of no consequence. As soon as he gave her leeway, she would take him out and return to the compound.

As she bounced upon her abductor's shoulder, she paid little attention to the discomfort and pain. Such things were controllable. Her eyes stayed focused on her surroundings. Once she took care of her abductor, she would need to find her way out of the jungle. Her training hadn't included jungle survival methods, but she was confident she would find her way out. Giving up was alien to her.

"Shea, you're awfully quiet. Either you're unconscious or you're plotting something."

She remained silent and still. This name Shea he continued to use was not a name she was familiar with. Was it a term for something? Was he using a mind game on her, trying to trick her? She would wait and watch. When the time came, she would be ready.

Without permission, discomfort seeped into her thoughts. Nausea from hanging upside down and having her stomach pummeled against a hard, muscular shoulder caused physical reactions she could no longer ignore. As bile rushed up toward her throat, she began to gag.

"Okay. Hold on."

The voice sounded oddly soothing, as if he knew what she was going through. He slowed and headed to a small clearing. Sliding her off his shoulder, he dropped her on the ground. Big hands lifted her slightly to scoot her back against a tree and then pulled the gag from her mouth.

"No screams or I'll gag you again and ignore the fact that you're throwing up. Understand?"

Harsh breaths wheezed from her as she nodded her understanding. She would remain quiet and do as she was told until she was able to free herself. Then she would dispatch the assassin.

He'd been injured. She'd caught the scent of blood earlier. The hands that pulled her gag away were crusted with the evidence. Would he die from his injury? If so, she needed to free herself prior to his death. If he didn't die, his injury would make killing him easier.

Her head stayed down, her eyes focused on the dark green covering of the jungle floor. She'd been trained to never look into the face of her enemies. Had been taught that it weakened the warrior inside if she allowed eye contact. She could afford no weaknesses. This man was stronger and much more skilled than the others. All her training and resources had to be used.

"Here."

The gruff voice almost brought her head up, but she caught herself in time. When a canteen of water pressed against her mouth, she tilted her head back and drank, eyes closed to avoid seeing the man in front of her.

"We won't be able to stay here long. Rosemount's men are probably combing the jungle for us."

Her eyes focused on his boots, but she could feel his gaze on her.

"Dammit, Shea, are you going to just sit there? The least you can do is speak to me . . . tell me why you shot me. What the hell's the matter with you?"

When in a hostage situation, remain silent, keep your abductor off guard and wary. Do not allow him to see a weakness, as he will take advantage of it. She bit her lip, somewhat surprised that she did want to speak. She wanted to ask him why he had taken her, why he hadn't killed her when he had the chance. And why did he keep calling her Shea?

The man blew out a curse as she watched his booted

feet move a few feet away from her. His blood-encrusted hands opened a pack and pulled bandages and antiseptic wipes from it. He was tending his wound. Until he'd confirmed it, she hadn't realized her shot had found its mark.

He expelled another harsh curse, then went silent as he treated the wound. Her eyes flashed upward briefly and caught sight of his injury, a bloody crease across his side. Her bullet had only grazed him.

She tugged at her bindings, testing their strength: no give. This would be an excellent chance to run. Unfortunately, until he at least untied her feet, she would remain his hostage.

Several minutes later, having bandaged his wound, he came to stand in front of her. Muscled, tree-trunk legs before her revealed a large, well-built man in excellent shape. Another reason she'd been unable to best him. His strength was much greater than hers. She would have to rely on tactics other than strength to outwit him.

"Get up. I don't have time to play the silent game with you."

Bound hands pressed against the tree behind her, she stood and waited, prepared to be hauled up onto his shoulder again. When he untied the bindings on her ankles, she almost looked at him. Why had he done this? Was his injury so great that he could no longer carry her? Or was this perhaps a trick to throw her off? Did he want to see her run and then shoot her in the back?

"Just because I'm letting you walk doesn't mean I trust you." As he said this, he used the material he'd had on her legs to tie her belt loop to his. "Let's go."

Without waiting to see if she would comply, he took off. She had no choice but to follow. When he stopped abruptly, she slammed into his back.

"Turn around."

She turned as far as she could, once again surprised

when the binding at her wrists loosened. Before she could react, he twisted her around and immediately tied her hands in front of her.

"You can't keep your balance with your hands behind you." He stood quiet for a second, as if waiting for a response. Finally, he growled in a voice heavy with weariness, "Let's go."

Following him was easy. Her eyes stayed on the heels of his boots. When he slowed, she slowed. When he stopped, she did the same. She was in excellent shape, so the miles they traveled were not difficult. The sun was almost obliterated by giant trees; dense vegetation surrounded them. Air thick with the scent of dark earth and heavy with humidity cloaked them but had no effect on her. She often trained in the heat for hours and was accustomed to its intensity.

Limbs and branches fell away as the man cleared a path with a large knife. Wild creatures squealed around them, and large birds cried as they found their prey.

When he stopped, she raised her head to see why. He looked around for a brief moment and then started again. She told herself to lower her eyes but couldn't make herself do it. This was the first time she'd seen him without the need for survival blurring her thoughts. He was, indeed, a big man. Broad-shouldered, lean-hipped, very tall. She believed herself to be around five feet five; he stood almost a foot taller. An olive green T-shirt, dark with perspiration, covered his torso; underneath it, his muscles rippled and flexed as he moved. His hair was a conglomeration of blond colors. Gold, almost white, wheat, and light brown blended together. Shaggy and unkempt, hanging down to his shoulders. She was accustomed to clean-cut, well-groomed men at the compound. It was apparent that the man in front of her did not have the same degree of care for his appearance.

A face flashed into her mind. Craggy. Handsome. Arresting. Rough-hewn and suntanned, the face had a long scar down the side of a broad cheekbone, disappearing under the chin. The eyes were a brilliant shade of light green that darkened and lightened with fascinating shadows. She'd seen the face from time to time when she'd been forced to go without her vitamin shot. Though she hadn't seen this man clearly, she instinctively knew that this face belonged to him.

Her mind scrambled for an explanation. Since she saw the man only when she had to go without her shot and the demons chased her, she had to assume he was evil.

Her vitamin shot. What would she do if she didn't make it back to the compound before her shot was due? She would become weak, unable to function. That couldn't happen. She needed to escape as soon as possible, since it could take her hours to return home. If she was going to escape, she had to do it now.

She jerked to a halt, causing him to toss a glare behind him and growl, "What?"

"Water."

"So you can talk. I was beginning to think they'd cut your tongue out."

His mocking voice disturbed her for some reason. She ignored that as he pulled the canteen from a hook on his waist and handed it to her. She accepted it and took a long swallow, then rammed the canteen into his face.

Blood spurted. A vile curse erupted from his mouth as he grabbed his nose. Squatting, she snatched the knife he dropped. The sharp blade sliced the tie that bound her hands and the one that bound her to him. She took off. With blood pouring from his nose, he'd have difficultly following her for a few seconds. She had to make the most of his distraction.

Speed more important than stealth, she didn't bother to soften her footsteps. For an instant, she wished she hadn't left the knife with him but knew it was too cumbersome to carry. Branches cut and clawed at her skin as she forged through the thick green wildness. Gasping sobs raked over her lungs. A part of her felt surprise at that noise. It didn't sound normal coming from her. She felt no emotion other than the need to escape her captor; why, then, did it feel as though she might lose control?

A slight breeze of warning—then a hard, powerful body slammed into her, tumbling her to the ground.

Gut-wrenching fury almost overwhelmed Ethan. His nose pounded and his side throbbed, alerting him he'd started bleeding again. White-hot anger burned in his brain. Betrayal beat a heavy, agonizing tune against his heart. Shea had turned. There was no other explanation. Earlier today, she had tried to kill him. He had searched for an answer but hadn't come up with one. Now, without a doubt, he had the answer, though it clawed his gut to admit it. The one woman he had believed in, trusted above all others, had turned bad.

His body covered her as she lay facedown on the ground. Slender arms stretched in front of her; her shapely, firm ass jerked up, trying to knock him off. Despite the hurt and fury roaring through him, his body recognized the unique scent and soft femininity of his former lover. Ethan cursed his physical reaction, though he knew it was pointless. This beautiful woman was the only one who'd ever caused his libido to overrule his good sense. Just because Shea had turned into a killer made no difference to his hardening erection as it pressed against her, searching for her familiar soft, sweet heat.

With no small amount of regret, Ethan did the only thing he could do to save them both. Clipping the edge of her jaw to stun her, he pressed his thumb against her neck with the right amount of pressure, forcing unconsciousness. As her struggles ceased and her body re-

laxed, a part of him wanted to gather her in his arms
and howl with hurt fury at her betrayal, while another
part was furious for even caring.

Breath wheezing from his overtaxed lungs, he rolled
off her body and allowed himself a few seconds of rest.
Dim light filtered through the trees and indicated that in
an hour, perhaps two, the jungle would be in total darkness. There was little time to spare. He sat up, pulled a
wet towelette from a plastic container in his pack, and
wiped at his sore nose. Damn thing had thankfully
stopped bleeding. He knew from experience it wasn't
broken, but it throbbed like a toothache and would
most likely result in some colorful bruises.

The bloody towelette tucked away, he pulled out more
ties from the pack and bound Shea's hands and legs
again. Teeth clenched against the slash of pain in his
side, he hauled her unconscious form up and then over
his shoulder. He needed to find civilization before night-
fall. His cellphone had no signal, so calling for help was
out until they were closer to a town. How he would explain the tied-up, unconscious woman on his shoulder,
he'd worry about later.

As he trudged down hills, around tree stumps, and
over vines the size of elephant trunks, Ethan tried not to
think about the consequences of Shea's betrayal. He
knew there had been a few times when LCR operatives
had gone bad and had been dealt with. Noah McCall
was perhaps the most compassionate man in the world,
but when it came to one of their own betraying others,
there wasn't a lot of latitude. Few people asked what
happened to these traitors, but it was assumed that
whatever it was, the punishment was harsh and just.

What had happened to the warmhearted woman who,
though skilled enough to handle herself against the
strongest of men, could never bring herself to truly harm
anyone? Oh, she could disarm the meanest of bastards,

had no problem clocking someone to knock some sense into them. But her tender heart had never allowed her to cause true injury. Killing wasn't in Shea's nature. How many times had he chided her for those useless emotions? Her reaction was always the same . . . a gentle, breathtaking smile he'd felt to his soul.

Though he'd always thought her beautiful beyond description, the sheer joy of living Shea exuded, along with her warmth and compassion, were the things he'd loved the most about her. His years in prison had eaten away any tenderness he'd possessed. Shea's pure heart had filled that emptiness. God, what had happened to her?

The body draped over his shoulder woke and started squirming. "I don't feel well . . . let me down." The words were a demand, but the tone sounded weary and drained.

"Tough shit, babe. Should've thought about that before you tried to knock my nose through my skull."

"I won't run."

He didn't bother to respond to an obvious lie.

"I'm sorry I hit you."

Her apology sounded even more insincere than her promise not to run. He squinted up at the sky. "It'll be dark in about half an hour. Looks like we're going to have to sleep in the jungle tonight. I'll put you down then. If, however, you try to attract attention, I'll knock you out again. And believe me, baby, this time it'll hurt." He smacked her butt. "Understand?"

"Yes."

"Good. Now that you're awake and in a talkative mood, you want to tell me why the hell you went from a warm, courageous woman who saves people to someone who kidnaps and terrorizes innocent women?"

She didn't answer for so long, Ethan began to think she'd gone back to her silent treatment.

"I . . . do . . . what I am told." The words were said

haltingly, as if she wasn't quite sure what she was supposed to say.

"Oh, well. That explains everything. Thanks."

"You're welcome."

His sarcasm couldn't have been more evident, but she'd answered as if he'd really thanked her. Something was so off with her, and for the life of him he couldn't figure it out.

"I'm going to vomit if you don't put me down." This time, the distress in her voice sounded authentic.

Stifling a weary curse, Ethan stopped and slid Shea to the ground. A bite of conscience hit him when he heard the thud. He'd never treated a woman so roughly before, and for it to be Shea, of all people, tore at his gut.

She rolled over and tried to sit up, but her hands were tied behind her back. After watching for a few seconds, Ethan gave in and pulled her up so she could sit.

Blowing out deep breaths, she kept her face straight ahead, still not looking at him.

"Shea, dammit, look at me. Do you feel guilty for what you've done or do you just hate me that much?"

She was motionless for several seconds and then raised her head. "Why do you keep calling me Shea?"

The question almost knocked him on his ass. "What the hell else am I suppose to call you?"

A tiny frown appeared on her forehead, confusion flickered in her eyes, and then her expression smoothed into blankness. "You don't need to call me anything."

Ethan looked up to the sky for inspiration . . . for patience. "Look, you're tired. I'm tired. It's getting dark, and we're probably still about an hour or so away from a village. I'm going to tie you to this tree, go find someplace we can stay the night, and then come back for you."

For the first time, real emotion flared in her eyes . . . pure panic. "But I have to go back to the compound."

Since he didn't have an answer for such an asinine statement, he ignored it. Squatting, he untied her hands. Resisting the urge to caress the reddened skin around her wrists, he retied them in front, then pulled rope from his pack and wrapped it around the tree, then around her waist. After a strong tug on the knot to ensure that she couldn't somehow wiggle out of it, he stood. "I'll be back in a few minutes."

Her heart thudded against her chest as she watched her abductor disappear into the jungle. What was she going to do? She was due for her shot . . . she cast her eyes up at the darkening sky. It was past time for her injection. Soon, when it became dark, the demons would attack. She had sworn she would never go without her shot again. That she would do anything and everything to ensure that she never went through the agony. Now not only was she miles from the compound, she would be sleeping in the jungle beside a man who wanted to kill her. A wave of despair swept through her, and despite all her training, she couldn't seem to fight it. What was she going to do?

She pressed back against the hard surface of the tree, her eyes darting left and right. Animal sounds that had seemed normal earlier now sounded ominous. Fear dehydrated her mouth; desperate breaths wheezed through dry lips. The heavy pounding of her heart increased in speed, racing toward a foreign rhythm.

Darkness slid with easy familiarity over the jungle floor. A rustling in the bushes behind her had her panting and twisting, trying to see. He had her tied so tight, her body wouldn't swivel. What if something attacked from behind? What if he attacked her from behind? She still didn't know what he wanted from her. Why hadn't he killed her?

Sweat popped out all over her body. Breath rasped through her lungs as her pants increased, faster . . .

faster. Ink-black nothingness obliterated everything in sight. Tiny little sobbing noises pierced the night. Where were they coming from? She squinted, her eyes struggling to drill holes into the darkness. Holding her breath to listen, she was surprised when the sobs stopped. She resumed breathing, and they grew louder. Shock roared through her . . . they came from her.

Panic soared, overwhelmed all logic. Would he leave her here? Had he planned this all along? Abandon her and let wild animals devour her body?

Rustling steps grew closer and closer. Her heart would soon burst from her chest. She couldn't see anything in front of her. What was it? Who was coming toward her? Was it the demons? Were they attacking?

"Okay. I found us a . . ." A hand touched her face. "Shea? What's wrong?"

It was the demon. He had come for her. Tied up, knowing she was going to die, she did the only thing she could. She opened her mouth and released an unearthly scream.

four

Ethan slapped a hand across her mouth. Anyone within half a mile would've heard her screech. Muffled under his hand, her screams continued. Pressing his forehead against hers, he growled, "If you don't shut up, I'm going to knock you out again. Understand?"

His hand stayed firmly on her mouth until he felt her nod. Pulling away, he whispered furiously, "What the hell's wrong with you?"

"Someone is after me."

"No shit, Sherlock. With that banshee scream, you pretty much ensured they'll find you."

She clawed frantically at the rope at her waist. "We have to leave . . . I have to go."

"Finally, you said something sensible." Untying her, he put his hands under her arms to pull her to her feet. Her slender frame shuddered and shook. "What's wrong?"

"Need . . . to go . . . now."

"Okay, fine." He untied her feet but kept her hands bound. "This way." His grasp tight, he found the path he'd made a few minutes earlier and pulled her along. He kept looking back to watch her. Not that there was much light left, but he had good night vision. Something was wrong with her. Hell, what was he thinking? Of course, something was wrong with her. But now there was more. She was acting even odder than before. If he could get her to talk, maybe he'd get some answers.

"I found a small cave. It's not the Hilton, but it'll do for tonight."

Silence.

"You hungry?"

No answer. What had he expected?

He brushed aside the limbs he'd used to cover the small entrance to the cave. "Come on, let's go."

"I n-need to-to go-go to . . . to . . . bathroom."

He untied her hands, then pointed to a tall bush a few feet away. "Over there. You got two minutes. If you run, you'll regret it. Understand?"

Her shadow moved behind the bush and squatted. She was headed his way in less than a minute. Would miracles never cease? She'd actually done as he'd asked.

"Get in. I spread a couple of blankets out. It won't be comfortable, but it beats being out in the open."

Without comment, she stumbled into the cave and plopped onto the blanket. After covering the entrance again, he placed his flashlight between them and dropped down in front of her. Taking two protein bars from his bag, he handed her one. "Tastes like crap, but it'll fill you up."

A slender, trembling hand grabbed the bar. Ethan's eyes narrowed as he studied the woman across from him. He'd missed several things in his need to get her inside, out of the path of anyone who might have heard her scream. Sweat poured down her face. The night was warm, but not hot enough to cause that kind of perspiration. Her shaking had turned to violent shudders. Before, when she'd spoken, she'd stuttered. He'd attributed it to an urgent need to empty her bladder, but now he wasn't so sure.

And why had she asked why he called her Shea?

An odd, sick thought hit him. "Shea," he said quietly, "look at me."

Her wobbling head lifted. Ethan's heart plummeted to

the deepest, darkest depths of his soul. Shea's eyes were wild, dilated, and watery. "Good God."

Never in the years he'd known her had she even drunk alcohol. Her mother and stepfather had been alcoholics and drug addicts. Shea couldn't even stand the smell of alcohol. The few times he'd ordered a beer when they went out, she'd gotten all quiet and watchful. So how did someone who had such deep convictions about putting mind-altering chemicals into her body become a drug addict?

"Who did this to you?"

He wouldn't get an answer. She was fast losing her battle with whatever was trying to control her mind. Hell, he didn't even know what she was addicted to . . . not that it would help. He had a little medical training, but nothing in the way of how to handle drug withdrawal.

He watched as she lowered her head and tried, without success, to open the wrapper of the bar. Her hands were trembling so hard, she dropped it twice.

Ripping open his own bar, he handed it to her. He was probably crazy for feeding her, because she'd most likely throw it up. But they'd been on their feet for over fourteen hours with no nourishment. She needed something inside her, even if most of it came back up.

His appetite now nonexistent, he took her bar, tore it open, and ate the cardboard-flavored food in three bites. He ignored the taste—nourishment was their primary function, not enjoyment. Besides, the next few days were going to be rough as hell on both of them. They would need all the strength they could get.

Relieved to see that she had managed to eat the entire bar without gagging, he took the wrapper and handed her the canteen of water. "Drink as much as you need."

Her teeth chattered so hard, they clanked against the

canteen opening. Finally, she swallowed several mouth-
fuls and handed the container back to him.

"Drink more."

Without questioning, she took several more sips, then
looked up at him as if waiting for more instructions.

His heart heavy, he took the canteen and stood.
"Come on, let's get you settled."

Stark desperation gleamed in her eyes, revealing how
close she was to losing control. He untied the laces of
her boots and slid them off. Pushing her gently down
onto the blanket, he covered her with another thin blanket and watched as she curled up into a fetal position.
The blanket shook violently as shudders rippled over
her entire body.

Ethan sat across from her in the small, dimly lit cave
and felt a helplessness he hadn't experienced in years.
Forced at an early age to withstand more hardships than
many people faced in a lifetime, he'd become a hardened, unemotional man. But this . . . this was something
that ripped at him unlike anything else. A woman he
had once loved, admired, and desired with a fierceness
that sometimes stunned him was going through hell
right before his eyes and he had no idea what to do for
her.

How had this happened?

Weary beyond words, Ethan untied and removed his
boots, then his socks. Placing them beside him, he set his
gun beside the shoes. If Rosemount's men were still following, they'd most likely camp for the night and re-
sume their search at dawn. He'd covered their trail and
doubted they'd find any trace of them. However, he
didn't know how long they were going to be in this cave.
From what he knew about withdrawals, Shea wouldn't
wake up in the morning perfectly fine and ready to go.
By morning, he figured, she wouldn't even be lucid.

He unbuttoned his shirt to check his wound. With a

slight wince, he stripped the tape away, revealing an angry-looking gash about six inches wide, but only about a half inch deep. Probably could've used some stitches, but sewing himself up while people were looking to shoot more holes in him was kind of hard. Besides, he'd had worse. What did one more scar matter?

After cleaning the wound with an antiseptic wipe, he applied ointment and slapped on another bandage.

"Does it hurt?"

Startled at the soft voice, he looked up to find Shea's eyes open and watching. Though her body still shook, she seemed lucid and aware.

He shrugged into his shirt. "Not really . . . aches a little."

She closed her eyes; he thought she might have fallen asleep. He was about to get up and stretch out beside her when she opened her eyes. "Who are you?"

"Ethan Bishop."

"Are you going to kill me?"

The question made him furious, but the anger wasn't directed at her. Shea had been Rosemount's victim just as much as the women she'd kidnapped. "I came to rescue you . . . take you home."

Would she even believe him? She closed her eyes, and he waited to see if she would speak again. After a few minutes of silence, he lay down beside her and switched off the flashlight. Her body continued to shiver . . . the hard ground transmitted each shudder to him.

He closed his eyes, hoping for a short nap before the real trouble began. Within seconds, the shivering increased to shaking so violent, he thought she was convulsing. Her teeth clattered as the involuntary movements of her body increased. With a vile curse at the bastard who'd done this to her, Ethan did the only thing he knew to do. Scooting closer, he wrapped his arms around her and held her tight.

"Shea, you're fine. You're going to be okay." Ethan repeated the words over and over, with the hope that somewhere in her ravaged mind she understood and was comforted. The blanket covering her was soaked in perspiration, hers and his. Her ice-cold skin was coated in moisture.

He held her until her breathing slowed from harsh, heavy pants to lighter, easier breaths. He blew out a long sigh, relieved that she'd finally succumbed to exhaustion.

Holding her like this brought back good memories. This was the way they used to sleep together, with her back to his front. She'd once whispered she loved to sleep this way because she felt surrounded by him. Hopefully, she felt some reassurance now. He inhaled her sweet, familiar scent and felt his body loosen from the tension that had gripped him all day.

Ethan jerked awake; his arms were empty. He reached for Shea and was rewarded with a fist to his jaw as she thrashed and rolled beside him.

"Shea, stop it."

Agonizing sobs tore through her, and Ethan realized that as her arms flailed around her, she struck at creatures only she could see.

"No! Stay away! No! Don't let them get me. . . . Please, God . . . help me!"

Ethan tried to wrap his arms around her again, but her legs began powerful bicycle kicks. Cursing, but knowing he had no choice, Ethan turned on the flashlight and pulled out the ties he'd used earlier. Holding her down, he tied her arms together and then her legs. Heart-wrenching sobs tore through her, and he was surprised to realize that tears poured down his own face. Whoever had done this to her would pay.

The night was long and excruciating. Since she couldn't move freely, she ended up jerking most of the night, sobs and screams coming intermittently. She cried about demons coming to kill her, monsters that would shred her to pieces and devour her.

Every time she cried out, he soothed her with promises. When her body jerked with spasms, his was there to comfort her. He lost count of the times he wiped her body down. She was losing so much fluid, he worried about dehydration, so in her saner moments, he held water to her mouth for hydration. Most of the time, her eyes were closed. The few times she opened them, the hopelessness in them made him want to howl.

In the early afternoon she fell into a deep sleep, and Ethan was relieved to be able to untie her. Slumped back against the wall of the cave, his body ached as if he'd battled the very demons she'd had chasing her. Shea's face was still unnaturally pale, but her breathing was only slightly elevated and her heart rate almost normal. He didn't fool himself that the worst was over. Her body had shut down from exhaustion, but when she woke, she could be just as bad or worse.

He took advantage of her sleep to go out and check their surroundings. So far, there'd been no sign of Rosemount's men, but he doubted they'd given up so easily.

The heat and humidity of the day had peaked. Within a few minutes, thunder would rumble and the almost daily deluge of rain would explode from the sky. Feeling as though he needed a thorough cleansing, he stood in the open and waited for the storm. A light, distant patter against the leaves grew quicker and harder, and then with a forceful rush, torrents of water gushed from above.

As rapidly as it had come, the rain ended, and hot steam rose with the afternoon heat. Wringing the water from his hair, Ethan shook himself like a giant wet dog and turned toward the cave. He skidded to a stop. Shea stood at the entrance. Her pale face drained even whiter as her eyes glittered with confusion and what looked like panic.

"Ethan?" Her voice was hoarse from the screams and sobs earlier, but he understood her.

"Shea?"

He took a step toward her. She took a step toward him. Then her eyes flared in a wild panic as her legs collapsed and she fell to the ground in front of him.

When he reached her, she was unconscious. He scooped her into his arms, carried her back into the cave, and settled her onto the blanket. Fiery strands of hair covered her face. When Ethan brushed them away, he was relieved to see her lids flickering.

"Can you hear me?"

She blinked rapidly, as if trying to focus. "Ethan?"

"In the flesh." *Thank you, God. She remembers me.* He hadn't dared hope it'd be that easy. Profound relief, gratitude, and a mass of other emotions filled him.

"What happened?"

"What do you remember?"

Her brow furrowed. "You rescued me?"

"Yes."

"Have I been sick?"

Ethan went still. How much did she remember of the last few months? He treaded carefully, not wanting to scare or damage her further. "You were sick for a couple of days, but you're going to be fine. We'll get home and get you some help."

Her gaze roamed over their surroundings. "Why are we in a cave?"

"Just came in here to take a rest."

"Was I injured?"

"No. You were given a drug that made you forget for a while."

She lifted up a few inches, then collapsed back against the blanket with a groan. "Who did this?"

"Donald Rosemount."

A strange glimmer in her eyes made him ask, "You remember him?"

"Name seems familiar." She closed her eyes and mumbled, "Need to sleep."

The telltale flicker of avoidance in her eyes, combined with a subtle twitch of her mouth. He recognized both. Shea was lying. Why?

She'd always been the worst liar . . . one of her biggest drawbacks as an LCR operative. When you worked for an organization that relied on subterfuge for most of its missions, the inability to lie could be a fatal flaw. Shea had numerous skills, but lying had never been one of them. At least that hadn't changed.

Did she remember Rosemount but for some reason didn't want to tell him? Or had she faked regaining her memory, hoping to catch Ethan off guard? He waited to make sure she'd actually fallen asleep. He didn't like not trusting her, the gash in his side a reminder that he couldn't let his guard down again. After several moments of watching her deep, even breaths, he pulled himself up and headed outside again. He needed time to himself, to think and to plan.

She blinked slowly. Her eyelids heavy and thick-feeling. Why was it so dark? Where was she? Had the demons taken her to a place of permanent darkness? She tried to move and caught herself in a groan. Agony pounded. Her head throbbed, and every muscle she possessed felt as though she'd wrenched it. Had she been tortured?

She shifted. A big, hard body lay beside her. The demon? If he slept, she could escape. Ignoring the pain tearing through her body, she got to her knees and crawled toward a small slice of light, assuming it was an entrance.

A low, sleepy growl stopped her. "Where're you going?"

"I . . . I need . . ."

"Hold on. I'll take you."

For a demon, he sounded surprisingly agreeable.

"I can go by myself."

"Shea, you probably won't walk two feet before you fall over."

Memory flickered. That name again. Why did he keeping calling her that name? Before she could move an inch more, he was at her side, helping her up and then pushing her gently through the small opening of the cave, into daylight. One step out of the cave, her legs turned to mush. A small cry left her lips as she felt herself falling forward. Strong arms wrapped around her.

"I got you."

He carried her to a large green bush. After lowering her feet to the ground, he held her shoulders till she could stand. "Need me to stay?"

Avoiding his eyes, she shook her head, strangely affected by the gruff but gentle tone.

He backed away without a word and gave her privacy. Her hand closed around a limb of the bush to steady herself as her bleary eyes looked around. Vegetation surrounded them. She should try to escape. The master would expect her to take advantage of this brief freedom.

Somehow, relieving the pressure on her bladder seemed even more important. Besides, judging by the pain radiating through her limbs and head, she wouldn't get but a few feet away before she collapsed. No, she would wait until she felt better; then she would make her escape.

After she finished, she turned . . . and the world kept turning. As the ground rose up to meet her, hands caught and held her tight. "I'm here." Scooping her up in his arms, he carried her effortlessly to the cave.

Back inside, he eased her down on the makeshift bed and handed her a canteen. "I've tried to keep you hydrated as much as possible, but you've been pretty out of it. Drink as much as you want. I refilled it from the rain we had earlier. I can always get more."

A faint flash of something that felt like gratitude went through her mind. She mentally shook her head at such a strange notion. This man was her captor. If she felt anything for him, it should be hatred. He might not have killed her, but that didn't mean he wouldn't. He'd claimed he had rescued her. She hadn't needed rescuing.

She took several long drinks, her parched throat relishing the relief.

"How are you feeling?"

"Better."

He was silent for several seconds, and she knew he was looking at her, accessing. Then he asked quietly, "What were you called at the compound?"

Agony speared through her head. Her fingers pressed against her temples, which pounded in tandem with her pulse. A name? Why had she never wondered about this? Other people had names at the compound. She didn't remember anyone calling her anything other than "woman." The master called her *gatita* . . . little cat. But she didn't have a real name. Why?

"Not Shea?"

"No." Her head pounded harder. *Who was she?*

"Are you hungry?"

Her panic blurred as her stomach growled and rebelled simultaneously. She knew it was empty, but anything she put inside her would come back up. "No."

"Then why don't you try to sleep a little more?"

Why was his voice so tender and soothing? Earlier, when he abducted her, he'd been surly and mean. Was it just another ploy to throw her off her guard? If so, it wouldn't work. Nevertheless, she found herself lying down on the blanket and allowing him to cover her. She blinked hazily up at him. The cave was dim, and her head pounded with a relentless rhythm, but for a second, she thought she saw something in the way he moved, the way he turned his head . . . was it familiar?

When she'd woken earlier, the name Ethan had come easily to her lips. Did that mean something? Her exhausted mind veered from that wild thought. Of course it didn't. He'd told her his name, and she'd used it to her advantage. Keep your opponent off guard and uncertain . . . that's what she'd been taught. But hadn't his name caused a small blip in her mind? Did she know him after all?

She closed her eyes on this ridiculous thought. The man was her abductor, nothing more. She fell asleep with the knowledge that when she woke, she would probably have to kill him. For some strange reason, that bothered her.

five

Hours later, Ethan woke to the sounds of Shea thrashing around again, moaning about demons and beasts. Were these things in her subconscious because of the drugs or had they been fed to her along with the drugs?

Feeling like centuries-old dead dirt, he pulled her close to soothe her. "No one's going to harm you again, I promise."

"I hurt."

The little-girl voice tore at him as if he'd given her the pain himself. "I know, sweetheart, but it'll get better."

Her voice, weak and hoarse, was full of cautious curiosity. "Why are you being so kind to me?"

Ethan peered down at her. Was she acting or was she too weak to try to pretend? "Because I care about you."

"How can you care? You don't even know me."

Already making the decision to share small amounts of information in the hopes that it might help, he said, "You're Shea Monroe. Your birthday is May twelfth. You're thirty years old. You grew up in Omaha, Nebraska. Your mother and father split up when you were just a baby."

"Is that all you can tell me?"

About her childhood? Hell, yes. No way would he give her even more nightmares. "You work for an organization called Last Chance Rescue. You help people."

"I do?"

His chest tightened at the small note of hope in her voice. "Yes, you've saved a lot of people."

"I saved people?" She sounded as though this was a foreign concept.

"A lot of people."

She was silent for a few seconds, as if absorbing the information, then said, "And do you also work for this organization?"

"Yes."

She raised her hand and rubbed her forehead. "Why don't I remember?"

"Because someone's been giving you drugs to make you forget."

"Who? Why?"

"A man by the name of Donald Rosemount."

Her body went stiff.

"Do you remember him?"

Her eyes flickered closed as she shook her head. "I'm so tired."

Leaning forward, he kissed the top of her head. "I know you are."

"Are we lovers?"

"Why?"

"You keep caressing me. I just wondered."

"We were at one time."

"But no longer?"

"No."

"What happened?"

Ethan pulled himself up. Talking about their past . . . how stupid he'd been. Hell, he'd rather swallow rocks. But she was waiting for an answer. He could lie. Tell her the things he'd always told her . . . that he hadn't loved her, hadn't wanted to spend his life with her.

There were too many lies between them already, but he saw no point in unearthing more demons for either of them. Yet there was one truth he had never denied. "I thought you deserved better."

A hint of something like humor flickered in her face. "So you made up my mind for me? You sound very arrogant."

He grinned. That was a very Shea-like comment. "Yeah, I do, don't I?"

Confused green eyes searched his face, as if she was willing herself to remember him. A slender, shaky finger traced the scar on his cheek. "How did this happen?"

"Wrong place, wrong time."

The disappointment in her expression forced the truth. "Car wreck when I was a teenager." He touched his face. "My souvenir."

"There was more to your injury than just physical."

"Yes," he said quietly.

"Someone else was hurt?"

"Yes."

"You feel responsible."

A statement, not a question. He didn't bother agreeing.

She waited for several seconds. When he didn't answer, she asked, "Why are your eyes black? Were you hurt rescuing me?"

She didn't remember hitting him with the canteen? "Yeah."

"I'm sorry to be such trouble for you."

Shea Monroe was the least docile person he'd ever met. If she'd been herself, she would have laughed and told him he needed to do more training because he was obviously rusty. He missed her smart mouth.

Breaking off part of a protein bar, he handed it to her. "Try to eat this. I'm hoping by tomorrow, you'll feel well enough to travel."

"Where are we going?"

"Home."

"Where is home?"

Good question. Shea had a house in Key West, Florida. She and Cole had lived there after they married. But there was no way she could live on her own. First of all, she still didn't know who she was. Secondly, Rosemount would probably be combing the country trying to find her. He gave her the only answer he could, knowing deep down that he wanted this more than anything.

"You live in the United States . . . in Tennessee." He paused. "With me."

Tilting her head, she looked a little startled and then, doing what she'd done since they'd started this conversation, she accepted what he'd said as fact. "It will be nice to go home."

"Yes, it will."

After she ate, she slept for several more hours. When she woke, it was early afternoon, and though she seemed weak and confused, she was docile. Ethan figured that was the best he could hope for right now.

She shifted on the blanket and he knew her body had to be sore and uncomfortable. Going through withdrawal anywhere was no picnic. Experiencing it while on the floor of a cave in the middle of the Mexican jungle with a stranger you thought was your enemy would be a piece of hell.

"Do you need to go outside?"

Her mind even more exhausted than her body, she shook her head. The demons had quieted in her nightmares and the pain had lessened, but the insidious doubts remained. This man seemed to believe what he told her. If he spoke the truth, she'd been drugged and used. All her memories were gone. If, however, he was lying, planning something evil, she should try to escape. Her mind felt so muddled and confused. Should she believe him? Should she try to escape? Indecision wasn't something she was used to, or knew how to comprehend.

Still weak and helpless, she could only wait and see what happened.

"Feel like sitting up and eating something?"

"Yes."

His arms rock hard and steady, he scooped her up and leaned her back against the stone wall of the cave. The trees and bushes he'd used to block the entrance had been removed, and dim light flooded the small space.

An unwrapped protein bar appeared in her hand. "Eat it slowly, as much as you can. Your stomach may not be ready for a whole bar, but you need to get your strength back."

Taking a small bite, she chewed with determination. It tasted like artificially sweetened cardboard, but she soon found herself feeling stronger.

He arched a golden brow. "Better?"

"Yes." Then, surprising herself, she said, "Thank you."

"You're welcome."

After several swallows of water from the canteen he offered, she asked, "What is this Last Chance organization you said I work for? What is its function?"

"Pretty much what I did with you." A broad shoulder shifted in a lazy shrug. "We rescue people who've been abducted."

"And that happens a lot?"

His rusty chuckle caused an odd stirring within her. "Yeah, a hell of a lot more than most people think."

"Why are these people taken?"

"Ransom. Extortion. Sexual predators. Slavery. Prostitution. You name it, it's been done. Selling human beings for all sorts of vile acts has become big business."

"That is . . . interesting." She'd almost said "sad" but had stopped herself. What was or wasn't sad was not something she could differentiate. Nor was it her place to try.

"Yeah . . . interesting, but mostly sad."

Uncomfortable that he'd stated her thoughts, she shifted on the thin blanket. Her bottom had gone numb, but finding a comfortable position seemed impossible.

"Why don't we go outside and let you get some fresh air. After all that water, you probably need to relieve yourself."

Bodily functions were normal and nothing to be ashamed of. Why, then, did she feel her cheeks redden? Embarrassment? Could she be feeling an emotion that only a few days ago she had no concept or understanding of, other than to acknowledge its existence?

"You okay?"

Nodding, not wanting him to question her, she pulled herself to her feet. When she swayed, his hands were there to steady her.

"Take slow, small steps till you get your balance."

She shuffled toward the cave entrance. Once outside, she pulled in deep breaths. Though the air was heavy and thick, it still felt fresh and sweet on her skin and in her lungs.

Birds skittered across branches, while insects and other small creatures created a symphony of clashing sounds that for some reason seemed both exciting and scary. When was the last time she had listened to nature? Her days were always filled with training and following orders. Nights were filled with duties . . . she blinked as her vision narrowed, tunneled toward darkness. Swaying, she reached out a hand; the man beside her grabbed it and held her tight.

"I got you, Shea. You need to sit down?"

She shook her head quickly, hoping to clear it. For a moment, a vision of something truly horrific touched her mind. Unable to comprehend the meaning, she veered away from the thought.

"Let's get you to a place where you can relieve yourself, then back inside."

He helped her across the small clearing, then stopped at a bush. "You okay to do this by yourself?"

"Yes, I'll be fine."

He backed away from her. She noticed that not only had he moved several feet off, he'd turned his back to give her privacy. Why would he do this when he knew she could try to run? Did he think she was too weak to escape? He couldn't trust her—didn't he know this?

Unable to come up with a viable answer, she unzipped her pants and relieved the pressure on her bladder. She had just zipped them back up when the first rustle of sound reached her ears. Something or someone headed their way. She twisted her head to look at Ethan. He stood silent and still, his eyes filled with a question. Would she give them away? He appeared to be waiting.

Male voices came closer and closer. Though the language was Spanish, she easily understood the words. "We have to find her. Can't return until we bring her back . . . and kill the man who took her."

Frozen with indecision, her mouth trembled with the need to say something. Any sound or movement would catch their attention. The men were now only a few feet away from her. She could see them through the dark green vegetation.

One word and she would be rescued.

One word and Ethan would be killed.

She didn't move.

Several breath-holding minutes later, the men moved on, never knowing that the object of their hunt had been inches from them.

Confusion and fear swamped her as the world swirled

around her. Turning to the man who claimed to have rescued her, she whispered, "Ethan, I'm scared."

Everything went black.

Shea's eyelids flickered, alerting Ethan that she was finally waking. He kissed the hand he'd been holding and let it go. An interminable fear that'd been pressing in on him eased up, but only slightly. For almost twenty-four hours, she'd been in some sort of deep unconscious state, literally scaring the hell out of him.

Seconds after Rosemount's men had passed by, she'd fainted. Thinking it would be like the other time and she would immediately awaken, he'd carried her inside. When he couldn't wake her, he'd come as close to panic as he ever had. Calling her name repeatedly, he'd thought she had gone into some sort of a coma and he would never get her back.

"What happened?" Her voice sounded fragile and worn, but to Ethan, it was the most beautiful sound in the world.

His throat raw from pleading with her to wake up, he sounded like a sick frog. "You passed out. Been unconscious for nearly a day." Turning away, he grabbed the canteen sitting beside his backpack. "You're probably thirsty."

"A little."

Cradling her head in his hand, he lifted her, allowing her to sip the water. After several small gulps, she touched his hand, telling him she was finished. Ethan lowered her head and watched as she tried to assimilate and focus. He had no idea if, after being out of it for so long, she'd remember what had happened before she passed out.

"Those men were looking for us."

So she did remember. A good sign . . . finally. "Yes. You didn't give me away. Why?"

Her smooth forehead furrowed. "I don't know."

"I do. You may not think you remember me, Shea, but something inside you does."

For several long seconds her gaze roamed over his face. Ethan held still, willing her to remember. Finally, unable to wait for her verdict, he urged, "Tell me you remember me, Shea."

"Your face is familiar . . . I often saw it in my nightmares."

Ethan turned away before she could see the crushing impact of her words. The knowledge that she saw him only in her nightmares didn't surprise him, since he'd hurt this woman over and over again. Regret, born of a thousand mistakes, ate at him daily. If he could go back and make right everything he had done in his life, he'd have to start at a much younger age. At the tender age of nineteen, when with stupidity and arrogance, he'd taken a young girl's life.

"We'll go as slow as you need to. The village we're headed to is only a couple of miles away."

Forcing her stiff lips into a small smile, she allowed him to help her over a fallen tree. This Ethan person believed she trusted him. That she accepted the ridiculous lies he'd spouted. Fooling him gave her an odd sense of satisfaction. He'd apparently been told to continue the fabrications until they reached their destination. He wasn't going to kill her yet.

She'd woken this morning feeling weak and worn, her mind muddled and fractured. Yesterday, she had almost allowed herself to believe him. Something *had* kept her from calling out to the men searching for her. Was she protecting Ethan? Or had it been mere indecision on her part?

Ethan continued to insist that somewhere inside, she did remember him. If so, why did his face appear only in her nightmares? When her subconscious was at its weakest, why would he be involved in her most horrific moments if he really meant her no harm? There was only one conclusion to make: Ethan was indeed her enemy.

Escape would have to wait until she had recovered more of her strength. He claimed that they were headed to a village. Once there, with proper food and rest, she would find a way to escape. Until then, she would pretend to be this subservient woman he seemed to think she was.

Out of the wild growth, at the top of a hill, she stopped. Increasing her breath slightly, as if she needed to rest, she surveyed their location. Small houses and a church steeple indicated that a village lay only a short distance below them. Blue cloudless sky, fresh air, and sunshine surrounded them. After the darkness of their cave, the world seemed bright and new.

An unusual sense of optimism hit her. Just a little while longer and she would find a way to break free. Perhaps she could ask Ethan to get her some food. He seemed intent on pretending to care for her and would most likely continue that act until they reached his intended destination. She would make sure that didn't happen.

After a couple of minutes of allowing her rest, he took her hand and pulled her with him down the hill. She noticed that he kept a close watch on her, as if concerned with her well-being. Another act, of course.

Determined to trap him in a lie, she continued to question him. "How did we meet?"

"We were both in training in Florida. LCR's headquartered in Paris, France, but there are branches throughout the world. We did some training in France too. That's where Noah lives."

"Noah?" Did she know the name?

"Noah McCall. He's the head of LCR." He gave her a sharp look. "His name sound familiar?"

She shook her head. There had been another small blip inside her head, but that didn't mean she remembered the name.

"What kind of training?"

"You name it, we did it. Languages, self-defense, history, geography, tactical planning. LCR people are well versed in a lot of different areas."

"I excel in languages."

He chuckled. "Yeah, you never minded bragging about that. Modesty was never your strong suit."

Shoulders straight, a familiar mantra sprang to her lips. "Modesty is a lie to myself and others. I am proud of what I accomplish for the master. Regardless of my infirmities, imperfections, and doubts, I go forward with my duties. My master's intelligence is superior, and his will always wins out."

"Your master?"

To avoid his penetrating eyes, she looked toward their destination. The master would have her beaten if he knew she'd talked about him in this manner. The excuse of being weak and disoriented would not be tolerated. She'd been trained to never speak of him, never reveal his existence. How could she be so careless?

She pressed fingers to her temples, hoping the little-girl act would work again. "My head hurts."

He pulled her to face him, and held her head in his hands. "Look at me."

The disappointment on his face tugged at something inside her, as if his opinion mattered. "What's wrong?"

Instead of answering, he took the ties he'd shoved into his pocket when they'd left the cave and bound her wrists. "You've been playing me the entire time. And I fell for it." He shook his head. "I'm an idiot."

"I don't know—"

"Save it," he barked. Pulling her behind him, he began to walk faster. His shoulders and back were so tense, she could almost feel the anger bouncing from them.

Despair and panic mingled. She used to be so much better than this. He must have drugged the water to disorient her. Also, her inability to attain her daily vitamin shot weakened her.

Since it would do no good to protest her innocence, she instead looked around. She had to escape. Now that he'd realized she'd been acting, he would give her no opportunity. If he took her to the United States, she might never be able to come back here. She had to get away from him before they reached the village.

"I can feel your mind working." He turned and glared. "Understand this: you *are* going back with me. I don't give a damn if you think you're Cleopatra, Attila the Hun, or Bluebeard's Ghost. You are Shea Monroe, and you will fucking be Shea Monroe again. Do you fucking hear me?"

"I'd say the entire world fucking heard you."

They both jerked around. A tall, dark-haired man stood on a small rise, only a few feet away from them.

Ethan blew out a long sigh. "Damn, Gabe. How the hell did you find us?"

"Tracked your cellphone signal."

"Sure hope that means you've got transportation."

"Got a bird a few yards down that way." He nodded toward what looked to be a clearing beyond a copse of trees.

"Good."

The woman beside him tugged on her bindings, evidently realizing that her hope for escape had just become impossible. Ethan pulled her closer. "Shea, this is Gabe Maddox. Gabe, you remember Shea. Unfortunately, Shea won't remember you."

"What do you mean?"

Holding tight to Shea's bound hands, he headed toward his friend. "I'll tell you on the way. The sooner we get in the air, the sooner I can relax."

Behind him, Shea made small whimpers as she continued to twist and jerk, no doubt looking for an escape route. Forcing himself to ignore her sounds of desperation, he brought Gabe up-to-date on what he knew and what he suspected.

Gabe shot a glance back at Shea. "So you're telling me she doesn't remember who she is and what she's done?"

"Doesn't remember a thing. We need to get her some medical care. I don't know what they've been giving her."

"Noah wants her in Florida."

Ethan couldn't argue. Having Shea at his home, where he could keep an eye on her and help her, was one thing. Having a woman who had no idea who she was and thought he was the enemy was something altogether different.

They came within sight of the helicopter, and Ethan knew he'd never seen a more welcome sight. Tightening his grip on Shea, he headed to it.

Using his arm as leverage, Shea kicked her feet out, knocking Gabe to the ground. She then whirled and shoved her knee toward Ethan's groin.

Ethan swerved just in time. "Dammit, Shea. Last time you did that you almost killed me."

Her eyes hard with determination and panic, a long, lethal leg shot toward him. Ethan jumped out of the way of a gut kick. Just when he knew he was going to have to do something drastic to restrain her, Gabe came up behind her and put a choke hold around her neck.

"Settle down or I'll choke you for real," Gabe said.

Shea clawed at his arms, shifting her body to throw him off. Gabe tightened his forearm against her throat.

"You're hurting her, Gabe."

"All she has to do is stop struggling."

Shea's face was red from exertion and lack of oxygen. "Shea, he's not kidding."

She went still, and Gabe loosened his hold. Shea immediately swung her foot back, kicking Gabe in the shin.

Not bothering with another warning, Gabe thumped her on the side of her head. Ethan caught her before she fell to the ground.

Gabe frowned down at the unconscious woman in Ethan's arms. "Doesn't seem like she's changed that much to me. If I'm not mistaken, last time she saw you, she knocked the hell out of you."

Ethan carried Shea to the helicopter and placed her on a mat on the floor. "She had good reason to be pissed at me then."

Gabe jumped into the chopper. He waited until Ethan had settled in against Shea, then said, "Cole acted on his own, whether either of you agree or not. He's the one who got himself killed."

As their ride rose in the sky, Ethan pulled Shea closer. No matter what Gabe or Noah told him, he knew the truth. And somewhere in her damaged mind, so did Shea.

six

Ixtapa, Mexico

Donald stood at the giant arched window of his new residence and observed the gardeners working frantically to bring order and beauty to the grounds. This was the least favorite of his many houses, but hidden as it was within the densely treed mountains, it was the most secluded. No one could find him here. Unfortunately, he hadn't kept an eye on the place and it had become overgrown with weeds and wild vegetation. The fury he'd displayed on seeing its condition had provided incentive to improve his home's appearance. People were working night and day to remedy the situation. Disorder was chaos. He hated it.

His sigh heavy with sadness, he turned from the window. The big, empty room was a stark, painful reminder of his loss. The pristine white comforter called out for a beautiful creature to lie on it, eager to please. The white sofa across the room cried for his beauty to curl up beside him and give him the attention he craved. He missed his *gatita* . . . his kitten . . . much more than he'd thought possible. His men had been unable to find her and would soon be punished. Then not only would he have to extend his search beyond Mexico, he'd have to find at least ten more men to replace the ones destroyed.

Business would suffer until he could get things back in order. Though his fortune was secure and the people he paid would continue to be highly compensated, ensuring their cooperation and loyalty, the interruption of business would cut into his profits. One more thing LCR would answer for when he took them down.

He had no concern that the woman would remember enough to threaten him. Her thoughts would be so fractured from the drugs, he doubted she'd ever be able to function properly again. Within days, her mind would be filled with shadowed images. In a week, maybe two, a dark film would cover most of the remaining memories of her time with him. Any that were left would be scattered, like flotsam. Her description of him would be vague and unhelpful. When questioned on her daily duties, she would be uninformative and sketchy.

The injection she had received each day had been just enough to keep her in line and on the edge, needing the drug with an intensity that would make her do anything to get the reward of relief. Without her daily dosage, the withdrawal would be painful and damaging.

Sad really, that she had to go through such pain, but fitting as well. She had failed him. Her training had included intensive reinforcements that if she were ever taken, she must come back to him.

No matter how furious he was at her failure, he had to get her back. The companionship she'd provided was of paramount importance to his happiness. In the months they'd been together, he'd felt a contentment he'd never dared dream of.

Every evening after she'd been given her shot, they would have dinner together and he would share with her. She would nod as if she understood and could totally identify with his worries and concerns. He told her all the things he'd held inside himself for so long. Things he'd never told anyone else. She knew him inside and out . . . even if she didn't remember.

After dinner, he would instruct her to curl up beside

him on the sofa. She would sit there for hours, never complaining, never speaking unless he asked her to. And when he wanted it, a small smile would curve her lips in approval. She never commented, never questioned him, and never criticized his actions. She was the perfect companion. The perfect pet. He had to find her!

A knock at the door pulled him from his morose thoughts. Victor, one of his most trusted men, entered. A scrawny teenager, hardly bigger than a child, shuffled into the room behind him.

Of course, Donald knew that the teen wasn't a child. This young man was malnourished and, as a result, looked years younger. It would take weeks before proper training could begin. In the meantime, he would be fed well and given only minor duties. When the time for training came, his having experienced starvation would be a huge bonus.

Knowing his place, Victor stood quietly and waited for Donald to speak. The man had been trained by the best . . . himself.

"What have you come to tell me?"

"Everything is in place for the exhibition."

His heart jumped with excitement. He had been so consumed with sadness, he'd almost forgotten today's entertainment. "Excellent." Donald turned his attention back to the young man beside Victor. "And how is our new recruit?"

Victor touched the boy's shoulder. "Answer him."

After several audible swallows, the boy said, "Fine, sir."

"Good." Donald began a slow circle around the young man. Despite his gaunt, desperate look, he was an attractive specimen. Of course, he wouldn't be at the compound if he wasn't.

"Raise your shirt."

Dark brown eyes widened. "What?"

"Do not speak unless I ask a direct question! And never question my orders! Raise. Your. Shirt."

Skinny fingers trembling, the kid swallowed again, then raised his shirt, allowing Donald to see his torso. Though his ribs were still quite prominent, Donald knew the young man had gained a good ten pounds since his arrival a couple of weeks ago. Still, to Donald's knowledgeable eyes, it would take another month or more before he could begin his discipline and training regimen.

"What is your name, boy?"

"Raphael . . ." Wary eyes skittered over to Victor and then went back to Donald. He added, "Sir."

Donald examined the bone structure, the length of his torso and legs. Sleek, elegant . . . almost like a greyhound or a Great Dane. Yes, that was a good name for him. "You can keep your name."

The boy's eyes widened with surprise—and was there maybe a hint of arrogance, too? Donald's heartbeat increased in anticipation. When was the last time he'd had a challenge? Not since his little kitten came to stay. This young man's training might be even more fun than he'd first thought.

Donald nodded at Victor. The big man's hand clamped on to the boy's bony shoulder, pressing deep into the muscle. He said, "Lower your eyes to the floor and repeat after me: Thank you, sir, for allowing me to keep my name."

Donald noted a small, mutinous twitch of the boy's mouth before he lowered his head and said, "Thank you, sir, for allowing me to keep my name."

Feeling quite pleased with himself and this new upcoming challenge, Donald turned to Victor. "Let's go."

Victor opened the door for Donald. They walked out of the bedroom, Victor and the boy at least five feet behind him.

With a spring in his step, Donald headed down to the courtyard. At last the people responsible for his unhappiness would be punished. This kind of entertainment always put him in a better mood. Then he would see about getting his kitten returned.

Tampa, Florida
LCR Clinic

Impotent fury pounded through Ethan as he gazed down at a helpless, terrified Shea. She'd been unconscious for much of the flight from Mexico to Florida. When she'd woken, she had been quiet and watchful. It was when they arrived at the small private clinic that she'd gone wild, kicking and screaming like a feral animal. Fortunately, she'd still been tied, but the stark fear in her expressive face cut deep.

Now, she lay strapped to the bed, but her eyes . . . God, her eyes held such desperate panic. Her expression reminded Ethan of a trapped, helpless animal. He could only imagine what was going through her mind. Gasping sobs and small helpless whimpers were the only sounds she'd made. He'd tried several times to get her to talk. So far, she hadn't uttered a word.

Ethan pulled his eyes away and turned to the gray-haired man standing beside the bed. "There's got to be something you can give her."

Barely over five feet tall, Dr. Lawrence Norton was one of LCR's leading physicians. The older man's normally twinkling eyes were dimmed with concern. He had known Shea even longer than Ethan had. They'd been friends from the start of her service to LCR.

"I can't give her anything until we know what she's addicted to. From the look of her buttocks, she's been getting regular injections of something. Based upon what you've told us about her memory loss and behavior, we can't risk giving her something that might exacerbate what's in her system."

Slumped beside her in a chair, Ethan caressed her hand, hoping that somehow, the sane, beautiful woman he'd known was somewhere inside her and would feel comforted. "Shea, I know you're scared, but I promise you . . . I swear on my life, no one is going to hurt you. We're going to find out what the bastards were giving you, and then we're going to make you better."

Green eyes, once bright with joy and love for him, glittered with helpless anger. He knew exactly how that felt. How it was to have no escape. How it felt to wake each morning, knowing captivity was a part of his life and he couldn't get away no matter how he tried. But he'd been in prison and had deserved to be there. How much more difficult was it for Shea to not know her captors? She believed they'd taken her for evil reasons and trusted no one.

"Can't you at least give her something to sleep?"

"Not until we know something." Dr. Norton looked at the heart-monitoring machine and jerked his head toward the door. "Can I talk to you a few minutes?"

After one last squeeze on her hand for reassurance, Ethan followed the doctor into the hallway. With his back propped against the wall, he blew out a weary, frustrated sigh. "I feel so damned helpless."

"I think she feels safer with you."

His head snapped up at the doctor's words. "What makes you say that?" He'd seen only the hot blaze of hatred in her eyes.

"Because she calms down as soon as she sees you. She listens to you talk. She may not be speaking, but wherever you go in the room, her eyes follow you. When you took her hand a minute ago, her heartbeat slowed." The doctor raised his hand before Ethan could start questioning him. "Now, I'm not saying she remembers you, but for some reason, there's a level of trust for you that she doesn't have for anyone else. I think she knows you don't mean to harm her."

"What should I do?"

"Stay with her till she falls asleep. We're rushing the lab work as fast as we can. Last time I talked to our lab guys, they were having a hell of a time identifying what they'd found in her blood."

Shoving his hands through his hair in frustrated anger, Ethan thanked the doctor and headed back into Shea's room. Something flickered in her face. He didn't know if it was because of what he'd been told, but Ethan could swear he saw relief.

A heavy weight of weariness pulled at him as he slumped in the chair beside the bed. He'd only taken the time to shower before coming back to her room. Since the clinic was exclusively for LCR operatives and family members, the accommodations were similar to those of a small hotel, along with an advanced medical facility. He'd borrowed some clothes from Gabe until he could go out and get some. His appearance was the least of his concerns.

Stroking her hand, Ethan spoke softly, "You need some sleep, Shea. It's been hours since you've rested. I'll be right here. No one will hurt you, I promise."

"Ethan?" Her voice was low and raspy.

His heart jumped at the first words she'd uttered in hours. "Yes?"

"Why are you doing this?"

"Shea, baby, I'm trying to protect you. I know you don't believe that, but I am. Some bad men took you, gave you drugs . . . made you forget who you were . . . your life." Unwilling for her to be tied up and without hope any longer, he untied the restraint on her right arm, took her hand, and held it against his mouth. "We have a history together, Shea. You have a life . . . a very valuable life. I'm not going to let you throw that away because you're afraid."

"I'm not afraid."

He smiled against her skin. That statement actually sounded like Shea.

"Okay, not afraid. Maybe confused."

"I don't believe anything you say . . . but tell me again how we met . . . how we know each other."

He caught a glimpse of the tray of food she'd refused earlier. "On one condition. You eat something."

She twisted her head and stared at the tray. "It's drugged."

Ethan snorted, picked up the plate of food, and slid it on the small swing table beside the bed. "It's not drugged." Lifting the silver cover, he sniffed appreciatively. "They have a great cook here."

"I don't—"

"Tell you what . . . I'll eat a bite for every two you eat."

She bit her lip and then nodded.

Wasting no time, he cut a piece of chicken and put it in his mouth. As he chewed, he cut another piece and held it to her mouth. He almost whooped in delight when she opened her mouth and took the bite he offered.

Within minutes, they'd demolished the chicken, mashed potatoes, and steamed vegetables. A feast by no means, but the most either of them had eaten in days. A small amount of color already bloomed on her cheeks.

"You haven't told me anything," she said.

He pressed the button on the bed to put her in a more comfortable position, then rearranged the pillows. "Settle back and I'll tell you."

Surprising him, she snuggled into her pillow and looked up at him expectantly.

As he settled back into the chair, a small smile kicked up at his mouth.

"Why are you smiling?"

Because, for a moment, she looked like the old Shea. For the first time since seeing her again, he felt as if he were talking to the woman who'd stolen his heart all those years ago. "I was remembering the day we met."

Her eyes fluttered as she fought sleep. "Tell me," she whispered.

"It was just down the road from here . . . at the training facility. I walked into a room and heard the most joyous laughter. I turned around and saw three beautiful women. All three were drop-dead gorgeous, but it wasn't until the one in the middle laughed again that I realized who was the most beautiful."

"I laughed?"

She asked the question as if surprised. God, that broke his heart.

"Sweetheart, you have the kind of laugh that makes everyone smile. It's one of those deep, luscious, full-bodied laughs that's just a natural part of who you are."

Her emerald-green eyes darkened, became more haunted. "I don't remember laughter."

"You will, Shea. I promise, you'll remember how to laugh."

What looked almost like a small smile played around her lips as she whispered, "I'd like that." Her eyes fluttered closed and she finally slept.

Taking her hand, he held it against his face and wished with all his might that things could have been different for them. By the time he'd realized he couldn't live without her, he'd broken her heart and pushed her into the arms of his best friend. Cole had been decent and honorable, so much better for Shea than Ethan ever could have been. And from the moment Cole met Shea, he'd loved her.

Ethan had told himself it was Shea's fault for pushing. What they'd had together was incredible. A chemistry that could set the sheets on fire, but also an ability to read each other's thoughts and actions. Their partnership as LCR operatives had been legendary. Working together, they'd been unstoppable. If only that had been enough for Shea. She had wanted more. She'd wanted promises . . . she had wanted forever. And the way she'd tried to ensure their forever had been his breaking point. Unfortunately, he'd almost broken her instead.

Ethan stood and, reluctantly, tied Shea's hand again. If she woke and was the wild creature she'd been before, she could hurt someone or herself. He couldn't take the chance.

He headed toward the bedroom he would be staying in until it was determined what could be done for Shea. Noah was on his way, and Ethan hadn't had a chance to discuss Shea with him. He didn't know what Noah had planned but was determined that Shea wouldn't suffer anymore. If that meant Ethan spending the rest of his life protecting her, then that's what he would damn well do.

How he was going to convince Shea of that was another matter.

Ixtapa, Mexico

Donald stalked into the arena. His people had done a good job of clearing the small exhibition area. What had once been a training area for horses would become a training venue for soldiers. His people stood on the outskirts, behind a short bricked-in area. He noted expressions of fear and confusion. Those emotions stoked his excitement and ratcheted up his enjoyment. He'd never staged such a large event before. Many of them had no idea what he had planned, but they knew something major was about to take place. This was an excellent introduction to Donald's high expectations.

The few privy to his plans knew what was coming and looked on with anticipation. Some of them would enjoy this almost as much as he did.

For everyone, it was a lesson: If orders aren't obeyed, punishment is quick, brutal, and often lethal.

The guilty men stood in a circle in the middle of the arena. Their hands tied behind them, their feet bound together, they collectively shook. Some of them wept, others cursed, while a few stared stoically at him. They all knew what was coming. They had failed him. His punishment was just.

Heading to the chair prepared on a hastily made dais, Donald seated himself and addressed his audience: "Today is all about obedience and following rules. My home was invaded. My property stolen. Those who allowed this to happen and those who failed to find her must be punished."

Not a sound, breath, or voice could be heard. Everyone waited in rapt silence. As he looked around at their fearful and respectful faces, power surged through him, followed quickly by a hot flush of pleasure. He waited for several seconds, allowing the excitement to build. Then, when the anticipation was almost at a crescendo, he waved his hand and commanded, "Bring him."

Heavy footsteps stomped closer and closer. Those who had seen the creature's work before, and knew what was about to happen, lowered their eyes. The newer recruits stared in awe as he entered the arena.

Donald's eyes slid up and down the animal standing in the middle of the arena, awaiting his orders. Dressed in only a loincloth Donald had had specially made for him, the creature stood before him. Six feet, five inches of pure, brute strength. His 240-pound prized trophy. The creature's dark hair gleamed blue-black beneath the hot

Mexican sun, and his golden skin glistened with healthy male sweat. Flawless and beautiful. Strong and lethal. The perfect killing machine.

The condemned men gave a collective gasp, and then the weeping, begging, and screaming began anew . . . this time louder and more anguished. Satisfaction and sheer exhilaration brought Donald to his feet. Pointing at the bound men, Donald shouted his order: "Kill them!"

His face an empty mask of blind obedience, the creature marched forward. Wrapping his hands around the first man's neck, he snapped it as if it were a twig and dropped the body to the ground. As each man waited his turn to die, their screams grew more desperate, their pleas for mercy more anguished. Their faces grew darker, masks of sheer terror at the horror that awaited them.

At last, ten dead men lay on the ground. The silent crowd watched as the creature turned to his master and bowed. His goal had been accomplished . . . his master was pleased.

Donald smiled.

seven

Her mouth sandpaper dry, she blinked sleep away and tried to focus. Where was she? Her eyes roamed over the large room. Creamy pastel walls and colorful paintings did their best but couldn't disguise the stark impersonality of a hospital room. She shifted, tried to move, and couldn't. Her heart picked up a frantic rhythm as she realized that her arms and legs were restrained.

Sun streamed in from a window beside the bed. She lifted her head and peered out. Only a few yards away, elegant white swans glided over a pond sparkling like diamonds. Surrounded by swaying weeping willows and moss-covered trees, the picturesque sight gave her an unexpected feeling of serenity.

"Good morning, Miss Monroe. Here's your breakfast."

She jerked her head toward the door and squinted as artificial light flooded the room. A cheerful-looking middle-aged woman headed toward her with a tray.

"Where am I?"

"You're in—"

A tall stranger stepped into the room, behind the woman. "I'll take care of this, Melanie. Thanks."

The woman turned and smiled brightly at the stranger. "Oh . . . of course, Mr. McCall. I just brought Miss Monroe's breakfast."

Anger and suspicion swamping her, her eyes narrowed at the stranger. "Who are you?"

The man flashed a smile at the older woman as she handed him the tray of food. Then, turning toward her, his face softened and became oddly sad. "How are you, Shea?"

She leaned back against her pillows with a tired sigh. "And I suppose I should know you, too?"

He placed the tray on the swing table beside the bed. Frowning at the restraints on her arms and legs, he untied them. "We don't really need these . . . do we?"

Though profound relief shot through her, she kept a wary gaze on the stranger as she pressed the button to raise the bed. Just because he'd untied her didn't mean she could trust him. Until she knew more . . . knew something, she could trust no one. Sitting up, she gave a tentative stretch of her muscles. Why did she ache everywhere?

"Feel better?"

She lifted a shoulder in a silent message that she would give him no leeway.

"Would you like to freshen up before breakfast?"

Surprised but still suspicious, she nodded. She had no idea how strong or weak she would be, but she was willing to take the risk to actually be able to stand, on her own, without being restrained in any way. Twisting her body, she threw her legs over the side of the bed and put her feet on the floor. The cool tile felt wonderful against the soles of her bare feet. She looked down at her attire. At some point, someone had undressed her, exchanging the pants and shirt for a long, blue cotton nightgown.

She gripped the bed rail for balance as she stood. The man stayed beside her but didn't offer to help. Strangely grateful for his allowing her this small independence, she headed toward the small bathroom. Her feet slid across the floor like a zombie's. By the time she'd made it across the room, breathless, her legs wobbling like overcooked noodles, she felt triumphant, as if she'd achieved a major victory.

With the door closed behind her, she turned and swallowed a gasp, startled at the person staring back at her in the mirror. A stranger's face. Deathly pale skin, dull green eyes, wild auburn hair. She knew this face, yet she didn't. A wave of dizziness washed over her as vague, blurred scenes and images swept through her mind. People she should know? Things that had happened?

Not only did she not know her name, she could barely remember events from a few days ago. Every time she reached for her memories, they flitted away from her, leaving vague images of darkness and horror. Yesterday a man who claimed to be a doctor had told her it was the drug she'd been given. Could she believe him?

Fingers grasping the sink for support, she closed her eyes and tried to make sense of it all. Was all of this possible? Could she really be Shea Monroe?

A knock on the door shook her from her panicked thoughts.

"Shea, you okay?"

"Yes . . . I'll be out in a minute." She relieved herself and hurriedly drank a glass of water. Making use of the toiletries on the counter in front of her, she washed her face, brushed her teeth, and combed her hair. An odd sense of accomplishment swept through her at the completion of these mundane and normal tasks.

Feeling somewhat refreshed and more capable, she pulled the door open and shuffled out. The man who'd been kind to her stood beside the window, across the room. Ethan, the man who'd been alternately kind and gruff, sat in a chair beside the bed.

"Good morning, Shea," Ethan said.

That deep, graveled voice now sounded so familiar. Was it from her past or because she'd heard him so much over the last few days? If Ethan was truly evil, why was he constantly taking care of her instead of harming her? Was she beginning to accept what he'd told her?

"Shea, you okay?"

She gave a rapid shake of her head, hoping to clear it from the incessant shroud of fogginess. "Why does everyone keep saying 'Shea'?"

"Because you need to learn your name." Ethan sounded angry for some reason.

The other man shot a surprised glance at Ethan and then nodded toward the breakfast tray. "We'll talk while you eat."

She bit her lip, uncertainty warring with the need to fill the gnawing emptiness in her belly. Yesterday, the food had been fine, but what about today? "I don't know . . ."

"Your food is not drugged, dammit," Ethan growled.

The stranger frowned at Ethan. "You get up on the wrong side of the bed this morning, or what?"

"I'm just tired of her questioning everything we do. It's time she learned to trust."

Her spine stiffened. "I don't think your attitude inspires trust, Mr. Bishop." The voice, crisp and alert, surprised her, even though it came from her mouth.

Ethan's laugh was rusty and gruff, as if it hadn't been used in a while. For some reason, the sound caused all sorts of tingles and leaps inside her body. *How odd*.

"Now, that sounds like the Shea Monroe I used to know." Ethan nodded toward her tray. "Eat your breakfast."

She felt a strange compulsion to refuse, so that he would lose his temper. Why? She never challenged others. She performed her duties, did what she was told to do. The master always . . . A hot flush of dizziness swamped her as her legs buckled.

Ethan was there before she could fall. "I've got you, sweetheart. You're fine."

The gruff tone had disappeared and the gentle, concerned man had returned. He carried her to the bed and sat her down.

"Better?"

She swallowed past the fear. "Yes."

"What happened?"

"I don't know . . . I . . ." Closing her eyes, she shook her head. "I just had a strange sensation that I . . ." She reached for the memory and couldn't find it. "I don't know."

Ethan uncovered the plate of food, revealing scrambled eggs, bacon, toast, fruit juice, and coffee. "Eat and we'll talk."

Knowing she had no choice but to at least trust him in this, she took tiny bites and felt better with each swallow.

The man beside Ethan spoke. "We've not been properly introduced. . . . I'm Noah McCall."

"The head of LCR." She remembered Ethan telling her this.

When Noah McCall smiled, she blinked again, this time in shock. How had she not noticed how incredibly handsome this man was?

"Do you remember anything else?"

She shrugged. "I only remembered that because Ethan told me."

"Can you tell me what you remember about Donald Rosemount?"

"The man Ethan said drugged me?"

"Yes."

"My mind is blurred. The name seems oddly familiar but I don't know why. I see vague, blurred images. . . . I'm not sure what they are, when they were . . . if they even exist."

"What do you remember about the past six months? Where have you been? Why did you go off on your own like that? How did you find Donald Rosemount?" Noah McCall delivered the questions with the subtly and speed of an AK-47.

Her eyes darted from Noah McCall to Ethan. Both men's expressions were cool as they examined, assessed. Her mind searched, grasping for information . . . anything. This was the first time she'd been questioned. She'd felt no pressure to give information before this. Now she could see that they both expected something from her, and she could give . . . nothing. Her heart pounded in tandem with her head. Pain exploded. The food she'd swallowed headed back up her throat. "I . . . I don't . . ."

Ethan stood and touched her shoulder. "That's enough, Noah."

The dark brown eyes that had looked so cool and remote seconds ago turned warm and compassionate once more. "I'm sorry, Shea. I needed to see for myself."

Understanding that she'd been under some kind of test, she shrank away from both men.

"Don't start that again," Ethan snapped. "We are not going to hurt you."

Cold chills shuddered through her as she realized something astounding. She had begun to trust Ethan. Noah McCall's questions had made her want to go to Ethan, to ask for his help and protection.

Ethan shoved away the table holding the tray of food and sat beside her on the bed. "Stop looking like that."

"I was beginning to trust you."

"You *can* trust me . . . you can trust both of us. Noah only wanted to—"

"Shea, this is my wife, Samara," McCall said.

A petite young woman stood beside Noah McCall. Dark-haired, very pretty, and obviously pregnant, Samara

McCall smiled at her—the first smile she'd seen that didn't seem to have a hidden agenda behind it.

"Ethan, you and Noah need to go. I think you've scared Shea enough for one day." Though her voice was soft, Samara McCall's tone indicated her seriousness.

Ethan shook his head. "I didn't—"

Samara stared pointedly at both men. "She doesn't need any more pressure right now, from either of you."

"Fine." Ethan took the hand he'd been holding and pressed it to his mouth. "You're safe now. Remember that, if nothing else."

A ragged sigh of relief blew through her lips as the two men left the room.

Her expression gently understanding, Samara McCall sat in the chair close to the bed. "They mean well, but they can get a bit intense, don't you think?"

Confusion added another layer of pain to the constant dull pounding in her head. She was a trained warrior. Dangerous to anyone who got in the way of her master's orders. Why had they left this small, unarmed, pregnant woman alone with her? Did they not realize what she was capable of?

"Shea, what's wrong? You look as though you're full of questions."

"Why would they leave you alone in here with me? I could kill you in an instant."

The compassionate look on Samara McCall's face was a surprise and increased that odd, vulnerable feeling inside her. Why was this woman being so kind? Samara's words, however, were even more astonishing. "Because Shea Monroe is not a killer. They know that and, soon, you will, too."

Ethan clicked the door closed behind himself and growled, "You son of a bitch. You didn't have to do that."

Noah raised a brow. "Still defending Shea, I see."

"Somebody needs to."

"Relax, Ethan. Shea's a lot stronger than you give her credit for . . . she always has been. I needed to be sure."

"And?" Ethan challenged, still pissed.

"She's not lying," Noah said.

"No, she's not."

Both men turned at the sound of Dr. Norton's exhausted voice. He held a thick stack of papers in his hand.

"You got the test results," Ethan said.

Looking as tired as Ethan felt, Dr. Norton nodded. "Yes . . . though I wish I could tell you exactly what they gave her. . . . It's not that simple."

Dreading the answer, Ethan asked anyway, "What do you mean?"

"That poor child has been pumped so full of drugs. . . . Some of the substances we recognized, most we didn't."

"Dammit, Doc, what?"

"We recognized a substance that closely resembles GHB. Various steroids and antidepressants, along with other things we can't identify yet. There's also evidence of scopolamine. Which would explain her nightmares and hallucinations of demons."

"And her memory loss, too," Ethan said.

The doctor nodded. "It would take months, perhaps years, to develop a drug with all of these ingredients. He's apparently made a cocktail of them. Based on what we know about these drugs and Shea's symptoms, we can conjecture that memories, emotions . . . and any kind of free will are suppressed and manipulated. She probably knows only what she's been told by whoever did this to her. And even those things are beginning to fade."

"She mentioned someone she called 'the master,' " Ethan said.

"I could see that," Dr. Norton said. "With this kind of mind control, there would be one person who would tell her what to do, where to go, what to think. She would be on automatic pilot, with this man as her driver."

The breakfast Ethan had forced down churned in his stomach. He'd known Shea had been drugged, but knowing she'd had no control over anything in her life tore at his insides. There was no telling what Rosemount had forced her to do. The only good thing was she remembered little or none of it. But how long would that last?

"So what do we do? Is there something that can reverse it? Will her memory ever come back?" Ethan asked.

"I don't know. Some of these drugs can suppress the memory forever. For instance, people who have been given GHB don't remember many of the things that happened to them while they were under the drug's influence. Scopolamine often has the same effect. Someone who's received these drugs, day in and day out for months . . . Honestly, I'm surprised she's alive at all."

Ethan turned away from Dr. Norton. He wanted to hit something, kill someone. Rosemount. He wanted to kill Rosemount.

"Ethan, stop it."

Whirling around, he snarled, "Stop what, Noah? Stop wanting to kill the man responsible? Stop blaming myself, because if it weren't for me, she would never have gone after Rosemount in the first place?"

"Stop looking for someone to blame and figure out a way to help her."

"I'm going after the bastard." He glared at his former boss. "I'm not employed by LCR."

Noah's mouth quirked. "Is that the mercenary's version of 'You're not the boss of me'?"

"Take it any way you like."

"Ethan, you should know me better by now. This man took one of our own. We've been trying to get Rosemount for months . . . since he killed Cole. I had no intention of just letting it slide. Once you got Shea out of there, we planned to raid the compound. Half an hour after Gabe found you, we moved."

"And?"

"The place was empty, with the exception of one man with a bullet hole in his head. We couldn't find anyone else."

"I wounded a couple of guards . . . knocked out a few. I didn't shoot anyone in the head."

Noah grunted. "Probably Rosemount's punishment for allowing you to take Shea. The other men . . ." He shrugged. "Who knows."

Sick dread pulled at Ethan. "So Shea's our only lead."

McCall's eyes flickered with compassion, but his answer was resolute and firm. "Yes."

"She's going home with me."

Noah shook his head. "We need to get as much information as we can from her."

"Dammit, Noah, she doesn't remember anything."

"Not yet, but we need her here when she does remember."

Turning his glare toward Dr. Norton, Ethan growled, "Can you do anything to help with her memory without hurting her?"

"We can do our best. We'll try hypnosis first. Until we know what kind of effect the drugs continue to have on her, I don't feel comfortable treating her with more drugs."

Ethan drew in a breath, prepared to fight if necessary. "Do what you can. If she makes no progress, I'll take her home with me and continue to work with her. Maybe not feeling forced to remember will help her memories return."

Noah's dark eyes searched Ethan's face before turning to the doctor. "What do you think?"

Dr. Norton nodded. "Ethan and I talked about this last night. She feels safe with him. I think it might be a good idea."

Noah looked at Ethan. "You know Rosemount will be digging deep to find her."

"I'll keep her safe." Ethan turned back to the doctor. "What should I expect?"

Dr. Norton's expression revealed his frustration at the lack of clear-cut answers. "Hard to say. Based upon what you told me happened when you were in the jungle, she could have small pockets of memory, and then forget those memories. She might have tidbits of information emerge every day, or her memories could just suddenly reappear all at once. I just don't know."

"I think you need to pray she never remembers." The soft, husky voice drew the men's attention.

Noah reached for his wife and pulled her into his arms. "What's wrong, Mara?"

She pressed her face against Noah's chest for a second, then raised her head. Eyes glittering with tears, she swallowed audibly. "Sorry, I have a tendency to be extra-emotional these days." After a ragged breath, she said, "From what I can tell, just in general conversation, he used her not only as a weapon but also as his companion. She trained Rosemount's people, abducted women when she was told to, and . . ." She cast an anxious glance at Ethan. "Pleased the master."

Ethan turned away from her compassionate eyes. He'd known all along that she'd most likely been forced to have sex with the bastard. Having Samara confirm it didn't change the knowledge.

"How much of that does she remember?" Noah asked.

Samara lifted a slender shoulder and shook her head.

"She can't discuss it like it was an event. What little she reveals isn't in conversational form. It's like part of her is still on automatic . . . spilling information like a vending machine delivers soda." She winced. "Sorry, that sounds trite. I don't mean it that way."

"I know exactly what you mean," Ethan said. "It's like a computer giving out information. The words are just there, with no emotion. No real sense that what she's saying means what it means. It's like she doesn't know that what happened to her was wrong."

"Exactly."

"She's going to stay here a few days, and then Ethan wants to take her home with him," Noah said.

With a smile he figured Noah had probably fallen for fast, Samara told Ethan, "She mentioned your name several times. She's very curious about you."

His heart lifted at her words. None of this was normal or right. He despised what had happened to Shea. Hated himself for being responsible for it. But she would be home with him, where he could care for her and protect her. If and when her memories returned, he'd be there for her. He refused to ask himself what would happen when all her memories returned, including the things he'd done to hurt her.

eight

Ixtapa, Mexico

Donald sipped his specially blended tea, his senses savoring the subtle fragrance of orange and jasmine. "I do love a good cup of tea." Out of habit and ingrained politeness, he waited for a response from the creature who sat across from him. Not that he would get one, since the animal could respond only to a direct question.

Filled with an empty vagueness, the classically handsome face revealed nothing of the intelligence he'd once possessed. At the beginning of his captivity, Donald had delighted in pitting his wits against the man. Even chained, caged, and half starved, at the mercy of his captor, he'd been a worthy adversary. His arrogance and confidence had been such a challenge to suppress and destroy, providing Donald with hours of pleasure.

When the time came for him to assume his new position, Donald's designer drug had worked wonders. The man's cognitive powers disappeared, his memories were demolished, all will gone. That unfortunate incident at the beginning of his service was a distant, unpleasant memory. A mistake in the initial dosage had caused near-catastrophic results. A job got screwed up, money had been lost, property destroyed. His beautiful new pet had detonated. Crazed with pain, unaware of his actions, he'd destroyed the merchandise instead of restraining it, as he'd been ordered.

All of that was in the past. The doctor responsible had been fittingly reprimanded, becoming this creature's second victim. In the words of Shakespeare, "All's well that ends well."

Once his scientists figured out what had gone wrong and corrected the dosage, his mighty creature had performed amazing feats. Only to himself did he admit a certain fondness for this particular one. After Donald had acquired him quite by accident, the man had been able to go to work almost immediately. With his training and abilities, all he'd needed was the proper incentive. The wonder drug had provided that motivation.

Donald leaned forward, feeling the unusual need to share his thoughts with someone who would understand what he was going through. "I really miss my kitten. She's the only one who has ever understood and appreciated me."

Again, no change of expression. Donald held back his frustration. At least with his other creatures, he could get a small amount of reaction. This one, because of his immense size and unpredictability, had to be drugged even deeper. Except when Donald—and only Donald—issued a direct order, evoking any kind of response from him was impossible.

His little cat, on the other hand, had always reacted just the way he wanted. He'd learned to manipulate her emotions so that when he needed them, she would provide just the right amount of personality. And she'd been so easy to talk to. He'd never had to worry about what he said because she'd been interested in everything. It was like pulling a string; she would be anything he wanted.

Not that this creature didn't perform exactly as he wanted. Last week's exhibition had been all that he could have wanted and more. Admittedly, creating a big event for the execution was a bit self-serving. After all, he could've just shot the men himself and been done with it. But allowing the creature before him the opportunity to practice his lethal skills accomplished several things. A good training lesson had been taught; public viewing of punishment allowed others to observe what happened when the master was betrayed; and, though he'd never admit openly to anything so base, it'd been exhilarating to watch.

Watching a man's neck snap. Hearing that distinctive pop. Seeing his eyes go wild with fear, then blank with death . . . Donald shuddered, shifting uncomfortably in his chair at the erection the memories evoked. The sheer thrill of watching an execution gave him a pleasure unlike anything he'd ever known.

But his little cat . . . ahh, she brought out tender emotions he'd never experienced or anticipated. If he'd known how important she would become to him, he would have protected her identity better. Despite her beauty, he'd assumed that within a few weeks boredom would replace the excitement of having captured such a prize. That hadn't happened.

Really, though, wasn't it her fault? She'd been the one to fail to disguise her identity, not him. She'd been taught to protect him above anything else . . . and this would have included hiding her identity.

When his kitten returned, she would be exquisitely punished and he would enjoy several weeks of what he'd always considered one of his greatest talents. It took a huge amount of creativity to devise his special types of torture. Donald had always considered himself fortunate to be one of the few people on earth who truly enjoy their profession.

And now he knew where she was. Donald looked down at the printed email message, the first of many he'd received over the last few days.

*You don't know me. We're in opposite fields but
have a similar interest. We both despise a certain organization. If you're interested in a profitable business arrangement, reply via email and we will talk
further.*

A friend

Yesterday he'd talked to the handsome young man via
videoconference, confirming his suspicions of the man's
identity and employer. A sly fox in the proverbial hen-
house, indeed.

"I'm bringing my woman home soon. I might need
your help." He waited several seconds and then said,
"You will help me, won't you?"

The creature gave his usual answer: one nod of his
head and then a "Yes."

"I've already sent someone after her. We'll be glad to
see her, won't we?"

For an instant, the man across from him looked
faintly puzzled; then once again he nodded and said,
"Yes."

Donald blew out a sigh and gave up. At least with his
kitten, he could get a smile and the occasional laugh.
This creature could do nothing like that. Would Ethan
Bishop respond differently to the drugs?

Based on the description he'd been given, Donald had
suspected it was the woman's former lover who had
taken her. The conversation he'd had yesterday confirmed it.

He knew quite a lot about Mr. Bishop. The woman
had rambled endlessly about him when she first came,
describing him in detail, and providing many scintillating, intimate tidbits. Through punishment and drugs,
he'd managed to drain all those memories out of her.

The way she spoke about the man, though . . . Ethan
Bishop sounded both fascinating and intriguing, like a

giant golden lion. Of course, they'd have to do something about the hideous scar on his face. Physical perfection was a necessity.

The flawlessly handsome face across from him brought back a flash of bitter resentment. His parents would have been proud to call this animal their son. Simon and Lenora Whitman had made Donald's life miserable. His father had been an avid outdoorsman; his mother, a health-food nut, always cramming vile garbage down his throat in an effort to make him bigger and stronger. They'd wanted an average kid . . . they'd gotten a genius . . . above average in every possible way. Neither of them had been able to understand or appreciate the supreme being they'd unwittingly created. Eventually he'd stopped trying to be what they wanted him to be, and they'd given up. And then the fun had begun.

Donald couldn't remember the day he finally realized and accepted his superiority. The knowledge had just suddenly come to him. He had finally understood that though he might have been born to human parents, he was far from human himself. His intelligence went far beyond the normal realm. He was above everyone . . . all creatures. His parents had been ignorant, never realizing the gift they'd given the world. Their loss—not his.

The creature in front of him suddenly blinked and Donald's mouth went dry. Now, that was the only thing he'd liked to change about him . . . his eyes. An eerie gray-blue, the color of glaciers he'd seen on a National Geographic program once. Sometimes those eyes would look at him, and if he didn't trust his drug so well, he could almost believe conscious thought and awareness gleamed in them. Even though it was an absurd idea, a quiver shot through him. If this man ever became cognizant again, Donald knew he'd be dead in an instant.

"Look at me."

Eyes, dull and dazed, stared at him without a flicker of intellect or awareness. Relief loosened Donald's limbs. Only his vivid imagination working overtime . . . nothing more. With his kitten missing, he was disoriented . . . filled with nerves that made him see things that weren't there. There was nothing to worry about. Control of this creature was in his hands.

"I have a new job for you. You will fly to Ohio, where you'll retrieve two young men. They meet once a week at a bar. Since they always drink too much, a cab is normally called for them. You'll be in the cab with Henry, who will be the driver. You will be able to handle both with no problem.

"Once you have them, Henry will drive you to a warehouse. You'll stay there until I call. Then you and Henry will take them into the woods and drop them off. Neither will be damaged."

He waited to make sure comprehension was attained. Since the face never showed emotion, Donald was limited to waiting for a small signal that the information had not gone through. A chill speared through him as he stared into the cold, soulless depths of those creepy eyes. This creature could snap a man's neck like a twig. Swallowing past a frozen lump of fear, he opened the middle drawer of his desk and fingered his pistol. One click and that face would go even blanker and any threat would be gone.

He chewed his lip in indecision. If the plans he'd put into place didn't result in getting the woman back, he would have to use this man. The need for his pet versus his fear of this creature. A brief glimpse of emerald eyes and dark red hair flashed through his mind. No, he couldn't do it. He had to keep him.

"That'll be all. Go to the training room."

Despite the wide desk that separated them, Donald scooted his chair back when the creature stood. He was just so damned big. Without any kind of expression, the animal turned and stalked out the door, closing it softly behind himself as he'd been taught.

Only when the door clicked shut did Donald look down at his shaking hand, the one that had grabbed the gun. Perhaps after his kitten returned, he should go ahead and dispose of the creature. While he hated to destroy such perfection, the only other alternative would be to have his eyes jabbed out. And though that might be entertaining to watch, he'd be left with a useless animal. Pointless beyond the occasional playful amusement.

Yes, as much as he would miss him, it would be for the best. But only after he had his little cat back. And perhaps he could snare a golden lion, too?

Marching toward the training room as his master had commanded, he pondered what had just happened. The master was nervous. Sweat had beaded above his mouth; his hand had trembled on a gun he hid in the desk. His master feared him, though he wasn't sure why. Perhaps he had displeased him in some way.

Learning that the redhead had been taken from him had upset him, evidenced by his command that the guards were to be punished. He had handled this order within minutes of it being issued. The master had seemed pleased with him, but only a short while later, he'd appeared to be displeased with everyone.

Perhaps losing the woman had created more problems for the master. Not that he was concerned with such issues. The master told him what to do, and he carried out those orders. The others in the compound served the same purpose. They existed only to serve.

The master had a certain fondness for the red-haired woman. He'd often been in attendance when the master and the woman were together. The concept of affection wasn't something he could comprehend, but if it pleased the master, it had to be a good thing.

A garbled scream waking her, Shea shot up in bed and covered her face with her hands. Memories, blended with nightmares, played cruel, malicious games. Awake or asleep, they peeked out for barely a second, taunting her with elusive knowledge or a vague horror. A grasp for meaning resulted in their disappearance, leaving only a nebulous sadness and foreboding.

Dr. Norton had assured her that the poisons were slowly being eliminated from her body. He wasn't sure how long it would be, if ever, before her memories returned. The dark void in her mind constantly searched for meaning, for knowledge. So far, other than tiny pockets of memory, she still had no idea of who she really was . . . other than Shea Monroe, former LCR operative and former lover of Ethan Bishop. And that was only because it was what she'd been told.

When she'd finally accepted that she was indeed Shea, she didn't know. It was a gradual knowledge and understanding of something good and right. These people cared about her. She liked that feeling . . . didn't want to lose it.

Even Ethan, beyond his grumpiness and gruffness, was kind to her. Though he did seem to delight in irritating her to the point of anger. For some reason, her temper amused him. Admittedly, anger felt so much better than the constant fear and sadness that pervaded most of her thoughts.

Pushing those thoughts aside, Shea pulled herself out of bed. She was tired of being afraid. Marching to the bathroom for her shower, she told herself to be grateful for what she did have. Her strength was slowly coming back. The lost, hollow look in her eyes had disappeared.

She had people who wanted to help her. She no longer felt alone.

She had Ethan.

Under the hot blast of the shower, Ethan appeared in her mind. He was rugged and handsome, the savage scar on his cheek only adding to the character etched in his face. Green eyes, the color of clear peridot, could cut with a glance, but they could also grow warm with emotion. And his hair . . . she loved his shaggy mop of hair. How many times, when he wasn't looking, had she fantasized about running her fingers through it? Wild and untamed, the look suited his personality.

Wringing her hair out, Shea pushed the shower door open and grabbed the towel from the hook. She stepped from the shower and gasped. Ethan stood in her bathroom.

Time froze.

She thought she'd seen his eyes reveal every emotion. This was a new one. Green fire flared, then blazed. Warmth spread through her body, and though she knew the heat should be from embarrassment, she was woman enough to recognize that it wasn't. Ethan's eyes burned with desire, and her body responded in kind.

Endless seconds later, he spoke in an odd, hoarse tone. "I knocked. When you didn't answer, I got worried."

Water dripped, pooled on the floor, and still she couldn't move. A voice inside her whispered, told her to tell him to leave. She ignored the voice. The towel she held gave minimal concealment, yet she made no effort to completely cover herself. While his eyes roamed over her as if he were dying of starvation and she was a feast laid out before him, she stood, allowing his perusal. All the while, the heat inside her intensified, bloomed to a brilliant glow.

Coming to his senses well before she did, Ethan turned and stalked out the door. "I'll be in your room."

Stunned at the disappointment of his departure, Shea wrapped the towel around her body. Not only had she wanted him to continue looking at her, to touch her, she had wanted to touch him, to answer the fire blazing in his eyes. What was happening to her?

Ethan paced across the room. Pushing his fingers through his hair, he cursed himself. Just what the hell did he think he was doing? Staring at her like that? How was she ever going to trust him when he looked like he'd jump her bones the second he had half a chance? She'd been abused. Treated as if she were nothing other than property to be used and discarded. He had no business thinking what he'd been thinking. And he was thinking that Shea was more beautiful than ever.

Her skin looked as soft and silky as he remembered . . . like cream satin. How many times had they showered together and he'd ended up licking her body dry? The area behind her knees was especially ticklish, a spot at the small of her back could have her moaning in seconds, and his tongue on the inside of her silken thighs peaked her arousal to fever pitch. He closed his eyes as his erection grew and memories pounded.

The door opened and Shea entered the room, wearing jeans and a sleeveless green blouse. The expression on her face was impossible to read. Ethan fought the now familiar fury. This was another reason he would tear Rosemount from limb to limb when he finally caught him. Shea no longer wore her emotions for the world to see. Rosemount had destroyed that wonderful spontaneity she had once radiated. Every emotion she'd felt had been revealed on her beautifully expressive face.

Ethan swallowed his anger and forced himself to address what had just happened. "I'm sorry about barging in on you."

Her brow furrowed in a confused frown. "You seem angry . . . shouldn't I be the one who's angry?"

"I'm not angry, and neither should you be. I made a mistake. It won't happen again."

Her mouth trembled as if she wanted to say something. Instead she nodded and darted around him.

"Dammit, Shea, I'm not going to hurt you."

That stopped her in her tracks. "Well then, stop looking like you want to bite my head off."

Fighting the image of what his mouth would like to do to her, he turned away and dropped into a chair across the room from her. "How are you feeling this morning?"

"Okay. A little groggy."

"Any flashbacks?"

"A few. Nothing substantial."

"Such as . . . ?"

She rubbed her forehead, and though he'd rather eat glass than give her more pain, he needed to know as much as he could of what she remembered.

"The memories are vague . . . even more than they were when I first got here."

"Dr. Norton said that's to be expected. Apparently, withdrawal from the drugs is causing those memories to fade. We need to catch as many as we can before they totally disappear."

She nodded. "I know . . . it's just there's so little. I remember wearing white . . . a uniform, I think. I remember a room filled with mats . . . and there was fighting. I don't remember faces . . . all the images are blurred."

The plastic sack he'd dropped and forgotten when he couldn't get Shea to answer his knock caught his attention. Ethan leaned forward to pick it up and handed it to her. "Here."

"What's this?"

"Art supplies."

"For what?"

Another thing she didn't remember. "You're a very talented artist, Shea."

Surprise and wonder flickered. "I am?"

Despite the reasons for bringing the supplies, Ethan was glad he could tell her something that at one time had given her great joy. "Yes, you've done some amazing sketches."

She opened the bag and peeked inside. The vulnerable expression on her face when she looked up tightened his chest. "What if I've forgotten that, too?"

"Impossible. Something like that can't disappear. It may take you a while to get the hang of it again, but you'll remember. I promise." He hoped to hell he was right.

Her smile of delight made him hesitant about telling her why he'd brought her the supplies. He forced himself to ignore the regret. The sooner they identified Rosemount, the sooner she could get her life back.

"When you get an image in your mind, I want you to draw it."

Her mouth lost its upward tilt for barely a second. Then the grit and determination he'd always admired returned along with her smile. "That's a great idea. I'll work on that this afternoon."

"Your hypnosis starts tomorrow. You up for that?"

"Absolutely. I want this over and done with. I'm tired of not knowing."

"Good. Any nightmares last night?" Ethan knew the answer . . . he wondered if she did.

She shrugged. "A few . . . they're getting better."

She didn't remember, which was a good thing. Every night since she'd been here, he'd come into her room while she slept. Her nightmares had been violent. Her screams and cries could be heard all over the building. Each time, Ethan had crawled into bed with her and wrapped his arms around her. Every single time, those nightmares dissipated and she slept deeply. At dawn, he'd force himself out of her arms and away from her before she woke.

Ethan stood. "I'll check back with you in a few hours."

"Wait . . . I'd like to go out for a while."

His heart stuttered. "Go where?"

"Outside."

"You go outside every day."

Her soft snort of disgust told him what she thought of that small freedom. "I sit out on the patio, surrounded by a brick wall."

"Where do you want to go?"

"I want to go shopping, eat in a restaurant. Do normal things."

"That's not a good idea."

"Why not?" Eyes flashing, delicate chin lifted in a mutinous slant, her beautiful mouth plumped to a luscious fullness.

Ethan ground his teeth as every ounce of his willpower was tested. Everything within him wanted to pull her to him, wrap his arms around her, and ignite the fire that had so often come close to consuming them. That look of furious passion was such a Shea look.

Rigid determination kept his feet rooted to the floor. "You've got someone out there who wants to either abduct or kill you. That's why."

"So I'm just supposed to stay here forever?"

"No, just until we can get Rosemount."

"What if you never get him? Am I going to be held prisoner forever?"

"You're not a prisoner."

She twisted around to stare out the window.

"I'll get him, Shea. I promise."

She whirled around, her eyes wide with something like fear. Was she worried for him? "Why you?"

"Because I can get the job done."

"Others can't?"

"Not to my specifications."

"You want to kill him."

"Yes . . . and I will." Ethan turned and stalked out of the room, the need to hold her an increasing compulsion. She looked so lost and dispirited. Her confinement had only just started and it was already wearing on her. Shea's independent nature was quickly making itself known. It was one of the many facets of her personality he'd always admired.

He forced another regret away. Until Rosemount was caught, this was the safest place for her. No one could find her here.

nine

Columbus, Ohio

The two young men lay clumped together on the floorboard of the taxi. They had been easy to handle. Inebriated and unstable, neither was able to put up any kind of fight. When they'd staggered out of the bar toward the waiting cab, singing an off-key duet, he'd come up behind them, grabbed them by their necks, and knocked their heads together. The taxi door had been open, and he'd tossed them inside. The entire deed had taken less than a minute.

The master would be pleased.

A slight movement, then a moan, came from one of them. He pressed fingers against the man's neck. Not too hard. The master didn't want these men damaged. Just taken and then released. He had performed this particular function many times.

The car door opened. Henry, the master's employee said, "We're at the warehouse. I'll help you carry them in, then I'll hide the car."

Grabbing one of the men under his armpits, he hauled him up and threw him over his shoulder. Henry followed, dragging the other man.

"Be sure to keep your head down," Henry said.

He knew to do this, but it was something he was always reminded about. Keeping his face hidden was a priority to the master. His enemies would torture him if he was ever captured. He didn't know who his enemies were or why they would want to hurt him, but he understood the pain from torture. From time to time, the master tortured him, but only to reinforce a lesson or to make an important point. That was his right. The people who sought to capture and torture him for their pleasure he wanted to avoid at all cost.

He lowered the young man to the concrete warehouse floor. Henry dropped the other man next to his friend.

"I'll be right back. Stay here," Henry said.

He stood next to the unconscious bodies. They didn't move, but he wouldn't take his eyes from them. This was his one and only purpose, and the master depended on him to carry out his orders exactly as he commanded.

A gasping, breathless Henry ran into the building. "We gotta get out of here."

"But the master said—"

"All that's changed. We've been found. The master said we have to leave."

His pulse pounded as uncertainty hammered. "The master says it's okay?"

"Yes. He said your enemies have found you. They'll capture and punish you."

That sounded like the master, always looking out for him. Without a backward glance at the men on the floor, he ran out of the warehouse, behind Henry. The taxi, within a few yards, was a welcome sight.

The whirl of helicopter rotors sounded overhead. He looked up at the sky to see bright, flashing lights from a low-flying helicopter.

"Keep going!" Henry yelled.

He dashed toward the taxi and threw himself in the passenger side. Henry jumped in the driver's side and took off. Gravel spun from the vehicle's wheels. Dust, created by the helicopter, blew around them, turning the dark night to pitch-black nothingness.

As they zoomed down the road, he looked back to see if the helicopter followed them.

"Keep your head down!"

Though Henry wasn't the master, he knew the words were from the master. Turning back around, he bent forward till his face touched his knees.

Henry's cellphone rang. "Damn, I've got to get off this road. I can't talk on the phone and drive, too. You'll have to talk to him." Henry threw the phone at him. With his head down, it thudded to the floorboard.

Uncertainty grabbed him again. Talking on a cellphone was a foreign and unusual activity. He picked up the phone, held it to his ear. "Master?"

"Yes, it's me. What's going on?"

"We're being chased by a helicopter."

"Did anyone see you?"

"No. I kept my head down."

"Good. Tell Henry if anyone sees your face, he is to shoot you in the head and throw your body in the woods. Do you understand?"

"Yes."

"Tell him to call me as soon as he ditches the tail. Understand?"

"Yes."

He waited for several seconds for the master's next command. The master blew out a long sigh. "Close the phone."

He closed the phone and twisted his head to look up at Henry. "The master says that if anyone sees my face, you are to shoot me in the head and throw my body in the woods. And you are to call him as soon as you ditch the tail."

"You poor stupid idiot. You'd stand there and let me shoot you, wouldn't you?"

He didn't understand Henry's words or the compassion that flashed in the man's eyes. He understood only one thing. "I have to obey the master."

Henry shook his head and glanced in the rearview mirror. "Looks like the chopper went back. Let's go home."

Home. Yes, that sounded like a good plan. And the people chasing them had not seen him, so Henry wouldn't have to shoot him in the head. The master would be pleased.

Donald stood at his desk, unable to sit . . . his fury so immense, he could barely speak. "You failed me."

Though the connection was filled with static, he heard the cocky young man blow out an exaggerated puff of air. "Hey, man, I told you about the kids. Gave you the information to make the grab. I did my job. Your people screwed up, not me."

"My people were almost captured. There were helicopters and cars swarming only minutes after my men arrived. How did that happen?"

The man's condescending chuckle had Donald envisioning cramming the phone down the bastard's throat. No one laughed at Donald Rosemount and lived to talk about it.

"Like I said, man, your people screwed up. All I was supposed to do was supply you with the names and location. Maybe the kids have some sort of GPS tracking system on them or something. I can't be responsible for what happens after I deliver the information."

"How did LCR know about the operation, if not from you?"

"They've got eyes and ears everywhere. Like I said, bro, your people fucked it up . . . not me. I did my job."

He was being played. Donald had known all along that this brazen young man would pit him against LCR, and that once someone came out on top, that's where his questionable loyalties would lie. The lack of morals and character in the man worked to Donald's advantage, so he couldn't really be too angry. After all, the man had provided what he sought most. Plans were well under way to retrieve his little cat.

A long, impatient sigh came through the phone line, as if this man had more important things to do than talk with Donald Rosemount. The sound solidified Donald's decision. Once he had his kitten back and LCR was destroyed, this arrogant young prick would pay a high price for his greed and insolence. Until then, Donald would play along.

Though his entire body ached with the effort to speak the words, he said, "You may be right." He could envision the young man's smug smile at his admission.

"By the way, you haven't delivered the payment for the other job. I gave you the location of the woman, didn't I?"

The phone tightened in Donald's hand. The blatant disrespect for his power and wealth was almost intolerable. "Your payment will be deposited tonight. If, however, the information you provided doesn't secure her, you'll be expected to make other arrangements."

"Hey man, that wasn't our agreement."

"You're the one who contacted me. Don't you dare try to back out now. Either provide what I ask for, when I ask for it, or our relationship will end."

The silence on the other end told Donald he'd scored a powerful point. Satisfaction lifted his mouth in a grin. Two could play this game. No one outwitted Donald Rosemount.

As expected, the man immediately began to backtrack. "Wait a minute, I didn't say I wouldn't. I just—"

"Good. After the woman is secured, we'll discuss future projects." Content that he'd made his position clear, Donald hung up the phone. Outmanipulate a master manipulator? He didn't think so.

Ethan raced down the hallway. He'd been headed to Shea's room to see if she would have dinner with him in the dining room. Not the restaurant she wanted, but it was better than the four walls of her room. The screams echoing through the hallways told him something dire had happened. Another nightmare?

He shoved the door open. The scene facing him would have been comical if it wasn't so sad. Shea stood on a small table in the corner of the room. Jolene, one of the clinic's volunteers, was in the opposite corner, drenched with some kind of liquid. It was hard to tell which woman was screaming louder.

Ethan stepped in front of Jolene and barked, "What the hell happened?"

Her eyes still on Shea, the woman continued her screams.

"Jolene, shut up and tell me what happened."

Jolene's screams stopped abruptly. Milk drops flew in a white spray at the rapid shake of her head. "I just came in to give Miss Monroe her meal. When I handed her a straw for her milk, she picked up the glass, threw it at me, and started screaming."

"And you thought it would help to scream back?"

Her eyes flashed. "She scared me."

"Of all the stupid—"

"Jolene, why don't you go on back to your station?" Dr. Norton's calm voice interrupted Ethan's scathing words.

Wiping her face with her sleeve, Jolene scooted toward the door. "I'm sorry, she just scared me."

More concerned with Shea than Jolene's milk-drenched face, Ethan turned to her and his heart wrenched. She was now crouched on the table. Wild fear gleamed in her eyes as her breath came in desperate gasps and tiny sobs. Reaching out a tentative hand, he touched her knee. "Shea, come down from there. You're fine."

A deep breath shuddered through her as she collected herself. Then green eyes glared, as if she despised him. "Get out."

"Not until you come down and tell me what set you off."

"She tried to inject me with something. You said I was safe. That he couldn't get me here."

"She tried to give you dinner, nothing more," Ethan said.

She shook her head. "No, I saw her . . . she had a needle . . . she pulled it out of her pocket."

Dr. Norton stayed a nonthreatening distance away and spoke soothingly, "She had straws in her pocket. She was handing you a straw for your milk."

Another emphatic head shake. "No, I saw her . . . she . . ." Covering her face with her hands, she shuddered. "At least I think it was a needle."

Ethan held out his hand again. "Come down here. No one's going to hurt you."

Ignoring his hand, she stepped from the table to the floor. Her face averted, she darted around him and headed to the bathroom.

"Where are you going?"

"Away from you. This may be my prison, but I can and will lock my bathroom door for privacy."

"I can knock a bathroom door down just as well as any other door."

Eyes flashing, she snarled, "Try it and see just how far you get."

"Don't push me, babe."

"Children," Dr. Norton chided, "while this is vastly entertaining, it's not getting us anywhere." He pointed to a chair. "Shea, unless you're in dire need of the bathroom, would you humor me a moment and have a seat? I need to know why you think Jolene was trying to harm you."

Furious eyes raked over Ethan. "Only if he leaves."

"Come over here and make me."

"Ethan, either stop your childish taunts or get out," Dr. Norton said.

Ethan knew a quick moment of shame. The doctor was right. Sparring with Shea was getting them nowhere. Though seeing her eyes flashing brought back some good memories, he needed to remember that her anger was caused by fear, not temper.

"I'm sorry, Shea. If I promise to behave, can I stay?"

When she didn't answer, he assumed her answer was no. As she seated herself in a chair, Ethan headed toward the door.

"Stay." She softened her tone. "Please, stay."

Nodding, Ethan leaned against the wall and watched as Dr. Norton questioned her.

"When Jolene came in, what did she say?"

"Nothing. She just put the food down and took something out of her pocket." Her throat worked as she swallowed hard. "It was long and white . . . it looked like a needle."

"Have you had any more flashbacks like that?"

She jerked, obviously startled at the news. "You think it was a flashback?"

Dr. Norton lifted a shoulder. "You were injected with a drug daily. And you indicated that it was usually at the end of the day, before your evening meal. Most likely, seeing the straw triggered a memory. Have you had any other feelings as though someone was going to hurt you?"

"I thought someone was in my room early this morning. I woke up . . . saw a flash of something going out the door. I got up and looked out. No one was there."

"What time was this?" Ethan asked.

"Around five or so."

As much as he didn't want to admit this, he couldn't have Shea thinking people were entering her room to harm her. "It was me."

"What were you doing in my room?"

"I wanted to make sure you were sleeping okay."

"Why wouldn't I be sleeping?"

He had wondered if she knew he was there and just hadn't mentioned it to him. Apparently, she still trusted him only when she was asleep. The thought depressed him.

"Sometimes you have nightmares. I just wanted to check that you were okay."

A tender expression flashed in her face, so fleeting he figured he'd imagined it.

"I don't remember the nightmares."

"Good."

Dr. Norton had been watching the exchange quietly. Apparently satisfied that they'd explored the subject enough, he stood and patted Shea's hand. "You're doing well, young lady. Better than I thought you could have after what you've been through. We'll start the hypnosis tomorrow and hopefully find out some things that will help you."

Wanting to discuss this new paranoia of Shea's, Ethan followed the doctor to the door.

"Ethan . . . wait. I would really like to go out."

Ethan turned back to her. "Hell, Shea, we've already talked about this."

"But you could come with me." She looked down at the pants and blouse she wore. "Samara was kind enough to purchase these clothes for me, but I'd like the opportunity to buy my own."

"No." The very thought of her being out in the open shot terror clear to his bones.

"Why not?"

"I've already told you. It's too dangerous. Rosemount could have men anywhere."

"If you believe that, then you can keep me safe."

"How do I know you're not going to run from me?"

Her slender body quivered with anger. "So it's not only Rosemount. You don't trust me."

If that kept her inside and safe, she could believe anything she liked. "Is there a reason I should?"

"Is there a reason I should trust you?" she repeated.

"I rescued you . . . saved your life."

"How do I know that? All of this could just be a huge fabrication. Everyone could be lying."

"For what reason?"

"For whatever reason you want."

Ethan snorted his disgust. "I'm not going to argue about it, Shea. You want to believe we're keeping you here for our own wicked reasons, that's your problem, babe, not mine. Either way, you're not going anywhere. You're safer here than anywhere else . . . you go out and there's no way to guarantee your safety."

Her mouth set in a mutinous line, she said, "You know, I could just walk out of here on my own. The doors aren't locked."

Ethan snorted. "I trust you not to be that stupid. Don't make me have to lock you in, because I will."

"Trust is a two-way street."

"I'm not the one who's been kidnapping innocent women."

Like a delicate bloom in the bright blazing sun, she wilted in front of him. The remark had been a direct hit. A low blow she hadn't deserved. He had no excuse other than his worry that if he let her out of his sight, or if she were out in the open, she could be taken again. That couldn't happen if she stayed here. Within the confines of these walls, with him, she was safe.

Her expression froze into a mask of blank indifference. "Very well. You've made your point." She turned to look out the window beside the bed. "Please leave."

Aw shit. "Shea, dammit . . ." Blowing out a ragged sigh, he said, "I'll take you shopping. Okay?"

Whirling around, she gifted him with a genuine smile. The first real one he'd seen from her. She looked like the old Shea. Pretty lips curving up, slender, feminine nose slightly scrunched, beautiful eyes glinting. When Shea smiled, her entire face participated in the event. Ethan's heart thudded like a stampede of cattle.

"Thank you, Ethan."

Ethan nodded and stalked toward the door.

"When can we go?"

Without turning, knowing she'd see things he didn't need her to see, he snapped as he went through the door, "Tomorrow, after your hypnosis session."

When the door closed behind Ethan, Shea slumped into her chair. Exhaustion beat within her like a caged lion. If she ever let it loose, it would consume her totally. When others were around, she tried to put on a strong, brave front. Deep inside, she felt like a frightened child.

And now, apparently, nightmares and vague memories weren't her only problems. If the woman she'd thrown milk at was any proof, her flashbacks could endanger others. Strangely, though, her first instinct had been to run and scream instead of attack. Perhaps she was a danger only to herself.

Great, at least I'm not a dangerous lunatic. Just a self-destructive lunatic.

She pulled herself to her feet. No matter how depressing her day had been, Ethan had agreed to take her out for a few hours tomorrow. The thought of leaving the clinic for even a short duration gave her a healthy boost of optimism.

She knew that everyone here wanted to help her and keep her safe. But the longer she stayed and the fewer drugs she had in her system, the more she despised her confinement.

Shea was learning many things about herself, and one of the biggest was a fierce need for independence. To be able to make decisions for herself and be her own person. Rosemount had denied her all these things for the months he'd held her, which made the determination even stronger. She was damn tired of being a victim of her circumstances.

Memories or not, Shea wanted her life and her control back.

ten

Ethan sat in the corner of the darkened room and watched Shea's slender body sink with boneless grace into the leather recliner. The therapist, Dr. Karen Greyson, spoke to her quietly, drawing her deeper into a hypnotic trance. Even in the dimly lit room he could see a serene expression soften the tension Shea often wore around her mouth and eyes. The constant battle against her memories and nightmares had taken their toll on her youth and vitality, often giving her a pinched, tense look. It physically hurt Ethan to see her suffer day after day, without any relief in sight. Her memories continued to bombard her with teasing reminders of horror and pain, but with no reward of any substantial information.

This would be their third attempt at hypnosis this week. The other two had resulted in nothing other than frustration for them and a blinding migraine for Shea. In an effort to relax and hopefully prevent the agonizing headache, she'd tried yoga prior to today's session. He hoped like hell they could gain something significant this time.

"Shea, can you hear me?" Dr. Greyson asked.

"Yes."

"Where are you?"

"At the compound."

"What do you see?"

Holding his breath, Ethan waited. Her eyes closed,

Shea's brow furrowed as she apparently tried to concentrate on what she was seeing.

"Can you tell me what you see?" the therapist asked again.

"Men . . . fighting," Shea said softly.

"Why are they fighting?"

"Training."

"How many men?"

"Three . . . no, four fighting . . . one instructor."

"Can you describe the men fighting?"

She bit her lip, her brow furrowing deeper. "Young. Late teens . . . early twenties. They're terrified. One is crying. The instructor is shouting at him." Her voice changed, became harsh as she repeated what she heard: "You useless piece of garbage, shut up and fight!"

"Describe the young men . . . what do they look like?"

"Two white, one black, and one Latino. They're all tall . . . but skinny." Her voice softened. "And so scared."

"What about the instructor?"

Her slender body shuddered, revulsion flickering across her face. "He is white, medium height, very muscular. His hair is cropped short, it's blond and gray."

"What is his name?"

"Sir."

"What?"

"His name is sir. We have to call him sir."

"Is he the master, Shea?"

An emphatic shake of her head. "No, he is sir."

"Okay, leave that room and go to another one." Dr. Greyson waited a few seconds and then asked, "Are you in another room?"

"No."

"Where are you?"

"Outside . . . at the cages."

Ethan locked eyes with the therapist as she asked, "Cages?"

"Yes. Where we begin our training." Her voice trembled as she added, "Or we are sent for punishment."

"What happens in these cages? What kind of punishment?"

"Torture," Shea whispered.

"What kind of torture?"

She was silent for so long, Ethan began to wonder if she had come out of the hypnosis. Finally she said, "Whatever he thinks will hurt the most."

"Who, Shea? Who's in charge of the torture?"

"The master."

"Is anyone there . . . in the cages?"

"Yes."

"Who?"

"Five young men."

"What are they doing?"

She bit her lip and was silent for a while. Finally, she blew out a sigh and said, "Sleeping . . . crying . . . screaming in pain."

Nausea rose at the picture Shea painted in his mind. What kind of monster was Rosemount? What did he do besides drug his victims to ensure their cooperation?

"Okay. Leave there . . . go to a room inside the compound."

Shea blew out a soft sigh, as if relieved to be going somewhere else.

"Where are you now?"

"My bedroom."

"Do you share this room with anyone?"

"Sometimes."

"Who do you share it with, Shea?"

"My master."

Bile rose in Ethan's throat while fury boiled in his blood. If Shea remembered the abuse, how would this affect her? What she had experienced . . . been forced to do. . . . Hell, he'd give his life for her not to remember that horror.

"What happens when he stays with you?"

Ethan cursed, and Dr. Greyson shot him an admonishing frown.

"After my shot, he allows me to bathe. He watches me . . . sometimes he bathes me himself."

Another curse formed on Ethan's lips. He swallowed it back.

"Then he dresses me and we have dinner. He talks to me, tells me things."

Ethan jerked at this news. What had Rosemount told her? What secrets lay in Shea's subconscious?

"What does he talk to you about?" the therapist asked.

Shea's brow furrowed again as she tried to concentrate. Her face went white with strain, and then she breathed out a sigh. "He will kill everyone I love if I tell."

"No, he won't. He can't touch anyone you care about. Tell me what he's told you."

Shea's pretty mouth crimped, as if she'd been told to keep it shut. Her long silence indicated that the information would not be forthcoming. Rosemount had trained Shea to keep his secrets . . . even under hypnosis.

"Okay, Shea. Let's try this. Is this master in your room now?"

"Yes . . . and another man."

"What does your master look like?"

Furrowing her brow again, Shea tensed her body and then relaxed. "He has my vitamin shot."

"Who, Shea. Who has your vitamin? Your master?"

"Yes."

"What does he look like? Look straight at him and describe him."

"He's frowning. I've angered him."

"No, he's not angry, Shea. Tell me what he looks like."

With her eyes still closed, tears rolled down her face. Her breath turned to pants. "He's angry. He's not going to allow me my vitamin shot."

"Yes, he will, Shea. He will give you the shot, but you must tell me what he looks like."

Auburn hair swished back and forth, slapped against her face, as she shook her head wildly. Her voice thickened with emotion. "He says I've disobeyed him. That I must be punished."

Wanting nothing more than to go to Shea and ease her agony, Ethan gripped the arms of his chair. He had been warned that this would be difficult, but no matter what, he had to stay silent.

"Okay, Shea. Look at the other man in the room. Can you describe him?"

As she recognized the reprieve, a ragged breath shuddered through her. "He's very tall. Muscular. Black hair. Blue eyes. He never speaks. He stands in the corner at the master's order and watches."

"Do you know his name?"

"Creature. Animal. Trophy."

"All of those names belong to one man?"

"Yes."

"What does this man do for the master?"

"Kills."

The stark, one-word answer sent chills down Ethan's spine.

Dr. Greyson returned to her earlier questioning. "And the master. What does he look like, Shea? What color is his hair? How tall is he? Describe what you see."

Her head swung slowly back and forth. "I can't," she whispered.

"Yes you can, Shea. He can't harm anyone you care

about. He can't touch you. You must tell me what he looks like."

"He won't give me my vitamin shot . . . he's going to punish me."

"No, he—"

She jumped from the leather recliner and fell to her knees. Forehead touching the floor, her voice thick with tears, she begged, "I'll be good, I promise. Please don't punish me."

"Tell me what he—"

"That's it." Springing from his chair, Ethan grabbed Shea's shoulders and glared at the unrelenting therapist. "Damn you, stop it. Can't you see what you're doing to her?"

Heartbreaking sobs tore through Shea's body as she whispered over and over, "I'm sorry. Please don't punish me. I'm sorry."

"Shea." Dr. Greyson's calm voice interrupted her terror. "You're fine. When I count to three, you will remember everything you've told me, but you will not be afraid. Remember that. You. Will. Not. Be. Afraid." She paused for half a second. "One. Two. Three."

Sobs still shuddering through her, Shea pulled away. Opening her eyes, she looked up at the man holding her. "What happened?"

Ethan's thundercloud expression showed his concern. "Don't you remember?"

Her temples already beginning an agonizing throbbing, Shea held her head. "I remember coming into this room. I remember you holding my hand and telling me everything would be okay."

Ethan glared at the therapist. "I thought she was supposed to remember everything."

The woman shook her head, clearly astounded. "She should have. Whatever drug she was given has apparently prevented the memory."

Drawing a deep breath, Shea struggled to her feet. She ignored Ethan's outstretched hand, feeling the need to do this small thing on her own. "Did I give anything helpful?"

Before Dr. Greyson could answer, Ethan nodded. "Yes, you did."

Already knowing Ethan well enough to recognize his protective voice, she peeked around a broad shoulder and sent the therapist a questioning look.

The older woman smiled as if she knew what Shea was thinking, but nodded her agreement. "Actually, you did. You told us about his training facility." She frowned. "And I'm beginning to get a clearer picture of how a lot of that training is done."

Ethan's voice rumbled, "Yeah, me too." He dropped his gaze to Shea. "How are you feeling?"

Feeling like the biggest wimp born, she managed a weak smile. "I've been better . . . I think."

His mouth curved up at her small attempt at humor, and despite the hammering headache, her heart leaped. Ethan didn't give indiscriminate smiles. When he offered one, she felt as though she'd won a prize. The smile softened his stern, somewhat harsh face, making him appear almost boyish and carefree. Silly, really, but seeing him smile made her feel better.

"Let's get you back to your room before the pain gets too bad."

Despite her newly acknowledged need for independence, Shea could only halfway nod as a wave of nausea roared through her and her head pounded harder. Ethan lifted her into his arms and carried her down the hallway. She would have protested, but as in the previous sessions, the pain was fast becoming hideous. Now all she could do was hang on until she could get to her room, take the medicine waiting for her, and ride it out.

Thank God Dr. Norton had been able to prescribe a

painkiller that didn't interact with any of Rosemount's drugs still in her system. The blinding pain was almost more than she could bear.

Shea shifted slightly to press her head more deeply into Ethan's shoulder. Despite the agony radiating through her, she treasured the few moments of being in his arms. Each day, he seemed to retreat more and more from her.

Reaching her room, Ethan pushed open the door and gently deposited Shea onto the bed. "I'll get your medicine."

Closing her eyes against the pain, Shea took deep, even breaths. Underneath the fierce throbbing, her ears picked up the sounds of Ethan closing the blinds at her window. Seconds later, he said softly, "Here are your pills, sweetheart."

Warmth swept through her at his endearment. He called her sweetheart when he was the most worried for her. She took the pills and water he held out to her and swallowed them quickly. She no longer marveled at her complete trust in Ethan. Taking any kind of drug after what she'd been through should have been impossible. But she trusted Ethan—he would never do anything to hurt her. And in turn, she trusted the doctors that Ethan trusted.

Praying for quick relief, she closed her eyes.

A warm, wet cloth settled on her forehead. "I'll leave so you can get some sleep."

Her eyes flew open. "Stay. Please"

Though the room was dim, she could still see his concern. When he nodded, she closed her eyes and allowed her head to sink into the pillow. "Tell me something good," she whispered.

As was the custom since they'd begun their "Tell me something good" game, Ethan began to relay another of their adventures. His low, gravel-rough voice spread through her like warm honey, comforting and soothing. "We were on assignment in Missouri. Pretty routine. A woman wouldn't return her children to their father, who had primary custody. He didn't call the authorities because despite the fact that she was breaking the law, he didn't want the kids' mom going to jail."

"Sounds like a decent guy," she mumbled.

"Yeah, he was. Problem was, his ex-wife wasn't all that decent."

"So, what'd we do? Go in like gangbusters and nab the kids?"

At his low, rusty laugh, vibrations of pleasure caressed her senses. That laugh should be bottled and sold to women everywhere.

"I wanted to go in and nab them. You had a different idea."

"Uh-oh. Hope it was a good one."

"It was . . . though we argued about it."

"Doesn't surprise me. I've already discovered that you can be quite stubborn."

To her astonishment, she felt a quick kiss on her lips. "Be quiet and let those pills work."

Her heart hammering from the unexpected caress, Shea did her best to act normal. "Arrogant, too," she murmured.

He chuckled and continued, "Anyway, your idea was to go in and talk to the mother. We had a little of their history. You were convinced that the woman still had feelings for her ex-husband, and that was the reason she was holding on to the kids.

"So you walked in—without any kind of protection, I might add—and confronted the woman. Took you two hours. I was getting antsy. Just knew she was going to pull something. But sure enough, you walked out with the two kids. They had cookies in their hands, chocolate on their faces, and didn't appear to realize they'd been involved in any kind of drama."

"I'm glad it had a happy ending. What happened to the mother?"

"You convinced her to go to therapy. Both of you looked as though you'd been through the wringer."

"What do you mean?"

"Apparently, while the kids were feasting on chocolate chip cookies in the kitchen, you and the woman had a tear fest in the next room."

Her eyes flew open. "I cried?"

"Buckets."

"Why do you look so pleased about that?"

Something dark and heated touched his face as his eyes settled on her mouth. "Because I got to take you home and comfort you."

The pills had worked their magic, easing the pain in her head. Now a new, pleasurable need arose. A hot flush of awareness raced through her.

Ethan's deep voice added to the throbbing awareness. "You keep looking at me like that and I may have to—" He surged to his feet, an expression of anger replacing the sensual moment.

"What's wrong?"

"That was inappropriate, Shea. I'm sorry."

"I didn't mind."

Ethan leaned over and pressed a kiss to her forehead. "Get some sleep. I'll be back in a few hours. Since we didn't get to go shopping the other day, if you feel like it, we'll go out for a few hours this evening."

He turned and stormed out of the room. Shea smiled. Ethan had his thundercloud expression back in place. Normally this would have upset her, and it had, until he'd stood. The erection pressing against his zipper wasn't something he could hide. He wanted her. That should scare her, but it didn't. She trusted Ethan with her life. And someday, very soon, she would trust him with her body.

Stalking to his room, Ethan pushed the door open and slammed it shut. Deciding that hadn't been hard enough, he opened the door and slammed it again. Just what the fuck did he think he was doing? Shea had been sexually violated. Forced to do unspeakable things, and he'd practically come on to her as if nothing had happened. Disgust at himself, mingled with the hard throb of unsatisfied desire, resulted in a frustrated anger he could barely contain.

Stripping his clothes off, he pulled on shorts and running shoes and headed out the door. He might not be able to catch the demons that chased him, but he was damn well going to try.

"What the hell's the matter with you?"

Ethan clicked the door closed and looked up to see Gabe in the hallway. Since he had an apartment in town, Ethan assumed Gabe was here either for an assignment or to talk to him. Suddenly all his anger was aimed at his former friend. The man who'd made no secret that he doubted every word that came from Shea's mouth.

"I'd like to ask you the same question. What the hell's the matter with you?"

Gabe shook his head and turned away. "You're spoiling for a fight. I'm not in the mood."

"No, you'd rather sit in your apartment, down a bottle of bourbon, and stare at pictures of your ex-wife."

"She's not my ex-wife."

The hollow tone in Gabe's voice calmed his anger. "What the hell do you mean?"

Gabe turned and shrugged. "Just that. . . . She's not my ex-wife. She's my wife."

"I thought you got a divorce."

"She never signed the papers."

"When did you find out?"

"Few years ago."

The stark emptiness in the other man's eyes told the story. Gabe was still desperately in love with his very famous wife. A woman many considered to be the most beautiful and eligible woman in the world.

Ethan blew out a sigh, his anger now completely demolished. "Holy hell, Gabe. You're even more screwed up than I am."

Humor glinted in Gabe's dark blue eyes. "Now, that's about the meanest thing I ever heard you say."

Ethan glanced at his watch . . . a little after four. "You want to go fall into that bottle of bourbon or take a run?"

"Neither. Noah called me in for an assignment. I was just about to go in and see him."

Nodding, Ethan turned away.

"Ethan."

Looking back over his shoulder, he said, "Yeah?"

"I know you want to believe she's telling the truth. . . . Be careful, my friend. Lies are easy to believe when it's what you want to hear."

Ethan shook his head. "Someday you're going to have to tell me exactly what your wife did to make you distrust every woman."

Evidently not wanting to get into an argument neither would win, Gabe said, "Just be careful," and walked away.

eleven

"*It's time to come home.*"

The voice, horrible and familiar, sounded real and terrifyingly close. Shea swallowed a sob, willed herself to wake from the nightmare.

"*You've been a bad little cat, but I won't punish you if you get up and walk out right now.*"

No, she didn't want to leave. She felt good . . . safe here. Besides, Ethan was here. . . . She couldn't leave Ethan.

The voice grew harder and louder. "*Get up before I have to hurt you . . . or what if I hurt that hero of yours? What would you do if Ethan Bishop died because you wouldn't obey me?*"

Tossing and twisting on the bed, Shea demanded, "You leave Ethan out of this . . . leave him alone."

"*Then get up . . . now!*"

A slight sting on her arm jerked her awake. Shea rolled away from the pain.

A harsh feminine voice said, "Shit. I didn't get it all in her."

"*Bring her!*" The harsh voice demanded.

"Who's there?" Her muscles locked from fear, Shea's eyes roamed around the room without her head moving. Darkness surrounded her. *A nightmare . . . just a nightmare.* A chillingly familiar voice had threatened Ethan. Was this a new kind of horror? Having Ethan threatened? Thank God, it was only a nightmare.

Rasping breaths filled the room. Shea held her breath . . . the sounds continued. Her heart thudded, threatened to break through her chest. Someone was in the room!

Bright light flooded the room. "Get up," a female voice said.

A scream caught in her throat. Shea looked up at the hard-faced woman lurking over her bed. "Wh . . . what?"

"Get up. He's waiting for you."

"Who's waiting for me?"

"The master."

Cold doom and inevitability pervaded her senses. He had come for her . . . as she had known he would. Hadn't he told her over and over that she could never escape him? The sting in her arm . . . already vague fogginess blurred her mind. The drug . . . she'd been given the drug again. How long before she crashed? She had to act.

Drawing on all her reserves, Shea sprang from the bed. Her feet had barely landed on the floor before she jerked the woman up by the shoulders. "Where's Rosemount?" she snarled.

Eyes wide with alarm, the woman clawed at Shea's fingers. "Let me go. . . . You have to come. The master is angry. He's going to kill—"

Her vision blurring, fading, Shea shook the woman's shoulders. "Tell me where he is."

"Let. Me. Go!" The heel of a palm shot up, knocked against the side of Shea's head.

Swaying, her mind beginning to whirl and swirl with memories of horror, Shea was swamped by visions that almost brought her to her knees. Quickly losing strength and coordination, she felt her hands loosen. Knees buckling, she stumbled back against the bed.

The woman made another grab for her. Though Shea's vision wavered, she remembered the cup of tea she'd had before bed. Dodging the grasping hand, Shea sidled around the woman and reached out. Her fingers curled around the mug. As weapons went, it wasn't much, but it was better than nothing. She waited until the woman came at her again. When she was within inches, Shea swung. The vibration of the impact and a satisfying thud told her she'd made a direct hit.

A howl of fury. Then the woman muttered, "I'm out of here," and ran from the room.

Dark spots appeared before Shea's eyes, grew larger, but she couldn't let go. She had to stop her. . . . No one else to do it. . . . Had to be stopped. Legs stiff and uncooperative, Shea stumbled across the room and through the door. Her vision edged with darkness, she could barely make out the running shadow in front of her. Forcing uncooperative muscles to function, Shea followed.

At the entrance to the stairway, the woman turned back. "You'll pay for this, bitch!"

Fierce determination forced Shea to stay upright and moving. The metallic flavor of blood filled her mouth as she bit the inside of her jaw to stay awake. An inhuman scream emerged from deep within her being as she plowed through the door and stumbled after the woman.

Ethan headed down the hallway toward Shea's room. He'd checked earlier to see if she felt well enough to go shopping and found her still asleep. Despite his promise to take her out, he couldn't help but be relieved that for one more day, at least, she was inside, safe and secure.

An eerie, high-pitched scream echoed down the hall. Ethan took off, knowing the scream came from Shea. He rounded a corner just in time to see her disappear around the stairway door.

"Where the hell are you going?" As he sprinted down

the long hallway, Ethan's heart pounded in rhythm with the rapid stomp of his feet. She'd told him she could walk out of here on her own. Was that what she was doing? Envisioning the horror of what could happen if she was actually alone, out in the open, Ethan shoved open the door.

What the hell?

Shea and another woman were halfway down the stairs. Shea's arms were locked around the woman's torso. The woman surged forward; Shea hung on, almost riding her back. As the woman tried desperately to pull away, her hands clawed and scratched at Shea's face and arms.

The woman twisted around, her eyes big with fear, and caught sight of Ethan. "Help me! She's trying to kill me!"

Jolene. The volunteer who'd scared Shea a few days ago. Why was she even here at this time of night?

Ethan flew down the stairs, grabbed Shea's arms, and pulled. "Dammit, Shea, let her go."

"No!" Shea's wild shout held a strong edge of hysteria as her arms locked tighter around Jolene.

"Shea. Let go." Knowing he was bruising her skin but seeing no other way, Ethan gripped her arms and pried them open.

At last, with Ethan's help, the woman wrenched away from Shea. Eyes wild with horror, Jolene backed away from them. "I can't work here anymore. She's a lunatic."

Ethan scooped a softly crying Shea into his arms and snapped at the volunteer, "Follow me."

Dread flooded him as questions pounded. What could have caused Shea's loss of control? Was this a new symptom? Was she becoming dangerous to others? Had a nightmare triggered another flashback? Did this woman resemble someone from Rosemount's camp? Could that be why Shea seemed to have such a violent reaction to this particular person?

He kicked the door open and deposited Shea on the bed. Without turning, he asked the other woman, "What happened?"

No answer.

Ethan turned. Jolene had apparently been too terrified to come back to the room. He'd question her later. The most important thing was to find out why Shea had attacked an unarmed woman.

Wincing at the scratches and bruises already standing out against her creamy skin, Ethan brushed her hair from her face. Silent tears slid from beneath her closed lids. "Shea, what happened?"

No answer.

Ethan shook her gently. "Come on, talk to me, sweetheart. Did you have another nightmare? Why did you—"

Her eyes flew open. A dazed, blank-eyed stranger stared up at him.

Holy God.

Grabbing the phone, he punched a button. "A woman in a volunteer's uniform is trying to leave the grounds. Detain her and get Dr. Norton in here. Now!"

His hands cupped Shea's face, shook her lightly. "Shea, can you hear me?"

No emotion. No expression. Her beautiful green eyes were dilated and glassy. Shea had returned to hell. The woman she'd feared was going to inject her with something had been given a second chance and had succeeded. Because Ethan had believed her instead of Shea.

"Shea, baby, look at me. We'll get you some help. I won't let you go again."

"Ethan, what's wrong?" Dr. Norton asked.

Without taking his eyes from Shea, he snarled, "That bitch drugged her."

Dr. Norton took one look at Shea and picked up the phone. "Get a nurse in here." He slammed the phone down. Nudging Ethan aside, he grasped Shea's face and tapped her cheek. "Shea, it's Lawrence Norton . . . can you hear me?"

Still that blank-eyed stare. If Ethan hadn't seen her chest moving when she breathed, he wouldn't be sure she was alive.

A nurse rushed in. While Dr. Norton and the nurse drew blood for a tox screen, Ethan stood over her. He'd told her she would be safe here. Had dismissed her fears. Even insinuated that he couldn't trust her because of what she'd been forced to do for Rosemount.

"I don't think she gave Shea much of the drug," Dr. Norton said.

"Why do you say that?"

"Her pupils are already responding. My only concern now is what this will do to her recovery. She was just getting those drugs out of her system."

Ethan shoved his fingers through his hair. "How the hell did that bitch get in here as a worker?"

Dr. Norton's mouth flattened in a grim line. "That's what I'm about to find out."

Standing beside the bed, Ethan ran a finger down Shea's pale, delicate cheek. "I'll stay with her."

Patting Ethan's arm as if he were a child, the doctor gave Shea one last worried look and walked out the door.

Ethan cursed himself, knowing he had failed her again. But, dammit, this was the last time. When she was well enough, he would take her home with him. He didn't care if he had to battle Noah and every LCR operative in existence. Never would Shea be left vulnerable, as she had been here. If he had to stay awake twenty-four/seven, he'd damned well do it. No matter what, Shea would never be threatened again. He'd kill anyone who got in his way.

Ixtapa, Mexico

With a roar of fury, Donald threw the phone handset at the wall of his office. The whiny, simpering voice continued from the speaker at his desk. "It's not my fault. She was too strong for me."

Pulling out the stress ball he kept inside his drawer, Donald squeezed hard, pretending it was this woman's neck. He had to keep his cool until he got what he could from her. "How much of the drug did she get?"

"Not even half of it . . . not nearly enough to incapacitate her."

"No one can trace you, right? And you left no incriminating evidence? Such as the drug?"

"No, I still have it. No one can find me."

A smug smile curved his mouth. That wasn't true, but she didn't need to know that yet.

"I know you're disappointed, but I did my best," she said.

Revulsion surged, threatened to spill bile from his mouth. How he despised the wheedling tone of a weak woman. Her lack of accountability would only make her suffering more severe and his retribution and punishment all the more pleasurable.

"You did what you could. That's all anyone could ask."

"I'm still going to get paid half, though . . . right?"

"Of course—that was our agreement. I'll leave the money where we originally agreed."

"I still don't see why you can't just wire the funds to a temporary account."

"We've already discussed this, my dear. I can't risk

having something like that traced to me. Believe me, this is much safer for us all."

"Okay, if you're sure. I'll go to the bus station tomorrow at ten."

"And your payment will be there. Never fear."

"Thank you."

Donald punched a button to end the call, no longer able to keep the hatred out of his voice. Not only had the bitch failed to get his woman, she'd left part of the drug in her bloodstream. They would be able to take her blood and determine the compounds. . . . His magic potion might be discovered, and even worse, drugs could be developed to counteract it. All his wonderful work could be lost forever.

Sniffling, Donald stood and trudged to the corner of his office to retrieve the phone. Loneliness washed over him. With a sobbing sigh, he plopped down on the floor. His glasses fogging up, he pulled them off, then pressed his forehead against his knees and allowed the tears to flow. Nothing had gone right since she had been taken from him. He had no one to talk to, no one who understood him.

A buzz at his desk alerted him of an incoming call. Taking deep breaths to calm his shattered nerves, he pulled himself up, trudged back to his desk, and pressed the speaker button. "Yes?"

"Still want me to pick up the woman at the bus station?"

"Absolutely."

Anticipation washed over him, and a hefty dose of optimism replaced his grief. He had an execution, Rosemount-style, to set up. That always made him feel better. Then he would begin new plans to go after his female.

All was not lost. Donald Rosemount was not a loser!

*   *   *

As he marched toward the main house from the barracks, his mind struggled with unfamiliar indecision. Yesterday, a woman had been brought in for a reprimand. Soldiers had rushed into the building at the master's command. In the excitement, the man responsible for administering his vitamin shot had forgotten. Last night, he'd lain alone in his bed, battling monsters and demons. Today, though he was still strong, his mind felt fractured, blurred with confusion.

The master didn't like him to speak unless he was asked a direct question. So he wasn't sure if he should mention that he'd hadn't received his shot. If that made the master angry, he would be punished. He had been punished in the past by having his shot delayed. While he suffered the effects of this, the master had ordered the other men to throw him into the training cages for torture. Though it wasn't his place to question the master's orders, he wanted to avoid punishment if possible.

Knocking on the door to one of the main labs, he entered as the master's voice snapped, "Come."

Two men stood beside the master. They held a dark-haired, middle-aged woman between them. She was nude, her body bruised and bloody from beatings. His senses picked up the scent of semen. The master's men had used her . . . she had been punished. He had no idea why. It wasn't his place to ask. If the master chose to punish, the right was his.

Another man stood several feet away, holding a camera. That was normal. All punishments were recorded, so that everyone could see how the master's will should always prevail and, when it didn't, how punishment was meted out.

The woman's eyes were swollen from the multiple blows she'd taken. She looked up at him and something inside him snapped, piercing the confusion. The woman was suffering, hurting. That wasn't a good thing. No one should hurt like this. No one should be treated so cruelly. He blinked as more uncertainty fogged his mind.

Fingers snapped to get his attention. His gaze shifted to the master, who looked more animated than he'd ever seen him. Perspiration beaded on his upper lip; his eyes, behind his thick glasses, glittered with excitement; and his small body vibrated with energy.

Pointing at the woman, the master ordered, "Snap her neck."

His heart thudded against his chest. For the first time ever, he did not want to follow orders. This woman, whatever she had done, didn't deserve to be treated this way. How could he tell the master this? He wasn't allowed to speak. Words trembled in his brain, on his lips. Words of refusal . . . denial.

"Well, what are you waiting for? I said kill her."

Now the master's eyes bulged with fury. Indecision and dread made his heart pound even faster. Disappointing the master, having his anger directed toward him, filled him with terror and sorrow. He had to do what the master ordered. It was his place, his only reason for existence . . . he had to follow his orders.

He moved closer to the woman. His big hands encircled her throat.

"Please . . . no, don't kill me. Please. I beg you."

The one eye that wasn't swollen shut was filled with tears. She was begging him not to kill her.

His hands tightened against her throat . . . he had to obey . . . the master demanded his obedience. . . . Pain sliced through his brain. Myriad images filled his mind . . . blurry, unformed. A soft, female voice whispered words he didn't understand, emerged from a memory he no longer possessed.

Loosening his hands, he stepped away from the woman.

"What's wrong with you, you idiot?"

The master stood in front of him, glaring up at him. Purple veins bulged in his forehead. His face crimson with rage, he spat, "Kill her or suffer the consequences."

A word, wrenched from somewhere deep inside him, burst from his mouth: "No."

Shocked silence filled the room. The only sound was the pitiful weeping of the woman in front of him.

The master whirled toward the woman, raised his gun, and shot her in the head. Brain matter and blood splattered the men who held her. They dropped her and jumped back. The woman thudded to the floor. Blood spread like a slow, dark stain across the creamy white tile.

He stared at the stark image. The thick, dark liquid crept closer to his boots. His mind screamed. Under a roar of increasing panic and pain, he heard the master's words: "Punish him."

Terror filled him; he knew what was coming. His mouth opened on a bellow of anguish as four men jumped him, wrestled him to the floor. He kicked them, bit them, screaming with fear. Fists pounded into his face, pummeled his stomach. Under the roar of pain, he heard the master shout, "Harder . . . hit him harder!"

Booted feet kicked his ribs, his back. Fists thudded into the side of his head, stunning him, abruptly stopping his struggles. Dazed and winded, on the edge of consciousness, he lay prostrate on the floor.

In a vague, otherworldly way, he felt the burn on his body as he was pulled across the floor, into another room. Hands picked him up and slammed him face-first against a wall. Blood spurted from his nose and mouth. His hands and feet were bound to ties on the wall. Pain reeked through every pore. When he heard the distinctive whoosh and snap of the whip, his muscles locked. Someone ripped the shirt from his back. From deep in his soul came the tortured cry of an animal in torment. The thin blade of a whip sliced into his back.

Agony roared.

twelve

Shea shot up in bed, her eyes popping open as a scene of horror flashed through her mind.

"Shea?"

Ethan's gravelly voice brought her head around. He sat in the chair beside the bed. From the look of him, he'd spent the night there. His hair was wild around his face, as if he'd combed his fingers through it a thousand times.

"Go back to your room, Ethan. I'm fine."

"The hell you are."

She pulled herself up in bed, wincing at her sore muscles. Though she didn't exactly feel fortunate, she knew she was. The drug the woman had given her had been much less powerful than what Rosemount had fed her on a daily basis. Dr. Norton had given her a shot, reversing the effects almost immediately. But not soon enough. For the last two days, she'd drifted between unconsciousness and wild, screaming demons of memories. She remembered. Sweet heaven, she remembered. Not a lot, but too much.

"Are you okay?"

Throwing her feet to the floor, Shea stood. Her voice hoarse from crying, she winced as she snarled, "If I had a dime for every time someone's asked me that question in the last two days, I'd be able to hire my own army to kill Rosemount."

"I know you're angry . . . you have every right—"

Shea whirled, then caught herself when the world kept turning. She grabbed the back of a chair, waving off Ethan's attempt to help her. "Angry? Why should I be angry? You told me I'd be safe here. You wouldn't let me leave the building. You said this was the only place he couldn't get to me. That woman tried to attack me before . . . tried to take me back to Rosemount. But you didn't believe me. Now, why the hell would I be angry?"

Ethan's face was an infuriating mixture of anger, sorrow, and amusement. The anger she could handle. Even his amusement. But she was damned tired of the sorrow.

Chin lifted, back straight, she drew in a calming breath. "I'm going to put some clothes on. When I get back, you and I are going to have a talk. I understand why you and Noah didn't want to tell me about Rosemount before, thinking it would color my memories. Well, those memories are coming back. I want to hear about Rosemount from you, and I'll tell you what I remember. Agreed?"

The mouth she'd had some interesting thoughts about twitched—with humor or words? She didn't know. But he nodded in agreement, and that was all she needed. Grabbing a handful of clothes from a drawer, she marched into the bathroom, slammed the door, and sank to the floor.

Pretense. It was all she had right now. Despite Ethan's assertions that she would be safe from Rosemount, she knew she wasn't. Now that parts of her memory had returned, an acidic flood of terror swamped her, eating away at any security she'd felt. She needed information. She had information to give. Then she would determine what should be done.

Run away? Hide? She still had no memory of her life before Rosemount, but something told her she wasn't the type to run. An image of pure evil flashed in her mind, followed by the memory of severe agony. She shuddered and shook her head. She might have not been the type to run before, but that didn't mean she couldn't change.

The knock on the door had her stifling a scream. "Shea, Noah's on his way in. Are you about ready?"

"Yes." Her voice was barely above a whisper.

The door handle jiggled as Ethan turned the knob. Thank heaven she'd locked it. "Shea?"

"I'll be out in a minute."

She hadn't meant to snap, but since the drug had been in her system, that's all she'd been doing. Dr. Norton had assured her that the surly mood would go away. Some type of steroid fueled the anger, supercharging even the slightest aggravation into rage. Yes, she was angry, but the violence surging through her felt unnatural and wrong.

With a heavy sigh, Shea picked herself up from the floor and pulled on the jeans and shirt she'd brought with her. She was determined to get through the next few hours without going either ballistic with fury or weepy like the overemotional bundle of nerves tap-dancing through her screamed for her to. Taking the time to braid her hair and apply makeup might seem foolish to some. To Shea, it provided a feeling a normalcy she desperately needed.

She stood back and surveyed the damaged woman staring back at her. With her translucent skin still too pale, the black beauty mark below her left eye looked like a black dot in a sea of white; shadows under her green eyes made them look sunken and dull. She had no concept of what she'd looked like before Rosemount got his hands on her, but she was damned sure that what she saw in the mirror wasn't what she wanted to continue to see.

Shea turned and marched out the door. Determined to

get hell over with so she could get the hell on with her life.

Ethan ushered Shea into a small living room the staff members used when they were on a break. Noah and Samara sat on one sofa. Gabe sat in a chair in the corner, far removed from everyone. Though his friend had made his doubts about Shea known, Ethan was glad he had enough sensitivity to allow her the space, whether he believed her or not.

Dr. Norton rose from his chair when Shea and Ethan walked in. He pointed to the sofa across from him. "Sit over here, my dear. We'll try to make this as easy as possible."

Shea took a step toward the couch. Ethan grabbed her hand and walked with her. She might be mad as hell at him, but there was no way she was going through this without him by her side. She could slug him later if she wanted.

A soft groan left her lips as she lowered herself to sit. He'd heard her tell Dr. Norton that every inch of her body ached. After she told them what she could, Ethan had every intention of giving her some relief. He just wondered how much he'd have to battle her to get her to agree. Didn't matter. In this, he would have his way.

Noah leaned forward. "Before we get started, Shea, I want to apologize for what happened. Jolene's credentials were reviewed thoroughly. She passed every security check we put her through. We don't know how Rosemount found our facility, much less how he put one of his people in it." He glanced over at Gabe. "We've got some theories, but nothing concrete yet."

As all eyes turned to Shea, Ethan felt a shuddering breath go through her. He knew she was gearing up to go through hell.

"Take your time, Shea." Samara's soft voice lessened the building tension in the room.

"My memories are still scattered. Some have a concrete basis. Others have no meaning. Most have no beginning or end. I see images. Thoughts and knowledge, but most of them are there without comprehension." A slender shoulder lifted. "Does that make any sense?"

Dr. Norton nodded. "Yes, it does. You're saying you have pockets of knowledge without knowing why. That's normal." His bushy eyebrows met in a frown. "Well, as normal as this can get."

"I remember watching a group of men fighting . . . they were training. I'm standing in the door . . . a gun in my hand . . . I don't know why. I remember feelings of anger . . . sorrow. I don't know the cause."

"That may have been when you first found Rosemount—before you were captured," Noah said.

"Maybe . . . I just . . ." Fingertips rubbed her forehead. "I wish I could remember."

Ethan placed a comforting hand on her shoulder, while everyone else looked on, waiting for her to continue. No one spoke or urged Shea to go on. This was a nightmare no one should encourage . . . even if it was something that had to be done.

She closed her eyes on a small sigh. "I woke up in a bed. My head is pounding. My feet and legs are bound. I'm furious at myself for getting caught. For not doing what I had come to do." Her eyes opened, flickered up at Ethan. "I still don't know what that was."

Ethan swallowed hard. At some point, very soon, she would need to know.

When he didn't speak, she turned her gaze back to the other people in the room. "A soft, evil voice . . . high-pitched but masculine . . . tells me . . ." She swallowed audibly. "He's going to enjoy taming me."

Teeth gritted, gut clenched, Ethan worked hard to show no reaction.

After another long, drawn-out breath, she whispered, "I remember pain . . . torture. He enjoys this immensely." She closed her eyes and said, "I hear high-pitched laughter . . . almost like squealing. I know it's his. I think he designs the torture based on what he thinks would be the most degrading and painful."

When she opened her eyes, Ethan wanted to howl at the stark pain reflected. "I was hung upside down naked . . . and sprayed with cold water. Then he would have them cut me down and leave me lying there, my hands and feet bound, for hours. This happened over and over again. The days blurred together into one giant nightmare.

"Then, something changed. For some reason, after those first weeks, he started treating me differently. I still don't remember exactly what he did to me. There are still so many blank spots. But I do know that the pain stopped, I was allowed to bathe, and had clothes to wear.

"I remember pulling a woman into a van. I don't know when or where. She's crying, begging us not to hurt her." Another hard swallow. "While men held her down, I injected her with a drug. We took her to a warehouse." Her brow furrowed with concentration. "I don't know what city we were in. . . . The voices I heard were American. . . . I think she was American. We stayed there for a few days. She was tied up and blindfolded. I sat in a corner and watched her."

In a voice thick with emotion, she said, "I felt nothing for her. No remorse. No emotion. I listened to her cry, day and night, and didn't care." She shook her head as if unable to comprehend, then after a shaky breath, added, "Later, we took her in the van again. Untied her and left her on a back road in a wooded area. Then we came home.

"I did this several times. I don't know how many or where we were. I was told who to get, and that's what I did." She stopped, blew out a long breath, and looked at Noah. "There's not a lot more. . . . Can you ask me questions? Maybe something will click."

"Do you remember who gave you the orders?" Noah asked.

"No." She rubbed her forehead. "Crazy, I know, but the information is just there, without any idea how it came to me."

"What about a location? Any idea where Rosemount's main headquarters are?" Ethan asked.

"I don't remember the names of locations. I know we moved around frequently . . . because I remember being in a van a lot . . . but I don't know if it was when we were abducting women or if we moved from one of his locations to another. Those images are blurred. I remember hearing Spanish . . . much more than English."

Ethan took her hand. It felt small and vulnerable in his—and ice-cold. "Can you tell us what Rosemount looks like?"

Breath shuddered through her. "He's below average height . . . I think. I remember standing next to him and I didn't have to look up."

"What about ethnicity?"

"White . . . very pale . . . as if he doesn't spend a lot of time outside. He has light red freckles on his hands."

"What else?"

She shook her head. "I don't know . . . I can't see his face. I'm not sure I was allowed to look directly at him."

A loud, disgusted snort came from the corner where Gabe sat.

Noah shot him a dark look. "You got something to say, Gabe?"

"A short pale man with a high voice and freckles. Hell, let's go get him right now."

"Shut the hell up, Gabe," Ethan snarled.

Gabe waved an arm at Ethan's anger. "We're not getting anywhere with this kind of questioning. Either she remembers him or she doesn't."

Shea whirled around and glared. "What exactly do you want me to do, Mr. Maddox?"

"I want you to tell the truth."

"You think I'm making all of this up?"

Gabe's stare told her exactly what he thought.

"Gabe, if you don't have anything constructive to share, maybe you should keep your prejudice and opinions to yourself."

Though furious at Gabe, Ethan couldn't suppress a small grin of appreciation at Samara McCall's gentle reprimand. Noah's wife looked like a tiny angel, but she had a way of getting her point across very effectively.

Gabe grunted and slumped back into his chair.

Shea gave Gabe a frustrated, irritated glare, then turned back. "Maybe if you told me what you know about Rosemount, that might trigger something."

Noah leaned forward. "Donald Rosemount came up on our radar about five years ago. A man went missing. His daughter called us a few weeks after the authorities ran out of leads. We dug in, found some things out about the daughter's husband. Turned out he'd had his father-in-law kidnapped for ransom. Rosemount split the ransom with him."

A grim smile curved his mouth. "After it was over and the man was returned . . . the son-in-law spilled the beans . . . confessed it all. We got enough information to realize there was a kidnapping organization starting up but never got close enough to pinpoint who or where. Eventually, Rosemount got better, not only at choosing his jobs but also at the actual event. We gave the authorities what leads we had, but somehow, the creep always seemed a step ahead.

"From what we know, he gets his clients in a variety of ways. We believe most of them come from the Internet. He's also used personal ads in the paper, along with recommendations from one satisfied customer to another."

"So he kidnaps just for ransom?" Shea asked.

"Can't prove anything yet, but we suspect he also kidnaps and sells his victims . . . some women, some kids."

Fierce denial crossed her pale face. "No, I don't remember any children. There were just women. And I believe they were all released." With agony in her eyes, she turned to Ethan. "Please tell me I'm not responsible for kidnapping children."

"No, as far as we can tell, you were only involved in abducting wives of wealthy men."

She released a sobbing laugh. "I never thought I'd be relieved to hear that."

Ethan squeezed her hand.

Noah continued. "Rosemount's a recluse. We know that's not his real name, but we have no clue what it is. He obviously had plenty of money before he got started in the abduction business. Where it came from, where *he* came from, is a mystery. You're the only one we know who's gotten away from him alive." He gave Ethan an unfathomable look. "Last year, we set up a sting. Sent out an ad on the Internet and Rosemount responded. One of our operatives went undercover to get kidnapped."

Ethan stiffened. How much would Noah reveal?

"The op went bad. The kidnapping didn't take place, but one of our finest men . . . Cole Mathison . . . was killed."

Shea twisted her head and looked up at Ethan. "So that's the reason you want to get Rosemount so badly."

Ethan searched her face, saw nothing to indicate that she remembered anything about Cole. Aware that she was waiting for an answer, he muttered, "One of the reasons."

Noah shot Ethan a hard glance and then looked back at Shea. "Then there was another abduction. Family called us almost immediately. It had Rosemount's stink all over it. We were barely into our investigation when we got a call saying the man had been found dead . . . his neck broken."

"Why do you think this was Rosemount?"

"Had all the markings of one of his abductions. Ransom demand within a certain amount of time. Drop-off point for the money in a public place. We were told where the victim could be found. Alive. Phone calls and emails were similar to those used on his other jobs. The family was wealthy . . . the wife had gathered the money, did everything she was told to do. We were going to make the drop for her and do our damnedest to capture Rosemount's people." Noah shrugged. "Never got the chance."

Noah glanced at his wife. "Samara and I went to visit the widow. Needless to say, she was devastated."

"Do you think something went wrong? Or was he planning to take the money and kill him, too?" Shea asked.

"Hard to say. There haven't been any other deaths like that."

"Except for the Lancaster woman," Gabe said.

Everyone glared at Gabe, except Shea, who asked, "What happened with the Lancaster woman?"

Noah blew out a sigh. "She was found dead. Washed up on a beach in Miami . . . her throat cut."

Shea shook her head. "I don't . . . I don't . . ." She swallowed hard. "I'm almost sure I haven't killed anyone."

Ethan put his arm around Shea's shoulders. "We don't think you did either, Shea." He glared at Gabe again. "Gabe was out of line."

She pulled away from Ethan. "No, even though he doesn't believe what I'm saying, I need to know as much as I can." Her eyes touched on everyone in the room. "Please don't keep anything from me to protect me. I need to know everything."

Ethan's heart thudded. This would be the time to tell her that the operative killed had been her husband. That they believed she was on a mission to avenge his death when Rosemount took her. He and Noah had discussed this. Noah had agreed it would be Ethan's call when to tell her.

A breathless silence permeated the room. Everyone, no doubt, was waiting for him to speak. Shea shuddered out a sigh. The moment passed.

"I don't know . . . I don't feel as if I've helped at all. None of this triggers anything for me."

"Whether you realize it or not, you have helped tremendously, young lady," said Dr. Norton.

"I have?" The hopeful note in her voice tugged at Ethan's heart.

Noah nodded. "Actually, you have, Shea. Based upon the information you gave us in your hypnosis sessions and today, we have a clearer idea of what the facilities are like. It sounds as though he's got a hell of a lot more people working for him than we first thought. Question is, where are they coming from. He—"

"They're homeless," Shea said.

"What?" five people asked at the same time.

"I had to train many of the new recruits. I remember one young man crying, saying he wanted to go home. The man in charge of training taunted him and said, 'Don't you remember? You don't have a home. Just like

the other pricks around here. We gave you homeless idiots a chance and you don't even appreciate it.' "

"That makes sense. There are so many street kids in
the world that no one misses a few of them when they
disappear," Samara said.

Noah stood, indicating that the meeting was over.
"That gives us an angle we've never even considered.
Great work, Shea." He frowned and added, "Ethan,
why don't you take Shea back to her room before she
collapses."

Ethan was already scooping her up in his arms. She
looked as bad now as she had when she'd first started
going through withdrawal. Horrific memories, along
with her most recent trauma, were finally catching up
with her.

As Ethan carried her toward the door, he looked over
his shoulder at Noah. "I'll be back in a few minutes. We
need to talk."

Ethan figured Noah already knew what he was going
to say. Merely a courtesy warning. He would give Shea
a few hours to rest and then he was taking her away
from this place. Their location had been compromised.
No one was safe anymore. Especially Shea.

thirteen

A hand touched her shoulder, pulling her from the depths of dreamless sleep. "Shea, wake up."

Squinting up at Ethan, she asked in a groggy voice, "What's wrong?"

"Nothing other than we're leaving. Our plane takes off in half an hour."

She rubbed sleep from her eyes, trying to get her bearings. "What are you talking about?"

"You're coming with me."

"To where?"

"My home."

"I can't leave." Shea struggled to sit up, then flipped on the bedside light. "I'm just now beginning to remember things."

"You can remember them just as well in Tennessee as you can here. Maybe even better."

"But why—"

Ethan threw some clothes onto the bed. "You've got ten minutes. You're not ready . . . I'll carry you out in pajamas."

Her feet thudding to the floor, she stood. "You know, that he-man attitude might be attractive to some, but not to me."

"Darlin', having you attracted to me is something we can explore at another time. Right now, speed is my number one priority. I've got a plane waiting just a few

minutes from here. Now, are you going to get dressed or
do you want to go like that?"

She told her somersaulting heart to ignore Ethan's endearment and that slow, sexy growl in his voice. Main-
taining her glare was difficult. "What does Noah have to
say about all of this?"

Ethan stopped in the process of stuffing her clothes
into a bag and grinned. "Said he couldn't believe I'd
held out this long."

When Ethan smiled like that, something inside her
just melted. Despite his heavy-handed arrogance, she
wanted to please him. No doubt about it, she was a lunatic.

Grabbing her clothes, Shea stomped to the bathroom.
If she said anything else, he would probably realize that
she wasn't all that upset about going with him. The man
was too sure of himself already. No way was she going
to give him more ammunition.

Shea emerged seven minutes later to find Ethan
sprawled in a chair, flipping through the sketches she'd
drawn. Finding out that she was a talented artist had
been both surreal and exciting for her. She'd feared not
remembering her talent. The instant she'd held the
sketchbook and touched the pencils, though, the fear
had disappeared and peace had descended. So far, other
than the blurred image of a high forehead or a beaky
nose flitting through her memories, the only real
sketches she'd done were of the people she'd met at the
clinic. For some reason, there were an inordinate number of drawings of Ethan.

He looked up at her. "You're even better than I remember."

Without getting too close, she peered at the one he'd
just flipped to. One of him, of course. She'd drawn it a
few days ago, right after an argument. He'd stalked out

the door, and she'd immediately picked up the book and begun to draw.

Incredible green eyes flashing, that devilishly sexy mouth pulled into a straight line that only emphasized its sensuality. His hair had hung down around his face, and he'd been wearing a black T-shirt and jeans. It was a full-body sketch, emphasizing his size, his muscles, his masculinity. The drawing was now her favorite.

He stared at it for a long time, then looked up at her with a slow smile that fired heat to every known and unknown erogenous zone she possessed.

"Let's go home," he growled.

East Tennessee

Shea didn't remember enough to believe in anything yet. But if there was a heaven, this had to be what it looked like. The mountains of Tennessee rose green and majestic all around her, highlighted at the top by what looked like plumes and clouds of blue smoke. Every time she arched and twisted her neck to look at another beautiful sight, Ethan made that rusty, gruff laugh. Though she would never admit it to him, she overdid the twisting just so she could hear that laugh.

She caught him once again glancing in the mirror. Since they'd walked off the plane and gotten into his truck, he'd had one eye on the road and the other in his rearview mirror.

"You still believe Rosemount's going to come for me, don't you?"

He shot her a grim glance. "Don't doubt it for an instant. He was able to infiltrate one of LCR's private facilities. That means we have a mole somewhere in LCR. It also means he's willing to risk a lot to get you back."

"But why?"

Another look, this one even grimmer. "After you went

to sleep last night, I talked with Noah and Dr. Norton. Based on the things you've told us over the last few days, we've gotten a fairly good profile of Rosemount. We believe he's obsessed with you."

Shea's mouth went dry. "Obsessed? In what way?"

As if uncomfortable with the question, Ethan lifted a broad shoulder in an awkward shrug.

"You mean sexually."

Ethan blew out a ragged sigh. "Sexually, maybe. But we think it's more than that. You mentioned that he had conversations with you, told you things. We believe he looked upon you as a companion . . . perhaps even a girlfriend."

Revulsion shot straight to her stomach, where it churned and writhed violently. She turned toward the window, looking for peace in the mountains around her, wanting to deny the horror of his statement. *Rosemount's girlfriend? Oh, God.*

"You'll get through this, Shea. And we'll get Rosemount, I promise."

"I still don't understand why he took me in the first place. No one's told me anything. Was I on assignment somewhere?"

After a surprisingly long pause, Ethan said, "We think you went after Rosemount." His mouth curved into a wry smile. "Actually, we'd love to know how you found him, since Noah's had a team on his ass for years."

"Why would I go after him on my own?"

Another long pause. "The man Rosemount killed. He was a . . . friend. We think you went undercover to get revenge . . . and you got caught."

"This man—he was a friend of yours, too?"

"Yes, one of the best men I've ever known."

She didn't remember the man, but he must have meant a lot to her if she'd wanted to avenge his death. From the look on Ethan's face, he'd taken the loss of his friend hard. "I'm sorry for your loss."

"It was a loss for all of LCR."

Shea stared out at the beauty of the Tennessee hills but could no longer appreciate the sight. "So this is my fault, after all."

"Like hell. Don't you dare blame yourself. Rosemount's the one who did this. You got caught in a trap."

Perhaps he was right, but she couldn't let go of the fact that if she hadn't gone off on her own, all of what had happened could have been prevented.

"Stop looking like that. Rosemount's the bastard who did this. Okay?"

Shea swallowed past the regret. What was done, was done. If she could go back and change it, she would in a heartbeat. Now the key was to regain her health and, most important, her memories, so that Rosemount could be found and brought to justice.

And the reason she had the opportunity for recovery was due to the man beside her. Without Ethan, she'd still be a drugged-out slave. Gratitude swept through her for this brave, heroic giant of a man. Though he could make her furious with his dictatorial attitude and arrogance, she owed him her life and her sanity.

"Ethan, thank you."

His body jerked as if the words surprised him. "For what?"

"Rescuing me. Saving my life . . . my sanity. I owe you so much."

Instead of looking pleased or modestly embarrassed, he clenched his jaw and growled, "You don't owe me a damn thing."

Recognizing his discomfort with her gratitude, Shea changed the subject. "What's going to happen to the clinic now that its location has been compromised?"

"Knowing Noah, he'll probably donate it to the city

and move the clinic somewhere else. Having any of our people at risk isn't something he'll take lightly."

"And you really believe LCR has a mole?"

"No other way the location could have been found. All LCR locations are secret, and most of the people who work for the organization do so in anonymity. A compromise in security could have fatal consequences. Not only do we need to find Rosemount, we've got to dig out the mole."

Shea leaned back in her seat with a sigh. The incessant throbbing of her head and the never-ending exhaustion reminded her that she was far from being well. All this talk of apprehending Rosemount and chasing down moles exhausted her. Perhaps getting away from the constant stress of trying to remember was exactly what she needed.

"This is the most activity you've had in weeks. How are you feeling?"

"Okay . . . not as cloudy or achy as last night."

"Still have a headache?"

"A little."

His hand landed on the back of her neck; strong fingers rubbed her tight muscles. Shea bit her lip to keep from moaning in delight. Once Ethan had learned that rubbing the back of her neck helped ease the pain and tension, he'd often obliged. Last night, her pounding head had nearly brought her to the point of tears. She'd fallen asleep with Ethan's warm, solid fingers massaging her taut, aching muscles.

"Feels good, huh?"

"What?"

"You were moaning."

"Oh." Heat flooded through her. She pulled away and answered quietly, "Yes . . . thanks. It's better."

She closed her eyes, and for an instant, a face flashed

in her mind. Shea blinked. Closed her eyes tight. Blinked again. Thin. Cruel. Intelligent. Mocking. Rosemount?

Twisting around in her seat, she pulled her sketchbook and pencils from her bag, hoping to capture that image before it disappeared.

Satisfaction filled Ethan as he watched Shea draw. She had an extraordinary artistic talent. So far, all of the complete sketches had been of people she had met at the clinic, but with her memories slowly returning, hopefully some new faces would emerge.

The one she'd drawn of him from a few nights ago intrigued him. He'd been frustrated and angry when he left, and she'd drawn his fury quite well. What had gotten his attention was her drawing of his body. Ethan knew he was in good shape, but having Shea draw his body in that way surprised him. She'd drawn a detailed sketch of his biceps and broad shoulders as well as the shape of his ass. Not something he'd figured she'd noticed. What else had she been thinking about him?

Ethan slammed the door shut on those thoughts. Taking care of Shea. Protecting her with his life, making sure she never suffered again . . . that was his goal, his only purpose. Thinking about his attraction to her . . . hell, his obsession with her accomplished nothing. Shea was his job. His only obsession now was to keep her safe. Full stop. Period.

The one person he'd cared about above all others had suffered tremendously because of his mistakes. He'd never have Shea again. A second chance with her would never happen. He hadn't deserved her years ago, and he deserved her even less now. But he did have a second chance at keeping her safe. Until Rosemount was found and dealt with, Shea would stay with him.

Last night, after talking with Noah, he'd gone back into Shea's room to find her tossing and crying from a nightmare. Ethan had held her, and in the midst of her nightmare, she'd called Ethan's name. He'd been there for her. He would always be there for her. Until she no longer needed him.

When the time came to let Shea go, a new hell would begin for him. But until that time, Shea would be safe and Ethan would take what heaven he could.

Ixtapa, Mexico

Donald pushed open the door to the infirmary. His shoulders drooped with sadness; grief pervaded every shuffling step he took. His favorite creature had become unreliable. He was heartsick over the decision he had to make. Though he'd already decided to have the animal destroyed after the retrieval of his woman, he'd been teetering with indecision. Destroying such a valuable commodity seemed so wasteful. Now there was no choice; he'd become too volatile to keep.

Lying facedown on the bed, the creature was covered by a white sheet from the shoulders down. His eyes were closed, his handsome face relaxed; green-and-blue bruises covered every exposed inch of his big body. Donald held back a cry of distress at the marring of such perfection.

He noted that the doctors didn't trust the creature even unconscious and in severe pain: his powerful arms were shackled to metal straps on the floor.

Tentatively, he stroked the animal's head, his thick, black hair soft and resilient beneath his fingers. How he would miss him. "How is he?"

Dr. Kline grunted as he looked down at his patient. "Your men went too far with him this time."

Donald's heart skittered. No, he couldn't die yet. There was still one more mission he had to perform. "How bad?"

The doctor pulled the sheet away from the man's back. Donald swallowed a moan. From his shoulders to his buttocks, his skin looked as though someone had taken a meat grinder to him. The once smooth back was now a mass of strips of flesh, thick welts, and angry bruises.

Donald's stomach flipped over, the meal he'd enjoyed a few minutes ago surging toward his throat. He waved a hand at the doctor. "Cover him. Now."

The doctor pulled the sheet back up, hiding the hideous sight. "I don't know if he'll make it this time."

Swallowing back bile, Donald said, "He has to . . . he still has work to do."

"I'll do my best, but it could take weeks to get him back to full strength."

Donald had accepted that the punishment his men had meted out might well delay his plans. When the creature had defied him, his reprimand had taken precedence over other needs. This animal might not be long for this earth, but while he was on it, he would do what he was told. Disobedience could not be tolerated.

"Get him well as fast as you can."

"I'll need to cut his dosage in half to keep him weak and docile."

"That's fine. Just keep him chained and out of my sight. Once he's well, we'll give him a few weeks to get strong again."

Donald gave one last lingering look to the body on the bed before he turned and walked out the door. Though he'd already made his peace with the fact that the creature would have to be destroyed, it still depressed him. He'd even been thinking about keeping him . . . perhaps just bringing him out on special occasions. An amusement he could enjoy whenever the mood struck. Now that hope was gone. Not only had he defied an order, he was no longer perfect. Donald's men had scarred him, and there was no way to make him beautiful again.

Donald stepped into the elevator. Aware that the cameras in the corners would pick up any expression, he glared at the door, his face stoic and hard. Whoever occupied the monitor room would see only a tough, icy exterior. No one could tell that deep inside, he was in terrible emotional distress.

The opulence and splendor of his home brought no comfort or pride as he left the elevator and trudged toward his bedroom suite. He needed solitude. With his kitten still missing and the perfect, beautiful animal he had created now marred and soon to be destroyed, he was depressed and lonely. Killing the bitch who'd failed him hadn't brought him the joy he'd anticipated. When his creature had refused his order, everything had been ruined.

He sniffed back the tears, determined not to lose control until he was alone. His people didn't need to see this sensitive side of him. They believed that Donald Rosemount was tough . . . invincible and deadly. That's what they needed to believe, the persona he'd perfected. If they realized how tender his heart really was, he'd lose control of them. The more they feared him, the better they performed. When he got to his room, away from curious eyes, he would mourn his loss in private.

fourteen

Sunshine flooded the homey, comfortable bedroom. Soft, cozy warmth permeated her body as Shea snuggled deeper into the bed. Had she ever felt so safe and content? With almost no memory, it was hard to say, but she couldn't imagine feeling more secure than she did at this moment.

Yesterday, after a stop at a grocery store, where Shea had watched Ethan fill two carts with an enormous amount of food, they'd driven for miles, deep into the mountains. When he pulled into a gravel drive at the top of a hill, Shea lost her breath. She thought she'd seen heaven on the drive up, but that had been a mere appetizer.

Ethan's two-story log home sat on the crest of a giant hill. Wraparound porches, on both levels, overlooked lush valleys filled with enormous trees, wild vegetation, and deep green secrets. Tall and massive, the mountains loomed in the distance, adding a breathtaking majestic beauty. She'd gotten out of the car the moment he'd stopped and just stood there, unable to comprehend such paradise.

As if recognizing her awe, he'd shot her a smile, and her heart had leaped. Unlike any other smile he'd given her, this one went straight through her, infusing every cell with a hot tingle of awareness. She must have given him some kind of indication of her feelings, because his face had darkened with a sensual heat. Her body had responded with a pulsing flush she'd felt to the soles of her feet. Then the oddest thing had happened. Ethan's eyes had turned cool, his expression once again unreadable.

Inexplicably, Shea had had the overwhelming urge to sit down and cry.

With a gruff "Come on in the house," Ethan had gently pushed her inside. Though she'd wanted to explore what appeared to be a beautiful home, inside and out, exhaustion had washed over her and she'd stumbled through the doorway. Without a word, Ethan had swept her up into his arms and carried her to a bedroom upstairs. Before he'd settled her on the bed, she'd been asleep.

The sun shining through the huge window told her she'd slept through the night. And as unbelievable as it seemed, she had no recollection of any nightmares. Excitement spiraled through her . . . she was really getting better.

Shea stretched in the bed, glorying in this new sense of well-being. Pushing herself up, she settled back against the pillows and surveyed the bedroom. Pretty without being feminine. Light green walls created a cool beauty, while exposed wood beams overhead gave it a rustic feel. The old-fashioned oak furniture was a nice contrast to dark hardwood floors and colorful area rugs. Giant windows on two walls gave a glorious view of the outside beauty while allowing the sunshine to cast lights and shadows to highlight the colors inside.

Ethan didn't seem the type of man to care about decor, but the room reeked of elegant simplicity.

A light tap on her door and Ethan poked his head in. "Morning. Breakfast is ready."

Her stomach twisted, and the smile trembling on her lips went south. Her appetite since she'd been injected with the drug again had become nonexistent. Whenever food was mentioned, she usually found herself running to the bathroom. Dr. Norton had assured her that this was just her body's way of ridding itself of the remaining poison in her system. He said the additional drugs had most likely heightened and hastened these symptoms. His assurance that nothing more serious was wrong had reassured her. Unfortunately, the nausea was an unwelcome side effect and would have to work itself out. Until then, she would suffer the consequences.

"Come on, Shea. It's just a little oatmeal and some toast. Surely you can eat that."

Knowing she had no choice, since she had to have sustenance, Shea nodded. Glancing down at the jeans and shirt she still wore from yesterday, she said, "Let me change clothes and I'll be right down."

Ethan clicked the door closed and fought a deep sense of contentment at seeing Shea in his home. No matter how right it felt, this was a temporary arrangement. She was here until Rosemount was caught. Thinking of her staying any longer than that was not only stupid, it was futile. Despite that warning, the contented feeling lingered.

His head shaking at his stupidity, Ethan ambled down the stairs, stopping midway to take a second to appreciate the new additions to his home. A few days after returning from Mexico, he'd called his builder. Already determined to bring Shea here to help her recover, he'd wanted her to be comfortable. The lack of furniture had never bothered him. He usually came inside only to sleep or eat. But that was him. Shea deserved more.

The builder's wife was a decorator, and Ethan had given her carte blanche, the only instruction being not to go too froufrou. He liked the results. The woman had shown that she knew a thing or two about understatement. The deep brown leather couches, colorful Indian-weave rugs, and leather recliners placed strategically in front of the giant rock fireplace created a comfortable, inviting atmosphere. Restful and simple.

Morning sunlight peeking through mountain mist added a glow to the oak beams. His Tennessee grandfather, the only family member who hadn't disowned him, had left this chunk of land to Ethan. After leaving LCR, his intent had been to live here in absolute privacy and seclusion. Staying the hell away from people was his gift to the world. The magnificence of the surrounding mountains had been lost on him. Fortunately, his builder had been able to maximize the beauty without forfeiting his client's privacy. Months had gone by before Ethan had even noticed the view. Shea had noticed it immediately.

Shea. What was he going to do about her? The feelings he'd forced himself to bury when she and Cole were married had reemerged, stronger and deeper than ever. He wanted her healthy. He wanted her safe. Hell, he just wanted her.

He slammed a mental door. Nothing could happen between them. He'd broken her heart once already. Damned if he'd do it again.

Muscles knotted with renewed tension, he rubbed the back of his neck as he returned to the kitchen. A dark oak pedestal table and four chairs had replaced the rickety old table and chairs he'd purchased at a thrift shop. This one was a bit fancy for him, but he had to admit that it looked a hell of a lot better than the one he'd had before.

He grabbed the pan of oatmeal and poured a large amount into each bowl. A soft, whispering breeze floated across his skin. Ethan twisted to see Shea standing on a small side porch. Perhaps that's why he'd moved here after all. Shea had always loved the mountains. She'd said that if anyone ever doubted the existence of God, they should come to Tennessee. Even while he'd forced his mind to forget, his heart had remembered. Instead of selling the land, as he could have, he'd chosen to live here. And now, Shea was with him.

Not forever, his mind whispered.

"Ethan!"

Letting the bowls clatter to the table, Ethan took off running. Stopping with a skid behind her, he snapped, "What?"

Shea turned, tears pooled in her eyes.

Wrapping his arms around her waist, Ethan grabbed her up and strode back inside the house. "What's wrong? Did you see someone?"

She pointed toward the valley. "Deer."

Ethan peered down to see a doe and her fawn nibbling on vegetation. Relief battled adrenaline. He'd thought Rosemount's men had come for her. Clenching his jaw to refrain from snarling at her for scaring the hell out of him, he managed to nod instead. "In the evening, just before dusk, there's about fifteen or so that come out."

"Really?"

"Really." He held out his hand. "Come get breakfast and we'll take a walk around the place."

She stood on her toes for one last glimpse of the deer. When she turned back to him, her smile was a beautiful glimpse of the old Shea. "I think I'm going to like it here."

Ignoring how his heart wrenched at her words, he led her to the kitchen and pulled out a chair at the table for her. Then he set a bowl of oatmeal in front of her, along with brown sugar and butter.

A frown of uncertainty furrowed her brow. "I don't remember oatmeal. Do I like it?"

"Yes. It's what you always ate for breakfast when we weren't on assignment." He didn't mention that she'd also used artificial sweetener and fat-free spray butter. Shea needed all the extra calories she could get.

She added sugar and butter, tasted it, frowned, and then added more.

Satisfied to see her eating, Ethan took a swallow of coffee and approached a subject they had yet to discuss: her safety. "Shea, I want to believe you're safe here. Rosemount shouldn't be able to trace me here, but that doesn't mean it's impossible."

"Why can't he trace you here? Don't you own the land or house?"

"Yes, but under a different name."

Knowledge touched her eyes. "Your real one."

"Yes."

"Can you tell me what it is?"

Could he? When they were together, he'd kept even that small part of himself from Shea. Not trusting that she wouldn't delve deeper and discover his secrets. Hell, did his secrets even matter anymore? Once she remembered everything, she would hate him anyway.

"Ethan Andrew Maurice Standifer."

Because of her memory loss, the Standifer name wouldn't mean anything to her. To the rest of the country, it meant wealth and power.

Her pretty feminine nose scrunched. "That's a mouthful. I like Ethan Bishop better."

"Me, too."

"Where's your family?"

"Texas."

"Do you see them often?"

"No." Before she could ask why, he said, "Back to Rosemount. There are only two people who know where I live. I trust both of them with my life. More important, I trust them with yours. Thing is, he was able to infiltrate the clinic, so I'm not discounting his ability to somehow find you. You need to be aware at all times. No going off on your own. Wherever you go, I go."

She blew out a frustrated sigh. "So I'm still in a prison, just a prettier one?"

"You're not in a prison. But until Rosemount is captured, you'll just have to limit your adventures."

"I think I've had enough adventures for a while."

"Once you get your life back, and Rosemount's no longer a threat, you'll want to jump back into things."

"Like what?"

"You're a young, talented woman. Artistic and creative . . . there's a lot you can do."

"After this is over, maybe I'll go back to LCR."

"No." The word was out of his mouth before he could stop it. Hell, diplomacy with Shea had never been his strong point.

"Why not?"

"Because you've been through enough. There's no need to put yourself in danger again."

"Ethan, I appreciate your concern, but once I'm fully recovered, there's no reason I can't continue my work. If I thought it was important before this happened to me, I'm sure I'll feel the same once I get my memory back."

He'd stupidly thought that after her experience with Rosemount, Shea wouldn't want to put her life in jeopardy again. How could he have forgotten that Shea never backed down and never quit? Another one of the reasons their relationship had been so volatile . . . they were so much alike.

That stubborn expression on her face was one he recognized all too well. It wouldn't do any good to try to talk her out of it now. They were months away from her fully regaining her memories, if she ever did. When that time came, he'd deal with it.

He was relieved to see that she'd eaten almost half of her breakfast. Not enough, but it was more than she normally consumed. "Why don't we take a walk outside? The sun will do you good, and maybe it'll increase your appetite."

Unwilling to argue with him further, Shea stood. There was no reason to discuss her returning to her old life until Rosemount was caught and she had recovered her memories. Ethan was just trying to protect her. The look on his face when she'd told him she wanted to go back to work for LCR had been filled with horror. When the time came, she would make the decision on her own. Arguing about it now would accomplish nothing.

Following him to the front door, she stepped out onto the porch and inhaled deeply. Fresh mountain air, tinged with the scent of evergreens, honeysuckle, and rich earth, suffused her senses. "How could you ever leave such paradise?"

Satisfaction curved Ethan's mouth as if he was pleased with her comment. "You've always loved the mountains."

"Really?" Shea took in another deep breath. If this didn't cure her, nothing would.

His big body in front of her, Ethan pointed at the gravel road leading up to the house. "That's the only access to the property. Anyone trying to come a different way will have to climb up steep hills and rock."

She peered over Ethan's shoulder, wondering why he didn't get out of the way so she could see clearly. She moved to the other side, and he blocked her again.

"I can't see," she complained.

He shifted, but only slightly.

"Ethan!"

He turned and frowned down at her. "Maybe coming here wasn't a good idea, after all."

"Why not?"

"If you go outside, you're totally exposed."

"You just got through saying that the only way here was up the hill."

He turned around, his eyes searching, as if expecting a threat from anywhere. Blowing out a sigh, he turned back to Shea. "Okay, but remember, you don't go out alone. Anywhere. For any reason."

Shea snorted softly and tried to walk around him. She got half a step before he stopped her. Wrapping his hand around her arm, he pulled her back around.

"I'm serious, Shea."

"Ethan, I'm not going to be a prisoner here the way I was at the clinic. Don't start that again."

"You're not a prisoner, but your safety is my number one priority. If that gets in the way of a few of your personal freedoms, deal with it. I'm not going to change."

Shea drew in a breath. While the independent part of her snarled at the restrictions, the vulnerable and scared part was in total agreement. Rosemount had come too close to her only a few days ago for her to feel safe. Until his capture, Shea knew she would have to abide by Ethan's overprotective rules.

"Fine. But just so you know, the minute Rosemount is no longer a threat, this big brother act is over."

"Believe me, the last thing I feel for you is brotherly." And with those enigmatic words, he gave another sweeping look around, grabbed her hand, and pulled her down the steps into the yard.

Ethan's land seemed to stretch as far as the eye could see. Gentle green hills rolled down into heavy wooded areas. Shea wanted to explore every nook and cranny. She sighed with pure pleasure.

The man beside her chuckled in that growly, grumbly way of his, and her pleasure increased tenfold. There was just something about Ethan's rusty laugh that created little dances of delight inside her.

"If you keep sighing like that, you're going to hyper-ventilate."

She threw her hand out with a broad gesture. "I can't help it. Everywhere I look, I see paradise."

"So you like it here?"

"I love it. But something's been bothering me. When we were in the jungle, you said I lived here with you."

He lifted a broad shoulder. "I thought it'd be easier for you to trust me if you thought you lived with me."

She nodded. "So where do I live?"

He hesitated, and Shea knew he was remembering Dr. Norton's warning before they left. *Try to let her remember things on her own.* "I don't think knowing where I used to live is going to cause any damage, Ethan. Please, I want to know."

"We hadn't been in touch for a while before you disappeared, but as far as I know, you lived in Key West, Florida."

"Alone?"

His mouth tightened. "Yes . . . alone."

"That seems like such a small thing to remember . . . yet I don't."

"Don't push it. It'll come back."

To get her mind off her careening emotions and unnamed fears, she pointed at a giant red barn in the distance. "Do you have livestock?"

A smile curved his mouth, and Shea was startled to realize something she couldn't believe she'd missed. Ethan had a dimple in his right cheek. Yet another flutter of her heart.

"Yeah . . . come see my livestock."

As they walked toward the barn, Shea inhaled the fresh air and felt more relaxed with every step. At the entrance, she immediately heard the sounds of Ethan's livestock. Little mewling sounds.

Taking her hand, he drew her inside and to a ladder. She climbed up to the loft and was welcomed with a loud *"Meow."*

She turned around and beamed at Ethan as he came up behind her. "Kittens."

"I found them this morning. She must've had them a few days after I left." He picked up a little gray fur ball and held it in the palm of his hand. "See, their eyes are already open."

Shea thought the tiny, helpless creature in Ethan's giant hand should look out of place, but somehow it didn't. The gentleness he displayed as he cupped the kitten and the tender way one large finger stroked the fur, told Shea more about him than any of his other actions. Behind Ethan Bishop's surly, gruff exterior was a gentle and soft heart . . . one he rarely revealed.

"What's the mama's name?"

"Don't know. She showed up at the door one day. I gave her some food, and she's been here ever since. I just call her Cat."

A blip hit her mind and her heartbeat increased. Frowning, not sure what had caused the reaction, she focused on the furry creatures in front of her. "Every creature deserves a name. I'm going to name her Stella."

"Stella?"

She kneeled beside the proud, purring mother and gave her a loving pat. Scooping up a kitten, she held it next to her cheek. The silky, warm fur against her skin brought tears to her eyes. One of the sweetest sensations she could imagine. "I love cats. When I was growing up, I always wanted one. Already had the name Stella picked out and everything. Mama said she didn't have enough money to feed us, much less a cat."

The stiffening of Ethan's body was the first realization that something significant had happened. She glanced up at him in concern. Before she could ask what was wrong, comprehension hit. Hands shaking, she put the kitten beside its mother before she dropped it. Her bottom plopped down onto the loft floor in shock. "My God, Ethan. Just like that, a memory of my childhood flashed through my mind."

Ethan sat beside her, giving her time to come to grips with a new memory. Though he didn't touch her, she was more than aware of his presence, and it comforted her.

What else did she remember? A stabbing pain shot through her head as she tried to force something else into her mind. *Kitten*. The kittens in front of her? No. He had called her Kitten. Rosemount?

Agony speared through her head. Why couldn't she remember? Why wouldn't it come all at once? Why did a memory pepper her thoughts, then close up? She pressed fingers to her temples. Lights exploded behind her eyes; shards of glass speared through her head.

"Shea . . . stop it." Ethan's gruff voice penetrated the roaring in her ears. "You can't force it. Do what the doctors told you to do. When a memory comes, take a deep breath and savor that memory, but don't try to force any more. All it will do is give you a migraine."

"I know . . . I know." She shook her head. "I just . . . I just feel so stupid and slow."

Ethan's calloused hand massaged her neck, and Shea bit back a moan of delight. Nothing in the world felt as good as Ethan's hands. A scene flashed in her head, shocking her to her core. Jerking away, she stared up at him. "We made love on a kitchen table."

Ethan looked as shocked as she felt. "God, Shea. You remember that?"

"Yes." Her eyes closed as pain pounded.

"Let's get you back to the house and get one of those pills the doctor gave you."

Allowing him to help her up, Ethan climbed down the

ladder in front of Shea. The pain increased with every step she took down the ladder. Finally, on the first floor, Ethan scooped her into his arms and headed back to the house.

Though agony pierced her head, Shea couldn't help but feel a sense of triumph and immense relief. She was actually beginning to remember. And finally, she'd had a memory of Ethan. They had definitely been lovers. In the brief flash before pain chased the memory away, she'd seen herself lying nude on a kitchen table. Ethan had been standing between her legs, thrusting into her. Despite the pain, a hot flush of sexual heat flooded her at the image.

Under half-closed eyes, she watched Ethan's face as he carried her into the house. Jaw clenched, mouth flattened into a grim line—his concern was obvious. Even as agony pounded through her head, Shea recognized a certain peace. Everything Ethan had told her was true. It might take weeks or months to remember everything, and she might not remember her entire life, but she was on her way back. Thanks to the man who held her close in his arms, she was finally on her way back.

Ethan drove the axe down, barely aware of the hard impact's vibration through his body. Wood split and splintered. He tossed the firewood into a wheelbarrow, picked up another log, and slammed the axe down again. Sweat poured from his face, beaded and pooled over muscles taut with fatigue and anger.

Shea was remembering sooner than he'd thought she would. Hell, they'd only been here one day. Her recollections in the barn had been pure memory, untainted by anything he or anyone else had said to her. His mind grappled with conflict. For her to remember their lovemaking had been elation, as well as agony.

How he wanted her to remember the good times. The

laughter they'd shared, the love they'd made. The rush of adrenaline when they were working an op. The fierce satisfaction when they saved a life.

That their lovemaking was one of her first memories meant a lot. Soon those memories would be tainted when the bad ones returned. The shouting. The anger. The accusations. Cruel things he'd said trying to convince her to leave, and all the while feeling as though he was cutting his heart out of his chest. Shea's fury, her hurt, and then her tears. That last dreadful day, when he'd made vile accusations and she'd demanded an apology. He hadn't relented. She'd stalked out the door. Weeks later, their world fell apart.

Ethan threw the axe onto the load of firewood. Swiping at his brow, he squinted up at the sun. He needed to go check on her again. Last time he'd checked, maybe an hour ago, she'd been sleeping soundly. The pills for her headaches always knocked her out. Still, he couldn't help but look in to make sure she was okay. If she was having more nightmares, he needed to be close.

As he headed inside, one question hammered at his brain. When would she remember Cole? He should tell her. Dr. Norton hadn't thought it was a good idea, but despite that warning, guilt ate at him. Keeping something so important from her seemed wrong. He'd even told the doctor that he would reveal everything at some point. That if anyone should tell her, it should be Ethan. So why the hell hadn't he?

Ethan knew he had many faults, but only now did he realize that when it came to Shea, he was a coward. Years ago, he'd felt he didn't deserve her. That she deserved a man who epitomized strength, character, and integrity. Cole had been all of those things. Though it had ripped his heart out, he'd pushed Shea toward Cole, knowing he was the better man. Now, with new eyes, he wondered if he hadn't pushed her away simply because he was too much of a coward to take a chance on losing her once she discovered how incredibly flawed he was.

Stomping into the house, Ethan went to the kitchen. Pouring a glass of water from the sink, he drained the contents. Inward analysis of his emotions was about the lowest priority on his list of things he liked to do. Now he knew why. The truth was damned uncomfortable.

fifteen

Ixtapa, Mexico

The pain was immense. His back throbbed and rippled with endless waves of agony. Even more excruciating was the horror of fleeting memories. Like small feathers, they floated toward him, then flittered away before he could grasp their meaning. He heard voices . . . sweet, wonderful voices filled with love and laughter. Childish giggles. A tender, feminine hand caressing his face; soft, sweet lips kissed his mouth. Innocent and precious words like "Daddy" and "darling" drifted through his mind. He felt loved. Knew love. Who and why? He had no form or reason for his thoughts. They were only snippets between unconsciousness and drugged oblivion.

For days, he lay on his stomach, his arms chained to the floor. The doctors treated his injuries with unfeeling but deliberate care. Though the hands touching him were rarely gentle, he somehow knew they were doing all they could to help him recover. Their words terse and detached, they never harmed him and seemingly tried to alleviate the immensity of the pain.

At some point, when he was unconscious, he was turned over. He woke to being able to see something other than the cold, ceramic floor. A face appeared before him . . . the doctor who'd been caring for him. A middle-aged man with a cold and humorless expression. Even in his fractured thinking, he knew this man didn't care what happened to him but was going to make sure he lived.

Injections of his daily drug had continued, but for some reason, they didn't block thought as they had before. Though he still felt dim and slow, often blank, an occasional coherent thought would interrupt or long seconds of clarity would burst through. Scary but also reassuring. He was able to realize that he was actually a real person . . . cognitive thought and reasoning were possible. Though these moments were rare, he treasured each one. Anything was better than blank nothingness.

In the middle of one of these drifting moments of cognitive awareness he heard the voice. The voice of evil. The one he had called master. He kept his eyes closed, intent on learning as much as he could before another black void claimed him once again.

"How's he doing?" the evil voice asked.

"Improving. His vital signs are stable. He should be able to be up and around in a week, maybe two."

"He'll be ready that soon?"

"Ready to walk . . . not ready for training or any kind of mission."

An exasperated sigh. "Then when will he be ready for a mission?"

"A month . . . maybe less. He's extraordinarily strong and healthy, so he's healing better than I thought he would. Once he's able to train again, it'll take him a couple of weeks or more to regain his strength."

"Does his back still pain him?"

"Yes. But the drugs have dulled the worst of it."

"Is there . . ." An audible swallow. "Do you still think there will be scarring?"

"Yes . . . I told you. There's nothing I can do about

that. If you had wanted to keep him flawless, you should have told your men."

"Don't you dare reprimand me, you imbecile."

A long sigh. "I'm merely saying that it's too late with this one. Any future ones you want to keep, you'll need to tell your men to take care. These kinds of injuries aren't mere bruises. He'll be scarred for life."

"Doesn't matter. Once he performs one last duty, he'll be destroyed."

A grunt.

"What?" the evil voice asked.

"Well, if you're not going to need him, I thought perhaps we could use him in the lab."

"How so?"

"I've been working on a few other things I thought might be useful to you. Not only mind control, but heightened sexual arousal and increased intelligence. Also, my research has led me to some interesting ways to enhance the five senses, making them more animal-like than the average human's. It'd be helpful to have a few human guinea pigs to test the new stuff."

"Hmm. That does sound intriguing." A long pause. "If he stays alive, you'll have to keep him out of my way. I don't want him even in the regular cages, where I might see him. I can't abide being near him anymore."

The doctor's voice warmed with enthusiasm and friendliness. "We'll set up a cage in the lab, cover it with drapery unless we're using him. After he helps get your woman back, you'll never have to see him again."

"Mmmm. It would be nice to be able to sell some of your new creations on the market."

"Then let me keep him. It'd be a shame to destroy such a valuable creature."

His body wanted to leap at them, tear them to pieces. His teeth gritted against the fury unfurling inside. Damn them. He wasn't a fucking lab rat!

"I'll give it some thought."

The sound of footsteps told him the evil man had left. He expelled breath he hadn't been aware he was holding.

"You can open your eyes now. I know you're awake."

He opened his eyes and looked up at the demon doctor. There was no compassion, no feeling. This man might have a different agenda for keeping him alive, but it was all for his benefit.

He opened his mouth, but nothing but a garbled groan emerged.

The doctor nodded. "Your tongue's swollen. The drugs do that." He moved away for a moment. When he returned, he held a cup filled with ice chips. "Here. This'll help."

Not caring why the doctor was helping, he opened his mouth like a baby bird and allowed the doctor to spoon small chips onto his tongue. The relief was instantaneous and gratifying.

"Feel better?"

He nodded.

"Want to ask a question?"

Swallowing, he opened his mouth again and huffed out a word. "Who?"

"Dr. Richard Kline." The man stuck out his hand as if to shake his and then pulled it back. "Sorry, forgot you were a bit tied up." He laughed at his own joke.

Holding back his fury wasn't easy, but he wanted answers. After he got them he'd figure out a way to make this man pay. "Wh . . . why?"

"Why am I doing this?"

He moved his head in a small nod.

The doctor looked away and pulled up a chair to sit beside the bed. "Because I've worked my entire life for this." The man's expression of barely contained excitement churned his guts, but if answers were revealed, the discomfort would be well worth the price.

"A few years after I graduated from MIT, I got caught doing some unauthorized experiments for a pharmaceutical company I was working for. Nothing severe, mind you, but the damned board of ethics fired me and then tried to bring me up on criminal charges. I had to leave the country. Donald found me and offered to fund all of my research. I've been working for him for almost ten years now. I'm just now getting to the point where my hard work is paying off."

The doctor leaned forward as he warmed to his subject. "See, the mind's a fascinating organ. Endless avenues to explore—controlling it, manipulating it, expanding knowledge and then removing that knowledge. I've dedicated my life to its study."

Evil eyes gleamed with cold amusement. "I know what you would say if you could. It's wrong. Unethical. But who's to say that in a few years, the drugs I'm creating won't save thousands of lives." He chuckled. "Though I have to admit that's not really my goal, it might well be a side benefit."

The effort to speak brought tears to his eyes, but he forced the words out: "How . . . many . . . here?"

"What? You mean how many people do we have working here?" Another grin. "You think you're going to be able to escape, don't you? You think if I tell you all this, you'll be able to come up with a plan." He slapped his thigh in delight. "See, that's one of the reasons I want to keep you. That incredible strength you have isn't only physical. You've got some sort of innate optimism in you. I saw it when we first brought you in. I find that very intriguing."

When the creature didn't say anything to his statement, the doctor shrugged. "I might as well tell you.

Keeping your hope alive will be an excellent test for one of my new drugs."

Chin in hand, his eyes were distant as he thought about the question. "There are five scientists and four assistants. Donald has about thirty soldiers. Some are drugged on a daily basis, trained to do what Donald tells them to do. Not drugged like you. They're given just enough to keep them obedient, but they do have some cognitive thought. Others aren't drugged at all. They just like the money and excitement."

A glimpse of brilliant auburn hair and emerald eyes glinting with humor flashed into his mind. Who was she? "Woman?"

"You're wondering about Donald's female companion, huh?"

Pain sliced through his head. Was that who he saw in his mind?

The doctor shook his head. "She hasn't been found yet. That's something Donald will need your help with. We'll get you healthy and strong again so you can help get her."

His eyes stinging from the strain of keeping them open, he closed them briefly, trying his best to hang on to his sanity. He wasn't to be killed yet . . . or to be given new drugs until he obtained the woman. That meant he had time. Time for what, he didn't know. He couldn't hold a thought for longer than a few seconds, but in those seconds, he saw hope. He had to hang on to that.

The doctor stood. "I need to get back to work, so we'll have to delay any further chatting for another day."

His eyes flipped open in time to see a needle inserted into his IV drip. Anger roared though him. No, he couldn't let go . . . he couldn't.

"Now, now. Don't fight it. Won't do any good. I'm only giving you enough to keep you semisedated. You'll still have an occasional independent thought . . . not that it'll do you any good."

A thick film of darkness began to cover his thoughts. His mind screamed as memories and reason vanished . . . and then, once again, there was nothing.

sixteen

Ethan stuck his head out the door. "Feel like a picnic?"

Shea pulled herself to her feet, relieved by the interruption from her thoughts. "Absolutely." She'd been sitting on the deck all morning, morose and blue. Nightmares from the last few nights had cloaked her in a shroud of numbness. Hazy images of grief, horror, and pain without any substantive reality continued to swamp her. What more had she gone through and what had she seen?

Right now, a simple, uncomplicated picnic sounded like heaven.

Though his mouth moved up into a smile, the solemn look in Ethan's eyes told her of his concern. He'd been with her during the worst nightmares. Soothing and comforting her. What would she have done without him?

"There's a stream that runs through my land about a half mile down the valley. It's got some nice shade trees. Great spot for dozing in the sun, too."

She smiled, delighted at the idea. "Sounds wonderful."

Birds twittering above and the crunch of loose rock and broken twigs under their feet were the only sounds as they made their way down the grassy hill. Back to their left was a small cleared-out area where Ethan told her he intended to plant a vegetable garden. And to their

right was the corral he planned to use when he purchased some horses. When she'd asked him when he
would do that, he'd shrugged and said, "When things
settle down." Meaning after Rosemount was caught and
she had recovered.

Ethan's generosity continued to surprise and amaze
her. How many people would put their life on hold the
way he had? She shot a glance at him. She'd been so preoccupied with her thoughts, she'd just realized that
Ethan hadn't uttered a word since they'd started walking. "Is something wrong?"

"Just thinking about how quickly some of your memories are returning."

"Amazing, isn't it? A week or so ago, I was imagining
trying to have a life without any kind of past." She grimaced. "Looks like the bad stuff's going to come in the
form of nightmares . . . which I guess is totally appropri-
ate."

"I called Dr. Norton this morning, before you woke
up. Told him what was going on. About your memories
and your nightmares."

"Was he surprised?"

"Not really. He's said all along that if you were in a
more relaxed environment, you'd be less likely to try to
force your memories. He did have an interesting theory
. . . said that your subconscious is trying to shield you by
giving your worst memories back to you in nightmares."

"How is this shielding me?"

"He seems to think that it's a way to ease you back
into the bad experiences."

Shea snorted softly. "Doesn't feel like an easing to me.
They're becoming more and more hideous without giving me any kind of real information."

Ethan squeezed her hand in sympathy. "I know."

They halted under a giant oak tree that loomed over
and shaded a grassy level area. The gurgling rush of

water from the stream below them made the setting perfect for a picnic. "This look okay to you?"

Ethan watched Shea turn in a circle, as if assessing the entire scene. After several seconds of silence, she looked at him with a smile that could rival the sun for brilliance. "Can't imagine a more ideal spot."

Doing his best to ignore what Shea's smiles always did to his heart, Ethan handed her the blanket. With a quick flick of her wrists, it floated and covered the ground.

Toeing her shoes off, as he'd seen her do a thousand times, she kneeled beside the basket and peeked inside. "What's for lunch?"

Ethan dropped down across from her. He really couldn't remember what he'd put in there. "A little bit of everything."

"I'll say. This basket probably weighs as much as I do. You must've been hungry."

He was, though not for food. Shea's memories might be returning gradually, but his memories were ever present and crystal clear. When her mouth curved up, he was reminded of how her full, luscious lips tasted under his. When she breathed out a sigh, he thought about the little hitch of breath she would release just as he slid inside her. His gazed lowered and his hands clenched at the memory of her perfect breasts, how the warm, soft mounds felt when he cupped them, and the way her pretty nipples would bead into little ruby-red nubs when he sucked them.

With a stifled groan, Ethan shifted on the blanket. He was doing nothing but torturing himself. Their lovemaking was in the past. Hot, delicious memories he could relive on cold, lonely days. They didn't belong here today. Thinking about what they'd once had together would only create more problems. He had more than enough already.

His body twisted away, blocking her view of the erection pressing against his zipper. Thankfully, she seemed preoccupied in unloading the basket. For the first time since rescuing her, he didn't see any shadows or pain in her face. Her eyes held a sparkle much like the old Shea's.

An uninhibited giggle jerked him from his thoughts. "Do you want to start with the salad, the veggies and dip, or the cheese and crackers?"

"What's so funny?"

"Did you bring everything you had in the fridge?"

"Too much stuff?"

Another gurgle of laughter. "Not if we were planning to camp out here for a week . . . maybe two."

"Sorry, it's been a long time since I went on a picnic."

"Don't apologize. It looks wonderful. I just don't know if I can do it justice."

Grabbing a cracker from the plate she'd put in front of him, he said, "Eat what you want. I can carry the rest back."

"Okay." She leaned forward and grabbed something from the basket. "Think I'll go with this first."

Ethan's chest tightened as he watched her bite into a fudgy brownie. He must have made some sort of a sound because she stopped in the middle of taking another bite.

"What's wrong? Why are you looking like that?"

He moved his head back and forth in wonder. "Even though you don't remember a lot of your life, Shea Monroe is definitely coming back."

"What do you mean?"

"Whenever you could, you always ate dessert first. Your reasoning was, 'Why wait for the good stuff?' "

She looked delighted at this new knowledge. "Really?" Taking another bite, she swallowed and said, "There's so much stuff you can tell me about myself. You probably know me better than anyone."

Apparently noticing something in his face, she rushed on, "Surely it can't hurt to tell me some of my habits or idiosyncrasies."

"You hate broccoli, but you love spinach."

She covered her mouth to stifle a soft snort. "Any other scintillating details?"

Ethan lay back on the blanket, stared up at the flawless sky, and remembered. "You like sappy romances and chick flicks, but hate war and horror movies. At the theater, you'd always buy popcorn and chocolate-covered raisins and eat them together. Your favorite flower is the daisy, your favorite tree is the weeping willow. You're afraid of spiders, but if you found one in the house, you'd always call me to put it outside. You can ice-skate and snow-ski like a gazelle and swim like a fish. You love to watch football and basketball games, both college and pro. Baseball make you sleepy, hockey makes you cringe. And you suck at golf."

"Wow."

Hearing the thick emotion in that one word, he glanced over at her. "What's wrong?"

Her throat worked as she swallowed hard. "I know it's silly, but knowing those kinds of things means so much. Most of my memories so far have been so hideous."

"I'm sorry, Shea. I should have told you sooner."

Her eyes gleaming with tears, she smiled. "You're telling me now. That's all that matters."

Hoping to lighten the mood, he gave her another fact. "You sing like a crazed hyena."

"I do not!"

"The neighbor's dogs howled every time you sang."

Another soft snort.

He smiled at the familiar sound. "Oh, and you snort when you disagree with something."

"I do not."

Propping his head on his hand, he turned toward her. "You also love to argue."

"No, I don't—" She caught herself and giggled. "Okay, maybe a little."

Ethan lay back and closed his eyes, allowing the music of her soft laughter to sink into his soul. Yes, he knew almost everything there was to know about Shea Monroe. Her likes and dislikes, her politics and beliefs, the little quirks he'd sometimes found irritating but most of the time endearing. He knew her open and loving nature, her fiery temper, and the special place on her body that required only a slight pinch before he had her screaming in orgasm.

He also knew who and what had once destroyed her. A bastard named Ethan Bishop.

Propped up on her left arm, Shea blew out a long breath of contentment. Stuffed from all the food Ethan had crammed into the picnic basket, she was pleased that her appetite was returning but felt as though she wouldn't want food for at least another week.

Ethan lay next to her, eyes closed, looking more relaxed than she'd ever seen him. She already knew he didn't sleep much. Every time she woke from a nightmare, he was there. She smiled down at him, in awe of his kindness. Saving her life, taking care of her, opening his home to her and protecting her. Whether he wanted to admit it or not, he cared deeply for her. Which made her wonder. Why had they ended their relationship?

She opened her mouth to ask, then caught herself. If he was sleeping, the last thing she wanted to do was wake him. He needed his rest as much as she did.

Stifling a yawn, Shea fought the temptation to take a nap, too. Surrounded by giant trees, blooming summer flowers, and the sweet scent of wild honeysuckle, she wanted to stay awake and relish the beauty. If she slept, she might miss something.

The gurgling of the little stream a few yards away called to her. Wading in the cold water sounded heavenly. She shot one more look at Ethan. He hadn't moved a muscle. Slipping her shoes on, she got to her feet and tiptoed away. Her heart clip-clopped in anticipation, as if this were a major event. Playing in the water just seemed so innocent and carefree.

Perched on a giant rock, Shea slid her shoes off and plunged her feet in. She caught herself with a gasping squeal and jerked back out. *Oh man, that's cold.* More hesitant this time, she dipped her toes in, then out. Her skin acclimating quickly, she plunged her feet in again, kicking and splashing like a kid.

"Shea!"

Startled at the alarm in Ethan's voice, she twisted around and shouted, "Down here."

Within seconds, he appeared at the top of the small hill and stalked toward her. She'd often thought he looked like a thundercloud when he was angry. The expression on his face now made his thundercloud expression look like a fluffy cloud. He was furious.

"What the hell are you doing?"

"I'm just playing in the water."

"Get your ass up here."

Her spine stiffened. "Excuse me?"

"You heard me. You've got someone dying to grab you again and you go off on your own like that. Are you crazy?"

She waved a hand at the quiet serenity of their surroundings. "I really doubt that Rosemount is going to jump out from behind a bush."

"You don't know that. Didn't I tell you not to go off on your own?"

By now, Ethan stood directly in front of her. Shea

jumped to her feet and glared up at him. Inches from his face, she could almost feel the heat of his fury.

"Stop snarling and treating me like a three-year-old. I was just a few feet from you."

"Well, that's not going to do you a whole lot of good when a bullet hits you, is it?"

"If you think he's going to shoot me, then you shouldn't be close to me."

"Why?"

Now as angry as he was, she snapped, "Because I don't want him to shoot you, you moron!"

Ethan's hands grabbed her shoulders and shook her hard. "You listen to me. When I tell you to do something, I expect you to obey. Understand?"

"How dare you," she gritted between clenched teeth. "I just left one master. I'll damned well not have another one."

"Dammit, I'm trying to take care of you."

Shea pressed her lips together to prevent another snarling response. Fine, so he was trying to protect her, but did he have to be such an ass? She settled for a glare, almost daring him to come up with another smart comment.

His eyes raging with more emotion than she'd ever seen from him, Ethan jerked against her and slammed his mouth onto hers. Shocked, she didn't respond for a millisecond. Then, recognizing that this was exactly what she'd wanted for days, she wrapped her arms around him. Pressing closer, she opened her mouth and invited him in.

A ragged groan came from Ethan as his tongue plunged deep, as if he couldn't get enough of her. Shea gloried in the hot, wild sensation. He had treated her gently for so long. Even when he'd growled at her, he'd acted as if she were fragile and breakable. Now she was simply a woman in his arms, and she loved the feeling.

Thrusting his tongue deeper, Ethan grabbed her hips and pressed her against him, the steel hardness of his erection creating an unbearable ache. A soft sob rose inside her that was smothered, then devoured, by his ravaging mouth. Shea lifted up on her toes and matched the center of her sex to his arousal and rubbed back and forth. Her actions elicited another groan from him, this time sounding tortured and sexy.

His mouth moved from hers and traveled down her face, then to her neck, where he nibbled lightly, his teeth scraping against her skin. Arching into his embrace, Shea savored the feel of his mouth on her skin, the chafe of his beard stubble an erotic thrill. When his lips reached the V-neck of her shirt, she gasped, hoping he'd go further, not daring to believe he would. A button popped and his mouth covered the open space. Thrusting her chest toward his mouth, wordlessly she told him exactly what she wanted. When his mouth covered her breast, she swallowed a silent cry of need.

"Shea . . . ?"

Raising her hands to his head, Shea threaded her fingers through his hair and undulated against his body. "I'm yours, Ethan. Don't you know that?"

Moving his mouth to her other breast, Ethan gently bit her nipple. Shock waves pulsed, desire spiraled, hot and wild, shooting sparks through her body and igniting a wildfire of need.

"Please, oh please . . ." Shea distantly realized she was pleading, groaning. She didn't care. Her body remembered Ethan and wanted him with a desperation that would be terrifying if it didn't feel so wonderful.

Hot green eyes, glazed with a burning intensity, looked down at her. "You're sure?"

Relief and excitement clashed. "Yes."

Calloused hands slid under her shirt, caressing her midriff, they made a slow glide toward her breasts. Nipples peaking in anticipation, Shea closed her eyes and let desire take over.

A distant sound barely penetrated her senses. Ethan stiffened. Raising his head, he gripped her hard with his hands as his eyes combed the woods surrounding them. Another sound came, and this time Shea recognized it. A gunshot.

Before she could speak, Ethan scooped her up in his arms and was carrying her up the hill.

"Ethan, wait."

"We've got to get out of here."

"No. Listen. It's at least half a mile from here. It's probably someone hunting."

His big body vibrating with tension, he stopped and listened. Another shot, sounding even more distant.

Dropping her gently onto the blanket, Ethan drew in a ragged breath.

She gestured around them. "We're fine. See? No one's around."

"We need to go."

His cool tone and granite-hard face shocked her. What had happened to the wild, aroused man?

"What? Why?"

Without answering, he went back for her shoes and dropped them in front of her. As she slid them on, he turned his back to her and repacked the basket, haphazardly throwing in plates, glasses, and food.

"Ethan, what's wrong?"

When he didn't answer, she reached out a tentative hand and touched his arm.

Ethan twisted away from her. "I said, we need to go."

Shea snatched her hand back and stood. In silence, she picked up the blanket and folded it into a neat square. Ethan took it from her, grabbed her hand, and started walking.

"The least you can do is tell me what's wrong. Why are you acting this way?"

His jaw was clenched tight, and Shea knew he was going through emotions she had no understanding of. What had made him switch from tender, passionate lover to this cold-blooded stranger?

"Dammit, talk to me."

He whirled her around so fast, she stumbled and slammed into his chest. He caught her, held her at a distance. "Let it go, Shea."

"No, I'm not going to let it go. What happened? We were seconds from making love and then you turn into a snarling bear. I have a right to know why you're acting this way."

"Fine. I'm angry at myself. I should never have kissed you."

"Why?"

"Because it's wrong. Okay?"

"Why is it wrong?" Nausea churned in her stomach as a hideous thought occurred to her. She told herself Ethan wasn't that shallow, but she couldn't prevent the words. "Is it because of what Rosemount did?"

"Not the reasons you think."

"Then, how?"

"You feel some sort of gratitude to me for rescuing you. I should never have taken advantage of you."

"You jerk. Gratitude had nothing to do with my response. I wanted you."

"You're too vulnerable right now. You sure as hell don't need me pawing all over you."

"Don't you understand? I wanted you. After all that's happened, to know I can feel desire . . . that I'm not afraid . . . is amazing and thrilling."

His strides still eating up the ground, Shea quickened up her pace to keep up with him, anger and hurt giving her extra energy.

He stopped so abruptly, Shea almost slammed into his back. He turned and looked down at her. "I'm glad you can feel that. More than you'll ever know. But nothing can happen between us. Not now . . . not ever."

"Why not?"

"Because, dammit, it can't."

"I deserve an explanation, don't you think?"

Looking as if he was on his last thread of patience, he snarled, "Fine. You want to know why we can't be together, I'll tell you. I broke your heart, Shea. When we were together, you wanted more and I couldn't give it. I couldn't do it then, and I can't do it now."

"Why?"

"Hell, woman, do I have to spell it out? I fucked you for as long as I wanted to and then, when you wanted more, I told you to get lost." He pulled her till her nose was inches from his. "I didn't love you then. I don't love you now. Is that clear enough?"

Ethan clicked on another site. Every morning he searched the Internet, looking for any hint of Rosemount. If he was getting most of his clients online, there had to be some way to identify him. LCR people were working this angle, too, but another pair of eyes couldn't hurt. One way or another, Rosemount would be found.

His gut churned from too much coffee and mountains of regret; his eyes burned from no sleep. After the vile words he'd thrown at Shea yesterday, closing his eyes had been impossible. Every time he tried, the stricken look on her face blasted into his mind. Why the hell had he spewed those words at her?

He'd tried to apologize and had done a lousy job. His "I'm sorry, I was out of line" had gotten the response it deserved. She'd shrugged and said, "Hey, I asked for the truth." They'd finished their return to the house in a thick, tense silence.

As soon as she'd closed the door to her room, he'd gone down to his basement and beat the hell out of his boxing bag. The exercise hadn't helped. If he'd been able to beat on himself, he would have felt much better.

After that, he'd stalked around the house, muttering and cursing himself like a madman. Then he'd made a decision. He couldn't do this to her. After almost destroying her one time, no way in hell would he do it again.

Wanting to get it over with, determined to do the right thing for once in his life, he'd put in a call to Noah.

In a somewhat groggy voice, McCall had answered, "What's up?"

Only then had Ethan looked at his clock. His mind was so screwed up, he hadn't even looked at the time. It was six hours later in Paris . . . three in the morning.

"Damn, I just looked at the clock. I'll call you tomorrow."

"Don't worry about it. I'll go to another room so I won't wake Mara. What's wrong?"

"I need you to find someone else to protect Shea."

"Why?"

"Because she can't stay here any longer."

Noah blew out a resigned sigh. "What did you do?"

Ethan swallowed a humorless laugh. Noah McCall knew him better than anyone. "So far, nothing more than hurt her feelings. If she stays here, there's no telling what else I'll do."

"She's only been there a week or so. I figured you could keep things together for at least a month. Besides, she needs you."

Alert to every nuance and word from his former boss, Ethan jotted a note, released a silent sigh. "You're right. I'm just being a selfish prick."

Noah snorted. "Some things don't change."

"I'll try to keep my mouth shut."

"Maybe that's your problem."

"What's that supposed to mean?"

"It means opening up is damn hard for some. Especially for people like us. But once you open up with the right person, life improves tremendously."

Despite the underlying message, Ethan knew Noah was referring to his own shaky and volatile relationship with Samara before they married. Ethan had seen their pain up close. Though it had worked out for them, they'd gone through hell to get there.

"What I did was unforgivable," Ethan said.

"How do you know unless you ask for it?"

Ethan changed the subject. "Anything else on the mole?"

"Not yet. How about on your end—any promising sketches?"

"Not really. Mostly half drawings and a few side profiles. Nothing that's going to tell us anything."

"Keep in touch. Give some thought to what I said. Women have an amazing capacity for forgiveness. Something I'm grateful for every day."

Ethan had hung up the phone without responding. He didn't deserve Shea's forgiveness and seriously doubted she'd give it to him if he asked. Either way, she was here for the duration.

Now he picked up the sheet of paper he'd scribbled on last night. It'd been almost a year since he had worked for LCR. He didn't think he was rusty, but he wanted to make sure he understood Noah's message. Then he would destroy what he had written.

LCR had its own code. Created and taught by Noah, it was known to only a select few operatives. They were the elite, chosen by Noah to be the eyes and ears for the organization. LCR employed hundreds of people for a variety of jobs, but only twenty such operatives existed with this particular knowledge. They were the most trusted. Ethan and Shea had been part of that group.

Based upon certain words in a conversation, Noah could communicate another message. As technology advanced, so did the possibility that unwanted ears could be listening. Noah had developed the most simplistic method to communicate the most secretive of messages. And the hell of it was, it worked.

Noah's comments last night indicated that the mole was close to being identified. If they broke away from their original plan, he might suspect something and pull back. Noah felt it'd be a month, maybe more, before they could confirm his identity.

As much as Ethan didn't like it, he knew Noah was right. If they made changes now, the mole might back away. They couldn't take the risk.

He slid the piece of paper into his shredder and listened to the satisfying munching of the machine.

He'd made the vow to protect Shea, and that's what he'd damn well do. Not only from Rosemount, but also from himself.

Ixtapa, Mexico

"I need you to find my woman again."

"I already found her for you one time and your people screwed up . . . *again.*"

The miles separating them didn't mask the young man's condescension. Donald grabbed his new stress ball. Since he'd become acquainted with this young twerp, he'd gone through three of them. Someday very soon, he was so going to enjoy making this punk eat his words. Only by envisioning his dazed blank expression when he had served his purpose could Donald even stomach talking with him.

Donald made sure his voice in no way indicated his antipathy. "The woman was an amateur."

"You hired her."

The grip on the stress ball went tighter. "You, however, are a professional. You can get the job done better than anyone."

"Huh?"

Ah yes, not so certain now. "I want you to retrieve Ms. Monroe. You'll be highly compensated, of course. But I also want you to bring me Mr. Bishop."

An obnoxious snort assaulted Donald's ears. "You'd have to pay me freakin' millions to risk that."

"All right."

"What?"

"You heard me. You bring me my woman, I'll pay you two hundred and fifty thousand. Bring Mr. Bishop also, I'll give you a million."

"A million for the Monroe bitch. Two million more for Bishop."

"Done."

Donald grinned at the audible nervous swallow. Money was a powerful motivator . . . second only to his special drug. However, this man would be torn. Capturing two LCR operatives, one of them as lethal as Ethan Bishop, would be virtually impossible. Donald had nothing to lose. If this young man was unsuccessful, he had no information to give on Donald's whereabouts. If, however, he succeeded in bringing in both prizes, Donald would not only have his woman back, he'd have Ethan Bishop and this young man in his grip. And if only his woman returned, no matter. He'd have his woman and still get the young man. A win for Donald any way he looked at it.

"It'll take me some time to come up with a plan. Bishop's taken the woman off somewhere. Only a few people know where they are."

"I'll leave all the tedious details to you. Just contact me when the job is going to be done and I'll make the arrangements for transfer."

Satisfied with the call, Donald replaced the handset on the base. Tossing the stress ball into the air, he leaned forward to catch it. The chair rolled backward, and he fell to his knees. The ball bounced across the room and landed in a corner. A brilliant heat flushed his cheeks; he peeked over his desk to make sure the door was closed.

He picked himself up from the floor, straightened his clothes, and returned to his desk. *Damned chair should be outlawed.*

His coordination was off because of his need for his kitten. He had suffered tremendously in her absence. The original plan of using his damaged creature had been delayed; he hadn't recovered as quickly as Donald had hoped. An infection in his lungs had developed into pneumonia, and only then had they learned that his designer drugs reduced the effectiveness of antibiotics. His poor pet had almost died.

His condition had improved, but he was still weeks away from full recovery. If the cocky young LCR operative didn't return his woman, his secret weapon would be waiting in the wings.

seventeen

Warm summer breezes, glorious searing sun, and the quiet peaceful beauty of the Smokies turned into the perfect healing combination. Time passed at a slow, undemanding pace, and Shea grew healthier and stronger. Memories still erupted like the popping of tiny bubbles in her mind. Though they were not all pleasant, Shea forced herself to treasure each one for what it was—a piece of herself. Each memory made up the woman she'd become, and more than anything, she wanted to rediscover that person in her entirety . . . warts and all.

The nights continued to be the worst as nightmares continued to stoke the memories. She often waited until she no longer had a choice before she went to bed, knowing that the instant she closed her eyes, it would begin.

Last night had been one of the most awful. Ethan had come to her room several times, but she'd refused his comfort. She knew he wanted to help. The anger and helplessness sparkling in his eyes told her he shared her torture. Despite his obvious concern, Shea was determined to handle things on her own. She no longer allowed Ethan inside her room or her nightmares.

They existed as polite strangers. Though his protection and concern for her were obvious, he maintained his distance, setting up a barrier she didn't know how to penetrate.

She stayed out of his way as much as possible. The

deck at the back of his house gave her the air and sunshine she thrived on, as well as the privacy. Ethan rarely ventured out there. Most of the time, he was working outside, coming in only for meals and sleep.

They had eased into an odd and lonely routine. In the mornings, he would prepare breakfast, and as she ate he gently but inexorably interrogated her about her nightmares and memories. She rarely saw him again until dusk.

Dinnertime was the most awkward. Since he made breakfast, she had taken to making their evening meals. Ethan always ate quickly, rarely saying a word until he finished. Then he would thank her politely for preparing dinner and disappear once again, either into his office or the gym downstairs.

She told herself she should be happy he'd made his position clear so soon. Prevention of a needless heartache. Unfortunately, it was too late. Her heart already ached.

Now, as the sun forced the moon into hiding, Shea rubbed gritty, sleep-deprived eyes. Her mind blurred from exhaustion, she contemplated what last night's nightmares had revealed. Putting a positive spin on these memories was difficult. Though she wished she could say they were simply nightmares, with no base in reality, she recognized the truth. The recollections of abuse and neglect were real. She'd had a horrific childhood.

A knock on the door was barely a warning before Ethan's golden head appeared. "Feel like breakfast?"

The concern in his eyes steeled her resolve. So what if she'd had a bad upbringing. Many people had experienced much worse and still lived productive lives. So could she.

"Give me a few minutes to shower and I'll be down."

His expression revealing that he wanted to say more, he nodded and closed the door.

She showered, slipped on a pair of jeans and a

sweater, and quickly braided her hair. Ethan would have breakfast waiting, and she needed to spend as much time on her face as possible. She applied makeup, paying special attention to the shadows under her eyes. After surveying the results, she released a disgusted sigh, grabbed a tissue, and wiped half of it off. A clown's face wasn't any more attractive than that of a washed-out insomniac.

At last, halfway satisfied with the results, she stuck her tongue out at the image, whirled around, and headed downstairs.

Ethan stood beside the kitchen table. Tall, ruggedly masculine, and as out of reach as the sun.

Pulling out a chair, she sat down and took a bracing gulp of Ethan's strong coffee. Before he could begin his questions, she asked, "How much do you know about my past . . . before I came to LCR?"

Across from her, Ethan scooped scrambled eggs onto a plate, his stony expression a good indication that he knew a lot. He took a sip of his coffee before replying gruffly, "Enough to know that if you never got your memories back, you'd be a hell of a lot better off."

"You know about my stepfather?"

A wary look came over his face. "A little."

"Did you know that from the time I was twelve until I ran away at fifteen, he raped me repeatedly?"

"Yes," Ethan said quietly.

"My mother knew about it. Told me I shouldn't complain because he bought the food and my clothes."

His grim, unsurprised look told her he knew that also. "What else do you remember?"

She lifted a shoulder in a halfhearted shrug. "Bits and pieces. I don't remember my real father. Before Mama married my stepfather, she had enough boyfriends to fill a football stadium. They never touched me. Once she married, that changed. To Mama, it wasn't a big deal.

The first time it happened, she forced me to drink a glass of wine because I couldn't stop crying when she told me what she wanted me to do. After it was over, I threw up on him."

"You never told me about that."

She shrugged again. "It kept him off me for almost a month. Then, one night, he came into my room. He'd been drinking. He poured something vile down my throat. Told me if I threw up on him again, he'd kill me. I still threw up. Just went to the bathroom to do it after it was over.

"The older I got, the more I resisted. He continued to force alcohol down me, trying to make me more cooperative. One day, I hit him with a lamp. Mama had to take him to the hospital for stitches. I ran away. The police tracked me down. He'd always threatened that if I ever told anyone, he'd kill me. I couldn't take it anymore, figured death had to be better. So I finally told them what had happened. He and my mama went to jail, and I went into foster care."

"What do you remember about that?"

"That it wasn't much better."

"You had one good experience . . . do you remember it?"

Her mouth moved up into a small smile. "Allison and Todd Hobart." The young couple with two little kids had taken her in with open arms and understanding smiles. For the first time, she saw how a normal family behaved. Parents who loved each other and loved their children. The Hobarts had given her such hope. She'd lived with them for three months. Had just begun to feel safe and secure when her mother was released from jail. After she'd convinced a judge that she was reformed and wanted her daughter back, Shea had been forced to go home. Having seen what life could be like, she ran away again days later.

This time, she made sure she didn't get caught.

"I couldn't go back to living with her after living with them."

"What else do you remember?"

"I got on a bus to Colorado. Lied about my age and worked two jobs till I got my GED. Went to college at night and got a degree in psychology. It felt good to be on my own. I was bone-assed tired most of the time, but it was a good feeling."

"I can't believe you remember all of this."

A grim smile tilted her lips. "Last night was a busy night."

"I wish you'd have let me help you through it."

Her eyes shifted to her plate. "I need to learn how to deal with them on my own." She cleared her throat and glanced back up at him. "Unfortunately, things get blurry after that."

"You don't remember calling Noah and telling him you wanted to work for him?"

She gasped. "I did?"

His clear green eyes glinted with something like pride. "Said you were tired of all the bureaucratic crap. You were working for social services in Denver. You told him you liked how he got things done."

"Did Noah tell you this?"

"No, you used to brag about it."

"I did?"

"Yes. Guess you don't remember that you were quite arrogant, too."

She was astounded that she'd been so cocky and confident. Laughter bubbled through her, then caught in her throat at Ethan's expression. "What's wrong?"

Ethan released a shaky breath. "My God, Shea. Do you know how long it's been since I've heard you laugh like that?"

A full smile curved her mouth. "It felt really good."

"Laughter and tears always came so easy for you."

"You sound envious."

He shrugged. "It's not that easy for most people."

"I know you've laughed, but you never cry?"

"Not in a long while."

"Sometimes I feel as though if I started crying, I'd never be able to stop. Do you ever feel that way?"

Ethan stood and turned away from her. "No." He gave a sidelong glance at her plate. "Are you finished?"

The stoic stone face Ethan presented didn't fool her for an instant. What had hurt him so badly in the past that he'd locked his emotions up from the rest of the world?

"Shea, are you finished?"

"Yes, sorry." She stood, knowing, as before, that once their discussion of her nightmares was over, they'd go their separate ways until lunch. "I think I'll go get my sketchbook and sit out on the deck."

Ethan watched her leave the room. From the deep shadows under her eyes, she needed sleep more than anything else.

Exhaustion beat at him, too. Last night had been an exercise in agony. Shea had refused his help, as she had for weeks. He wished it was just the return of her independent spirit, but he knew the truth. After he'd made it clear that she was only here temporarily and nothing would develop between them, she'd been determined to handle everything on her own. He counted himself lucky that she hadn't demanded to leave. Not that he'd let her, but fighting Shea when she was hurt and angry wasn't something he wanted.

Placing the dishes in the sink to be cleaned up later, Ethan headed to his small office at the back of the house. It was time for his weekly check-in with Noah. Closing the door quietly behind him, Ethan lowered himself into the leather office chair and picked up the phone.

"Anything new?" Despite his exhaustion, Ethan couldn't help but be amused at Noah's phone etiquette, so similar to his. No wasting time on niceties.

"Major nightmares last night." He paused. "She remembered her childhood."

"Hell, that's a nightmare all to itself." Noah's grim tone was an acknowledgment that there was little he didn't know about Shea's past.

"She handled it well. A hell of a lot better than I could. She remembers all the way up to getting her degree. Doesn't remember contacting you."

"That'll come soon."

"Yeah. Anything new on Rosemount or from Dr. Norton?"

"Not much on Rosemount. We think he's still in Mexico. Thought we had him . . . or at least some of his people. A few weeks back, got a tip two college kids were going to be nabbed. We rescued the kids, but Rosemount's men got away. Only description we got was two white males, one medium-sized with blond hair and one large with black hair." Noah blew out a snort of disgust. "Not a lot to go on."

"Think he's getting careless?"

"Maybe. Tip came in from one of our Web watchers. He saw an ad on one of the websites we know Rosemount has used. Thought it sounded similar to his kind of deal and alerted us. Turned out he was right. . . . Problem was, it took Jamie too long to find out where and who the kids were."

"Jamie?" Ethan asked sharply.

"Yeah. I know what you're going to say, but Gabe thinks he can turn him around."

"Yeah, well, Gabe wasn't there two years ago when Jamie sat with his thumb up his ass while one of our guys got killed either."

"He says he's not denying that the kid has problems,

but he thinks he can make something of him. Gabe's on assignment right now. When he gets back, he knows he's got only a short amount of time to whip Jamie into shape. In the meantime, Jamie's running down cyber-nappings. When he saw the ad for the two college kids, he brought it to me. Have to admit, I was impressed that he was on the ball like that."

Ethan grudgingly admitted, "It's been a while since I've seen him. Maybe the kid has changed. That's as close as you've been to Rosemount in a while."

"Thing is, since we got that close, I'm wondering if he's going to go deeper."

"Seems too arrogant to do that."

"Maybe." Noah paused for a breath and then said, "There is one piece of good news. I talked to Dr. Norton this morning. They're still working on developing something for Shea that'll return her memories without working adversely on her mind. One of the drugs they're experimenting with has had good results for people who've gone through trauma. Even though the memory returns, it dims the fear, making it seem like it's a movie."

"Hell, at least she'll be spared that, if nothing else. Anything else?"

"Might have something within a matter of weeks."

Ethan heard the warning. At some point, either through drugs or just through Shea's steely determination, she would remember all of her past. A sudden urge to see her had Ethan ending the call. "Thanks for the update. I'll check back next week."

"Stay safe."

Ethan hung up the phone and stared at the notepad where he'd made his scribbles. The mole had been identified and was being lured. Gabe would be handling the setup and Ethan was to be ready.

Shredding the note, Ethan shot to his feet and headed

to the back deck. Shea's favorite spot. It was also the only place outside where she could go without him. Due to the sheer drop from the deck, it would be almost impossible for anyone to gain access.

Shea came out here almost every day for what she called her bit of private heaven. The scenery seemed to fill her with serenity. He tamped down the thought of how much he wanted to give her his own idea of serenity. Though he fought it every day, the desire he'd always felt for her was greater than ever. With no outlet, his fantasies and memories of her kept him awake late into the night. Even when Shea's nightmares or his own weren't keeping him awake, his unappeased libido refused to allow him rest.

He stepped out onto the wooden deck and found a sleeping beauty. For right now, at least, no nightmares plagued her. She looked peaceful and so damned beautiful, his erection rose and pressed with urgent intent against his zipper. Accustomed to the intense desire he knew would never leave, Ethan ignored his needs. About to walk silently back into the house to allow her to rest, he stopped short when he spotted her sketchbook beside her lounge chair.

Every few days, Ethan faxed sketches to LCR in the hopes that one of them would be recognized as Rosemount. Most of the sketches were only half finished. Her mind held on to the face for only a few precious seconds, barely long enough to get the full image in her brain.

Ethan picked up the sketchbook, hoping she'd been able to come up with something they could use. His heart made a hard thud against his chest on its way to his feet. Shea had indeed drawn a new image. More complete than any others. One she hadn't drawn before.

He paid little attention to the spiral binding biting into his hand as he gripped the sketchbook. His whole world was about to slam down around him. And though the expression on the face looking up from the page had no emotion or expression, he couldn't help but see a glint of accusation in the smoky blue eyes. Cole Mathison's eyes.

"Ethan?"

Jerked out of hell, he moved his gaze to Shea. "You drew a new picture."

She looked at the sketchbook and grimaced. "Yeah. Still have no idea who he is. Just another face that flashed through my mind. For some reason, this one was easier to draw than the others." Her eyes widened. "Do you think it's Rosemount?"

"What? No . . . I . . ."

Shea watched his throat work as he swallowed. A powerful emotion seemed to be working inside him. The cool green of his eyes had turned dark.

"What's wrong?"

The sketchbook dropped from his hand. In the next instant, Ethan pulled Shea from her chair and into his arms. Before she could protest or agree, his mouth was on hers.

With a moan, Shea wrapped her arms around Ethan's shoulders, pressed her body against his, and returned the kiss with all the fervor that had been building up inside her for weeks. Since that day he'd kissed her, she dreamed about kissing him again. Had been so afraid it would never happen. She felt as though she'd been waiting for this forever.

At her response, Ethan moaned against her mouth and deepened the kiss. Shea opened up, allowing his tongue to surge inside, slide, then tangle with hers. His taste was wonderful . . . coffee and Ethan. Desire swirled, then whipped through her, heating her blood and causing a hot, welcoming moisture to pool between her legs. Feelings she recognized as want and need made her pull away slightly. The deliciousness of the moment was something she wanted to savor.

"Shea?"

Ethan's eyes glinted with desire. Was she ready for this? After all she'd been through, could they make love without horrific memories hounding her? The answer came with an immediate and resounding *yes*. Perhaps if it were anyone but Ethan, she couldn't. But this was the man she'd once loved . . . the man she was falling in love with again. A sense of rightness blended wit. lesire. She wanted Ethan to make love to her.

"Shea, please . . . don't look at me like that. I didn't mean to scare you."

"I'm not scared, Ethan. For the first time in forever, I finally feel alive."

His thumb came up and gently wiped the moisture from her mouth. Shea's tongue peeked out and licked. A harsh, tortured groan came from deep inside Ethan. Shea opened her mouth, closed her lips around his thumb, and suckled.

"Shea." His body pressed against her and she felt his rigid arousal.

As she suckled his thumb, showing him what she'd liked to do to the hard, throbbing organ pressed against her, Shea pushed against Ethan, opening her legs, and shifted till her mound fit against him just so. Her eyes fluttered closed as the mounting desire spiraled toward an ecstasy she could only imagine.

Ethan pulled his thumb from her mouth and cupped her bottom with his big hands. Eyes open, she watched his face as he pressed deeper. With each hard rub, tension built between her legs, inside the depths of her sex. She was going to climax, and Ethan's fiercely intent expression told her it was what he intended, what he wanted. As she breathed out a groaning sigh, her eyes slid closed again.

"Open your eyes, baby. I want you looking at me when you come."

Eyes wide open, Shea kept her gaze locked with Ethan's as a glorious, pulse-pounding tension developed, winding tighter and tighter, stoking a hot glow of fierce need. The pleasure . . . so great, so profound, it was hard to fathom the exquisite intensity. At the edge, just when she was sure she would soon scream with the mounting need to just let go, climax slammed through her. Her breath hitching, Shea bit her lip and rode the hard ridge of his erection till the final surge of explosion, breathless pants, and small whimpers of need blended with nature. Ethan continued to watch her, his eyes glinting with something hot and wild, a fierce satisfaction etched on his taut face.

When the last orgasmic throb pulsed through her, she slowly released the grip on his shoulders. His erection was steel hard, but she already recognized denial in his face. He'd given her the release, but had no plan to take it further.

She drew in a shaky but determined breath. "Make love to me, Ethan."

Pressing a soft kiss against her nose, then her mouth, he whispered against her lips, "No. That was for you."

"And I'm not allowed to give back?"

He blew out a ragged sigh. "I can't deny that I want you, but—"

"But what? Do you think I'm looking for some kind of commitment from you?"

Ethan pulled away. Before Shea could protest, he dropped into a cushioned chair and pulled her into his arms. Shea sank into his embrace, loving this new intimacy, wanting with all her heart for it to go further.

"You've been through hell, sweetheart. Still recovering. I don't want to do anything that's going to hurt your progress."

She lay in his arms, quietly contemplating his words. She didn't doubt that he wanted her. The hard throb of his erection pressed against her hip like a hot iron poker, clear evidence of his desire. And despite his denial weeks ago, he cared deeply for her. But something held him back.

Allowing him to use the excuse of her recovery wasn't easy. She knew she was ready. Now she just needed to determine why Ethan wasn't.

"Okay, I'll wait." She pressed a kiss to his mouth. "But when I tell you I'm ready, no arguing. No overthinking or worrying. I'm not looking toward the future, just the here and now. Okay?"

The words were meant to reassure him that she expected nothing more from him. That the here and now was all that counted. So why did Ethan's expression remain haunted and agonized?

eighteen

Ethan threw the covers off and stared up at the ceiling. No sleeping tonight. After that interlude with Shea, he couldn't think of anything else other than the need to go into her room and finish what they had started. How he wanted her. And she'd been willing. That was the amazing part. After the hell she'd been through, after what he'd said to her, he'd feared that she'd never be able to abide his touch. But she'd been warmly responsive. More than that . . . she'd practically exploded in his arms.

He hadn't been able to take it further, though. Seeing Cole's face. Knowing that at any moment she would remember . . . how was he going to explain why he hadn't told her? A lame excuse that the doctor thought it was best wasn't going to fly with her. She would know better.

Keeping the truth from her no longer made sense. Shea was well on her way to recovery. Her memories were returning on their own. Her health had improved tremendously in the last few of weeks. Hell, she'd endured remembering her childhood with more strength and courage than he'd thought possible. Shea was a strong woman. She could handle hearing about Cole.

So why the hell hadn't he told her? She would hate him again, yes. But that wasn't the number one reason. If he told her . . . if she realized everything he'd done . . . she would try to leave. He knew she would leave anyway at some point, but only after Rosemount was captured. Having her leave before that was something he couldn't allow. So until Rosemount was captured or she remembered, she would stay here and she would be safe. No matter what he had to go through. No matter how much she hated him when this was all over. She had to stay safe. He had made too many mistakes already. Risking Shea's life was one mistake he would not make.

His eyes closed against regrets. How could one man screw up so many lives? With that thought heavy on his mind, sleep, at last, claimed him. And then, with the stealth of a lightning bolt and the ferocity of a hurricane, his past roared toward him.

Warm wet liquid poured down his face, blurred his vision. His limbs were weak and shaking; he raised his hand to wipe at his eyes. A glance down at his fingers revealed the name of the liquid. Blood. God . . . blood everywhere. What had happened?

"Ethan!" Abby's soft, sobbing voice had him jerking his head around. Pain speared . . . shot through his neck. What the hell . . . ?

He closed his eyes. Had to get his bearings. Once he knew what had happened, he could figure out the rest. With unconsciousness a sliver away, Abby's voice penetrated the dark.

"Ethan, help me . . ."

He jerked awake. "Where are you?"

"I don't know." Another sob. "I can't move."

The desperation and fear in her voice forced him from unconsciousness. Ignoring the pain roaring through him, he pushed to sit up. Wiping more blood from his eyes, he looked around. Though it was dark, the full moon glowed down on him, allowing him to see the distant shadow of hills surrounding him. What was he doing outside?

Still unable to comprehend what had happened, he

pulled himself to his knees. Abby's soft sobs led him toward her. Crawling toward the sounds, he barely felt the sticks and rocks digging into his skin.

"Ethan . . . help me."

"I'm coming. Hold on."

Finally on his feet, he wobbled briefly. Gritting his teeth against the hideous pain in his left leg, he hobbled toward Abby's cries. At the sight that met his eyes, he stopped, almost tumbling over. An anguished scream built up in his chest. Stumbling, then falling, he crawled forward.

His car was upside down. How it got there, what had happened, was a mystery. That could be answered later. Nothing compared to the horror of seeing that the car lay on top of Abby. Her head and shoulders were the only parts of her body he could see. The rest of her was covered in steel and rubber.

"Sweet Jesus, Abby."

Another soft sob, this one fainter. "I'm scared, Ethan."

He got to his feet and hobbled around the perimeter of the car, his dread increasing with every second. Though it was a small sports car, he wasn't strong enough to lift it. What if she went into shock? What if she had internal injuries and lifting the car off her without medical help killed her? God, he couldn't let that happen.

"I need to go get some help. I'll be right back."

"No! Don't leave me. I'm scared."

Going to his knees, he brushed honey-blond strands from her forehead. Her skin was ice-cold. "I've got to find some help. I can't find my phone. You need an ambulance, and I can't lift the car by myself."

"Maybe someone saw us go off the road."

Memory finally slammed into his head. He'd been

going too fast. A deer ran out in front of them. He'd swerved to avoid it, lost control, and soared off a hill.

"It's early morning, hours till daylight. I've got to find help now."

"Please don't leave me, Ethan. I'm so scared."

Tears poured from his eyes, blending with his blood. He swallowed a sob. "I promise, I'll be right back." After pressing soft kisses to her forehead, her tear-damp cheeks, then her mouth, he stood. "Hang on, Abby. Please. I'll be right back."

Panic and fear overrode pain; he clawed and crawled up the hill. Abby's soft cries followed him, begging, pleading for him to come back to her, growing weaker and weaker . . .

Ethan jerked awake. His hand went to his wet face. No blood, but the tears were real. After fifteen years, he should be used to the nightmares, but as usual, when they came, the memory and agony were just as fresh as if it had happened yesterday. At least he hadn't dreamed the most agonizing moment. The memory of finally bringing help for Abby only to find her cold, lifeless body.

"Ethan?"

He jerked again, surprised to see Shea standing beside his bed. When had he become so complacent that he no longer heard people while he slept? The thought chilled him. In his early days of prison, he'd learned a painful lesson. Awake or asleep, always be on guard.

Light from the hallway reflected the concern on her face. "Are you okay? I heard you shout."

"I'm fine. . . . Sorry I woke you."

Instead of leaving, as he hoped she would, she drew closer. "Did you have a nightmare?"

Ethan sat up and leaned against the headboard. "Yeah, something like that."

"Do you want to talk about it?"

Always his question to her when she had a nightmare.

"No."

She sat on the edge of the bed, her soft hand covering the fist he hadn't realized was clenched. "It helps to talk about it."

He shook his head. "I don't deserve any help. Go back to bed."

"Why not?"

A middle-of-the-night discussion of his past sins wasn't Ethan's idea of a good time. Regrets talked about could never demolish the sins. There was no point.

He flinched as a tentative finger traced the slash of scar from his left brow, past the stubble on his chin, and followed it under his neck. "Is this one of the things you have nightmares about?"

A ragged breath shuddered through him. "Not the injury. How it happened . . . yes."

"What did happen?"

"Car wreck."

"It was a serious accident."

"Yes."

"You lost someone."

He jerked at her perception.

"I'm sorry," she whispered.

Without meaning to speak, Ethan heard himself say, "I was a kid, thought I had the world by its tail. Turned out, the world caught me by the balls and held on tight."

He stopped. Hell, what was he doing?

"Tell me," Shea's soft voice urged.

He shook his head. "No, it's not something I—"

Soft hands cupped his face. "You can."

Ethan stared into the beautiful, luminous face, the purity and caring in her eyes a mockery to his doubt. Did Shea not knowing change anything? What was the point of keeping it from her any longer? Once she found out all he'd kept from her, any good thoughts she had about him would be completely destroyed anyway. Besides, hadn't he owed her the truth for years?

Releasing another ragged breath, he said, "I'd just started my sophomore year in college. Abby was two years behind me, still in high school. I was playing football on a full scholarship at the University of Texas. We had it all planned. After I graduated, I was sure to get a pro offer. Once Abby finished up college, we'd get married. We were young. Our families wealthy beyond most people's dreams. Both of us had everything given to us before we even wanted it. I was arrogant, thought I was so damned smart. So damned untouchable. Turns out, no matter what kind of plans you make, if fate wants to fuck you, there's not a damn thing you can do."

He shook his head, disgusted with himself. "Ah hell, it wasn't fate—it was me. Totally my fault. We were coming back from a party. I'd only had a few beers, thought I was okay to drive. The road was wet. I was going too fast. A deer ran out in front of me. I swerved, missed the deer, and went off a hillside." He took a breath. "Abby died."

"What about you?"

"Me? Hell, I was fine. Messed up my leg, lost my scholarship, but that didn't matter."

"And this?" She touched his scar again.

He snorted. "My mother was all for getting it fixed. Said it'd make it easier to forget." His harsh and humorless laugh bounced across the room. "Like I was going to forget that I'd killed Abby."

"So you kept the scar as punishment?"

"State of Texas took care of that."

"What do you mean?"

"Went to prison for involuntary manslaughter."

"For how long?"

"For taking Abby's life? Not long enough."

"You punish yourself still."

He shrugged. The truth was the truth. "Abby's dead; I'm alive."

"What about your parents?"

"What about them?"

"Couldn't they help—"

With the memory of his mother and father's cold, accusing expressions still as clear today as it had been fifteen years ago, bitterness and resentment boiled through him. "Do you mean, couldn't they keep me out of prison? They tried their damnedest."

"You wouldn't let them, would you?"

"How'd you know?"

"Because you wanted . . . needed to be punished. If they'd kept you out of prison, that would have made you feel as though you hadn't paid for it."

Shea understood him well, maybe too well.

"Was prison hard for you?"

He snorted. "A rich kid who knew nothing about hardships? They made sure I learned the rules fast."

"They?"

"Lifers."

Shea shook her head in denial. "How is that possible? You were just a kid. Why would they put you with hardened criminals?"

"Abby's parents. She was their only child. . . . They hated me almost as much as I hated myself. Were determined I was going to pay for their loss. Her father had political connections and deep pockets. Instead of going to a Texas prison, I got shipped out of state. A prison in Mississippi."

"If your parents were wealthy, didn't they have connections, too?"

"Didn't matter. By that time, they'd washed their hands of me. My father had decided I needed to learn a lesson." His laugh reflected his mood, hollow and grim. "They got what they wanted and then some."

He heard her swallow hard. She didn't ask . . . couldn't say the words. He said them for her. "First week in, I was attacked. Two of them grabbed me outside the laundry room."

Her hand gripped his arm. "Oh, Ethan, I'm sorry." The thickness of her voice told him she held back tears.

Her compassion astounded him. "You've been through worse, Shea."

"I never realized how you might understand what I'd gone through, but you do, don't you?"

"Some. At least the next time it happened, I had help."

"What do you mean?"

"A couple of weeks later, the same guys came into my cell. I was still this too stupid, wet-behind-the-ears kid, an easy mark. I knew I should be punished for what had happened to Abby. But deep down, I kept hoping my parents would burst through the door and save me. Turned out, I was saved, but not by my parents. Noah stopped them."

She gasped. "Noah?"

"Yeah, he'd been there a while longer than me. Beat the hell out of both of them. I never did ask him how he happened to be out of his cell. It's not something we ever talked about after that night."

"What happened after that?"

"I got put in the infirmary. Noah got time added to his sentence."

"For saving you?"

Ethan shrugged. "In that particular prison, it was kind of an accepted practice. Lots of guys were broken in that way, especially the young, clueless ones. A sort of a welcome to hell. Guys who interfered got worse punishment. By that time, Noah had a reputation. He was too tough for anyone to go up against him. COs had it out for him, though. They made sure he paid."

"So that's how you met. . . . Did LCR already exist?"

"Only in Noah's mind. He told me what he wanted to do. Said he planned to implement it as soon as he got out. To call him if I was interested."

"And you did?"

The exhilaration and relief of freedom that had zoomed through him that day was a feeling he'd never forget. "The day I found out about my parole, I called him. When I walked out the doors, he was waiting for me."

"And you've worked for him ever since?"

"No, I stopped working for LCR last year."

She drew back and frowned her confusion. "But you rescued me."

"You were a special case. Noah knew I'd do anything to save you."

"Why, Ethan?"

Needing distance from all he'd shared, Ethan got up from the bed. At the window, unable to face her too-perceptive gaze, he said, "I owed you."

"For what?"

"We were very close at one time."

"I know we were lovers. But we had broken up. Why would—"

"We were more than that . . . we were partners. We shared everything."

"Even what you just told me?"

"No, I've never been able to talk to you about that."

"Why not?"

"Shame, mostly."

He heard her come up behind him. She placed a tentative hand on his arm and asked, "Why shame?"

He stared down at her, surprised she even had to ask. "Hell, Shea, you overcame so many things in your life. Abuse, neglect. You triumphed. I had everything given to me and threw it away."

Even in the dim light, he could see the fire spitting from her eyes. "That's a load of crap. You could've gotten out of prison and resumed your life, but you didn't. You triumphed, too—you just won't give yourself credit for it."

"I couldn't have gone back to my old life. No one in my family will even acknowledge my existence."

"Maybe not, but how many people get out of prison and risk their lives to save others?"

"I enjoyed it."

"That doesn't mean you haven't done a lot of good."

"Maybe."

"Why did you leave LCR?"

"Screwed up an op."

"What happened?"

"My temper got out of control. Took out some people instead of bringing them in. . . . Noah wasn't happy with how I was handling myself. Thought I needed to be reeled in."

"You stopped caring."

"How'd you know?"

"Because I know you, Ethan. Maybe I don't remember us . . . but I know you now."

When she reached up to touch his face, Ethan jerked away and forced a deliberate harshness to his voice. "You don't know me, Shea. You don't even remember me. What you know is what I've told you. Big difference."

Her slender body stiff with hurt, she backed away. "Believe what you like. No matter what I say, you will anyway." She turned and stalked out of the room.

Everything within him wanted to call her back. Once again, he'd hurt her. If she had stayed, if he'd taken the comfort she offered, he'd have hurt her a hell of a lot more.

nineteen

"Ethan!"

He was on his feet and out of his bedroom before Shea's scream ended. Shoving open her bedroom door, Ethan halted at the foot of the bed. Shea was sitting up in bed, her hands over her face as her body shivered uncontrollably.

"Shea?"

When she didn't respond, he grabbed her shoulders and shook her gently. "Tell me, sweetheart."

Her hands dropped, and Ethan was stunned. The tears running down her face weren't unexpected. What shocked him was the joy in her expression. *What the hell?*

"He didn't rape me," she said.

His pounding heart almost skidded to a stop. "What? Who?"

"Rosemount didn't rape me. I thought he did because I kept seeing myself naked with him. But he never once touched me in that way."

"You're sure?"

Emerald eyes gleaming with tears of happiness, she nodded. "Absolutely."

"How do you know for sure? Have your memories come back?"

She shook her head. "No. This was a nightmare . . . like the others. Only this time, after I took my clothes off, I realized what he wanted. And I knew this was something he did over and over again. It wasn't sex he was looking for . . . I was more of a companion." A slight shudder went through her. "A pet. He called me *gatita* . . . kitten. He dressed me in pretty clothes, brushed my hair, talked to me, even sang to me . . . but when he touched me, it was more of a stroke of affection. There was nothing sexual about it." Her eyes grew wide with wonder. "My God, I can't believe this. He really didn't rape me."

His adrenaline-charged body was finally catching up with the excitement of the moment. Though it didn't negate the horror Shea had gone through with the bastard, to know she hadn't suffered the degradation of rape was definitely something to celebrate. Ethan eased onto the bed to sit beside her. "Can you remember anything else?"

She swallowed hard and let out a shuddering breath of air. "I remember being on my stomach and feeling the needle go into me." She looked up at him, her eyes suddenly vulnerable again. "If he had tried to rape me, I wouldn't have stopped him. I only wanted to be what he wanted me to be."

Ethan brushed a damp strand of hair from her face. "That was the drug, Shea . . . not you. Thank God he didn't want that."

As if she hadn't heard him, she said, "I wanted to just float away. Let everything go." She shook her head. "I didn't want to be me . . . didn't want an identity. Pleasing him was my only priority . . . my only thought."

"That didn't happen."

She drew in a shuddering breath. "You're right. He didn't rape me—that's the most important part."

"Do you remember anything else?"

She straightened her shoulders, her eyes becoming unfocused as she remembered. "I remember him drugging me. I think this was right after he captured me. When I came off the drugs, the torture began. I was hung up by my feet, totally naked. Soldiers would take turns hosing me down with hot and cold water. Then they would cut me down and leave me there, overnight. Flies and mosquitoes would swarm me. At daylight, they would start all over again."

She gave a tiny sob and added, "Once, they put me into a cage filled with raw sewage and threw food at me. My wrists were tied most of the time and my hands were so numb I couldn't catch any food before it fell to the ground. I was starving, but I couldn't make myself eat sewage."

Shea's image blurred as tears filled Ethan's eyes. What this beautiful, gutsy woman had gone through might destroy an average person. There was nothing average about Shea Monroe. Wrapping his arms around her, Ethan held her close and thanked God for the courageous woman in his arms.

Pulling away from him, she settled onto her pillow. Her expression a mixture of vulnerability and strength, she whispered, "Tell me something."

He smiled at the request. What had once been "Tell me something good" had progressed into "Tell me something." She wanted to know more than just the good things. Tonight, he would make sure she heard only good things.

"One time, about a year after we started working together, we were assigned a case involving a little boy. He'd been kidnapped for ransom. The money was claimed, but the kid wasn't returned. We got called in, as usual, as the last resort."

A small smile played around her mouth. "I hope this has a good ending."

Braced on his forearm, he brushed fiery strands of hair from her forehead. "The best possible ending. After some careful interrogation, where you, by the way, were the lead interrogator, we discovered that the grandfather had set it all up. Not only was he going to keep the ransom, he also had a huge insurance policy on his grandson."

She gasped. "That's terrible."

"True. But you coerced it out of him. You don't remember this yet, but you were one of the best interrogators LCR had. Few people ever escaped from you without spilling their guts."

"Really. Why?"

"You're hard as hell to lie to."

Her mouth curved into a slight smile. "You sound like you've tried before."

Damned if he wanted to get into that tonight. "Once you got the truth out of the old man, you and me and . . . some others went in and rescued the boys."

Her eyes brightened. "Really?"

"If it wasn't for you, that kid would've died. You were the only one who believed it was an inside job, and you pursued it to the end."

"So, I really have done some good things?"

"Sweetheart, you've done a lot of good things. More than most people accomplish in a lifetime."

"I'm glad . . . I wish I could remember them."

"You will. But until then, just ask me. I'll tell you how remarkable you are."

Gifting him with a smile he felt to his soul, she whispered, "Give me another memory?"

"Anything."

"Show me how it was between us."

His heart hitched. All his blood headed south. "What do you mean?"

"Show me how we were together. Let me see how good it was."

"Shea . . . I can't."

"I told you I'm not looking for promises. But I need this . . . I need you."

His mouth went dry. How in the hell could he say no when he wanted her more than he wanted his next breath? "What do you want?"

"Touch me. Let me touch you."

A lump of apprehension clogged his throat. Ethan swallowed hard and said, "Close your eyes."

She obediently closed her eyes.

He covered her mouth with his and pressed a soft, gentle kiss against her lips. A soft, surprised gasp escaped, which he joyfully swallowed. His lips feathered over hers, softly nipping and nibbling. With a groan of need, of surrender, Shea opened her mouth and Ethan delved deep, his tongue plunging and retreating. God, her taste . . . he'd never forgotten how delicious she was. He thrust deeper and then pulled back abruptly, afraid he was going too fast.

Panting slightly, she abruptly opened her eyes. "Why'd you stop?"

"I don't want to scare you."

She shook her head. "Ethan, there's nothing you can do to scare me. Don't you know you're the only one I trust not to hurt me?"

Guilt sliced through him, slashing at his already scarred soul. Not hurt her? That's all he'd ever done. He lowered his head again, afraid she'd read the truth in his eyes. Know him for the liar he was. Determined to give her pleasure, show her how beautiful and special she was, he traced her elegant jawline with his mouth and whispered soft kisses over her cheek, up to her delicate ear. "We used to make love for hours. Sometimes, we'd come in from a job and not even get our clothes off before I was inside you."

Her voice, soft with wonder, floated over him. "I can

almost feel you . . . almost remember what it felt like. Your heat . . . your mouth all over me."

Swallowing a groan at his memories, Ethan switched off his conscience, and went with the consuming desire that was always just a caress away when he was with Shea. "You were always ravenous after a job. We'd make love, then raid the kitchen." His mouth kicked up in memory. "Our kitchen table saw as much action as the bedroom."

"I remembered one of those times . . . how you felt inside me. It was wonderful. I felt powerful, invincible."

Fighting the need to rip her clothes off and show her just how good it had been, he held himself as still as possible. This was for Shea. His hands ached with the need to feel the familiar firm roundness of her breasts, the creamy texture of her skin, the goose bumps she used to get when he touched her in a certain way. He slid his hand up her top, the silky satin of her skin created a pulse-pounding pressure in his groin. "Your breasts . . . ah, baby, your breasts could make a saint come." His hand closed around a sweet mound. "Your right breast is your more sensitive one . . . did you know that?"

An inarticulate sound escaped as she shook her head.

"I don't know how many times I'd squeeze you, right here." He demonstrated by taking her nipple between his thumb and forefinger. "Then I'd slide inside you . . . you'd come almost immediately."

"Oh, Ethan . . . yes. Again. Squeeze me again, just like that."

Ethan felt the tension inside her building, body tight, already close to climax, her back arched as she thrust forward. As one hand continued to squeeze the nipple tighter, loosen, and squeeze again, his other hand slid between her legs and pressed hard, right at the top of her sex. Jewel-bright eyes flew open as she arched higher off the bed and released a keening cry as climax engulfed her.

Within seconds of his own explosion, Ethan reluctantly let go of her breast, but allowed his fingers the delight of skimming down her torso one last time as he withdrew. With a regretful sigh, he turned away.

A soft hand grabbed his arm. "Wait. Where are you going?"

"Back to my room."

"Why?"

"If I stay, I won't be able to stop."

"I don't want you to stop. I need this, Ethan. I need you . . . inside me. I feel like I've been waiting for this since I saw you again. I may not remember what we had, but I know, at this moment, that I've never wanted anyone the way I want you."

At those words, need overwhelmed, then consumed all his good intentions. Denying himself, denying Shea had just ended. With a growl, Ethan scooped Shea from the bed and stalked to the door.

"Where are we going?"

"My room."

"Why?"

Barely able to concentrate on walking, much less speak, he muttered, "Condoms."

With a soft moan of approval, Shea wrapped silken arms around his neck and pressed soft, sweet kisses to his chin and jaw. When her small teeth nibbled at his neck, it took every bit of his determination to continue to his room instead of laying her in the middle of the hallway and giving them both what they needed.

Finally reaching his room, he dropped Shea on the bed and moved over her immediately. Unable to speak for the emotions surging inside him, Ethan smothered his groan of need by covering her mouth with his. His tongue forged through, thrust deep, dancing, retreating, thrusting again . . . tasting, devouring, and giving all he had to give.

All the while, Shea's soft hands were busy caressing him. When her hand wrapped around his engorged erection, he almost came in her palm. It'd been so long, and Shea was the only woman who'd ever made him feel that he'd die if he didn't get inside her.

Backing away slightly, he gazed down at her. "You're sure?"

"More sure than I've been about anything since you rescued me."

He was a man, not a saint. A very flawed man who wanted, needed, and desired this woman above anything else. Sitting up, he pulled his T-shirt over his head. His pajama bottoms followed.

Shea lay there, watching. Her eyes held only a dark hunger. No fear. No hesitancy. She wanted him.

Ethan took a breath to slow down. This was like the first time with her . . . the first time she would remember. He wanted it to be perfect, beautiful. As beautiful as she was to him.

At the first touch of his hand on her breast, a smile of delight curved her delicate mouth. She seemed to recognize the difference in his touch. Heat and desire had led them here. Love and possession took over.

His hands glided under her pajama top, leaving her silky skin bared. Needing to taste her sweetness, he lowered his head and licked a nipple. Her gasp of pleasure urged him on. Closing his mouth around the hardened peak, he sucked. Her moans and groans let him know she loved what he was doing, wanted more.

He lifted his head, breathed against her skin. "Once . . . I sucked so hard, you climaxed."

"I can believe it . . . having your mouth on me . . ." She closed her eyes and shook her head. "When you suck on me, I can feel the sensation all through my body."

"What does it make you want to do?"

"It makes me hot . . . burning . . . makes me want to open my legs and—"

His mouth lowered, covered the sweet mound again, and sucked hard, then pulled back slightly. "What, baby? What does it make you want?"

"To feel you hard and hot . . . inside me . . . throbbing. Riding me."

"That's what I want, too . . . but first—" Grasping the bottom of her pajamas, he slid them down long, luscious legs. When he saw what awaited him, he stopped and almost exploded with rage. She was nude. None of the auburn curls he remembered protected her mound. Rosemount had permanently removed her hair.

"Is something wrong?"

Her voice, vulnerable and uncertain, grounded him. This was Shea . . . his Shea. No matter what that bastard had done, no one could touch or spoil her real beauty. He pressed a kiss to the flat surface of her creamy stomach. "I'd forgotten how beautiful you were."

His words, meant to reassure, aroused her instead. Her legs opened and the pink, moist flesh of her sex peeked out at him. Unable to wait another minute, Ethan lowered his head and licked, then groaned against her skin—her taste was as sweet as he remembered. Soft moans driving his own need, he kneeled between her legs, raised them over his shoulders, and devoured.

Sweet heavens, the pleasure. Shea grabbed at his head and arched up to meet his mouth . . . his tongue delved . . . went deep and then retreated. She screamed at the throbbing, urging him on. Wanting it to end . . . never wanting it to end. He plunged and she surged upward again. His hands grabbed her breasts . . . squeezed hard. Oh . . . the pressure at her nipples. She loved it.

Riding his tongue, she screamed Ethan's name as her world exploded into an oblivion of soft, velvet pleasure.

She barely registered that Ethan covered himself with a condom before he surged into her. Gasping at the incredible fullness, Shea wrapped her legs around his waist, certain she was too exhausted to do anything more than hold on and revel in his release. She was wrong. The hunger reemerged and sweet pleasure followed, softer and slower but just as lovely as before. Glorious heat flooded her from head to toe and then settled deep in her core, where mind-blowing pleasure bloomed. Grasping his shoulders, burying her face against his chest, she felt the surge and retreat of his powerful thrust throw her straight into an orgasm so explosive, more screams emerged before she could stop them.

And at last, when his release was upon him, shuddering through his big body, Shea held him tight and gloried in his satisfaction, his groans of release. The pulsing throb of his shaft inside her gave a different pleasure . . . one of deep contentment. This was Ethan. Her man. Her hero. Her rescuer. Her life.

As the last shock wave rippled through his body, Shea pressed tiny kisses to his hard chest, rubbing her face against the golden mat of hair, loving the sensation of roughness against her skin. Her mouth skimmed up to his broad shoulders, his neck, his chin, everywhere she could reach. When he shifted to pull away, the drag of his shaft against swollen, sensitive flesh caused another contraction, deep inside. Moaning, she arched forward, wanting to recapture the wonderful feelings she'd just experienced.

"I'm too heavy for you, Shea."

The growling gruffness of his voice swept over her, causing her muscles to contract and clasp down on his retreating penis. He gave one last involuntary stroke, then pulled away, dropped the used condom on the floor, and settled beside her. Then, before she could speak, he hauled her over him. The second her legs straddled his hips, he thrust, surging deep again. "I won't come again for a while. Ride as long as you want."

A half giggle, half moan emerged at the incredibly graphic and erotic invitation, but she wasn't going to argue. The wonderful intimacy they were sharing felt natural and beautiful. The explicit words they'd both uttered were a testament to their previous relationship. Shea felt as though there was nothing she couldn't tell him.

Needing to see his face, she put her knees on the bed and pushed herself to sit up. The erection that had been only a semihard arousal stiffened and plunged even deeper. Shea gasped at the steel-hard intrusion. Biting her lip, she held off the increasing need to take him up on his invitation. A part of her wanted a wild, fast ride so that the glorious release she'd just experienced would shoot her to oblivion again. Soon, but not yet.

Shea gazed down at Ethan. Her new lover, her former lover. His eyes glinted with arousal, desire, and a deep satisfaction. The beautiful mouth, often so stern and grim, which had only moments ago given her mind-blowing pleasure, curved slightly. She traced the curve of his smile with a finger. "Was it always like this for us?"

A shadow flickered, then disappeared. "Yes and no. It was always hot and passionate, sometimes wild. But this is better."

Hands pressed on his shoulders for balance, she allowed herself one small movement and gasped at the throbbing response deep inside. Her eyes fluttered closed for half a second, and then she asked, "How is it better?"

A grimace of pleasure crossed his face. "It just is."

Before she could pursue the question further, hard,

calloused hands covered her breasts. She gasped and shifted, pressing down, as he surged deeper. Shea forgot everything but the buildup of intense pleasure spiraling through her. When his fingers pulled on her nipples and then pinched tightly, her mind dissolved, went blank. Unable to ignore the need any longer, she began a wild ride, her inner muscles grasping and pulling at his shaft. Sparkling electricity flashed, fire ignited, and a wildness she had never anticipated shot through her. Gasping, crying, and then with a final, keening cry that was his name, Shea exploded.

Shuddering from the aftermath of an unbelievable fury of intense satisfaction, she opened her eyes. Ethan's green eyes were dark and glinting with fire and need. A flush high on his cheekbones and the way he held his breath told her he was within seconds of losing control. And in that instant, she knew that's exactly what she wanted. She wanted that iron control shattered, the grim stoicism he shielded himself with obliterated. A small part of her questioned her sanity. If Ethan truly let go of that control, could she handle it? Was she prepared for the consequences? An inner voice, one she had only recently acknowledged as part of her, answered yes. Every part of Ethan—his fiery temper, his hard, grim exterior, and his passionate nature—held an answering and compatible response from her. Ethan and Shea, a match in every way, equals in strength. Two parts of a whole.

Leaning down, his penis so hard and hot inside her, she knew explosion would take only seconds. With a tender sweep of her lips against his grim mouth, she whispered, "Give it to me, Ethan. Hard and deep."

A growl that began deep inside him emerged. His breath coming in restrained gasps, he rolled Shea onto her back, spread her wide, pushing her legs over her head, and plunged. Carnal, erotic, and coarse words were muttered in between the fast and furious plunge and retreat. Then with a low, feral groan, Ethan jerked out of her and spilled himself onto the sheet.

His breath soughing out of his body, he collapsed on top of her. Shea lowered her legs, wrapped her arms around his shoulders, and held him close, needing to show him that he was safe with her. He could let go, be himself, and she would always want him. She didn't know why she felt the need to communicate this to him, why it was so important. Recognition that this reassurance was what he needed? Or was it from long ago? An elusive memory that she hadn't been able to give him this promise before?

Ethan claimed he'd broken her heart. Why did she somehow suddenly suspect that she had really been the one to break his?

twenty

Ixtapa, Mexico

Gripping the hot steel bars, he ignored the blistering pain in his hands as his glazed eyes squinted at the setting sun. Flies and mosquitoes swarmed around him, their bites and stings inconsequential irritants. Sweat poured down his naked back, giving him the only relief from the searing heat. Three hours a day, they rolled his cage out of the lab for sunshine and fresh air. Soldiers, doctors, and strangers passed by him as if he wasn't there. As if he possessed no existence, no soul.

When he'd been lying in bed for days, drifting between a drug-induced haze and horrific comprehension, he'd thought he knew hell. He'd soon learned different.

He'd come close to death. The searing pain in his lungs had almost smothered him. The bastard doctor treating him had explained that the drugs he'd been given had weakened his immune system as well as rendering the antibiotics useless. They'd stopped drugging him long enough to get him well. And in place of the drugs, nightmares and vague, shadowed memories had emerged. Not enough to give him the information he sought. Just enough to torture. Just enough to have him screaming in agony.

And all the while, the fury built.

The doctors and scientists discussed him as if he were an inanimate object. As if he had no thoughts, no feelings, no humanity. Once he was well enough, the drugging began again. Since they believed he was nothing but a lump of something they could mold into whatever they so chose, they spoke freely in front of him. A blessing, really. They believed that, caged as he was, like a zoo animal, he posed no threat. Therefore, the drugs he'd been given were even less than before. He had several long moments of sanity before his evening injection. Not enough to remember anything of significance but sufficient for him to understand the utter inhumanity of his captivity and experience a fierce, writhing hatred.

Memories before this particular existence still wouldn't come—his name or how he came to be. He saw occasional glimpses of faces or flashes of past events, heard soft, sweet voices in his mind, but he was unable to hold them long enough to grasp their meaning.

They were getting him healthy for their own selfish and evil reasons. First, he needed to be strong enough to retrieve the red-haired woman for the man he'd once called master. Jaw clenched, he ground his teeth in rage. Revulsion clawed and ripped at his insides. No man was his master, and he'd die before he'd ever utter those words again.

Once that mission was accomplished, the doctors and scientists wanted to use him as their lab rat. There was no telling what they would inject him with or what he would be expected to do for them. He was their toy, to be used until he was used up.

He planned to kill them all. No way in hell would he continue to be subjected to this torture and humiliation. He didn't know when or how it would happen, but deep inside he knew it would.

After he killed them, he had no idea what he would do. Without any idea of who he was, where could he go? Did he have a family? People who cared about him? If so, why hadn't they helped him? Was he alone in the world? It didn't matter. Once he killed the bastards, perhaps he should die, too.

Perhaps his worth was only in the number of people he could kill. He had killed many. He remembered some of them . . . soldiers. They had been evil, and he had no remorse for their deaths. But there was someone else. Where or when, he didn't know, but he remembered stark terror in pale blue eyes just before they glazed with death. He remembered harsh voices screaming at him to stop. Man or woman? He didn't know, but he or she had been a victim. Not in league with these monsters. In his gut . . . in his soul . . . he knew he had the blood of an innocent on his hands.

Yes, perhaps after he killed the bastards who tortured him, he should die as well. Murderers didn't deserve to live.

Hot sultry summer slid toward a crisp, cool autumn. Ethan had told her that if she thought the Tennessee hills were beautiful in the summer, she hadn't seen anything yet. He was right. Colors of every hue and depth covered the mountains as far as the eye could see.

She'd been here for over two months, and in that time, so much had changed. She'd remembered much of her past. Still no real recollection of her time with LCR or anything significant from her past relationship with Ethan, though. Nor did she remember many of the things that had happened with Rosemount, but she had high hopes that all her memories would return someday.

Her health had improved, and though nightmares still plagued her from time to time, many nights she slept straight through till morning. Knowing that she hadn't been raped gave her tremendous relief, but she understood that the real reason for her lessening nightmares had one name . . . Ethan. He held her close each night.

In his arms, she knew true peace. He was her lover, her rescuer, and her best friend.

"Hey, Shea, I need to run to town for supplies. Can you be ready in half an hour?"

Twisting around, she gazed up at Ethan. He had changed, too. Though often still gruff and grumbly, he no longer wore that haunted, stony expression that used to shadow his face. When they made love, he was fierce and possessive, giving her pleasure beyond belief. Out of bed, his dictatorial ways could still make her more furious than a crazed hornet. She'd stood toe to toe with him on more that one occasion. And despite the fury spitting from his eyes, a little smile always played around his mouth, as if he enjoyed the fireworks. Truth to tell, she enjoyed them, too. Fighting with Ethan beat out just about everything for pure enjoyment and stimulation, with the exception of their lovemaking.

"Why are you staring at me like that? You okay?"

Shea jerked her attention back to the glowering man in front of her, concern furrowing his brow. "I was just thinking how handsome and sexy you are."

His eyes darkening with sensual heat, his gaze slid down her body like a steaming-hot caress. A shudder of awareness swept through her as her blood heated. Last night, Ethan had been insatiable, making love to her for hours on end. Every kiss and caress had ratcheted up the tension, until she'd exploded in his arms.

"You keep looking at me like that, you're going to find yourself on your back, with your legs spread and me inside you, before you can take another breath."

Her heart pounding at the vivid picture in her mind, she whispered, "And that's a problem why?"

A man of his word, Ethan plucked Shea from her chair and had her on the floor of the deck in seconds. He stripped her jeans and panties off, and between one breath and the next, his head was between her legs, his wicked tongue dancing and thrusting inside her.

"Ethan." She'd meant it to be a scream, but it came out a sigh. Twining her fingers through his hair, legs wrapped around his shoulders, hips thrusting upward, she rode his tongue.

Her taste . . . how he loved it. Salty sweet, warm musk, and liquid sunshine, Shea's sweetness and spirit spilled onto his tongue as she throbbed and spasmed in release. He loved how she tugged on his hair, thrust against his mouth, giving herself with an openness and sensuality that continually surprised him.

Sex with her had been good before, passionate and intense. He hadn't been able to explain to her how this was better. He knew the answer, though he couldn't give it. Their lovemaking was better now because of what they'd lost. The years that had passed, the pain of their separation, and the sheer hell of their experiences had deepened and intensified their sexual response to each other. Shea might not remember, but Ethan did.

With one last glide of his tongue, Ethan pulled away and sat up. With her beautiful face flushed with desire, her eyes glittering with need and that luscious mouth moist and plump, it was all he could do not to unzip his pants and plunge deep. Gritting his teeth against temptation, he stood and held out a hand to help her up. Her gaze moving from his face to groin, she shook her head slowly, telling him she had other ideas.

"Come on, babe. I don't have any condoms with me, and I need to get to the store before it gets dark."

With a graceful, languid movement, she went to her knees before him. When her hand rubbed his cock, Ethan growled, "Don't tease me."

"Who's teasing? I'm very serious." The rasp of his zipper being pulled down caused a throb of anticipation.

"Dammit, don't."

A soft hand caressed the thin cotton underwear covering the hard flesh. Without his permission, his hips surged forward. Taking this as acquiescence, she separated the cloth and soft, slender fingers wrapped around him and tugged. The gentle breeze of fresh air lasted only a second, until hot, moist breath bathed him with soft, sweet heat as her mouth closed over him. Eyes closed tight, he surged deep, going to her throat and then retreating. Shea's little tongue swiped and licked as he withdrew. Unable to prevent himself or deny her, he surged deep again. She moaned, and the vibration of her mouth shot lightning through him, causing a small amount of release to enter her mouth. Another moan let him know she was thoroughly enjoying his taste.

Ethan gave up all attempts to stop the madness. Grasping her head with his hands, he held her as he moved back and forth. In recognition and appreciation of his surrender, the suction of her mouth tightened, pulled harder. Electricity zipped down his spine, and Ethan knew his release was imminent. He jerked out of her mouth.

Gazing up at him in confusion, she asked, "What's wrong?"

Words almost beyond him, he managed to grind between his teeth, "I'm about to come."

"I want all of you, Ethan." Her tongue swiped. "Every." A long lick. "Last." Her pink tongue swirled over the head of his cock, licked at the center. "Drop." Her mouth closed around him again.

His heart almost exploded. Surging deep, holding her head, he plunged, retreated slightly, and then plunged deeper as his release burst forth, filling her sucking, hungry mouth.

Shudders rattled through him as he pulled away to stare down at the supremely satisfied woman still kneeling before him. Her lips were softly swollen, moist with his release. It took every ounce of willpower not to pick her up, throw her over his shoulder, and carry her upstairs. There was nothing he'd like better than to spend the rest of the day and night inside that beautiful body.

He ignored his hardening shaft, tucked himself back inside his pants, and held out his hand. "Come on, minx, before I take you up on that invitation gleaming in your eyes."

Shea rose with an artless grace that was so much a part of her natural femininity. Seemingly unembarrassed by her lack of clothing, she picked up her panties and jeans. With her back to him, she stepped into them and slid them up her body with a slow, erotic little shimmy. Her expression when she turned to face him told him she'd done it for his benefit. Judging from the smile on her face and her direct glance at his obvious arousal, she was pleased with the results.

He gave her advance warning: "Don't expect to sleep any tonight."

Eyes gleaming with anticipation and promise, she said, "I'm counting on it."

"Come on, let's go to the store and get back home."

"Let me run upstairs and comb my hair. Oh, and if we have time, I want to stop at that nursery on the way back and pick up some stuff."

"Like what?"

"That area on the right side of the house that's bare . . . I want to plant some flowers there. Maybe some tulips and crocus, so in the spring, we'll have some color. And then we can find other flowers so we'll have blooms all through the summer and into the fall."

A thud of dread slammed into him. This wasn't the first time Shea had mentioned something in the future, but comparison of the color she brought to his dark life and the blooms she wanted to plant formed too vivid an image to deny. How he wished their time together didn't have to end. Every day he railed at himself. It was his fault they'd become lovers. Now she was looking toward the future as if they had one.

"Ethan, what's wrong?"

Turning away from her, he growled, "We'll see. Let's go."

"You don't like to talk about the future, do you?"

Hell, he did not want to get into an argument, especially about this. He turned back to her and dug deep for a relaxed smile. "Let's enjoy what we have now. Until Rosemount's caught, we—"

"Are you saying that's all we're waiting on, for Rosemount to be caught?"

"I'm just saying we don't need to forget the real reason you're here."

"And when he's no longer a threat, what?"

Whether he wanted the discussion or not, it was apparently going to take place. "Once he's caught, you'll want to go back to your life."

"And that life doesn't include you. Is that what you're saying?"

"To put it bluntly, no, it doesn't include me."

"And this relationship we have . . . I'm just supposed to forget about it?"

"It would be better for you if you did."

"Can you do that? Can you just forget about what we've shared?"

Unable to answer that without giving his torment away, he glanced at his watch. "We've got to get out of here. It'll be dark in a couple of hours. There's a storm coming later—I'd rather not get caught in it."

Ethan felt her physical and mental retreat as she wrapped her arms around her waist and shook her head. "You go on. I'll be fine here."

He'd never left her alone, but he recognized her need for solitude. And he needed the time as well. Seeing the hurt on her face, and knowing he'd once again put it there, cut deep into the defenses that had become almost nonexistent against Shea.

"Fine. Keep the doors locked. Call me on my cellphone if anything comes up. I'll try to hurry."

She turned away, her shoulders hunched and defensive. Cursing himself for the bastard he'd always known he was, Ethan stalked away from her. Better that Shea go ahead and hate him now. That way, when she remembered everything, her disillusionment would be less devastating. Nausea roiled. Yeah, like that would make up for everything.

twenty-one

Sheets of rain slashed and beat at the window. Lightning flashed and despite herself, Shea couldn't prevent the tensing of muscles as she prepared for the next thunderous boom. As a kid, she'd loved thunderstorms. The fury of nature often matched the bubbling anger she'd battled inside. Admiring the way Mother Nature exploded, lashing out in fury with such drama and force, Shea had often envied that ability. After the storm, the blessed peace that followed matched her longing for her own kind of peace.

The hot bath she'd taken had removed most of the chill from her bones, but she still felt like a restless spirit, searching for solidity. The argument with Ethan filled her with an aching uncertainty she hadn't felt in weeks. Though she'd assured him that she wasn't looking for a commitment, they'd grown so close and their passion was so fierce, she had allowed herself to believe in the possibility. How could he make love to her as if she were the most important thing in the universe and then tell her that nothing was permanent? Why couldn't he admit his feelings? She refused to believe he didn't have any.

Shea turned from the window and surveyed the room. Without Ethan, the house seemed empty and forlorn. She'd told him she needed time to herself, and she had, but the flicker of relief in his face had cut deep. It was obvious that he'd needed distance from her as well.

Thunder boomed with a powerful blow, and the entire house shook. Uneasy awareness swept through her. Ethan should have been home by now. The storm had most likely delayed him. She'd already tried calling his cellphone and had gotten no answer. Telling herself she was just a worrywart, Shea turned back to the window. Lightning flashed again. In the millisecond of bright light, separated only by glass, a man stood in front of her. Not Ethan.

She froze. Surely she'd been mistaken. At the next flash of lightning, he'd disappeared. She blew a relieved sigh. Just her imagination working overtime.

The lights flickered once, twice. Everything went pitch-black.

Shea dropped to her knees. She knew the house well enough to crawl to the door of Ethan's office. He'd told her if she ever felt in danger, to get to his office and close and lock the door. It was made of some kind of bullet-proof material, he'd said; only a tank could come through that door. Scampering on her hands and knees, Shea dove into the room and slammed the door shut.

The lights flickered again, and bright light flooded the room. She rushed to the closet and pulled down a gun. A .38 Smith & Wesson AirLight Ethan said belonged to her. She'd held it a few times since then and had recognized some sort of familiarity. The weapon felt comfortable in her hand.

The thunder had diminished. Now only a distant and occasional rumbling echoed through the mountains. The quiet aftermath seemed eerie and suspense-filled. Who had been standing at the window? Could Rosemount's people have found her?

"Shea?"

She jerked at the sound of Ethan's voice on the other side of the door. "Ethan?"

"Let me in."

She pulled open the door. Ethan stood in front of her, a thunderous expression on his face. A soaked and dripping Gabe Maddox stood beside him.

"Gabe owes you an apology."

"Sorry, Shea. I knocked and no one came to the door. I was looking in the window, and I guess that's when you saw me."

The aftermath of adrenaline rush left her limbs weak. Holding the gun at her side, she slumped against the wall. "The storm must have drowned out your knock."

Ethan took the hand not holding the gun and kissed it. "You okay?"

Swallowing past dryness caused by fear, she nodded. "He just startled me."

Ethan shot a glare at Gabe. "Why are you here?"

Gabe's mouth quirked up. "Mind if we go into the kitchen and get a towel before we talk? I'm soaked."

Giving him a long look, Ethan, still holding Shea's hand, headed to the kitchen.

Opening a drawer at the kitchen counter, he pulled out a towel and threw it toward Gabe. Pulling Shea with him, he sat at the table and eyed his friend with an odd sort of cautious suspicion.

Gabe swiped at his face, then surveyed the room. "Looks a lot different than it did a few months back."

Shea frowned. "What do you mean?"

Ethan shrugged, his eyes still on Gabe. "I got some new furniture before you came. Why are you here?"

With a sigh, Gabe dropped into a chair across from Ethan. "Setting a trap."

An abrupt tensing of Ethan's body told her something was up.

"Shit. You let him follow you?"

"Yeah. Had to go slow, though. Turns out he's pretty lousy at tracking."

"How much time do we have?"

"Ten minutes, a little less."

"Is he alone?"

"Yeah, he's arrogant and stupid." Gabe's mouth tilted into a small smile. "Despite Jamie's opinion, I'm neither."

Shea felt slow and uninformed, two things she hated. "Somebody want to tell me what's going on?"

"Tell her, Gabe. You're the one who set her up for bait. You explain."

Gabe lifted a shoulder in a careless shrug. "She's not in any real danger." He glanced at Shea. "We've known for some time, since the woman attacked you in the clinic, that we've had a mole at LCR. We narrowed it down to a handful of people. One in particular seemed the most likely, and if he comes through that door in the next few minutes, we'll know we were right."

Gabe's casual attitude about her life infuriated her. "So what are we going to do—see if he shoots me and then you'll know?"

"Nothing so dramatic."

"Well, then what?"

Ethan shrugged, and Shea had the urge to shoot the next man who shrugged at her as if this was no big deal. "We'll play him . . . see where he leads." Wrapping his arm around her shoulder, he growled, "He'll never have a chance to hurt you."

"You guys have done this before, haven't you?"

"A time or two. Never with an LCR operative though. Should be interesting," Ethan said.

Shea pulled away from Ethan's arm. "Your idea of interesting and mine are a bit different. I'm going to bed."

"No."

Anger flared, which felt a hell of a lot better than the fear that had been surging for the last half hour. "Excuse me?"

The chuckle he gave told her he wasn't one bit put off by her anger. "We need your help."

"How?"

"Remember I told you that you used to be one of our best interrogators? Well, here's an opportunity to sharpen your skills."

"Ethan, I don't even remember that I had those skills. How am I supposed to know—"

"They'll come back to you, just like your artistic abilities did."

Before she could snap at him for his arrogance, someone knocked on the door. With a barely perceptible nod to Gabe, Ethan stood and looked down at Shea. "Follow our lead. If he doesn't expose himself in half an hour or so, we'll set a trap. Just go along with it." He leaned down and planted a hard kiss on her lips. "You'll be fine. I promise."

Since she apparently had no choice but to play along, Shea nodded and shot a glance at Gabe. "So you trust me on this?"

Gabe had the grace to look slightly guilty. "Sorry I've given you such a hard time. I was just worried about how Ethan would—"

"We've got a skunk at the door," Ethan growled. "Why don't you let him in?"

Gabe shot Ethan a hard look before he turned and headed to the door.

"What was he talking about?"

"Nothing." He held out his hand to her. "Let's see what kind of fun we can stir up."

Before taking his hand, Shea slid her gun into her waistband at the small of her back and covered it with her shirt. Despite Ethan and Gabe's lackadaisical attitude, she would not be caught off guard. This man wanted to take her back to Rosemount? No way in hell.

Shea watched the young man enter the living room. To

say he was beautiful would be an understatement. Only angels in heaven could compete with his physical beauty. A flash of knowledge hit her. If this man was indeed working for Rosemount, Shea knew without a doubt that he could very well end up like her. She remembered enough to know that Rosemount prized physical perfection over everything else.

"Jamie, what the hell are you doing here?"

Shea had to hand it to Gabe. He looked believably shocked to see the young man.

Jamie flashed an apologetic grin. "I followed you. I knew you wouldn't want me to come, but I couldn't resist."

Ethan glared, looking thoroughly pissed. "Did anyone follow you?"

A petulant expression crossed the young man's face. "Of course not. I was careful. I heard Gabe tell Noah he was coming here, and thought I'd come along and see if I could help out."

"Help out with what?" Gabe asked.

"Whatever you might need." His gaze swung over to Shea. "We've not met. James Jenson . . . Jamie to my friends."

Something Shea didn't expect came over her. A sense of completion and rightness, as if this was something she'd done many times before. She held out her hand and smiled with a gracious ease. "It's nice to meet you, Jamie. Won't you come in?"

She felt, rather than saw, Ethan throw her a look of appreciation.

As Jamie settled himself onto the sofa, Shea said, "I was just about to make a cup of cocoa. Would you care for one?"

Eyeing Shea strangely, as if she wasn't what he'd expected, he nodded. "Sounds great."

Pride filled Ethan as he watched Shea glide out of the

room. She was acting as if she did this every day . . . and she used to. Shea was one of the best interrogators he'd ever seen. Most people were caught off guard by her delicate femininity, underestimating her steely determination to get to the truth. One of the reasons she was able to carry it off so well was because Shea acted like the person she really was. Sweet and unaffected, she had a genuine interest in people. By the time most people figured out what she was doing, they had spilled secrets and revealed information others might have had to torture from them. Shea could accomplish miracles with a smile.

"Tell me why you're really here, Jamie. Did Noah tell you to follow me?" Gabe asked.

"Of course not. But I saw how pissed you were when you left. I figured whatever was going down, you could use the help."

Gabe nodded. "Yeah, I was pissed. We got word that Rosemount could have discovered Ethan's hiding place. Noah called Ethan to warn him, but I wanted to make sure he had help if things got bad."

"Glad I came then. Sounds like you can use all the help you can get." He glanced over at Ethan and then back at Gabe. "Why do you think the location's been compromised?"

Gabe shrugged. "Been hearing some chatter back and forth for the last few days. Tennessee hills have been mentioned."

Jamie had opened his mouth to say something when Shea came back into the room. Ethan jumped up and helped her set the tray filled with mugs of hot cocoa and a plate of sugar cookies on the coffee table.

Though she wore blue jeans and a Tennessee Volunteers T-shirt, no hostess could rival her for grace and elegance as she went about distributing the snack to each person. Cool and calm, she gave no indication that the man only a few feet away from her had come to take her back to hell.

After everyone had been served, Shea gracefully sat across from Jamie and gave him the disarming smile Ethan remembered so well.

"You have a bit of the South in your speech, Jamie," Shea said.

For a brief second, confusion replaced the cocky expression on Jamie's face. Had he expected Shea to be an emotional wreck? If so, he was about to get his socks knocked off.

He recovered quickly and offered her a charming smile. "I spent summers with my grandmother in Kentucky."

"Oh, I love Kentucky. All those green hills and valleys. Did she have horses?"

"Actually, she did. That's one of the reasons I loved going to visit her."

"I haven't ridden in years." The look she cast Ethan showed only a slight flicker of surprise. "The last time was that trip to the Bahamas. Riding on the beach."

Just like that, a new memory had emerged. A cold chill, having nothing to do with the traitor in their midst, rushed through Ethan. Another reminder. If he didn't tell her soon, it was only a matter of time before she remembered on her own.

Jamie looked startled at Shea's statement. Surprised she remembered her past?

As he listened to Shea's gentle inquisition, Ethan felt the fracture in his heart widen. Shea had almost completely recovered. The woman sitting across from Jamie, leading him to the truth, without his knowledge, was the Shea he remembered. The calm, professional LCR operative.

The weight she'd gained looked good on her, the bloom in her cheeks an indication of good health. Since they'd become lovers again, she slept in his arms every night. The nightmares that had haunted her for so long had disappeared.

It was time to tell her everything. He should have done so already, but he kept telling himself she needed to be healthy before he sprang the truth on her. That was no longer an issue. Actually, it hadn't been an issue for weeks, but he had relished being with Shea again. And the longer he waited, the more difficult it would be.

There was no future for them. Ethan knew that. Knew the inevitable would happen. And that he'd never be prepared for it. But Shea deserved the truth. She deserved to know about Cole. And she needed to know about Ethan. She would be hurt and angry, would most likely leave. If this interview with Jamie was successful, they would be able to get to Rosemount. Ethan would no longer be necessary in her life.

Ethan jerked his attention back to Shea's questions, knowing he'd be needed when she finished.

"I was in foster care, too," Shea said. "That was a particularly difficult time for me. How long were you in the system?"

As Shea gently prodded Jamie, gaining his trust, identifying with his difficulties, Ethan assessed him. Though he seemed relaxed, the white-knuckled grip on the mug he held belied his confidence. The man was on edge.

Ethan had worked with Jamie in the past. He'd assigned him low-level duties, mostly because despite the man's toothpaste-ad smile, Ethan had sensed his egocentricity. LCR had no place for egos. When the most important person was the victim, operatives came in second. Jamie never seemed to be able to buy into that concept.

A couple of years ago, Jamie had been on his team. A rescue of four children from a small fake adoption center. Should have been an easy grab . . . only problem was, Jamie, in his eagerness to show off, jumped the gun and got sighted, giving the man and woman holding the kids time to arm themselves. An LCR operative had paid the price for Jamie's arrogance and ego trip.

Ethan jerked back to the present to hear Jamie begin to question Shea.

"So your memories have returned?"

Shea lifted her shoulder in a delicate shrug. "For the most part. I remember enough to be able to go back to work soon."

"That's great. I hadn't realized how far you'd progressed."

His body showing none of his tension, Ethan allowed satisfaction and pride to enter his voice. "We haven't told anyone how far along Shea's come. We anticipate that she'll be able to give us Rosemount's location within the next week or so."

"Then I guess it's a good thing I came when I did."

Shea's heart lurched as Jamie stood, drew a gun, and pointed it toward Ethan, then Gabe.

"Now, that's just damn stupid." Ethan's relaxed drawl was belied by the fury glinting in his eyes.

Jamie snorted. "Not near as stupid as you both are."

Ethan shook his head, a little smile playing around his mouth. "If you think you're going to take Shea out of here without a fight, you're not just stupid, you're crazy stupid."

"Hard to fight when you're dead."

"So you think you're just going to shoot Ethan and me?" Gabe sounded more insulted than angry.

Jamie shrugged. "I was supposed to bring Ethan, too, if I could. The amount Rosemount offered would be enough to buy my own island. Unfortunately, I'm not going to be able to do that, so I'll just settle for the small fortune he's offered for Shea. Sadly, you two won't live to come after me."

"Jamie, I hate to burst your bubble, but Rosemount has no intention of paying you," Shea said.

His gaze never wavering from Ethan and Gabe, he snarled, "That's what you'd like to think. I know better. He's paid me some of it already. All I have to do is deliver you and I'll—"

"You'll be a drugged out zombie, just like I was."

"I'm too useful to him."

Ethan's harsh chuckle sounded unusually loud. "Useful how? You can't work for LCR anymore. Your usefulness will be at an end." He flicked a glance at Gabe. "I know you told me he was stupid and arrogant, but man, he's worse than that. He's a damned fool."

"Shut up!" Jamie screamed.

In seemingly synchronized and simultaneous movements, Ethan threw himself at Jamie while Gabe grabbed a lamp from the end table and swung, knocking the gun from Jamie's hand.

Shea dropped to her knees, her gun in her hand before she'd even realized she'd grabbed it. Holding the gun steady, she watched Ethan's fist slam into Jamie's pretty face.

The front door exploded inward. Two men charged through.

"Hold your fire, Shea," Gabe shouted.

Shea lowered her gun, recognizing one of the men as an LCR operative she'd met at the clinic. Gabe's backup had been waiting for a signal to come charging in.

The sound of fists slamming into a face penetrated Shea's shock. Ethan had Jamie on the floor, behind the couch, and was beating the man to a bloodied pulp.

"Hell, Ethan," Gabe growled, pulling Ethan from Jamie's unconscious body, "you're going to kill him and we won't be able to get any information."

Chest heaving with exertion, Ethan stood and twisted his head to find Shea. "You all right?"

A deep breath shuddered through her as she nodded and stood.

His face taut with a myriad of powerful emotions, Ethan crossed the room and wrapped his arms around her. "That got a little more intense than I wanted."

With Ethan's arms around her as if he would never let her go, she watched Jamie being picked up and carried out by the two men. Gabe went to follow them, but stopped before he walked through the door. "I need to talk with both of you about something, but it can wait till morning." He grinned. "I'll be back for breakfast."

"Bastard," Ethan growled softly as Gabe sauntered out the door.

As the door clicked closed behind Gabe, Shea pulled away from Ethan's arms. He resisted at first, and then, with a sigh, let her go. Her face pale but composed, she looked a hell of a lot better than he felt.

"Do you think he knows where Rosemount is?" Shea asked.

"Hard to say. Gabe will get it from him, if he does."

"Should I try to talk to him again?"

"No, I don't want you anywhere near him."

"Shouldn't that be my decision?"

Ethan blew out a ragged sigh. The bastard had come too close to getting what he wanted. What was supposed to be a controlled interrogation had almost flipped inside out on them. "Let's see what Gabe gets first. Okay?"

She nodded. "I think I'll go take a shower."

His heart bled as he watched her climb the stairs. Why the hell had he become her lover again? He'd known where this was headed the moment he'd found her in Mexico.

As the bleakness of his future loomed before him, Ethan realized he couldn't do this. If Shea was willing to put up with his shit, then he was damned well going to offer all he had to give. One day she'd probably leave him. Hell, not probably—definitely. Once she learned about Cole. Remembered how he'd treated her, what he'd done. Once she remembered how much she hated him. Hell yeah, she'd leave him. But until then, if she wanted him, he was hers.

Taking the stairs two at a time, Ethan ripped off his shirt. In the bedroom, he dropped his pants, then shoved open the door to the bathroom. Shea stood beneath the spray of the shower.

His heart in his throat, he approached her warily. She'd probably just as soon slug him as kiss him right now.

Even though the frosted glass blurred her face, he could see her mouth trembling. "Get out." Her voice was thick with tears.

Ethan tugged the door open. "I can't."

She shook her head in disbelief. "What do you want from me, Ethan? You tell me there's no future for us. That there's nothing between us but sex and your protection from Rosemount. So what is it you want? Just another fuck?"

Ethan flinched. Shea never cursed unless she was building up her defenses to hide her hurt. He should know. How many times had he heard her curse him? Every damn time he'd hurt her.

Naked, with no defenses, he held his arms out. "You've got me, Shea, for however long you want me."

Her eyes blinking back the pouring water, she stepped closer. "What are you saying?"

"That I'm no one's prize, but I'm yours for as long as you want me."

She stared at him for so long, he figured she was having second thoughts about wanting him for any time at all. Then, giving him the smile he'd fallen in love with, she held out her hand. "Then come wash my back."

Ethan stepped into the shower, pulled her close, and slammed his mouth down on hers.

Moaning into his mouth, Shea wrapped her arms around him as if she would never let him go.

Ethan refused to even wish for that kind of miracle.

twenty-two

Shea slid into jeans and pulled on a long-sleeved white shirt. An odd, desperate need to see Ethan hammered at her heart. After making love to her the entire night, he'd left just after dawn. In that growling whisper that always sent shivers of delight through her, he'd told her to get some sleep and he'd wake her for breakfast. That had been hours ago.

Shea spared another glance at the clock. It was past nine. She'd heard Gabe arrive just as she got out of bed. Instead of scampering downstairs in her nightgown, she had to take the time to shower and throw her clothes on. She slid her feet into socks but didn't bother to find her shoes. A strange tension radiated down her spine and though she told herself she was being silly, she had an odd premonition that Ethan needed her.

Pulling her hair into a hasty ponytail, she scurried across the bedroom and out the door. Last night with Ethan had been all she could want, with the exception of one thing. He seemed to believe that at some point she'd no longer want him. A ridiculous idea, but she felt the need to go to him and reassure him that she would always want him.

She ran down the stairs and then stopped on the bottom step, startled to see the two men glaring at each other in the middle of the living room. Ethan's face was a hard mask of fury. Gabe's expression was one of grim determination. She'd obviously walked in on an argument.

Politeness told her to back out and let them have their privacy. Self-preservation told her to stay put. These men were friends. Whatever they were arguing about most likely involved her. Gabe didn't like her, for some reason. And though Ethan's defense of her had been nice when she'd been ill, that time was over. If she needed defending, she'd do it herself.

Shea took the last step and stood between them. "What's wrong?"

Gabe's blue eyes seared her before returning to Ethan. "I came with some news. I'm not sure Ethan wants me to share it, though."

"I didn't say that."

The violent fury in Ethan's voice surprised her. What had happened?

"It's Shea's decision. Right, Ethan?"

"Of course it's her decision. I don't need you telling me that."

"Stop it, both of you." She placed a hand on Ethan's arm, surprised at the vibrating tension she could feel surging through him. "Ethan, I know you're trying to protect me, but I make my own decisions." Her eyes deliberately cooler, she looked at Gabe. "I can only assume you have news, and while I'm pretty sure you're not here with the intention to help me, you're right, I do deserve to know."

His eyes flickered with what looked like a small amount of regret. He nodded at Ethan. "Tell your watchdog."

She arched a brow. He wanted to act like an arrogant ass, she'd damn well show him she could do the same. "He's not my watchdog. He's my friend. Now, either tell me what you have to tell me or leave."

"Shea, you—"

Shea took Ethan's hand and held it against her heart. "It's all right. Whatever Gabe's got to say, I can handle."

After a visible swallow, Ethan growled, "Tell her."

"Dr. Norton's people have developed a drug to counteract what you were given. You should be able to regain full memory."

Well, so much for her spurt of courage. Nausea poured into her stomach as a cold wave of fear washed over her. She'd known they were working on this, and when it hadn't seemed feasible, she'd told herself it was what she wanted more than anything. Now the possibility of remembering everything loomed before her, and Shea no longer knew if she had the courage to face it.

Without conscious thought, she found herself wrapping her arms around Ethan's waist. He hugged her hard. This was why he had reacted as he had. He knew how hard this would be on her. How well he knew her.

Warm breath caressed her ear as he whispered, "Whatever you want to do, it's up to you. If you decide to go through with it, I'll be right beside you. But if you don't want to, everyone will understand."

A lump of emotion swelled inside her throat. Ethan had done so much for her, given her more than she could ever imagine. Her faith in him absolute, she tilted her head to look up at him. "But if I don't, Rosemount might never be caught."

"We still have Jamie. We'll try to get what we need from him."

Shea jerked her head around at Gabe's snort. "What?"

"Jamie doesn't know a damn thing. Except for one brief videoconference, every communication he's had with Rosemount was through email or by phone. The bastard gave him as little information as possible."

"How do you know he's telling the truth?"

A shadow crossed Gabe's face. "We know."

Shea got the distinct impression that she didn't want to know how they knew Jamie was telling the truth.

"If you don't want to do this, Shea, I'll find another way," Ethan said.

A flash of fear sent shivers rushing through her. Ethan wanted to kill Rosemount—he'd already told her that. Having him anywhere near that bastard filled her with much more horror than regaining her memories. She could deal with her past much better than she could deal with anything happening to Ethan.

Burrowing closer in his arms, she shivered again. Nothing could happen to Ethan.

"Want me to get your sweater?"

She nodded. Let him think she was cold. The last thing he needed was to know she was trying to protect him. He'd be furious.

With one last glare at Gabe, Ethan took off upstairs.

Her thoughts on what she knew she had to do, Shea turned toward the window, searching for peace in the beautiful serenity before her. Though she knew for sure that Rosemount hadn't raped her, she also knew other things had happened to her. What? What had he done to her? What had he made her do? Could she handle knowing all of it?

A soft curse of surprise had her whirling around. Gabe was looking at the sketches she'd done over the last few weeks, trying to come up with Rosemount's features.

The odd expression on Gabe's face confused her. "What's wrong?"

"You drew Cole. Ethan didn't tell us you'd remembered your husband."

"My what?" Her legs turned to jelly. Shea reached out for stability and awkwardly dropped onto the couch.

Gabe turned the sketchbook toward her. The features of the man who'd often haunted her dreams stared at her. She gasped for breath as air suddenly became nonexistent. "What do you mean . . . my husband?"

"Damn you, Gabe."

Shock roaring through her, she barely flinched when Ethan's fist slam into Gabe's jaw. The big man skidded across the hardwood floor. Ethan stood over him. "You bastard."

"What is he talking about? This man . . . he's my husband?" Shea gripped the arm of the sofa to keep from sliding off it, her voice a thin thread of sound. "I have a husband?"

His jaw working, Ethan shook his head. "You had a husband. He's dead."

"Dead?"

"Cole Mathison . . . the operative Rosemount killed in the sting last year," Ethan said.

Her eyes went to the sketchbook on the floor and then back up to Ethan's hard face. "That's why I went after Rosemount. You told me he was just my friend. My God, Ethan, how could you keep something like this from me?"

Shock turned to grief. Dear God, she'd been married. Was a widow. Ethan knew all of this. The reaction he'd had the first time he saw the sketch now made perfect sense. He'd distracted her by pulling her into his arms and kissing her, almost making love to her. She cringed as she remembered how she'd asked him . . . practically begged him to make love to her. And all the while he'd only done it to sidetrack her. As full comprehension hit, she recognized the manipulation. One he'd carefully orchestrated to keep her from finding out the truth.

"You lied to me. Why?"

Ethan's expression was one of deep regret, and yet, how did she know that wasn't a lie, too?

"To protect you."

"From a dead man?"

"You were hurt enough. Telling you about Cole wouldn't have changed anything. You didn't need—"

"Don't tell me what I didn't need. Ethan, I trusted you to tell me the truth. How could you keep this from me?"

When he didn't answer, Shea stood and walked slowly toward him, tears blurring her vision. "Talk to me. Please . . . why didn't you tell me the man I drew was once my husband?"

"I did what I thought was best."

"Why would it be best not to know that I had been married? That my husband had died?"

"I didn't want to cause you more pain."

"More pain than remembering that I kidnapped and terrorized innocent people? That I was the captive pet of a madman? That I'd been tortured? My God, Ethan, how much more painful could it have been? I asked you to tell me everything, even the most painful things." Shea swallowed past the lump of disillusionment clogging her throat. "I trusted you. More than anyone else in the world, I trusted you."

Ethan's grim voice repeated, "I did what I thought was best."

"That's it? You have no better explanation?"

Jaw clenched against pain, Ethan shook his head, unable to say anything else in his defense. What could he say? He had no real excuse. Hadn't he told himself all along that once she found out, she would hate him? Being right gave him zero comfort.

Shea's expression was one of deepest hurt as she whirled around and ran upstairs.

"I'm sorry, Ethan. I saw the sketch and thought she'd remembered him."

Though part of him wanted to rip Gabe's head off, Ethan knew his friend had only quickened what was going to happen anyway. Now his only worry was for Shea. Because of his inability to tell her about Cole, she would question everything he'd told her, leaving her wondering what was really the truth.

Within minutes, Shea was back downstairs, suitcase and coat in her hand.

"Shea . . . don't leave."

Without acknowledging him with even a glance, she swept up her sketchbook and made her way to the door. "I'll wait for you in the car, Mr. Maddox," she said, her voice dripping with ice.

Ethan reached out a hand to her, then let it drop to his side when he saw her shrink away from him. No matter how much she might hate him, he couldn't let her do this. "Wait. I'll tell you everything. You don't have to take the drugs."

"It's too late for that." Still not meeting his eyes, she shook her head as her throat moved convulsively. "How can I trust you again?" She turned and went out the door.

Gabe blew out a long sigh. "Hell, man, I'll try to make her understand—"

"Just go, Gabe. Shea's out there by herself."

Before Gabe went through the door, Ethan said, "One thing. You damn well better protect her with your life. If something happens to her because of what you told her, or what I couldn't, I won't rest until we've both paid. Understand?"

With a jerk of his head in understanding, Gabe left.

Hollowed out, Ethan's eyes roamed around the room. It looked the same as before but was totally different. Shea was gone, and with her, all the light and beauty had disappeared. The room, the entire house, was devoid of life.

Ethan closed his eyes against the glare of emptiness. He should have told her. Had known he'd pay the price at some point. And now, her trust was once again destroyed.

He stalked up the stairs. Regret and pain would continue. He had no choice in that. But he damn well wouldn't let her go through this alone. Protecting Shea was still his number one priority. She wouldn't like it, but when those memories returned, Ethan would be right beside her. After that, she would no doubt tell him to go to hell. That wouldn't be a problem. He knew from experience that without Shea in his life, there was nowhere else to go.

Tense silence filled the car as Gabe drove her to the airport. Shea kept her eyes straight ahead. She hadn't uttered a word since she'd gotten in the car, over forty minutes ago. Still stunned from the shock of learning she'd been married, she was swamped with unbelievable anguish at Ethan's betrayal. The one man she'd trusted above all others had kept this from her. Information vitally important to who she had been, what she had been. Why?

"For what it's worth, I'm sorry you found out that way," Gabe said.

She remained silent.

"Also, I want you to know that though I didn't believe you before, I believe you now."

Now, that statement required a reply. "Excuse me, Mr. Maddox, for apparently giving you the wrong impression."

Gabe shot her a confused look. "Wrong impression?"

"You seem to be under the misconception that I give a damn what you think about me. I don't. Whether you believed me or not hasn't made an ounce of difference to me. Do I make myself clear?"

His head gave a quick jerk of acknowledgment. "Crystal."

"Then please give me the courtesy of not talking. Further words are not necessary."

"Message received loud and clear."

She turned back to the window, and silence once more filled the car.

Several minutes passed. Then Gabe, who apparently couldn't leave well enough alone said, "You broke his heart once, you know. Almost destroyed him."

Shea tried to ignore the skitter of her heart, but wasn't this what she'd feared all along? That she had been the one to break Ethan's heart? Could she learn the truth from Gabe or just his version? "Is that the truth . . . or just how you interpreted it?"

Gabe shrugged. "Ethan was crazy in love with you. You up and married his best friend. How else should I interpret it?"

"My husband was Ethan's best friend?" God, that just didn't make sense. What would possess her to even marry someone else, much less Ethan's best friend?

"Yes."

"Why would I marry Ethan's best friend?"

"That's what I'd like to know."

She shook her head in denial. "There's got to be more to this."

"With your memory loss, I guess Ethan's the only one who knows the real truth."

Her eyes closed for a second. Like she needed a reminder of how much Ethan had kept from her. She twisted sideways to face Gabe. "Did you ever ask Ethan what happened?"

"Yeah, once. He said it was the right thing for you to do. He looked like hell. . . . You sure did a number on him."

Her eyes narrowed. "Maybe you only saw what you wanted to. You seem to have a skewed opinion of women. Did your prejudice blind you to what you didn't want to see?"

"I'm not prejudiced against women."

A soft snort. "Yeah . . . right."

"Ethan stopped caring whether he lived or not. He was a wild man . . . took the craziest chances. After Cole was killed, it got worse. He was on the edge. If Noah hadn't reined him in, he'd be dead by now."

She didn't like to think about that. No matter how much he'd hurt her, she couldn't bear thinking about anything happening to Ethan. She also didn't want to believe that she could be so heartless as to marry her lover's best friend. What had possessed her?

"I know it was a sting to get Rosemount, but how did Cole die?"

"I wasn't there, so I only know from the reports of the other operatives. Cole defied a direct order from Ethan to wait for backup. He ran into a building . . . and it blew up. Ethan blamed himself."

"Why would he blame himself if Cole ignored his order?"

"Beats the hell out of me. You blamed Ethan, too."

"I did? How do you know?"

"At Cole's memorial service, you slapped Ethan, told him he was responsible."

Shea covered her face with her hands. "Oh God, how that must have hurt him."

Gabe shot her a quick glance. "You still love him?"

Even after what she'd just discovered she couldn't deny the truth. "Yes, I love him."

After several seconds of silence, Gabe continued, "A few months after Cole's death, you disappeared. LCR operatives are free agents. We just assumed you were taking some personal time to grieve. Next thing we know, you're kidnapping women for Rosemount."

She rubbed the center of her forehead, where a small pain throbbed. "I still don't know how Rosemount got to me . . . or how I got to him." After a few moments of silence, she said, "Tell me about Cole."

"Only met him a couple of times. I was working most of my ops in South America back then. I know that after Cole trained in Paris, he started working on Ethan's team. I went on an extended mission. When I came back, you and Cole were married."

"Just like that?"

"That's the way it seemed."

"How long were you away?"

"Six months."

She gazed out the window, her mind searching and grasping for memories. For just one infinitesimal reminder of the man she'd called husband. There was nothing. "I don't remember him."

"If this drug works, you'll remember it all."

"Yes, I suppose I will."

An ache in her hand made her look down. She was clutching the sketchbook so hard the spiral binding was biting into her skin. Flipping it open, Shea turned to one of the pages where she had sketched the man she now knew was Cole Mathison, her husband.

Eyes squinted in concentration, she stared at the chiseled face of the man she'd been married to . . . been intimate with. With his striking good looks, he should be impossible to forget. Glacier-blue eyes, square, determined jaw, hawklike nose, and thick, dark hair. If she closed her eyes, she could see his face. But who he was and what he'd meant to her was still a deep, black hole of nothingness.

She couldn't even feel grief for him. Ethan had told her he was one of the finest men he'd ever known. And he'd told Gabe she had done the right thing to marry him. This man had most likely been a good, decent person. And she'd been his wife.

Alarm pounded as Shea became scared of getting her memories back for a whole new reason. Had she been the kind of woman to pit two men against each other? Had she broken not one but two men's hearts?

She had never imagined that recalling her time with Rosemount might not be the worst thing she could remember. What kind of person had she been?

twenty-three

Ixtapa, Mexico

They would come for him today. He'd heard them whispering yesterday. Excitement in their voices, making plans for him. Several of the doctors and soldiers had gathered at the other end of the room. They thought he couldn't hear them or couldn't comprehend their hushed conversation. He couldn't hear all of it, but he heard enough to know that the time had come for him to act. They believed he was still weak and unable to fight as before. They were wrong.

For weeks, when the sheets were draped over his cage, he worked like a madman to build up his strength. While the idiots slept in their soft, warm beds dreaming their dreams of evil, he was wide-awake and planning their death and destruction.

He had learned to act weak and defenseless and felt a fierce sense of satisfaction that he had been able to fool them. They believed he was controllable, manageable. They would learn the truth just before they breathed their last breath.

Last night, after he had completed his workout regimen of push-ups, chin-ups, and crunches, he had taken his weapon and ripped a small hole in the fabric that covered his cage. Now he would wait. Today would be the day. He could feel it in his bones. The bastards would try to inject their demon drugs into him, once again creating the animal-like monster whose only mission was to destroy. Little did they know, their drugs were no longer necessary. They had the monster they wanted. What they didn't realize was that the monster would destroy them, not their enemies.

He sat in the corner of the cage, empty except for a sleeping pallet and a bedpan. Until a few days ago, he'd resigned himself to using only his hands to wreak his vengeance. Since he'd relied only on his hands in the past, he knew he'd be able to take down three, maybe four, before they killed him. Fate had stepped in with the arrival of a new recruit. A young man named Raphael, who couldn't be much older than seventeen, had been given the task of feeding him.

He'd grown used to being hand-fed through the bars of his cage. Had learned to open his mouth and accept what nourishment they provided, knowing that if he didn't, he couldn't be strong enough to do what needed to be done. But Raphael seemed to have a problem with this.

At first, seeing the kid's hesitation had infuriated him. He'd thought the boy's reaction had been disgust, but after the roar of cold fury in his head calmed down, he'd begun to listen to young Raphael's mutterings.

"Treat you like an animal . . . must make them pay. I'll help you."

And then Raphael had given him a gift. Just as he'd finished spooning the last of the meal into his charge's mouth, he'd handed him a paper napkin. Inside that napkin had been another spoon. As weapons went, it was piss-poor, but it was a gift he'd never expected.

After the kid shuffled off, carrying the empty tray, the sheet was once more put in place. And then he'd begun his work. Sitting in his corner, he sawed night after night with that spoon against the bars of his cage. Though it was still a crude weapon, he'd worn it down to a sharp point. Sharp enough to slice open throats and stab soft bellies.

Now when they came for him, he would be ready. He would die . . . he knew that. His only thought, his only worry, was . . . how many could he take with him?

A soft sound alerted him that he was no longer alone. Was this it? He peered through the hole in the draping. Yes, there were only three of them, plus two doctors. His mouth curved upward and he couldn't resist putting his fingers on his lips, tracing what he knew was a smile. It felt strange and unusual, but good.

They crept toward his cage, most likely believing he was still sleeping. Though adrenaline surged and spewed like lava within him, he forced himself to lie down and wait quietly. The instant he heard the drapery being lifted, his eyes closed. His right hand, hidden under his thigh, held his weapon. His left hand lay on his stomach. The key turned in the lock, and the door made a soft squeak. He held his breath and heard their breathing. Heard the soft shuffle of their feet as they came closer and closer. And then they were beside him.

He sprang up. One hand swung out and jammed a fist into the throat of one man. His other hand gripping his weapon, he sliced into the soft sweet spot of another man's neck, severing his jugular. A third man roared toward him. He waited until the last second; then one powerful leg kicked up, knocking the man in the face and sending him soaring across the cage.

Breathing out ragged breaths, he stood and looked around him. All three were dead or dying. Only two remained. They stood frozen before him, as if stupefied . . . the doctors . . . the two he wanted most, almost as much as he wanted the head demon himself. He'd resigned himself to not being able to get the leader. If he got rid of these two, getting the leader was a real possibility.

He advanced toward the two terrified men and they finally went into action, running from the cage. He burst through the cage door and immediately felt a sharp sting in his shoulder. With a roar, he turned. The demon leader. The man he wanted to kill more than anyone stood beside the cage, a dart gun in his hand and a smile of delight on his thin face. He jumped up and down in excitement. "I knew it. I knew it. I told them you were faking. I was right!"

Laughter bounced against the walls, grew louder and louder. Pain speared through him. Grabbing his head, he screamed in agony. The evil face in front of him melted and blurred.

With the desperate cry of a helpless animal, he fell face-first onto the hard tile. His last thought was the terrible knowledge that once again, he would be the monster they wanted.

Tampa, Florida
LCR Clinic

The lights were soft in the small sitting room, dimmed in preparation for her treatment. Shea took a trembling breath as nerves clawed at her insides and dread and anticipation clashed.

Part of her wanted to just get this over with, while another part wanted to run from the room as fast and far as possible. Her nails dug into the arms of the leather recliner. She was determined to see this through, no matter how cowardly she felt.

Dr. Norton sat across from her, his kind face wreathed in wrinkles of concern. She twisted to get more comfortable, willing her body to relax as she listened to the doctor's warnings and instructions.

"Your memories won't return all at once. We're just giving you a small dosage until we see what kind of ef-

fect it's going to have on you. Once I know it's not ad-
verse, we'll increase the dosage."

He gave an absentminded glance at his watch and
then a quick glance at the door. Before she could ask him
if someone else was coming, he said, "Don't be disappointed if you don't have an explosion of knowledge."

That was a good thing. The thought of having knowledge of all of the things she'd forgotten slamming down
on her at one time tightened the knots in her churning
stomach. "But they'll all come back at some point,
right?"

"Yes, we believe so, though it may take a few weeks.
Since it could take some time, I'm going to show you
how to inject yourself. I would caution you against
doing it when no one's around."

"Why?"

"If you have a particularly bad flashback, it would be
best to have someone around. The most traumatic ones
should be vague. You'll still remember them, but they
won't be as vivid. You shouldn't experience the fear or
feel any pain."

She nodded, relieved to be spared that, at least.

Dr. Norton checked his watch again and bit his lip. He
seemed unusually nervous.

"Is everything okay?"

"Yes, of course." He cleared his throat. "There's
something I feel I need to explain. I understand from
Gabe that Ethan hadn't told you about your husband."

This was definitely something she didn't want to discuss with Dr. Norton. "That's true, but I don't—"

"Now. Now. Hear me out. I know that must have
hurt, but remember, I told you that hearing disturbing
things about your past before you remembered them on
your own could cause damage. Ethan was only trying to
protect you. See, it's really my fault. You shouldn't
blame—"

"Thanks, Doc, but Shea knows exactly who's responsible."

Jerking her head up, she stared at the tall, commanding figure standing in the doorway.

Dr. Norton stood. "Now, Ethan, I did tell you not—"

"You also told me that once she regained her health and appeared to be handling her memories well, I should tell her. That was weeks ago. No one's at fault other than me."

Shea scrambled to her feet. Despite the way her heartbeat had tripled in speed at seeing him, she wasn't ready to talk with him. "I don't want to hear any excuses, Ethan. Please leave."

His mouth tilted in that slightly crooked way that always made her want to kiss him, but his eyes remained resolute. "No. You may not want to talk to me, but you have a right to hear the truth. And you deserve to hear it from me." He gestured at the chair. "Sit down."

Shea was so focused on Ethan, she hadn't even realized they were alone. Dr. Norton had disappeared.

He blew out a sigh when she didn't move. "I know you're angry with me. You can't be angrier than I am with myself. But before you put yourself through this, I wanted to come clean with you."

"It's too late. You should have—"

"I know I should have, Shea." He shoved his fingers through his hair. "Let me do something right and decent, just this once, okay?"

She dropped back into her chair. "Fine."

"Everything I've told you, with the exception of telling you about Cole, is true. We met a few months after I started working for LCR. We studied and trained together. We became lovers and then partners. When we weren't on assignment, we lived in an apartment in New Orleans.

"Being with you was the best thing that had ever happened to me. After Abby died, I never felt I deserved happiness. I focused on the present . . . tried not to think about the future. Everything was fine until you started talking about getting married and having kids. At that point, I knew it was time for us to part. I couldn't give you the future you deserved."

She opened her mouth to protest and he held up his hand. "Let me finish."

Biting the inside of her jaw, she nodded.

"Cole started with LCR and we worked some ops with him. I knew he was attracted to you, though I don't think you ever saw it until I told you. You liked and admired him. The more I saw you together, the more I realized how much better he would be for you than I was.

"I started pushing you toward him. Making insinuations that you and I weren't a permanent thing . . . that I was thinking about quitting LCR and going out on my on. All bullshit, of course."

Shea could only shake her head. God, he was an idiot.

"The more you resisted, the harder I pushed. One day, I literally pushed you out of our home. I called Noah for an assignment and disappeared for a few weeks. When I got back, you two were married."

Shea didn't know when the tears started falling down her face. His eyes grim and full of sadness, Ethan picked up the box of tissues sitting on the table in front of him and handed it to her.

Wiping her eyes, she took a breath and said, "How long were Cole and I married?"

"Less than a year." He shook his head. "That's not the worst thing I did, Shea. I pretty much ruined your marriage, or did my damnedest."

"How?"

"I requested you and Cole on as many ops as I could. Noah allowed it because we worked so well together. He told me he trusted us all to be professional. The victims we rescued were the priority, not our personal issues."

"Why did you do that?"

"Hell, I don't know. To punish myself for being such a damned fool. Punish you for doing the right thing. Mostly, I think it was just to be able to see you."

Shea swallowed back her tears. He was breaking her heart all over again. "Were we able to handle it?"

"For the most part. The tension was there—we just did out best to ignore it."

Things were becoming much more clear as to why Ethan blamed himself for Cole's death. "And then one day, we couldn't?"

"One day, I couldn't. Rosemount had been kidnapping for a few years. We set up what we thought was a damned good sting. Our plan was to avert the kidnapping and get Rosemount, or at least his people."

"What happened?"

"I hadn't seen you in a few weeks. The minute you walked into the room, I knew something was wrong. You'd lost weight, and I could tell you'd recently been crying. You looked miserable. It pissed me off because I knew Cole had made you cry."

"And?"

"You left the room for a few minutes. I made a smart-ass comment. Totally out of line. Cole got pissed. You came back in. It was pretty obvious we'd been arguing. You asked what was going on. Cole muttered something about asking your old lover and stalked out of the room.

"After he left, you and I had an argument about me minding my own business. In the midst of the argument, Cole radioed in. The message was garbled, but I understood enough to know something was going down and he was going in without backup. I ordered him to wait. I couldn't understand his answer. We ran after him just in time to see him go into the warehouse. Seconds later, the damn thing blew up."

"Gabe told me I blamed you for Cole's death."

"Yes, as you should have. If I hadn't—"

Unable to sit still any longer, Shea jumped to her feet. "Stop, please just stop. How is it that everything's always your fault? Do you think other people don't have a say in their actions? Whenever anything bad happens, it's automatically because you did something wrong?"

"If I hadn't—"

"Dammit, Ethan, if I hadn't gone after Rosemount, several innocent women would not have had their lives almost destroyed. I feel hideous that I did that, but it's done. The only thing I can do is help try to find Rosemount so we can make sure it doesn't happen again. Guilt doesn't get you anywhere. Haven't you figured that out by now?"

"I'm so sorry I didn't tell you before."

"Why didn't you?"

"At first, we were afraid telling you might cause some damage. I didn't want to chance that. Then later . . ." He blew out a long sigh and rubbed his eyes as if he was exhausted. She knew he'd probably driven all night long to get here. It took every ounce of her self-control not to go to him and wrap her arms around him.

"Later, I couldn't figure out a way to tell you. I knew you'd remember at some point. The longer I waited, the easier it got not to say anything. I wanted to postpone the inevitable as long as possible."

"What inevitable? What did you think would happen if you told me I'd been married?"

"I figured it would trigger all the other memories. The ones where you hated me."

Even though she couldn't remember, she doubted very seriously that she had ever hated this man. Been furious and hurt, absolutely. The emotions Ethan created in her were often volatile and unpredictable, but hate? Having fallen in love with him, not once but twice, she didn't believe for a second she'd ever hated him.

"Why would I marry your best friend, Ethan? What kind of woman does that? How could I marry one man while loving another one?"

His broad shoulder lifted in a shrug, as if it were totally understandable. "Cole was a good man, and you cared deeply for each other."

Shea felt guilt, not only for marrying a man she obviously didn't love but also for feeling no grief for him. This man had been her husband, and she should mourn him. Yet all she wanted to do was go to Ethan and comfort him. She forced herself to stay put.

"When did I go after Rosemount?"

"Hard to say. After Cole's memorial service, I got assigned another op. You were pretty messed up. We weren't exactly on speaking terms. Disappearing from your life was the best thing I could do for you. A few months after Cole's death, Noah fired me. I hadn't seen you, but was told you weren't working. Everyone figured you needed time to grieve. Seeing me sure as hell wouldn't have helped you. I moved to Tennessee. A few months later, Gabe came and told me you were working for Rosemount. The rest you know."

Yes, the rest she did know. This man had rescued her, putting his own life in jeopardy. He'd saved her life, taken care of her, and brought her back from hell. How could she not love him?

"Thank you for finally telling me."

"I'm sorry, Shea . . . for so many things."

Shea could only shake her head. Loving Ethan meant understanding him. He was still punishing himself for a tragic accident years ago. He'd stayed with her as long as he didn't have to make a commitment for the future. Doing that would have required an acknowledgment that he had achieved some kind of happiness . . . something he didn't think he deserved.

If she'd known about his past before, would she have understood him and not pushed? It was hard to say, since she had no memory of their previous relationship. But she knew the truth now, and having promises of forever from Ethan wasn't paramount to her continued love. If they had forever or just one more day, her love wouldn't change.

His eyes solemn and sad, Ethan stood before her as if waiting for her final judgment. No matter what she said, she was damned. He knew she loved him but didn't believe he deserved it. If she told him to leave, he would.

Whatever their future held, it had to be his decision. The next few days would be difficult for her, but she couldn't depend on Ethan to see her through this. It was time to stand on her own.

"Thank you for telling me, Ethan, but you need to leave now."

"Shea, no. I know you despise me. You have every right to . . . but let me stay with you. You shouldn't go through this alone."

She took his hand and pulled him to sit beside her on the couch. Swallowing several times to dislodge the giant lump in her throat, she gave up and cleared her voice, hoping she could get through this without turning into a sobbing mess. "This is hard for me to say. So let me get it out." Hard though it was, she held his gaze, wanting him to see the sincerity and truth. "I don't despise you. Though I don't totally remember loving you before, Ethan, I know I love you now. You haven't said it, but I know you love me, too. And before you say anything, know this . . . I'm not looking for a commitment from you. That's not a necessity for me. The thing is, if we stay together, every day I'll wonder if this is the day you'll realize you're too happy and you have to leave. I can't live like that."

She brought one of his hands up to her mouth for a soft kiss. "You're an amazing man, Ethan Bishop. You have an incredible strength of will and a wonderful heart. You're a hero in every sense of the word. I believe you deserve happiness, but you need to believe it, too."

"Shea, please—"

She shook her head. "I need to do this without you. You've done so much for me and I thank you from the bottom of my heart, but it's time I stood on my own."

Pulling his hand from hers, he brushed his fingers tenderly against her face. "I wish I could give you what you deserve."

"And I wish I could erase your pain." She took a deep breath and stood. "I think Dr. Norton's anxious to get started."

Ethan stood and held out his arms. Knowing she would most likely lose control couldn't prevent her from going into his embrace. This might be the last opportunity to be in his arms. She couldn't allow a little breakdown to prevent this small luxury.

"You're the finest, most beautiful woman in the world, Shea Monroe."

Unable to speak, Shea put her head on his chest and listened to the hard thudding of his heart. She wondered if she could hear it fracture as hers was.

Taking one last bracing breath, Shea pulled away and whispered, "Good-bye, Ethan."

Ethan zoomed down the highway. Emotions slammed and twisted through him like steroid-charged wrestlers. She had asked him to leave, and he'd left. He'd done a lot of hard things in his life, but that had to be one of the most painful ones. He wanted to be with her. Help her. Protect her. But she was right. She couldn't really depend on him. Hadn't he showed her time and again how true that was?

So what was he supposed to do now? Just go back home? Pretend everything was all right? Pretend that the woman he adored wasn't going through hell? What would she do when she realized there was one more thing he hadn't shared with her? One more thing he'd been responsible for that he had never been able to voice? Was he going to just let her learn that on her own?

Hell, no. Checking the rearview mirror and seeing nothing coming, Ethan made a U-turn and headed back to the clinic. Even if she wouldn't allow him in the room with her, he could be close by in case she asked for him.

A vibration in his jacket alerted him to a phone call. Ethan snatched it up, hoping Shea was calling to tell him she'd changed her mind. He checked the readout. Curiosity flickered: *unknown caller.*

"Yeah?"

"Ethan, my boy. How are you?"

He jerked at the unfamiliar and slimy-sounding voice. "Who the hell is this?"

"Just the man you've been obsessed with for so long."

He froze, not daring to believe that Donald Rosemount could actually be calling him.

"I don't get obsessed with men."

"But you've made an exception with me." He giggled. "After all, we have a lot in common. We've both tasted and enjoyed the same little redhead."

Adrenaline surged even as triumph mounted. Rosemount didn't know how much Shea had remembered. The less he knew, the better. "You son of a bitch. How'd you get this number?"

"A mutual acquaintance. Sadly, I understand he's no longer working for LCR. Such a pity. I had hoped to continue our association. He's just so pretty."

Jamie.

"You're a freak, Rosemount."

"Now, now. Don't go getting all testy or I might change my mind about the little gift I have for you."

What was the bastard up to? Shea was under tight security. He'd checked it himself. No one could get to her.

"What gift?"

"They say a picture is worth a thousand words. I'm sending you one right now. Take a look."

Ethan pulled the phone away from his ear, pressed a key, and looked at the screen. His heart leaped into his throat. He stared hard. Rubbed his eyes, stared again. It couldn't be. Realization grew and settled . . . it was.

"You're a fucking dead man," Ethan growled.

"My, my, we're definitely going to have to clean up your language."

"What do you want?"

"Just a little exchange."

"You're not getting Shea."

"It's not Shea I want, Ethan. It's you."

"What?"

"There's a warehouse at Tenth and Burnham. Be there in ten minutes. Come alone. In case you didn't know it, you're being followed. If you don't do exactly as I say, the deal's off."

"How do I know you'll keep your word?"

"Well, I could just send you a picture of a dead body. Would you rather I did that?"

Grinding his teeth so hard he tasted blood, he said, "I'll be there."

"Excellent. Now, be a good boy and pull into that hamburger joint up on the right."

Ethan changed lanes. Ignoring the honking car he'd come close to clipping, he turned into the parking lot.

"Now what?"

"See that dark green BMW at the end of the parking lanes?"

"Yeah."

"Put your phone on the roof."

Pulling up behind it, Ethan shifted into park and got out with a casual leisure, giving himself time to search the parking lot. It was lunchtime, and the lot was almost full. He twisted around. Bastard had to be here somewhere.

"Ethan, I'm getting a little impatient with you. Now do as you're told."

Ethan stalked to the car. Just as he reached it, he heard Rosemount's cheerful voice, "See you in a few. Don't be late or I may change my mind."

Dropping the phone on the roof, he turned and jumped back into his car. He was at least seven minutes away from the warehouse. No time to call for backup. And with someone following him, no chance.

He had to do this on his own. Had no choice. Perhaps this was his destiny. Fate had finally caught up with him. But if things worked out, he could save a life . . . a very valuable life. And have one last chance for redemption.

twenty-four

Key West, Florida

Her mind reeling with memories, furious emotions pounding, Shea entered a code to the lock of the storage facility. One of the small but important pieces of information she'd been able to recall.

She'd arrived late last night, exhausted. Jagged and raw inside, as though someone had taken all of her emotions and ground them in a blender. All she'd wanted was to walk into her home and feel as though she belonged.

The way to her house had come to her as she drove the rental car out of the parking lot of the airport. Forty-five minutes later, she arrived at a pretty one-story, red-brick house with a neatly manicured yard and white shutters. A sense of well-being hit her, as if this place held some good memories. She opened the car door, put one foot on the paved driveway, and stopped as that new sense of peace was replaced with shock. She no longer lived here. She didn't remember why or how, but she knew she'd sold her home and most of the furnishings. The remainder of her things were in a storage facility about ten miles down the road.

She backed out of the drive quickly, unwilling to face the home owners and try to explain how she'd forgotten that she'd sold them the house. Past the point of being embarrassed about her memory loss, she just didn't have the energy to come up with a believable excuse.

Since it was so late, she located the nearest motel and fell into bed. Unfortunately, she spent a restless night with memories. Some sweet and some horrendous, they bombarded her like a hailstorm. When she woke this morning with the beginnings of a violent headache, a large part of her just wanted to roll over in bed and try to forget again. She refused to give herself that out. She'd come to here to find Shea Monroe. If all that was left of her was in a tiny storage facility, then she'd damned well find it and deal with the pain.

Three cups of coffee and a piece of toast at the attached restaurant revived her. Now she told herself she was ready, one way or the other, to face her past.

Regaining her memory was supposed to take time, maybe weeks or months. Dr. Norton had said her mind would remember each item when it felt it was ready. At the clinic, memories had returned like snow flurries. First, a single thought or remembrance; then another and another. The pace had been slow enough that she'd been able to relish each one, savoring the knowledge. Though not all of them were happy, they were real, and that, more than anything, was what she craved. The truth. No matter how painful, no matter how vile.

She'd left the clinic against Dr. Norton's wishes. Once she'd delivered all the information she could on Donald Rosemount, she'd had the intense desire to be on her own. Cautioning her on not overdoing it, he'd provided her with a handful of small vials of the drug and had shown her how to inject it. He hadn't liked the thought of her having memories with no one around to help her if they became too painful, but she'd been adamant.

She was well aware that Rosemount still searched for her and had taken care to make sure she wasn't followed. At least not by any of Rosemount's people.

The storage door slid open with a clang. Shea took a look around the perimeter of the facility. It was early morning, so the place was deserted. A familiar car sat a few yards down one of the aisleways, but the sight didn't alarm her. Why should it, when she knew the driver? She'd spotted him last night when she'd pulled into her former driveway. *Gabe*. On orders not only from Noah but, no doubt, Ethan, too.

His presence didn't bother her. As long as he stayed out of her way, she had no problem with a tail. She wasn't stupid. If Rosemount somehow found her, she would need all the help she could get.

Seeing no one other than Gabe, Shea entered the dark interior of the small storage room and flicked on the single lightbulb overhead. Boxes were stacked against the wall. Not so many, really, when one considered a life. Evidently, she had saved only those things she felt she couldn't live without.

She turned and slid the door closed. The last thing she wanted was for a passerby to glimpse inside and see an emotionally distraught woman weeping over a box. This was hers to endure and experience alone. Shea Monroe unveiled.

Willing herself courage, Shea strode to a large box on the floor, ripped it open, and plunged into her past.

Gabe switched off the car engine and settled in for a long wait. Shea knew he was here. She'd spotted him last night at her house. He didn't know why she hadn't gone inside. She'd just sat there for a few minutes before driving to a small motel a few miles away.

He'd spent the night in his car, his eyes on the room she'd trudged into after checking in at the front desk. His penance. Sure, he was here on Noah's orders and Ethan would skin him alive if anything happened to her, but there was another reason. Guilt. From the time Shea had returned from Mexico, he'd made it clear to everyone that he didn't trust her. The drugs in her system couldn't be doubted, but he'd had grave doubts about her memory loss and her motivation. Those doubts had disappeared.

After seeing her reaction to his comments about Cole, he knew she hadn't remembered him. No one could make themselves look that ill or devastated. And he'd been the one responsible for the way she'd found out. Ethan should have told her, but that didn't mitigate Gabe's part. His past prejudice against Shea had colored his opinion.

Ethan had once mentioned that Gabe had issues with women because of his ex-wife. No: *wife*. He had to stop thinking of her as his ex. She wasn't his ex-anything . . . yet. Maybe Ethan was right. The experiences he'd had could definitely skew a man's judgment. He wasn't proud of his bias, but at least he knew it for what it was. He wouldn't let it happen again.

He still didn't know what had gone on between Shea and Ethan. Had only determined that it had been Shea's fault, since she'd up and married Cole only a few weeks after their breakup. It hadn't been any of his business, but he'd always sided with Ethan. Seeing his friend's pain, he'd been sure Shea was to blame. Now, he just didn't know.

What had happened still wasn't any of his business, but he owed Shea for his treatment of her. So until she agreed to go back to the clinic for protection or Rosemount was caught, he would be her shadow.

The cellphone beside him buzzed. He looked at the readout. *Noah*.

"She okay?"

"Yeah, all's quiet. She's inside a storage bin right now. No sign of anyone following her."

"Good. With what she's given us, we're going to be

able to find the bastard. Still, there's more that she knows. If he finds her, I don't have to tell you what would happen."

"He won't find her. So she was able to give us some good leads?"

"The best we've had. We know his past. Where he came from, his real name. How he got started. He even explained to her how he set up an accident to kill his parents. That's where his initial wealth came from. We've got people digging into that. She also confirmed what we suspected about how he gets his victims. He advertises on the Internet on various lists, screens the responses, and goes from there."

Gabe grunted. "Guess our Web watchers are working that angle."

"Yeah. And she gave us some names and good descriptions of some of the people who work with him. Sounds like he's got scientists and doctors working round the clock on all sorts of drugs. He's marketing them, too."

"The man's nothing if not diversified."

"I'm hoping we can undiversify him real soon."

"Me, too." Shifting in his seat to make his long legs more comfortable, Gabe asked, "Did she say how she found him in the first place?"

Noah snorted. "He apparently found her."

"How the hell did that happen?"

"She still can't recall a lot of details yet. I'm hoping there's more to it than what she's remembered so far. Says she put out a couple of ads on a few sites, hawking her services as a freelance personal-protection guard, hoping he'd take the bait. Within a week, two of his men followed her home from the grocery store. Invited themselves in and offered her a job. Said she immediately knew who they were and went with them. Within a couple of days, she found herself trapped—he'd somehow figured out she wasn't legit."

"You're right. There's got to be more than that. The man had to have been tipped."

"Agreed. We just don't know how."

"Maybe the time with her boxed mementos will clear some stuff up."

"Hope so. Check in from time to time and let me know her status."

"Will do."

Flipping his phone closed, Gabe settled deeper into his seat. If, as he'd surmised, the storage room held Shea's possessions and memories, he figured he was in for a long wait. He grimaced in sympathy at what she must be going through, even if it was by choice. God knew, he'd just as soon eat coal dust as delve back into his own past. Revisiting past events was not an activity he'd willingly choose.

He'd escaped from hell, so why the hell would he ever want to go back to it?

Tears rolled down her face. Sniffling, she wiped her eyes against her sleeve as she closed yet another photo album. So many questions answered. Still so many unanswered. She and Ethan had shared an extraordinary life. Unbelievable adventures, incredible fun. The photographs also revealed a unique closeness. Despite Ethan's denial, there was no doubt in her mind that the couple in those pictures had loved each other deeply. What had happened?

She still had only minute remembrances of their relationship. The pictures had sparked a few vague memories, but nothing that gave her an idea of what had torn them apart. Ethan had insisted it was his fault because of his inability to make a commitment. That couldn't be the whole story. What would make her leave Ethan and, only days later, marry Cole? Nothing in her profile or in discussion with others gave an indication that she was flighty or shallow. Something had to have pushed her into the arms of Ethan's best friend. What?

She pulled another box toward her, this one filled with clothes and shoes. As her hands touched bright, jeweled colors and soft, silky fabric, Shea felt a small comfort of familiarity. These were definitely her clothes. She delved deeper, finding all styles of purses and a multitude of shoes. She picked up a clunky wedge-heeled shoe. Startled to see that the heel twisted, she peered inside the hollow space of an empty sole. Something she'd used on an op to smuggle a weapon?

Shaking her head at the odd idea, Shea pulled another box from the stack. It was smaller, older-looking than the others. As she turned it sideways to open it, her heart leaped at the word scribbled on the outside. *Cole.*

Heart thudding in anticipation, she ripped it open, feeling a desperate need to learn more about the man to whom she'd been married. A stack of cards, bound by a rubber band, caught her attention. She picked it up and slid off the rubber band. Confusion had her shaking her head again. Homemade cards for all different occasions filled her hands. All obviously made by a child. As she shuffled through them, her heart pounded with an unnamed dread. Every one of the cards had "Daddy" scribbled in childlike writing. Cole had a child? Where? Why hadn't anyone mentioned that to her?

She opened a Father's Day card and read, *I love you, Daddy. Your forever pumpkin, Cassidy.* She flipped through a few more—they were all signed in the same way.

The cards put to the side, she delved into the box once more and pulled out a small photo album. She opened the cover and found a family she'd never seen before. They were seated in a sleigh, with a large Christmas tree behind them. The caption at the bottom read, "Happy Holidays! Love, Matthew, Jill, and Cassidy Coulter."

She recognized Cole from the sketches she'd drawn of him. The woman, an attractive redhead with green eyes and a beautiful smile, had her arm wrapped around Cole's waist. A precious little girl, with reddish ringlets the color of her mother's hair and her father's vivid smoke-blue eyes, sat in front of them. Cole's wife and daughter? What had happened to them?

Each photograph was a depiction of a close and loving family. Vacations, holidays, sporting events. At one time, Cole Mathison had lived under a different name and had possessed an adoring wife and daughter. Something had happened to them.

Shea peeked into the box again and found another stack of cards. The top one said, "To my darling husband." Feeling too much like a voyeur, Shea put them aside.

She dug deeper into the box and found more photos, these of a younger-looking Matthew and Jill, most likely taken before the birth of their daughter. As she stared at the photos of Jill Coulter, she began to understand her own appeal for Cole. She and Jill could have been sisters.

Her eye caught sight of a newspaper clipping at the bottom of the box. Snagging the paper, she pulled it out. Her heart turned over in horror at the headline.

SCHOOLTEACHER'S FAMILY KILLED IN REVENGE FOR BAD GRADES.

As she read the article, her heart broke for the once beautiful family. Matthew Coulter had been a history teacher who had apparently given failing grades to some football players, who were then kicked off the team. In revenge, they'd broken into his home. The authorities didn't believe that they originally intended to kill any-

one, but one of the kids, high on drugs, went crazy and
shot both his wife and daughter.

Matthew had come from work to find that his life had
been destroyed.

Shea picked up the items she'd removed from the box
and closed it up. It wasn't until the small sob echoed in
the room that she realized she was crying. She might not
remember Cole, but the horror of what he'd experienced
would affect anyone.

Pulling in a ragged breath, she turned to another box,
this one even smaller than the others. The words on the
outside of it caused her heart to leap again. *Cole and
Shea*.

She now had a good idea why Cole had married her.
Now, hopefully, she would get some answers as to why
she would marry one man when she obviously loved another.

The box was pitifully light. She opened it and found a
few old movie stubs, a couple of photos showing her
and Cole. Neither of them looked particularly happy.
Her hand reached in for anything else. The tip of one
finger brushed against something velvet. She picked it
up.

A ring box.

Her heart thudded in an unnatural rhythm. Shea
closed her eyes as a wave of dizziness attacked. And in
that instant she saw him. In that instant she knew him.
And she knew what had happened.

*"Marry me, Shea. I know you don't love me. And you
know Jill was my life. But we could be there for each
other. That baby you're carrying needs a father. Ethan
might not be able to handle fatherhood, but I can."*

She had been pregnant? With Ethan's baby.

Frantically, her hands went to her abdomen. What
had happened to the child? Her fingers drifted over her
flat stomach. She'd seen herself in the mirror, and there

had been no indication that she'd once had a baby. No looseness of skin, stretch marks, incisions . . . nothing. The only explanation was that she'd lost the child. Another sob built up inside her at the loss of a baby she hadn't remembered.

Her vision blurred from tears, Shea opened the ring box. A beautiful diamond solitaire rested inside, glistening with promise and hope that had never panned out. She clicked the box closed and dropped it back into the box. An envelope holding legal-looking documents caught her attention. Her breath hitched as the answer to another question was exposed. She and Cole had not had a happy marriage.

Dropping the document back inside the box, Shea stood, exhausted and worn out. She had to get out of here. Every time she opened a box, either more questions arose or another heartache was revealed. The strain of trying to force her memories had drained her. She checked her watch. Five hours and counting. She'd go back to the motel and rest for a while. Then she'd come back and face the remainder.

Her cellphone jingled in her pocket. As she pulled it out, her heart leaped. Ethan? He was one of the few who knew her cell number. She looked at the readout. *Unknown caller.*

"Hello?"

"You've been a bad, bad kitty."

Panic ripped her insides. How had he gotten her number? Very few knew it. None of them would have willingly given it to him. Her legs shaking, Shea dropped to the dusty floor.

Deep inside she already knew, but she had to ask. "How did you get my number?"

"All in good time, little cat." His voice changed with exaggerated concern. "First of all, how are you doing? How are those pesky memory lapses? Still having migraines? Still waking up at night screaming about demons and monsters?"

"You bastard, tell me how you got this number."

"My, my. You've become a sassy bitch, haven't you? We'll just have to work that out of you again."

Her heart stuttering in her chest, panic set in. She closed her eyes and ground her teeth. *Focus, Shea.* "Where are you?"

"I'm close, my dear, very close. And I have a present for you. I'm sending you a picture right now."

A soft beep sounded. Shea pulled the phone from her ear and pressed a key to view the picture. A naked man was tied hand and foot to a wall. Horror slammed her senses. *Ethan!*

"As you can see, he's a bit out of it now. But I'll make sure he wakes up when you get here."

Shea stood, her spine stiff with determination. "What do you want me to do?"

An eerily familiar giggle caused her to shudder in revulsion. "That's more like it. I want you to go to slot 127 at Killian Bay. There's a small red-and-white speedboat docked there. I want you to get on it."

"If I do, what happens to Ethan?"

"I'll let him go, of course. You're the only one I want. Don't you know that? I love you."

"How do I know you'll let him go?"

"You'll just have to trust me. But you can be assured that if you don't come, he will die. I can guarantee that." He paused for a moment. "Want to see a demonstration of what I'll do to him if you don't come?"

"No. No. I'm coming. Just give me a few—"

"You've got fifteen minutes. If you're not here by then, you can forget ever seeing your golden hero again."

"Give me twenty. I can't—"

"You now have fourteen minutes. Stop wasting my

time. Oh, one more thing. Once this call is over, your cellphone will be unusable. Just a little insurance that you won't be calling for help."

"But I—"

"Thirteen and counting." Rosemount huffed out an exasperated sigh. "Apparently you don't care for Mr. Bishop as much as I thought."

"I'm coming. I'll be there. Just—"

The phone went dead. Shea pressed the On button again. No signal. True to his promise, Rosemount had somehow disabled her phone. Shea dropped it back into her pocket. In a flurry of activity, she set to work. Fortunately, she remembered where the bay was and could get there in less than ten minutes. She needed to use the remaining time to prepare for what lay ahead.

Somehow the bastard had captured Ethan. How and when didn't matter. Returning to that devil terrified her; losing Ethan scared her far more. This time, she would be prepared. This time, Rosemount would not win!

twenty-five

An earthquake was erupting in Ethan's head. Holy hell, it'd been years since he'd hurt this much. His eyes blurred from pain, he blinked and squinted, tried to focus. Twisting slightly to turn his head . . . he found he couldn't. Pain became secondary as the need to determine what the hell had happened became paramount.

Moving his arms and legs proved as futile as moving his head. Either he was paralyzed or in some sort of contraption that prevented any kind of movement. Since every particle of his body hurt, he was pretty sure it was the second theory, which was a relief. At least he knew that all he had to do was escape. The optimistic thought surprised him. That sounded more like Shea.

Shea. Memory returned, and with it fury and horrendous guilt. How stupid they'd all been.

Adrenaline pumped with no place to go. Ethan closed his eyes and forced himself to concentrate on what he could remember.

After leaving his phone on the car, per Rosemount's orders, he'd driven to the warehouse. Gun in hand, knife in his back pocket, and another gun in an ankle holster, he'd felt reasonably prepared. He hadn't spotted his tail, and the place looked deserted. The second he stepped out of the car, men poured from the warehouse. Carrying AK-47s and wearing the cold, soulless expression of trained killers, they surrounded him. Ethan dropped his gun to the pavement and held his hands up.

Then, like the parting of the Red Sea, they gave way, allowing a man to walk between them.

Despite the anger surging through him, a loud guffaw of laughter erupted at his first sighting of Donald Rosemount. A pipsqueak. With one hand, he could throw the shrimp across the parking lot like a football. And he'd fooled them all.

His chances of getting to Rosemount before he got his head blown off? Not good. All five men had their guns pointed straight to his head. Five head shots? Hell, it'd only take one to blow his brains out.

He threw a cocky grin at Rosemount. "Either your guys have heard of me or you're overcompensating for a tiny, shriveled—"

The hard-edged butt of a gun slammed into his head, cutting off the rest of his insult. Ethan remembered falling face-first onto the ground; then, instead of shooting him, which he would have greatly preferred, the men took turns kicking the shit out of him. He was at the edge of consciousness when Rosemount yelled, "Stop!"

Two men held guns against his head as Rosemount leaned over him. "I don't want you dead, Mr. Bishop. I just want you." Then he'd let loose a giggle, which scared Ethan a hell of a lot more than the guns. The guy was certifiable.

And then a needle was injected into his neck and he knew nothing more.

With his head in a vise, he could see only what was directly in front of him and in his peripheral vision. Concrete walls and floor. No windows. A basement or storm cellar? He was so screwed.

The door in front of him opened. A warm swath of air caressed his skin, and for the first time Ethan realized that he was stark naked. Well, hell, that couldn't be a good thing.

Donald Rosemount and another man entered. The

one he didn't know was taller than Rosemount, a little older. His expressionless face showed only cold disassociation. There'd be no getting help from this man.

Rosemount's eyes glinted with a supreme smugness. The creep thought he had him exactly where he wanted him. Ethan swallowed a laugh—what was he thinking? He *did* have him exactly where he wanted.

The other man came closer, his gaze shifting nervously to the ties at Ethan's hands. "You're sure he can't get loose?"

Rosemount huffed a disgusted breath as he drew closer to Ethan. "He can barely move a muscle, much less get loose. You're safe." A wide smile spread across his face. "Welcome to my humble little home, Mr. Bishop. I've been looking forward to this day for so long."

Ethan replied with a flippant arrogance, "Oh yeah? You should've said something sooner. I would've hightailed it down here to meet you."

"I do love a man with a sense of humor. It gives me a certain kind of thrill when I get to observe its total destruction."

Ethan snorted. "You're an awfully brave man around tied-up people, Rosemount. Why don't you untie me and let's see how big your balls really are."

Rosemount's beaky nose scrunched up in distaste. "Now, that's just gross. After all the work I've done getting one of the best plastic surgeons in the world to come and take a look at you."

Ethan stiffened. "What the hell are you talking about?"

"Simply that I can't have you working for me, looking like that." He pointed to Ethan's scarred face. "I can barely even look at you. Dr. Bromead is going to fix you for me."

"Thanks but no thanks to the job offer. And I don't want to be fixed."

"I'm afraid you have no choice in the work, and physical perfection is a must." Rosemount's eyes roamed up and down Ethan's nude body. "The rest of you—with the exception of the scars on your leg and side—is . . . well, let's just say I'm not disappointed. You're exactly how I pictured you. Like a big, golden lion, ferocious and bold, just begging to be tamed. But those hideous scars must be repaired. I can't allow you to stay with me unless you're perfect everywhere."

"You're a sick fuck, you know that?"

A sly smile slid up Rosemount's thin lips. "You'll soon change your tune." He turned to the doctor. "What do you think, Wally?"

Ethan had been so focused on Rosemount, he hadn't paid attention to the doctor, who had been staring at him as if he were a specimen under a microscope.

"The scars on his leg and side are easy fixes. But the one on his face." He shook his head. "I can make it better, but I can't get rid of it completely. It's too old, too deep."

"Are you sure?" Rosemount sounded like an ill-tempered five-year-old.

"I'm sorry, Donald. I know you wanted him perfect. I can make the scar less noticeable, but it'll still be there."

"No, he's got to be smooth. Flawless."

"It's not possible."

Laughter built inside Ethan and burst forth like a geyser. How ironic. The scar he'd kept on his face as a reminder of his past sins was actually going to save him from becoming one of Rosemount's zombies. This was priceless.

"Shut up." Rosemount glared at Ethan. "Do you think since I can't have you fixed you're just going to be set free?"

"We had an agreement."

"Ah yes, a trade of sorts. He's waiting right outside the door. Shall I bring him in?" Rosemount walked to the door and opened it. "Come in."

Fury unlike anything he'd ever experienced swamped Ethan as he stared at the tall, muscular man marching through the door. Smoke-blue eyes, glazed and lifeless, stared at him without any hint of recognition or emotion. Though he looked stronger and more powerful than Ethan remembered, the lines etched around his eyes and mouth belied his lack of emotion. The man had suffered, greatly.

Barely able to form words, Ethan growled between clenched teeth, "You're a fucking dead man, Rosemount."

Rosemount blew out a dramatic sigh. "Here I thought bringing two old friends together in a reunion would be something you'd appreciate. All three of us have something in common. We've all enjoyed the same woman. Why, I even let him watch us together. Very open-minded of me, don't you think?"

Ethan locked his jaw to avoid a response. The sick freak only wanted to rile him.

After a slight huff of disappointment, Rosemount turned toward the door. "I'm going to leave your friend with you for a while so you can revisit old times. Don't be too hard on him, though. He's not allowed to talk unless I ask him a direct question. And he has almost no cognitive thought, other than what I've given him. You'll have to carry the conversation." Before walking out the door, he turned back to Ethan and grinned. "On the bright side, he's an excellent listener."

Ethan ignored Rosemount's exit as he looked at the man he'd once called friend. How in God's name had this happened, and how was he going to get him out alive? Rosemount wasn't going to just let him go.

Could he understand anything? Comprehend what had happened to him? If these were the same drugs the bastard had used on Shea, not only wouldn't he recognize Ethan, he might well see him as his enemy.

How the hell could Ethan get through to him?

The big golden-haired man tied to the wall must have angered the master. Dried blood and bruises covered his face and torso. The scar on his cheek stood out like a white stripe against his battered face.

The man began to talk softly and slowly to him. "I am so damned sorry. We thought you were dead." His mouth twisted slightly. "Guess it won't do any good to ask if you recognize me?"

He moved closer. Recognize him? No, he didn't. The man looked distraught. Tears pooled in his eyes, rolled down his face.

After a deep, ragged breath, the man said, "Your name is Cole Mathison. You're an LCR operative. You have a wife, Shea. Do you remember Shea?"

Why did the man continue to talk to him? No one ever talked to him other than the master. He wasn't allowed to answer back—not that he would know what to say. What were the master's plans for this man? Would he want his neck snapped as he had so many others?

He knew he'd done something to displease the master. What or how, he didn't know. But he did know that he'd been punished. He had a vague remembrance of searing pain in his back. He was allowed outside for only a few hours each day, for training. And if the master came by, he had to hide. The master didn't want to see him. Today was the first time in weeks the master had asked for his help. If he pleased him, perhaps he wouldn't be punished again.

He turned around as he heard the master return.

"Did you have a nice visit?" the master said.

The golden-haired man said softly, "I'm going to tear your body limb from limb."

The master looked startled for a second and then smiled. "I'm afraid you won't have a chance." He turned away from the bound man and looked at him. "Are you ready to see my woman again?"

He nodded and said, "Yes."

"Then let's go." The master turned back to the golden-haired man. "We'll have another, even more special reunion when we return."

As he followed the master out the door, the man on the wall shouted, "No, damn you. Leave Shea alone!"

Gabe straightened in his seat when he spotted Shea coming out of the storage room. *Finally.* He'd begun to think she was going to stay the entire day. Not that he didn't have sympathy for her, but bodyguards were human, too. Give him a bathroom, a cup of coffee, and maybe a burger, then he'd gladly sit on his ass for another five hours.

She looked like hell. Even from a distance, he could see how upset she was. Poor woman was sheet white and looked as if— He stiffened. Shea was getting into her car, but her hand had given him a subtle but distinct signal. An LCR signal . . . *Follow me.*

Cranking the engine, Gabe waited. She started her car and drove toward the exit. Her head made subtle shifts every few seconds as she checked the rearview mirror as if assuring herself that he was still there. Something was very wrong.

He picked up his phone and pressed a key for Noah. "Something's up. She just left the storage facility. She looked scared as hell and motioned me to follow her."

"No one approached her?"

"No, no one's been near the building."

"What's she doing now?"

"We're heading down Marjorie Street. I'm about two car lengths behind her."

"Stay on the line. I'm calling in some of our locals."

"Okay, but instruct them to hang back. Something tells me she thinks she's being watched."

"Hold on."

Gabe switched on the GPS screen at his dashboard. Shea was heading toward the water. Killian Bay. He slowed, extending the distance between them. She knew he was there and he could see her, which was all he needed right now.

Noah came back on the line. "Okay, I've got your position. You're headed to Killian Bay. It's a large marina, busy place, lots of boats."

"What my backup ETA?"

"About eight minutes."

"Too late. She's already heading into the parking lot. I'll have to stay with her. Track me on my portable GPS. Tell our guys to follow when they can."

"Will do. Stay safe and report in when you can."

Shea parked several yards in front of him. Gabe snagged a parking place, hastily slid the small tracking device into his pant cuff, grabbed his pistol, and eased out of his car.

Shea jumped out of her car. Looking neither left nor right, she headed down a long pier and stopped in front of a red-and-white speedboat.

Gabe lowered his head and pretended to be looking at a dent on the hood as he watched Shea step up onto the boat. The instant her foot touched down, hands grabbed her. She disappeared from his view.

Stealth no longer an option, Gabe started running. The motorboat rumbled to life. If he didn't get on it soon, Shea would be on her own. Long legs eating up the distance, he took a flying leap and landed on its deck.

Pulling in gasping breaths of air, he flipped over. Two men stood over him with guns. Before he could open his mouth, the butt of a rifle slammed against his head.

Teeth clenched with determination and a pounding rage, Ethan tugged on the bindings at his wrists. He didn't know how long he had. If he didn't get out before they came back, they were all screwed. Damned if he'd allow that to happen. Cole was alive. He had to do something. And now Rosemount had threatened him with Shea. Had he found her, or was that a part of his torture? If he'd found her, then how? Wasn't she still at the clinic?

Cellphone. Shit, his cellphone had her number. If Rosemount called her, maybe sent her a picture of him or Cole . . . Hell, she'd do whatever the bastard wanted if she thought she could save their lives. She was that foolish and that heroic. Even after escaping from the hell Rosemount had put her through, she'd come back to it if she thought it would do any good. He had to get out of this room before they got to her.

Ignoring the blood streaming down his arms from the rips in his skin, Ethan twisted, tugged, and wrenched. As he struggled for freedom, his mind went back to that black day when all hell had broken loose and they believed Cole had died.

He and Shea had been in the midst of an argument when Cole's garbled message came through the radio. All he'd been able to make out were the words "something's wrong" and "going in." Ethan had ordered Cole to wait but had received no response.

In that instant, he'd met Shea's eyes and they'd been out the door. They made it outside just in time to see Cole run into the warehouse. He and Shea had started racing down the gravel road to the building. A few steps ahead of Shea, he'd glanced over his shoulder and shouted at her to go back. And in that instant, the entire building had detonated. He'd flung himself over Shea, covering her. Fiery pieces of wood and metal had rained down on them. Finally able to raise his head, he'd faced a blazing, decimated building. Nothing could have survived.

The fire investigators later determined that the cause of the blast was a combination of TNT and RDX, along with several pounds of magnesium. Since magnesium burns at around four thousand degrees and human bones turn to dust at two thousand degrees or so, no human remains had been found. Rosemount had somehow smelled a setup and been prepared. In the few seconds Cole had been in the building, he'd been captured. And Rosemount had made sure no one doubted Cole's death.

God, he'd been alive all along. Under the influence of Rosemount's drugs, completely helpless to think or act for himself. There was no telling what they'd put him through. Though he looked even more muscular than before, lines creased his face, evidence of his suffering. Whatever he'd gone through had caused him great physical and mental anguish.

The door clicked open. Ethan froze.

Rosemount sauntered in, his smug expression alerting Ethan that the man was satisfied with the way things were going. Did that mean he'd gotten to Shea? How the hell could he have done that without LCR knowing? Gabe had sworn he would protect her.

His body practically vibrating with excitement, Rosemount clapped his hands and bounced on his feet like a kid who'd just gotten his dream bike. "This has been the best day ever."

Ethan glared at the piece of shit before him. He kept

his voice soft and deliberate, wanting the man to understand the seriousness of his threat. "You're going down, Rosemount. Very soon. Don't •doubt that for an instant."

Ugly brown eyes flaring with fear, Rosemount pulled a gun from his jacket and swung it up toward Ethan's face. "I can kill you, right here, right now. You think you're so big, so powerful. Well, look who's got all the power now. Too bad your muscles didn't extend to your brain. Once more I've proven my theory: superior intelligence wins over brawn every time."

As if he hadn't spoken, Ethan let his eyes roam up and down Rosemount's body as he mused, "And you're a scrawny little creature, not much bigger than the maggot you resemble. The killing will be easy for me. Your pain will be immense. Your bones will crack like dry, dead wood. Puny little ribs will puncture your shriveled pea-sized heart. I'll make sure you stay alive until every single fucking bone in your weasel-sized soft little body is snapped."

Fire-red color shot up Rosemount's face. Holding the gun with two hands, he stalked over and pointed it up toward the center of Ethan's head. "I could just—"

A fist pounded on the door.

Rosemount brought the gun down and gathered his composure with a shaky breath. His mouth trembled and stretched into odd contortions. "You almost ruined it for me." He crossed the room and called to someone outside the door. "Bring her in."

Everything within Ethan went still and stiff with dread. One of Rosemount's goons pushed Shea into the room. His heart sank. The beautiful face that had only recently regained the vibrancy and life of the old Shea had disappeared. Emerald eyes, blank and empty, stared through him as if she saw nothing. Just as they had all those months ago.

"Shea," Ethan groaned.

Her face remained impassive, with no indication that she heard him.

"Shea, look at me, please."

Rosemount's evil gurgle of laughter bounced against the concrete walls. "I'm afraid Shea's no longer with us, Mr. Bishop. My kitten has been returned to me . . . thanks to you."

"What are you talking about?"

"Simple. I sent her a picture of you. She sacrificed herself to save you. Isn't that romantic?" He clasped his hands over his heart and sighed. "But I saved the best for last."

He turned to one of the men who'd brought Shea in. "Spread the plastic under him and several feet from the wall. I want nothing of him remaining when we throw his corpse out."

Their faces almost as expressionless as Shea's, the two men unfolded a thick square of plastic. Placing it at Ethan's feet, they pulled at the plastic until it covered half the room.

Rosemount grabbed Shea's hand and wrapped her fingers around the handle of a knife. "He can't be fixed, my dear, so do the honors, will you. Slice his gut open, just below his navel. I want his death to be slow. While he's bleeding, he can watch us get reacquainted. If you please me, I'll pickle his heart for you and put it in a jar."

Shea nodded. Knife in hand, she took slow, deliberate steps toward Ethan.

"Dammit. Don't do this. Wake up. Shea!" Ethan struggled against his bonds. Dying didn't terrify him as much as the knowledge that if Shea ever realized what she'd done, she would never recover.

A few feet in front of him, she stopped and stared. Was there anything of Shea inside her? "Shea, please, baby, wake up. Cole's alive. We can get out of here. Everything will be fine. Just. Wake. Up!"

Was there a tiny flicker of expression? Ethan's heart stopped. Had he seen a spark of life in her eyes or was it his wishful imagination?

"Go on," Rosemount urged behind her, "get it over with."

Taking several steps closer, she raised her arm, the knife grasped securely in her slender hand. Ethan looked into her face. If this was it . . . if he were to die, then Shea's beautiful face was the last image he wanted in his mind.

"Go on. Do it!" Rosemount shouted.

The knife glinted as her hand twisted to reposition it for the kill.

"I love you, Shea."

Her head tilted slightly. Beautiful lips curved up in a smile. She winked. The knife slashed down, slicing his bonds.

He was free!

twenty-six

A shrill scream, like an enraged hog, split the air. Shea whirled around as two men rushed toward her. She waited . . . waited. At the last second, she pivoted left. One man stumbled past her. The other stopped short and swiped a meaty fist at her face. Shea twisted, whirled, and kicked. Thankful for the wedge-heeled shoes she'd discovered earlier, she smacked the side of her foot into his jaw, hard, cracking it. His expression blank, he thudded to the floor.

A roar came from behind her. Shea turned halfway. The other man was back on his feet. Eyes glinting with unholy coldness, he ran toward her. Legs slightly bent, she prepared for his attack. A strong breeze of air rushed by as Ethan passed, throwing himself at the man. His fist slammed into the side of the man's head, then his gut. Assured that Ethan was healthy and more than capable of taking care of himself, Shea twisted around. Another man came through the door and ran toward her. Pivoting left, she side-kicked his head, her foot connecting with his nose. A satisfying crunch and then blood spurted. He fell facedown onto the plastic covering.

Panting slightly, she turned to see Ethan retrieving a gun from one of the unconscious men. "Where's Rosemount?"

Ethan grinned. "Ran out of here like a little girl."

"Hey, girls are tough, too."

He pulled her close for a hard hug. "Tell me about it."

Shea savored his arms for a second and looked up into his beloved battered face. "Were you serious? Cole's alive?"

"Drugged, but definitely alive."

"We'd better get out there then. There's no telling what Rosemount will do."

While Shea grabbed a gun from one of the fallen men, Ethan went to the largest of them and, with quick efficiency, pulled the man's pants off and slid into them. "Let's go."

Shea opened the door to a dimly lit, long, narrow hallway. Guns at the ready, they headed toward a door at the end. Running beside Ethan, she explained, "Rosemount called me. He sent a picture of you. Gabe followed me, but I don't know where he is. He probably wasn't able to get on board."

Ethan nodded. "I was unconscious when they brought me here. Do you know where we are?"

"Not really. Once I got on the boat, they put me below deck. We traveled about forty-five minutes from Key West. I know it's an island, but this is the only house I saw."

"Any idea how many men are here?"

"There were four with me on the boat."

Ethan grunted. "I had five, but three of them are back there on the floor."

"Rosemount's such a chicken, we'd better be prepared for an army."

In unspoken agreement, they slowed as they approached the single door on the left.

Ethan's eyes examined her. "How did you avoid getting the drug? I would've thought that'd be Rosemount's first priority."

"It was."

"What? Then how . . . ?"

"The drug Dr. Norton's people came up with . . . I had

several vials. I took a double dose in the hope that it would counteract what Rosemount gave me. It worked."

"Dammit, Shea, that could've killed you."

Dismissing the vile headache and nausea she'd fought during the first half hour of overdosing, she shrugged and flashed him a cocky grin. "Saved your ass."

He returned her grin with one of his own. "You're right."

At the door, they stopped. Ethan moved to the other side. Able to read his thoughts with just one look, Shea felt as if they'd never parted. She twisted the knob, and the door swung open. With stealthy quietness, gun at the ready, Ethan peered in low, then high, moving to avoid being a still target.

"Empty stairway," he said quietly.

Ethan went through the doorway; Shea followed. His long legs took the steps three at a time. They stopped at the door and Shea whispered, "Hold on."

Ethan jerked around. "What are you doing?"

Slipping her shoe off, she twisted the bottom and pulled out several vials of her new miracle drug. "Getting prepared in case I can get one of these into Cole."

"Shea?"

The husky tone of Ethan's voice had her looking up. His expression was a mixture of tenderness, grim acknowledgment, and pride. "You've remembered everything, haven't you?"

Recognizing and understanding every nuance of his expression, she answered with a simple and quiet "Yes."

He blew out a long breath. "We have a lot to talk about."

She straightened, pocketed the vials, and nodded. "Yes, we do."

Ethan turned back to the door; Shea grabbed his arm. "Wait. I don't want Rosemount killed."

The glare Ethan shot her told her he disagreed. "Why?"

"Because I want him to rot in prison."

A smile of understanding tugged at his mouth. "You're right. There are some things worse than death. And few people who deserve it more. I'll see what I can do to make sure he stays alive." He shrugged and added, "Healthy is another thing."

"Sounds good to me."

Shea turned the knob, pushed open the door. Ethan dropped low, took a look, and jerked back. "Kitchen's the next room. Rosemount's visible through the doorway . . . in the middle of the living room. Surrounded by four armed men. He's got a .357 Magnum to Gabe's head."

Shea closed her eyes. "Guess that answers my question about Gabe."

"Come on out." Rosemount's voice sounded strained and nervous. Not a good thing . . . especially for a coward with a gun in his hand. "Come join the fun."

Ethan took Shea's knife and slipped it into the back pocket of his pants, then shoved the gun into his waistband at the small of his back. "Stay back. Cover me."

She didn't argue. Ethan was better trained in hand-to-hand combat. She was a good shot. They needed to use their strengths to get out of this situation with everyone intact.

Ethan strode through the kitchen. At the living room door he stopped and took in the scene. Rosemount stood in the middle of the room. A tied-up and gagged Gabe sat at his feet. The gun, pressed against Gabe's temple, shook. One finger twitch and Gabe was a goner. Sweat rolled down Rosemount's face; his eyes, behind the thick glasses, darted back and forth, roaming all over the room. The man was scared as hell and desperate. A bad combination for someone as fucked up as Rosemount.

The four men around Rosemount all shared the same glazed expressions. Their guns aimed at Ethan indicated their intentions. *Well, hell.*

Ethan's gaze flicked to Gabe. His blue eyes were almost black with fury. When he got free, Rosemount wouldn't stand a chance.

Rosemount's voice, squeaky-high and shaking, grated on Ethan's ears. The nose of his gun ground against Gabe's temple. "I really want to keep him, but if you don't back off, I'll sacrifice him."

Ethan held his hands at his sides, away from his body. "You kill him, you'll be dead in an instant."

"Oh yeah, who's going to kill me? Not you. My soldiers will rip your body in half with one shot. And my woman may have disobeyed me, but she wouldn't hurt me."

Ethan just smiled. No words were necessary.

Biting his lips, Rosemount glanced around nervously. Then his eyes narrowed into lizardlike slits, a sly look replacing the fear. "I have another idea." Turning his gaze to Ethan's left, he said, "Snap his neck."

Ethan twisted around. *Cole.* His expressionless face and cold, emotionless eyes said it all. He would do whatever Rosemount wanted. Without any concept of right or wrong, he only knew he had to obey. Ethan turned fully toward him, his mind racing with how to take down his friend without killing him or getting killed.

Cole marched toward him; Ethan braced himself. Just before Cole attacked, Ethan kicked, his foot landing squarely on Cole's chest. Confusion flickered on Cole's face. He stumbled slightly, recovered, and started forward again. Ethan backed up and kicked again, targeting the same spot. Pain flashed in Cole's face before he dropped to his knees. Ethan scrambled behind him. Sliding his forearm under Cole's chin, he locked him in a choke hold. And squeezed. Cole gasped and gurgled. Pulled at Ethan's arms. Shifting left and right, he grunted as he tried to dislodge Ethan. Keeping the pressure tight but not lethal, Ethan held on. At last Cole slumped to the floor, unconscious.

Rosemount squealed, raised the gun from Gabe's head, and fired at Ethan. Ethan dropped and rolled. Catching sight of a leather recliner to his right, he sprang to his feet and leaped. Tipping the chair, Ethan rolled it forward with his body and ducked behind it for cover.

Raising his head slightly, he caught a glimpse of vibrant auburn hair at the doorway as Shea fired. Blood bloomed on Rosemount's shoulder, and he let out another squeal as he twisted his head and stared at the doorway where Shea had stood. His voice shook with hurt and betrayal. "She shot me."

With a wild sweep of his arm, he ordered the two men to his left: "Go get the woman. If you have to shoot her, fine, just don't kill her." He turned and shouted to the men on the other side, "Kill the freak with the scar. Now!"

Shit. Sinking behind the chair, Ethan pulled Shea's knife from his back pocket. Ears attuned, he heard the soldiers stomp closer. Praying that he'd gauged the distance correctly, as well as the height of the men, Ethan peered over the edge of the chair. Once he spotted the target, he let the knife fly. The blade landed inside the intended target: the man's groin.

An unholy scream erupted. Eyes rolling back in his head, the soldier dropped his gun. His hands clutched the knife as he fell to his knees, his screams turning to agonized whimpers. The other soldier never spared his comrade a glance as he continued forward. Holding his gun steady, Ethan squeezed off a shot. The bullet ripped into the man's hand. He howled, too, his steps faltering as he looked down at the blood. Then, his expression showing no emotion, he kept marching toward Ethan.

Resting his arms on the chair to steady himself, Ethan fired another shot, this time into the man's other hand. That stopped his forward progress. The gun fell as the soldier held both damaged hands and howled with pain.

Clambering from his hideout, Ethan ran toward the door. Shea and one pistol against two men with AK-47s? She didn't stand a chance.

"Hold it right there."

Ethan halted. Rosemount stood in front of him. Hands shaking violently, the bastard was close to losing all control.

Out of the corner of his eye, Ethan saw Gabe approaching. Because of Rosemount's tunnel vision and blind arrogance, he'd forgotten about the man he'd left tied up on the floor. To Gabe, having his hands tied behind his back was a slight and insignificant detail. There were dozens of ways to kill without using your hands. Gabe knew them all.

Worry for Shea pounded at Ethan. Every second counted, but Ethan forced himself to move toward Rosemount with a nonchalant ease. "Might as well give it up."

"Not bloody likely. Now it's just you and me, and looks who's holding the gun."

"That pea shooter?"

Eyes wild, Rosemount raised the gun higher. Exactly what he and Gabe were waiting for. Ethan ducked as Gabe rammed into Rosemount's back. The shot went wild.

Ethan lifted his head to see Gabe sitting on Donald Rosemount's back. The man was facedown on the floor, kicking, pounding, and sobbing, his feet and hands useless.

Wishing he had time to appreciate the picture, Ethan dashed toward the kitchen. The door leading outside was open. In the distance, he heard the blast of an AK-47. His heart almost exploded. About to run out the door, he was stopped by Shea's voice: "Hey, over here."

Ethan whirled around.

Shea emerged from a bottom cabinet. Grinning, she dusted off her clothes. "Donald's cabinets are nice and roomy, but he needs to dust more often."

His legs wobbling as if they were made of melted rubber, Ethan strode awkwardly toward Shea. "You scared the hell out of me."

"Not a scratch on me." Her eyes shifted to the door. "Where's Rosemount?"

"Come see. Gabe caught himself a little fish."

They stood in the doorway and watched Gabe make himself more comfortable on top of Rosemount. Multiple gunshots from outside drowned out Shea's chuckle. Ethan peered through the window. Seeing the distinctive blue jackets of LCR people, Ethan blew out a relieved sigh as they swarmed the grounds. He turned to Shea and said, "Cavalry's here. I'll go—"

A big body slammed into him. *Cole.* Ethan skidded across the carpet, landed on his shoulder. He heard and felt a pop. Twisting around, he tried to push Cole off, but his arms were trapped between their bodies. Big hands wrapped around Ethan's neck with one clear intent: he'd been ordered to snap Ethan's neck. Unconsciousness had delayed him, but it hadn't stopped him.

Ethan pushed with all his might. The roaring in his ears told him suffocation was imminent. Underneath the roar, he heard Shea's sobbing voice pleading. She hopped onto Cole's back, pulled frantically at his arms.

Ethan pushed harder. If he died, Cole might go after Shea next.

Black dots appeared before his eyes. His vision blurred. Ethan's knee shot up and rammed the other man's balls. A slight loosening gave Ethan air; then the hands tightened again. He could see Shea's face, wet with tears and wild with fear, just above Cole's shoulder. Her hand came up to Cole's neck, and she jammed a needle into the skin. Cole froze for an instant, his expression one of confusion. Then, with a roar, he threw Shea off and lurched to his feet.

His head in his hands as if in agony, Cole roared again, the heart-ripping sound an agonizing testament of a tortured soul.

Gasping and coughing, Ethan got to his feet, looking for Shea. She'd landed facedown several feet away. Ethan half-ran, half-crawled to her. His heart in his throat, he rolled her over. She blinked up at him with a reassuring smile.

Another agonizing roar. They turned to see Cole shoving Gabe off Rosemount. Donald let loose an ear-bursting screech. Scrambling on all fours like a frightened cockroach, he tried to escape. Cole scooped him up and dangled him by his neck. Rosemount's legs swung uselessly; his hands slapped ineffectually at Cole's arms as his face turned a brilliant purple. Then, like a pretzel stick, his neck snapped. With another roar, Cole swung Rosemount around and threw him across the room. His body made a nauseating but satisfying crack as it slammed against the stone fireplace.

Cole whirled around, his face wild with a horror Ethan could only imagine. Never had he seen such agony. With a soft sob, Shea jumped up and ran toward him. Ethan opened his mouth to shout at her to get back. Before he could say anything, Cole's arms wrapped around her. They dropped to the floor together.

It was finally at an end.

Ethan pulled himself to his feet, his dislocated shoulder and bruises a distant, ignorable pain. The couple on the floor was a demonstration of not only horrendous suffering but also incredible survival.

Pulling her head from Cole's shoulder, Shea looked up at Ethan. Tears poured down her face. An ungodly ache grew in his heart. What these two had endured was unimaginable, but they would survive. With their inner strength and support from each other, Cole and Shea could be the loving couple they were meant to be. As long as Ethan stayed out of their way. He'd sabotaged their marriage once before, and they'd all paid a hefty price. It was time to accept the inevitable. Time to let Shea go.

Offering her a small nod of understanding, he turned away. There was cleanup to do; reports had to be filed. Then he would go home, where he belonged.

twenty-seven

Washed out, ecstatic, weepy, and a whole host of other things, Shea shuffled out of Cole's room. He was finally and thankfully asleep. Dr. Norton knew much more about Rosemount's drugs now. Cole could be treated more extensively and more quickly. Though he was still confused and in pain, his prognosis for a full recovery was excellent. His physical strength would return much sooner than his mental stability. She knew from experience that it could take him months to overcome all the demons he faced.

"How's he doing?"

Ethan sat slumped in a chair down the hallway. Bruises and cuts stood out distinctly against his too pale skin. A sling held his right shoulder in place, and his wrists were wrapped in bandages. He looked as bad as she felt.

"He's finally asleep."

"Does he remember?"

She nodded, sad beyond measure at what he did remember. "Not all of it yet, but a lot. Too much, too soon. Dr. Norton gave him something to help him sleep. He couldn't handle any more today." She swallowed hard. "Neither could I." Still unable to believe the horror of his torture, her eyes swam with tears. "What Rosemount did to him, Ethan . . . I still can't believe it. I've never seen scars like that . . . all over his back. I can't imagine the agony he's endured."

His eyes stark with pain for his friend, Ethan said, "With your help, he'll make it through."

Shea swallowed a sob. What had she expected? Ethan hadn't changed his mind. She had to accept that and move on. But first, they needed to get some things out in the open.

"Can we talk a few minutes?"

Looking as though he'd just as soon eat razor blades, he gave a brief nod. Together they walked toward a staff lounge, thankfully empty.

The instant the door swung closed, she moved across the room and leaned against a table. She needed to be as far away from Ethan as she could get. If she stayed close to him, she'd end up in his arms. In her weak and vulnerable state, she couldn't trust herself. She had things to say, questions to ask, and apologies to make. Having all her memories back gave her a certain amount of peace, but also a knowledge of what she had done to precipitate so much of what came after. Ethan had taken all of the guilt on himself, and she couldn't allow that to stand.

Before she could find a way to begin, Ethan asked, "How much do you remember?"

"Everything."

His eyes closed. Regret or relief?

"When did that happen?"

Her shoulders lifted in a tired shrug. "That double injection I gave myself, coupled with Rosemount's drug on the boat, pushed all of it out. By the time we arrived on the island, I had remembered it all."

"Then you know about . . . ?" His clenched jaw indicated that he couldn't say the words.

"I know everything." Her head tilted. "I wonder if you do."

"What do you mean?"

"I was pregnant."

Regret and sorrow settled on his face. "Yes."

"You accused me of doing it on purpose . . . trying to trap you."

His throat working, he nodded.

She took a breath and admitted what she hadn't been able to then. "I did, you know." Her eyes closed briefly, battling tears. "You didn't want a commitment, told me over and over you didn't. But I knew you loved me . . . you never said it, but I never doubted that. I thought if I got pregnant, it would be easier for you and you'd have no choice. I thought you'd admit your feelings and that would be that." She closed her eyes again and whispered, "God, I was so stupid."

"I forced you into—"

Her eyes flew open. Furious, she pointed her finger at him and snarled, "Stop right there. You did not force me into getting pregnant. No man forces a woman to try and trap him. When you said the words, it was the first time I allowed myself to acknowledge what I'd done." She shook her head in regret. "I was so ashamed of myself. And angry . . . at both of us."

Ethan shook his head. "I handled it badly, Shea. Said those contemptible things to you. I knew I was hurting you, hurting myself. I was furious, but I didn't mean any of what I said. Having a baby with you would have been one of the greatest blessings of my life. Instead, I demanded that you get out. I've never hated myself more than I did in that minute."

Remembering that hellacious day wasn't easy, even the second time around, but they had to get past this. She and Ethan should have had this discussion long ago. "I came back a few days later. To apologize . . . talk to you. You'd left on assignment." She swallowed a sob. "In the foyer, boxes were everywhere . . . you'd packed up all of my things. All of my clothes, pictures of us together, even the gifts I'd given you. Your message was clear. You wanted nothing left of us . . . nothing that would remind you of me."

"I'm so damned sorry. I panicked. Behaved like a fool."

Despite her urgent need to go to him, ask his forgiveness, give him forgiveness, her feet stayed rooted to the floor. They needed to get this out in the open once and for all. "I took my stuff and drove to Florida to see Cole. I couldn't believe it was over. I needed to talk with someone who understood us both. He guessed immediately what had happened. I told him about the baby, what you'd said. He held me in his arms and I felt safe, no longer afraid."

She took a breath. Could she explain her fear to Ethan? Would he understand how her past had distorted her thinking? "All I could envision was my mother. How she was constantly looking for someone to take care of her and how she ended up with the scum of the earth. And there was Cole, so strong, so good. He'd lost his family and needed me, wanted me. Wanted the baby. I couldn't give him my love, like he deserved, but I could give him a family.

"When he offered marriage . . . it just seemed so simple. I knew you'd never change your mind. You were always throwing Cole in my face, telling me he was the better man. He seemed certain we could make it work. We loved each other in our own fashion. I told myself it was more than most people had. I hoped it would be enough."

Shea stopped for moment. Unable to go on . . . unable to say the words.

His voice thick with emotion, Ethan said them for her: "And then you lost the baby."

One of the most hideous memories of her entire life. God, how she'd wanted and loved that tiny being inside her that never had a chance to live. "I hated you then . . . hated myself more."

Ethan shook his head. "You couldn't have hated me any more than I hated myself. That was my baby, and I denied you both."

"The doctor said it was no one's fault. I didn't believe that for a long time. If it weren't for Cole, I don't know what I would have done."

"You and Cole probably could have made it work if not for me."

Shea gave a soft, disbelieving snort. "I know you'd like to think that, Ethan, simply because you always want to blame yourself for everything. Having to work with you was no piece of cake, but we could have said no." Regret hammered. "That last mission . . ."

"My fault, Shea . . . I started a fight with him. Told him how unhappy you looked. It was none of my damned business."

"You don't understand, Ethan. That last mission, Cole didn't want to go. I talked him into it." The tears that had been threatening rolled down her face. "Don't you see? It was my fault Cole was even there. If I hadn't talked him into going on the op, none of this would have happened."

"Shea, no, it wasn't—"

She swallowed a sob. "If you're planning to take all the blame on yourself, forget it. I screwed up . . . badly, and Cole paid the price." She wiped her face with the back of her hand, drew in a trembling breath. "But now he's safe and Rosemount's dead. That's the most important thing."

"So I guess it's back to the way things used to be."

Shea searched his face, looking for any hope, any hint that he'd changed his mind about them, and saw none. "Guess so."

"I'm headed back to Tennessee tonight."

She gripped the edge of the table behind her, her entire body aching with the effort to hang on to her composure. She made herself nod, hoping it didn't look as awkward as it felt. How she wanted him to ask her to come with him. But he wouldn't. Ethan had made his decision about them, and there was nothing Shea could do. She'd told him how she felt. If he didn't think their love was important enough to fight for, there was nothing more to say.

Determined to hang on, be strong for a few more seconds, she heard her voice say, "Have a safe trip home. Give Stella and the kittens a hug for me."

Ethan's grim mouth cracked slightly for a smile. "Will do." He turned to walk away and then stopped. Shea's heart stopped, too.

Turning back around, he said, "If you or Cole ever need anything, you know where I am."

Unable to do more than offer a half nod, she watched as Ethan walked slowly away, slipping out of her life forever.

Two Months Later . . .

Shea gazed at Cole across the table of what had once been their favorite restaurant in Tampa. She marveled at how much healthier he was beginning to look. "You look wonderful."

His stern mouth curved slightly, but his eyes remained shadowed and grave. Would he ever recover and be the warm, good-hearted man he'd once been? Would he ever again be the man who, though he'd suffered a terrible loss, had had the strength and determination to make the world a better place for others? Only time would tell.

"After doing nothing but eating and sleeping for almost two months, I should look good."

He made it sound as though he'd been on vacation. If only it had been that easy. Cole's memory had returned much more quickly than hers had, but he still had small pockets of memory loss they weren't sure he'd ever get back. And, like Shea, he suffered with migraines and his nightmares had been horrendous. Regaining his memories, regaining his life, had been anything but easy.

Remembering the senseless deaths of his wife and child had been as if he'd lost them all over again. The grief and fury had been fresh and real.

Added to that anguish was his extreme guilt over knowing he'd stood and watched Rosemount abuse Shea and had done nothing to stop it. After reading Rosemount's notes, they'd determined that Cole had talked about Shea . . . giving Rosemount valuable information about her. When Shea had advertised on the Internet site, searching for Rosemount, he had known exactly who she was.

Shea had repeatedly insisted that Cole's guilt was ridiculous. He hadn't been aware of what was happening and couldn't be blamed for something he'd had no control over. Nevertheless, he had the memory of it inside his head, and the guilt remained.

"I talked to Dr. Norton yesterday. He says you're ready to go home."

"Not really sure where home is anymore."

Shea grimaced an apology. "The house in Key West is gone. The money from the sale is still in the bank. I have a two-bedroom apartment here, so you can come stay with me."

Cole leaned forward, and Shea was surprised to see a hint of anger in his eyes. "You want to tell me why the hell you're here and inviting me to live with you, while Ethan's back in Tennessee?"

"Nothing's changed there."

"And you're just going to accept that?"

"What do you mean?"

"You're stronger now, Shea. Much more than when we first married. You were vulnerable and hurt. Ethan crushed you, broke your heart. If you'd been surer of yourself then, you would've made him admit his feelings. Hell, you would've followed him on that op he went on and wouldn't have backed down."

The words rang true. She *was* stronger now. Somehow, what she'd experienced had grounded her, made her more aware of not just her limitations but also her abilities. And it had given her a pride in surviving and overcoming horrific circumstances.

When Ethan had forced her to leave, she'd been pregnant and alone . . . an emotional wreck. Not questioning his treatment of her, she'd allowed him to manipulate their relationship. Insecurity and her own guilt over trying to trap him had blinded her.

Wiser and more mature now, she not only saw who she was, she saw Ethan, too. His strength and goodness had always been apparent. What she hadn't seen, until now, were the insecurities and flaws. And she loved all of him . . . every facet . . . forever.

"I was stupid, Shea . . . should never have asked you to marry me. Should've told you to go back to Ethan and demand an explanation." Cole shook his head, and for an instant, she saw the kindhearted man she'd married. "I had a hole in my heart and a gnawing void in my life. I needed to take care of you. Even if we'd never seen Ethan after our marriage, it wouldn't have worked for us. We love each other, but we were never in love."

She couldn't argue that point either. Even after they married, Cole continued to treat her as a friend, never a wife. Despite her resemblance to his former wife, he'd never been attracted to her in that way.

She'd always felt she'd failed him. But now she realized the truth. Cole had never wanted her to love him in that way. He'd only wanted to take care of her and protect her.

A half sob, half giggle broke out before she could stop it. "I guess we're one of the few married couples who've never slept together."

A wry smile tilted Cole's mouth. "I think we both felt we'd be cheating on the people we really loved. Ethan had your heart. And Jill . . ." He swallowed hard. "What can I say? I loved her. Even though she'd been gone two years, I still felt married to her."

Shea reached across the table and touched his forearm. "Thank you for being there for me."

"We were there for each other. I don't regret the marriage. I do regret making you feel as though you failed me, though. You didn't. We gave each other what we needed to survive. But now it's time for each of us to find our own way."

"I can't just leave you here alone."

"I'd feel a hell of a lot better if I knew that two people who were meant to be together finally got it right. You and Ethan, despite your fiery clashes, love each other the way Jill and I did. No matter where you go or how much Ethan runs from it, neither of you will be happy until you're together."

A shaky optimism surged through her. Could she do it? She'd always claimed that Ethan hadn't fought for their love, but how much had *she* fought for them? By telling Ethan she loved him? He'd known that forever. She'd never denied her love. But she had left the rest up to him. Had believed he should be the one to come after her. Where was her spirit? The determination to stop being a victim? Not fighting for Ethan's love made her a victim. And they both lost. It was time to show Ethan that her love meant she would be there for him, unconditionally and forever.

And if he didn't like that? Well, she'd just stick around

and persuade him otherwise. She knew from experience that she possessed some powerful persuasive skills when it came to Ethan.

A flicker of humor touched Cole's face. "Now, that's the look Shea Monroe should always have. Go to Tennessee, grab on to that mangy hair of his, and don't let go until he admits he can't live without you."

She swallowed a laughing sob. "He may go bald before that happens."

"Hell, it'll grow back."

"Where will you go?"

"Gabe's been in charge of the Rosemount cleanup." Bitter contempt darkened his eyes. "Most of the scientists and doctors were captured. There's one, though . . . one I'll never forget. He got away. And I'm going to find him.

"Some of the soldiers were for hire, and they've disappeared, too. A few of them were victims like us. . . . Noah wants us to do what we need to, to help them. I'm going to work until there's nothing left of Donald Rosemount on this earth."

"Then what?"

She instantly regretted the question as Cole's mouth tightened with pain.

"You know Rosemount kept records of everything. I read my file." He paused as if he had a hard time comprehending the reality of his next words. "I killed a man, Shea. On my very first job, they overdosed me and I went crazy. Thing is, I didn't need to read the file to know what happened. I can see his face, hear him crying. I killed an innocent man. I can't just act as if it didn't happen."

Shea grabbed his arm. "Dammit, Cole, you didn't know what you were doing."

"Doesn't matter. Rosemount's records indicate that it was a hired abduction. He never named names, but somebody, besides Rosemount, profited. That person may not have wanted the man killed, but he needs to be identified and dealt with. Noah told me the guy had a wife, a family. I can't stop thinking about them. I have to see them . . . make sure they're okay."

"Are you going to tell them the truth?"

His eyes reflected his continued agony. "I don't know."

Her heart hurt for him, but nothing she could say would change his mind. After the hell he'd gone through, Cole's sense of decency and justice remained steadfast.

He stood, pulled Shea to her feet, and hugged her hard. "Go after that stubborn idiot you adore. Tell him I hope we can be friends again someday."

"He was always your friend, Cole."

"Yeah, well, things got a little strained between us after I married the woman he loved."

Shea snorted. "He's the one who played match-maker."

A genuine grin curved his mouth. "True. Big dumb lug. Tell him I'll forgive him if he asks me to be his best man."

Returning Cole's hug, Shea felt hope spiral through her. Ready or not, Ethan Bishop was in for more than a few surprises.

East Tennessee

A soft, slender body pressed down on him; a hand covered his mouth. Instantly, he knew. He lay still, waiting, not daring to hope.

"Ethan, I'm taking you out of here. Understand?"

Beneath her hand, he smiled at the familiar words he'd whispered to her months ago. "Where are you taking me?"

Removing her hand, she breathed out a soft laugh. "I haven't decided."

"What are you going to do once you get me to wherever you're taking me?"

"I'm going to tie you up and do wicked things to your body until you admit you can't live without me."

Ethan rolled her over onto her back. "Hell, baby, you don't have to tie me up for me to admit that. But feel free to start on those wicked things."

"Good, because I'd much rather have your hands all over me when I ravish your gorgeous body."

The trees outside the window filtered the early morning light. Shea's beautiful face smiled up at him, her emerald eyes gleaming with love and determination.

"What about Cole?"

"We're not married. Our divorce became final just before that last op."

Ethan's heart skidded to a stop, then skyrocketed. "Why didn't you tell me?"

"I didn't think it would make any difference."

"That's why you'd been crying that day."

Snuggling against him, her head pressed against his chest, she nodded. "I felt so guilty. Even though it wasn't a real marriage, I felt like I had let him down."

What the hell did that mean? Pushing her away slightly, he looked down at her. "What do you mean, it wasn't a real marriage?"

"We never slept together."

More relieved than he had a right to feel, Ethan couldn't let that go. "Why not?"

"Because we didn't love each other in that way. When we got married, it didn't seem right because I was still in love with you. And I think Cole felt all sorts of guilt for marrying his best friend's girl. And he was still in love with his wife. Then I lost the baby, and that was a really rough time for both of us. After I healed, it just never came up again." She giggled and added, "I think we both felt like we'd be committing incest. We loved each other too much like brother and sister."

Ethan closed his eyes. How he'd hated Cole during that time, even though he'd had no right to feel that way. After all, he'd pushed them together. But he'd never been able to get the vision of Shea and Cole making love out of his mind.

"What's changed?"

She tilted her head to look at him. "What do you mean?"

"You said you didn't tell me you weren't married to Cole because you didn't think it would make a difference. What changed your mind?"

"I realized something . . . thanks to Cole pointing it out to me."

"What?"

"I'm not the same person I was before. I'm stronger. I'm not going to let you say no to me anymore. I kept waiting for you to fight for me. Expecting you to come running back to me and admit you loved me. I never fought hard enough for you."

"So what now?"

She pressed a kiss to his chin. "Up to you, big boy. I only know one thing . . . I'm not leaving . . . ever."

"You're serious?"

"Can't get any more serious than that."

When he didn't speak, Shea sat up, and though she tried to hide it, the vulnerability was there. She thought he was going to try to turn her away again. And though she'd bravely announced that she wasn't leaving, the fear of rejection was on her face. He had to make sure of one thing, before they went any further.

"Can you forgive me, Shea? For everything?"

"I think we need to forgive each other."

As he was about to insist that he had nothing to forgive her for, she pressed her fingers against his mouth. "Please, Ethan . . . listen. We both made mistakes. Very serious ones. But can't we put all of that behind us and look to the future? I'm not giving up on you. You seem to believe you don't deserve happiness because of what happened fifteen years ago. I didn't know Abby, but if you loved her, she must have been a wonderful person, and I can guarantee, if she loved you, she would want you to be happy."

Breath shuddered through him. He'd let her go once and regretted it for years. Had never believed he'd have a second chance with her. Never believed she could forgive him for everything he'd done. He wouldn't make the same mistake again. But he needed to know the answer to another very important question. He'd joined LCR with the intent of doing something good and valuable with his life. He'd put that on hold for too long. The need hadn't changed.

"What if I want to go back to LCR?"

Ethan knew that if he lived to be a hundred, he would never forget the beauty of the smile Shea gave him. "That's what I want, too."

"You wouldn't rather stay here?"

"No, but if you decide later on that's what you want, that's okay, too. Haven't you figured that out yet, Ethan? You're my home."

Could it be that simple? "So you're not letting me go, huh?"

"Nope."

"I let you go once, Shea . . . I won't do that again."

"I never wanted to go in the first place."

Leaning his forehead against hers, he whispered, "I was an idiot."

"We both were." Shea drew him down for a tender kiss. "Can you say it aloud, Ethan?" With a wry grin, she added, "Without me holding a knife on you? I really, really need to hear the words."

Ethan took her hand and placed it on his heart. "I love you, Shea. You're my heartbeat . . . my life. Stay with me forever. Be my partner, my lover. Be my wife."

"You're sure?"

"Absolutely." He pressed a kiss to her forehead, the tip of her nose, then her mouth. Before she could respond, he pulled away and added, "There's something else I want, too."

"What?"

"Babies."

A joyous giggle burst out. "Can we do both?"

"If anyone can, we can."

"You once said that this world was too rotten to bring kids into it . . . do you still think so?"

"When we're not making babies, we'll work at making the world safe for them."

She beamed up at him. "Sounds like a plan. . . . How many babies?"

"At least four."

"Four?" she gasped.

His heart whole for the first time ever, Ethan covered her mouth with his, swallowing her gasp. Then, lifting his mouth slightly, he growled against her lips, "Okay, five . . . but that's my final offer."

Gifting him with the beautiful laugh he'd fallen in love with years ago, she threw her arms around him and whispered, "Deal."

acknowledgments

I am truly a blessed person. Not only to do what I love, but to have the support of so many. Heartfelt thanks to the following people:

My husband, Jim, who continues to amaze me with his support and unending love, and my mom and sisters, who are always cheering me on.

The Romance Writers of America's Kiss of Death chapter, who were so generous in answering numerous questions on the Clues-and-News loop. And my wonderful home chapter, Southern Magic.

Friends Kelley St. John, Jennifer Echols, Dara Lace, Erin McClune, Jill Lawrence, Kay Keppler, and Karen Beeching for always being willing to listen.

Special thanks to Carla Swafford for dropping her own work to read the first draft of this book for me. To Marie Campbell for medical and drug advice and Milton Grasle for his assistance with explosives and non-lethal takedowns. Any mistakes are entirely my own.

Danny Agan, for his help and assistance.

My kind and talented editor, Kate Collins, and the entire Ballantine team for their wonderful assistance and support for this project.

And Kimberly Whalen, my incredible agent, whose enthusiasm is not only fun but also contagious.